About the Authors

Reese Ryan writes se... featuring a diverse cast ... presents her characters with family and career drama, challenging love interests and life-changing secrets while treating readers to emotional love stories with unexpected twists. Past president of her local RWA chapter and a panelist at the 2017 *Los Angeles Times* Festival of Books, Reese is an advocate of the romance genre and diversity in fiction. Visit her online at ReeseRyan.com

Sarah M. Anderson won RT Reviewer's Choice 2012 Desire of the Year for *A Man of Privilege*. *The Nanny Plan* was a 2016 *RITA®* winner for Contemporary Romance: Short. Find out more about Sarah's love of cowboys at sarahmanderson.com

Award-winning author **HelenKay Dimon** spent twelve years in the most unromantic career ever – divorce lawyer. After dedicating all of that effort to helping people terminate relationships, she is thrilled to deal in happy endings and write romance novels for a living. Her books have been featured in *Cosmopolitan* Magazine and E! Online. HelenKay loves hearing from readers, so stop by her website at helenkaydimon.com and say hello.

Secrets and Seduction

Secrets and Seduction:
Playing
with Fire

REESE RYAN

SARAH M. ANDERSON

HELENKAY DIMON

MILLS & BOON

First Published in Great Britain 2021
By Mills & Boon, an imprint of HarperCollins*Publishers*, Ltd
1 London Bridge Street, London, SE1 9GF

www.harpercollins.co.uk

HarperCollins*Publishers*
1st Floor, Watermarque Building,
Ringsend Road, Dublin 4, Ireland

SECRETS AND SEDUCTION: PLAYING WITH FIRE
© 2021 Harlequin Books S.A.

Playing with Seduction © 2018 Roxanne Ravenel
His Illegitimate Heir © 2016 Sarah M. Anderson
Pregnant by the CEO © 2018 HelenKay Dimon

ISBN: 978-0-263-30301-8

PLAYING WITH SEDUCTION

REESE RYAN

Dedicated to all the remarkable readers I've met during my publishing journey. You support African American and multicultural romance with your hard-earned dollars, valuable time, honest reviews and enthusiastic word of mouth. We are nothing without you.

Chapter 1

The click of high heels against the hardwood floors prompted Wesley Adams to look up from his magazine.

A mature, attractive blonde extended her hand, her coral lips pressed into a wide smile. "Pleasure to meet you, Mr. Adams. I'm Miranda Hopkins, executive director of Westbrook Charitable Foundation."

"The pleasure is mine." Wes stood and shook her hand. "But please, call me Wes."

"Wes, I'm sorry to tell you Liam won't be joining us for today's meeting." Miranda frowned. "One of the girls isn't feeling well, so he stayed home with her."

"No, I wasn't aware." Wes was surprised his best friend hadn't called him. After all, Liam had hounded him for more than a month to fly in from London for this meeting in Pleasure Cove. The woman looked worried he'd bolt, so Wes forced a smile. "But I'm confident he left me in good hands."

"You've managed some impressive events in the UK," Miranda said in her heavy, Southern drawl as she guided him toward a carpeted hallway. "We're so excited that you're considering taking on our project."

Wes nodded and thanked her, glad his friend had clearly gotten the point. He was here to assess the project and decide whether it was a good fit. Nothing was written in stone.

As they approached an open door of a glass-walled conference room, he heard the voices of two women. One of them was oddly familiar.

"Wes, this is our events manager, Lisa Chastain." He reached out to shake Lisa's hand. Then Miranda drew his attention to the other woman. "And this is Olympic champion and international beach-volleyball star Brianna Evans. Bree, this is Wesley—"

"Adams. We've met." Her expression soured, as if she smelled a rotting corpse. It sure as hell wasn't her glad-to-see-you-again-Wes face.

Bloody hell.

He hadn't seen Bree since the night they met at that little club in London's West End more than a year ago.

Liam, I'm going to strangle you.

He'd tell his friend what he thought of his match-making attempt later. For now, he'd play it cool. After all, he hadn't done anything wrong. But Bree, whose lips were pursed as she stared at him through narrow slits, obviously disagreed.

Wes widened the smile he'd honed while attending boarding school with kids whose parents made more in a month than his parents made all year. He extended his hand to Bree, despite the look on her face that dared him to touch her.

Bree shoved a limp hand into his, then withdrew it quickly, as if her palm was on fire.

What did, or didn't, happen between he and Bree was personal. *This* was business.

"I believe Miss Evans has a bone to pick with me." Wes pulled out Brianna's chair and gestured for her to have a seat.

She narrowed her gaze at him, then took her seat. As she turned toward the two women, who exchanged worried glances, Bree forced a laugh. "Wes predicted my alma mater wouldn't make it back to the Sweet Sixteen, and he was right. I'm convinced he jinxed us."

Nicely done.

Wes acknowledged her save with a slight nod. He slipped into the chair across from her—the only open seat with an information packet placed on it.

The night they'd met in London, her eyes, flecked with gold, had gazed dreamily into his. The coy, flirtatious vibe she exuded that night was gone.

Bree's face dripped with disdain. Anger vibrated off her smooth, brown skin—the color of a bar of milk chocolate melting in the hot summer sun.

Wes only realized he'd been staring at Bree when she cleared her throat and opened her information packet.

"Well, I…" Miranda's gaze darted between Brianna and Wes. "We're all here. Let's get started, shall we?"

The meeting was quick and efficient. Miranda and Lisa were respectful of their time and promised they would be throughout the course of planning and executing a celebrity volleyball tournament over the next six months.

Six entire months.

Liam had laid out a dream project for him. The perfect vehicle for expanding his successful UK event planning and promotions company to the US. However, working with Bree Evans for six months would be as pleasant as having an appendectomy, followed by a root canal. On repeat.

The meeting concluded with a full tour of the expansive Pleasure Cove Luxury Resort property. After they toured the main building, the four of them loaded into a golf cart. Wes slipped into the backseat beside Bree and tried not to notice how the smooth, brown skin on her long legs glistened. But her attempts to keep her leg from touching his only drew his attention.

The Westbrooks had gone all-out with the property. In addition to the main building there were four other buildings on either side of it that housed guests. There was a pool and spa house, four different restaurants, a poolside grill, tennis courts and two workout facilities. Large rental homes and a building with smaller, connected guest houses completed the vast property.

"Here we are at the guest houses, where you'll both be staying. Your luggage has already been taken to your individual guest houses," Miranda announced. "Wes you're in guest house five and Bree, I believe you're right next door in guest house six."

Of course.

"Makes it convenient to chat about the project whenever you'd like." Lisa grinned.

"It certainly does." Wes loosened his tie and stepped out of the golf cart. He extended a hand to

Bree, but she stepped out of her side of the cart and walked around.

"See you at the next meeting. If you want to knock around some ideas before then, just give me a call," Miranda said. She and Lisa waved goodbye as they zipped off in the golf cart.

Wes took a deep breath before he turned to Bree. "Look, I'm sorry I didn't call—"

"You're an ass." She shifted the strap of her purse higher.

She wasn't wrong.

Still, the accusation felt like a ton of bricks being launched onto his chest. "Bree, you're obviously angry—"

"Don't call me Bree. We're not friends." She folded her arms over her breasts, dragging his gaze there.

Wes raised his eyes to hers again. "Okay, what should I call you?"

Psycho? Insane? Ridiculously hot in that tight little black dress?

The corner of her mouth quirked in a grin that was gone almost as quickly as it had appeared. She'd caught him staring and seemed to relish his reaction. "Call me Brianna or Ms. Evans. I don't really care." Though, clearly, she did.

"All right, Ms. Evans." *Ms. Jackson, if you're nasty.* He bit his lip, scrubbing the image from his brain of her moving her hips and striking a pose. "I'd like to sincerely apologize for not calling when I said I would. It was rude of me. I should've called."

"You shouldn't have promised." Her voice was shaky for a moment. "Don't promise something if you don't intend to carry it out. That's one of the basic rules of not being an ass hat."

"Noted." He chuckled as he pulled his shades from his inside jacket pocket and put them on. "We good?"

"As good as we need to be." Brianna turned on her tall heels, which added length to her mile-long legs. His gaze followed the sway of her generous hips. She opened the door of her guest house and glanced over her shoulder momentarily before stepping inside and closing the door behind her.

Wesley sighed. He'd spent more than a decade building his event-planning-and-promotion business from a ragtag team of university misfits planning pop-up events for a little extra dosh to a company that routinely planned events for some of the hottest celebs and largest corporations in the UK. Taking point on the planning of the Westbrook's new celebrity volleyball tournament would help him establish a name with major players in the US more quickly.

But would Bree's animosity make it impossible for them to work together effectively?

He'd lived in London the better part of his life, and he loved living there. Still, the blue skies, warm sun and salty breeze drifting in from the Atlantic Ocean made him nostalgic for home.

But then he hadn't really gone home. He hadn't even told his mother he was in North Carolina.

Maybe he only missed the idea of home.

Either way, it was time to find out.

Bree tossed her purse onto the nearest chair and flopped down onto the sandy beige sofa. It was the same color as Wesley's pants. Not that she cared. She just happened to notice the color, and how well the material had hugged his firm bottom.

No. No. No. Do not think about his ass or any other parts of his anatomy.

She kicked off her shoes and headed to the bar. It was well-stocked, courtesy of Liam Westbrook. But she also had Liam to thank for bringing her and Wes together on this project.

The stunned look on Wes's face indicated that he was just as surprised to see her. Liam obviously hadn't told his friend that he'd invited her to work on the project.

But why?

They were best friends. Which meant Liam probably knew what had happened that night.

Her cheeks stung as she surveyed the bottles of wine. *No.* It was too early to drink chardonnay alone. She pulled out a split of champagne and a bottle of orange juice.

It's never too early for mimosas.

She took a sip of the cocktail and felt she could breathe for the first time since she'd laid eyes on Wesley Adams. His six-foot-three frame had filled out the navy jacket and beige pants as if they were made for him.

Bree checked the time on her phone. It was still early out in California. After a recent shoulder surgery, her best friend and volleyball partner, Rebecca Jacobs wouldn't be following her usual early morning workout routine. Still, it wouldn't hurt to text.

Bree sent a text message with one hand while nursing her drink in the other. Bex, you up?

Within seconds Bex replied. Uh-oh. How'd your meeting go?

Bree sighed. Was she really that transparent? Then again, she and Bex had been partners for the last seven years, so there wasn't much she could put past her friend. Meeting was great. Unfortunately, I would have to work with the devil himself. Don't know if I can do this.

The phone rang within seconds of her sending the text.

"What the hell is going on?"

Bree laughed. "Good morning to you, too."

"Sorry. Good morning. Now, what the hell is going on? Who was at the meeting that would make you want to pass up this opportunity?"

She sighed, her finger tracing the bar. "Wes Adams."

"The guy you met at the bar that night in London?" Bex let out a sigh of relief. "I know you're bummed he didn't call, but he's a guy. Don't take it personally. In fact, you should be glad you guys didn't sleep together. That'd be awkward."

"Today was awkward." Bree balanced the phone between her ear and shoulder as she wrestled with the plastic-wrapped gift basket filled with goodies. She could use some chocolate. Stat.

"Why? Because you guys fooled around a little? You are seriously out of practice, my friend." She laughed. "I told you not having a life would catch up with you."

"Volleyball *is* my life." Bree ripped open a chocolate truffle and stuffed it in her mouth.

"And it's a great life, but it won't always be there.

We're approaching thirty. Time to start thinking about life after volleyball."

"You aren't thinking of retiring on me, are you?" Bree mumbled through a mouthful of chocolate.

"No, but this injury has given me a lot of time to think. I don't want to wake up one day and feel like I missed out on the things that are really important."

"Like?" Her friend was surprisingly philosophical. It made Bree uneasy. She was usually the one reminding Bex to be more frugal and save for the future, when tournament money, appearance fees and endorsements were no longer flowing in, something they'd both been forced to think about more lately.

"I dunno. Like a husband. Maybe kids."

"Wow." Bree's mouth curled in a smirk. "So what's his name?"

"Shut up." Bex fell suspiciously quiet before releasing a long sigh. "His name is Nick. He's my physical therapist, and he is so cute."

"Uh-huh."

"But we're not talking about me right now, Bree. This is about you. Why is running in to this guy again such a big deal? Do you have a serious thing for him or something?"

"No." Even to her ears, her response sounded like that of a tween in denial, punctuated by an unladylike snort. Her mother would be so proud.

Bex paused, which told Bree that she heard her unconvincing denial, but chose to ignore it. "Then no harm, no foul. Certainly nothing worth giving up this opportunity. You could become the face of the hottest new beach volleyball event on the East Coast. Besides, Westbrook International Luxury Resorts is a worldwide organization. This could be the beginning of spreading your brand. *Our* brand. So don't wuss out on me."

Bree gritted her teeth and stared out onto the water. A huge wave licked the shore, the chilly waters chasing away a toy Pomeranian. "Okay, fine. I'll figure out how to deal with it. With him."

"That a girl. Whatever it takes. Just like on the court. Got it?"

Bree chucked the truffle she was about to open back into its box and nodded. "Got it. Whatever it takes."

She talked to Bex for another half hour, getting an update on her injured shoulder and her hot new physical therapist before finally ending the call. Bree changed into a pair of yoga pants, a T-shirt and a sweater. She stepped out onto the back deck and inhaled the salty ocean breeze. It was sixty-two degrees out. A fairly warm day for early February.

She flopped onto the chaise and tried to remember her friend's words. They hadn't slept together. So why was she still so pissed at him?

Because she'd wanted to sleep with him. God, she'd wanted to. She'd fantasized about it in the wee hours of the morning, when she couldn't shake the memory of his kiss from her brain.

She shuddered, remembering the touch of his hand when she'd been all but obligated to shake it and make up that story about why she was upset with him. There was some truth to the story.

A slight smile played on Bree's lips as she remembered their argument about what football team had a chance of winning the Super Bowl. She just left out the part where he'd asked her to come back to his place. Bree had turned him down. He smiled, his eyes filled with understanding. Then he gave her the sweetest kiss. Sweet and innocent, yet filled with the promise of passionate nights ahead. They'd only spent a few hours together, but he'd managed to make the kiss feel meaningful. Real.

Real enough that she'd stared at her phone for a week afterward, waiting for him to call. Like he'd promised after their kiss.

Her response that night kept replaying in her head. *Sorry, but I'm not that kind of girl.* She laughed bitterly. True, she wasn't the kind of girl who normally believed in one-night stands. In fact, she wasn't the kind of girl who got laid at all. Not for a very long time. Not since…

She tried to erase the memory of the scornful mouth and hard, dark eyes she'd once found so intriguing. Sexy even. She'd been wrong about that asshole. Apparently, she'd been just as wrong about Wesley Adams.

The man was handsome and tall with warm brown skin. An athletic body that had felt incredible pressed against hers on the dance floor. And a killer smile. One worthy of a toothpaste commercial. He had the straightest, most brilliant teeth she'd ever seen.

And she loved his laugh, which he employed often. Because he was funny. And smart. And he liked sports. Just like she did. But he wasn't intimidated because she was knowledgeable about sports and full of opinions she readily shared. He was the kind of guy she could see herself spending time with on those lonely nights she actually got to spend in her own bed back in Huntington Beach.

Wes was the kind of guy she wanted to spend more than one night with, so she'd turned down his offer to go back to his place.

She'd gone to the pub with Bex that night, determined to crawl out of all the insecurities that rumbled around in her head, barely leaving elbow room for her own thoughts.

She went to The Alley that night, intending to take someone back to her hotel. Just once she wanted to be a little naughty. To shed the good-girl image she'd worked so hard to perfect over the past two decades.

She was the scholarship kid who struggled to fit in at a private school, terrified that the kids would find out she lived in the run-down projects. Two of the front stairs missing and not a single blade of grass on their "lawn."

She'd spent the past ten years creating her image as the perfect spokesperson. A successful player with a feel-good story and the kind of good-girl image that garnered endorsements and kept them. Not the kind of girl who would stroll into a club and pick up a random guy for the night.

In the end, she hadn't turned him down to protect her shiny, good-girl reputation. She politely turned down his offer because she liked him.

Really liked him.

So she gambled on there being another night between them. Only there wasn't. Bree was angry at Wes for not keeping his promise. She was angry with herself for not taking him up on his offer.

Bree drew her legs against her chest, wrapping her

arms around them. If she was going to be working with Wes Adams for the next six months, she'd have to start thinking with her brain, not her libido. And she couldn't behave like a jilted lover.

Her heart fluttered, just thinking about how her hand felt in his, even for a moment. A glowing warmth arose through her fingers, making its way to her chest.

She put her head on her knees and sighed.

Letting go of her silly crush on Wes would be easier said than done.

Chapter 2

Wes rang Liam's cell four times.

No answer.

His best friend was definitely dodging him. It was probably best. He had a few choice words for Liam. No way it had just slipped his mind to mention that he'd selected Bree Evans to work on this project, too.

Not that Bree wasn't the ideal person to front an annual sports-and-music festival with the potential to be a huge draw for the resort. She was.

Bree was one of the top beach volleyball players in the world. One of the few players of color to gain endorsements and a huge following. She was genuinely nice. Frequently participated in charity events. And the camera loved her.

Every single inch of her. A gorgeous smile. A curvy frame anchored by her voluptuous breasts and an ass that would give any red-blooded man reason to adjust his trousers. Long legs. Strong, lean thighs. Undulating hips.

Wes scrubbed a hand down his face. Sitting there recounting the finer points of Bree's physique wasn't a productive use of his time, or a very good way to maintain his sanity. He glanced over at the wall that separated their units. Tried not to wonder what she was doing. If she'd slipped out of the thigh-hugging black dress she wore at the meeting.

He'd like to think she'd worn it for him. The surprise on her lovely face meant she clearly hadn't. Wes shook his head and sighed. Liam couldn't dodge him forever. In the meantime, he had business of his own to handle.

Wes grabbed the key to the loaner car Liam left for him and headed to the front door. Time to go home.

The gravel crunched in the driveway of the old bungalow his grandmother once owned. His mother had left England five years ago and returned to North Carolina to take care of his grandmother, who had taken a tumble down the narrow stairs and broken a hip. After his grandmother passed, his mother decided to stay in her childhood home. A home that held lots of memories for him, too.

Wes stepped out of the red Dodge Challenger with black leather. The loaner was another enticement from Liam to take on the project. Perhaps also an apology before the fact for springing Bree Evans on him without warning. He shut the door and headed up the driveway. There was no answer, so he knocked. Twice.

Finally he heard footsteps inside and the turning of

locks. The door swung open, releasing a dark, musty odor that made him wonder if he'd arrived at the wrong house.

"Wes? Baby, what are you doing here?" Lena Adams looked tired and slightly haggard. She ran her hand down the soiled apron she was wearing and smiled, then pushed open the screen door. "It's so good to see you."

He wrapped his long arms around his mother, her face buried in his chest. "Good to see you, too, Mom." His gaze traveled around the room. A thick layer of dust had settled on the furniture. Dust bunnies inhabited the corners. Stacks of books and papers were piled on various surfaces around the living room and dining room. If he wasn't holding his mother in his arms now, he wouldn't have believed he was in her house.

Lena had been the house manager for a wealthy family for two decades. She'd administered weekly white-glove tests, making her the bane of the housekeepers' existence. She would settle for nothing less than absolute cleanliness. Which led to much of her frustration with him, as a boy. Even while caring for his grandmother, she'd managed to keep the place immaculate.

What's going on?

His mother finally released him. She squeezed his hands in hers. "I can't believe you didn't tell me you were coming. I would've gotten the place ready and invited your brother up from Atlanta for a few days." She looked behind him. "Where are your bags?"

"This is a last-minute business trip. I'm staying at the new resort Liam's family built at Pleasure Cove." He tried his best to focus on his mother's face, and not the chaos surrounding them. "He wants me to work on a project for the resort. I haven't accepted the job yet, but I'm considering it."

"Really?" His mother pulled him into the room and toward the sofa. Shifting a pile of magazines from the couch to the floor, she made a place for him. She sat, then patted the space beside her. "All these years, you wouldn't take a job from the Westbrooks. Got your daddy's pride." Through years of practice she'd managed to make the last statement without malice. In fact, there was almost a hint of a smile.

Wes wished he could manage even a semblance of a smile at the mention of his father. The man that had up and left them so many years ago.

All because of him.

He cleared his throat. "I wouldn't be an employee. I'd be working with them as a contractor. And nothing is set in stone. We had the preliminary meeting earlier today."

"If it would keep you here, I'm all for it." She patted his hand and smiled. "But you seem worried. Why?"

Wes drummed the pads of his fingers against his knee. Whatever was going on with his mother, her innate sense of when he was perturbed was still intact. "It would mean working with a girl I met more than a year ago. Things didn't quite work out between us."

"Humph." She nodded, knowingly. "If you'd settle down and give me some grandchildren, you wouldn't have to worry about encountering ex-lovers at business meetings."

Wes sighed. "She isn't an ex-lover. We spent one night dancing and hanging out at a club in London. There was nothing to it really."

His mother laughed. "I'm guessing the young lady doesn't agree."

"Yeah, well it's nothing we can't work through."

"If you really believed that, you wouldn't be considering passing up on this job. And if you're considering taking money from the Westbrooks, it must be a game-changing opportunity." Her eyes twinkled. Sometimes he wondered if she didn't know him better than he knew himself.

Liam and Nigel Westbrook had been trying to get him to come on board at Westbrook International Luxury Resorts since his days in university. But he'd been a scholarship kid at the private academy he'd attended with Liam and at college after that. He didn't want a position just because Liam was his best friend. He wanted to earn his way in the world on his terms. Which was why his master's degree in business was collecting dust on the shelf in his flat back in London. During college, he'd discovered his gift for organizing events. Better still, he'd learned he could make a hell of a lot of money doing something he actually enjoyed. So he'd abandoned his plans to scale the corporate ladder at some conglomerate and struck out on his own.

As proud as Wes was of how the business had grown in London, he wanted to expand his business to the US. Another way to prove to his father that he was a success. The kind of person he should never have walked away from.

It was the only reason he'd considered Liam's offer.

Wes smiled. "Think you know everything, don't you?"

"Not everything. Just you." She squeezed his hand. "Why don't I fix us some lunch. You must be hungry."

"Don't go to any trouble on my account. In fact, why don't I take you out to eat? How about we go and grab an early dinner at the restaurant on the waterfront you're always telling me about?"

A slow smile spread across her face. "You sure? I could just as easily cook us up something. Won't take but a minute."

"I'm positive." He stood. "You go on and get ready. When we come back, I'll help with anything you need around the house."

The fair skin on his mother's cheeks pinked slightly. "I know things have gotten a little out of hand around here. Like I said, if I'd known you were coming—"

"It's okay, Mom." The last thing he'd wanted was to embarrass his mother, but there was something going on. Something she hadn't mentioned during their frequent calls. He needed to get to the bottom of it. "I haven't been home in a few years. I just want to help any way I can while I'm here."

Her smile slid back into place. "Okay, baby. Give me a few minutes to get myself together." As she stood, she seemed to lose her balance. He reached for her, but she'd steadied herself on the edge of the couch. "I'm fine." Her tone was defensive. She cleared her throat, then softened her expression. "Just the trappings of old age, I guess. I'll be back in a few. Excuse me."

He watched his mother cross the room and ascend the stairs. Her gait was unsure, and she gripped the banister as if her very life depended on it. The last time he'd visited she was practically taking the steps two at a time. Like always.

A sinking feeling settled in his gut and crept up his

spine. Wes walked back into the dining room and surveyed the books and magazines cluttering his mother's table. They were mostly health and nutrition magazines with little sticky notes protruding from them. He picked one up and turned to the marked page. A tightness gripped his chest, making it difficult for him to breathe. He put down the magazine and picked up another and another. Each sticky note marked an article about Parkinson's disease.

He shifted his gaze to the pile of books. The title on the top of the pile sent a chill down his spine. *Parkinson's Disease: A Complete Guide for Patients and Families*. The orange cover of the second book offered *300 Tips for Making Life with Parkinson's Disease Easier*.

A wave of panic rose in his chest. He steadied himself on a chair then flopped down in it. Lena Adams was one of the strongest women he'd ever known, rivaled only by his grandmother. She was wrong about Wes having his father's pride. Every ounce of strength and willfulness he possessed, he'd learned from her. She'd always seemed...invincible, so independent. Thinking of his mother slowly losing herself to this disease terrified him.

Wes heard his mother descending the creaky stairs. He should put everything back so she wouldn't know he'd been rummaging through her things, but he wouldn't. Instead, he turned to face her, brandishing the orange-covered book. "Why didn't you tell me?"

The smile on her face instantly disappeared, replaced by a look of guilt and apology. She didn't bother to chastise him for going through her books. "I—I was going to tell you the next time you brought me out for a visit."

"How long ago were you diagnosed?" He tried to keep his voice even, despite the fact he was so angry he could practically crawl out of his own skin.

Lena lowered her gaze before returning it to his. "Formally? About six months ago. I began to suspect a few months before then."

So she'd known on her last visit to London, just a few months ago. He rubbed his temple. Why hadn't he noticed?

"We need to talk about this."

Lena grabbed her purse off the chair. "No reason we can't talk and eat." Her cheeky smile almost made him laugh.

Wes looped his arm through hers and led her to the door.

"This is why I didn't tell you. You've known all of five minutes, and already you're treating me like an invalid."

"I'm not treating you like an invalid. I just want to make sure you're okay."

"I am." Her genuine smile and eyes shiny with tears warmed his chest. "Especially now that you're here."

On the ride into town, his mother chatted away, catching him up on what his aunts and cousins were up to. Her familiar laugh gave him a sense of solace. But he couldn't help noticing the slight trembling in her left hand as it rested on her knee. Or the limited gestures she used as she spoke. Both were unlike her, giving him more cause for concern.

Wes had been ready to call his friend and tell him he was passing on the project, but this changed everything. His mother needed him, whether she was willing to admit it or not. Establishing his business in the US, so close to his mother, was no longer a matter of ambition or pride.

It was a matter of family.

His mother had made so many sacrifices for him and his brother, a reality that plagued him with guilt. He'd never be able to repay her sacrifices in-kind. Didn't mean he couldn't try.

Not even if it meant checking his ego at the door and working with Bree Evans to put on the best event the Carolina coast had ever seen.

Chapter 3

Bree arrived fifteen minutes early for the meeting. Because she was always early. Also, because she hoped to get a quick word in with Wes. If they were going to work together over the next six months, she needed to keep things civil. Nothing had happened between them. Other than an amazing night together and a kiss that was so hot and sweet that it melted her insides and made her heart skip a beat.

Other than that, nothing at all.

Bex was right. She needed to let go of her resentment toward Wes. Count her lucky stars they hadn't slept together. Then things would've been unbearably awkward.

She would apologize and clear the air. Let bygones be bygones and all of those other ridiculous clichés. Not for him, but for her. Her participation in this event would expand their brand. Help her and Bex maximize the value of what remained of their careers on the volleyball circuit.

Bree entered the room. No one was there, except Lisa, who stood at the end of the table sorting documents. "Good morning, Bree. Can I get you a cup of coffee?"

"Good morning." She smiled brightly as she surveyed the chairs. Where would Wes sit? Probably next to Liam, who'd likely sit at the head of the table. She walked around the other side of the table and hung her bag on the second seat from Liam's probable chair. Lisa eyed at her expectantly. "Oh, the coffee. I'm fine. Thank you."

The corner of Lisa's mouth quirked in a knowing smile. "All right. Everyone should be here in a minute."

Bree's cheeks warmed. The other woman hadn't done a very good job of hiding her amusement over her careful deliberation about where to sit.

Note to self: take it down a notch. Your crazy is showing.

"Can I help with anything?"

"I'm about finished here." Lisa slid a few stapled sheets into a blue folder, then shut it. "There. All done."

Rather than taking a seat, Bree wandered over to the window and gazed out onto the water. She loved her life on the West Coast, but the Carolina coast was certainly beautiful, too. As soon as the water warmed up a bit, she would get out on a kayak and explore the Cape Fear River on the other side of the island. Right now, the water was still too chilly, despite the mild temperature outside.

Finally, Bree heard voices approaching. She waited until they were in the room to turn around, flashing her biggest smile. "Good morning."

"Good morning, Bree." Liam shook her hand in both of his, a gesture that was warm and welcoming. "Sorry I couldn't make yesterday's preliminary meeting. I had a family emergency, but I'm here now, and I'm thrilled you've decided to come on board with the project. It's going to be an amazing event. Good for the Pleasure Cove community and the sport of volleyball."

"I know. I'm thrilled. Thank you for inviting me to be part of it."

Miranda greeted Bree, then took the seat next to Liam, closest to the door. The seat she would've expected Wes to take. When Lisa slipped into the seat between her and Liam, that left only the seat across from her vacant. Which meant she'd spend the entire meeting pretending not to stare at him.

"Looks like we're all here," Miranda said. "Let's get started."

"What about… I mean, isn't Wes joining us?" The words spilled out of her mouth before she could stop them. She didn't dare look over at the amused half grin that was probably perched on Lisa's mouth.

Liam's eyes twinkled and his mouth pressed into a slow, subdued smile. "Wes had a family emergency of his own. He won't make today's meeting, but he should be here when we meet on Friday."

"Oh." Bree tried to filter the disappointment from her voice. She adjusted in her chair. *Way to look nonchalant.*

There was a brief moment of awkward silence that made Bree want to crawl into a ball and hide in a corner, until finally, Miranda started the meeting. She directed everyone to the agenda placed inside the front pocket of the folders in front of them.

They reviewed various possible formats for the event, based on ideas generated in the previous meeting. Miranda reviewed reports on current beach-volleyball tournaments in California and Miami Beach. Bree shared her insight on what worked at those tournaments and what could be improved, based on her participation in them in the past. Liam stressed that the event needed to entice notable celebrities who would draw people to the resort.

Lisa reminded everyone of the need to draw visitors who were not diehard fans, including locals. That was Wesley's expertise. Together they made a solid plan that they were all excited about.

After the meeting, Miranda leaned in toward Liam, her voice low. "Has Wes committed to the project?"

"Not yet. But I expect he will soon." Liam's polite smile indicated that his vague response was the extent of their discussion on the matter.

Bree had reacted badly to seeing Wes. She realized that now. Was he waffling on the project because of her?

Wes didn't seem like the kind of guy to let a little contention get in the way of something he really wanted. Still, if she was the reason he hadn't committed, it was more important than ever that she apologize to him. Before he walked away from the project.

Bree said her goodbyes and headed down the hallway.

Liam caught up with her. "Bree, can I give you a

ride to your guest house? I'm headed out for a lunch meeting."

She wanted to politely reject his offer. Spend the short walk back to her place lost in her own thoughts. Her feet, already tired of the four-inch patent-leather heels she was wearing, had other ideas. "Sure."

As they walked toward the front door, Liam stopped and turned to her. "I'm meeting with a few influential folks in town to quell their concerns about the commercialization of the island. It would be great if you came along. You'd be doing me a huge favor, if you don't have other plans."

She wanted to say no. She really did. But his pleading dark eyes and brilliant smile won her over. Besides, she'd taken the time to make up her face and wear a sexy outfit. She should get some mileage out of all that effort before heading back to the guest house and slipping into her comfy yoga pants and T-shirt.

"I'd love to meet some of the townspeople. Maybe even get them on board with the project early on. We're going to need a lot of volunteers."

Liam shook a finger, smiling. "I love the way you think. I owe you one."

"Two, actually." Bree held up two fingers. "The other is for not telling me Wes would be working on the project, too."

Liam pressed his mouth into a straight line, an eyebrow raised.

Busted.

"Perhaps I should've mentioned that. But I can't say I'm sorry I didn't. It would've been a shame if either of you begged off because of it. I think you two will make an excellent team." His smile widened.

She sighed. No apology, but at least he'd given an honest response. That, she could appreciate.

"You're right. I would've said no. That would've been a mistake."

Liam grinned. "You're both here. That's what matters."

Bree wasn't so sure. After all, she'd committed to the project; Wes hadn't. Maybe he'd decided that working with her wasn't worth it. She forced a smile and tried not to let the hurt that arose from that thought crack her smiling veneer.

Wes parked the Challenger in front of the guest house, stepped out of the car and stretched his long frame. He'd spent the last two nights in one of his mother's spare rooms. They had a delicious meal on the waterfront. By the time they ordered dessert she finally leveled with him about her Parkinson's diagnosis. She brought him up to speed on her doctor's prognosis and invited him to accompany her to her next doctor's appointment, which had been today.

He'd spent the last two days getting his mother's house back to the standards she'd always kept. He'd sifted through stacks of papers and mail, sorting and filing what was important, dumping what wasn't. He'd vacuumed carpets, scrubbed floors and cleaned the bathrooms and kitchen. Every muscle in his body ached. It reminded him of those brutal days on the rugby field at university. The days when he'd been sure he must be some guilt-ridden masochist to love the damn sport so much.

His mother's doctor appointment was two hours before his meeting with Liam and Bree. He'd hoped to get back in time to catch part of the meeting, but the doctor's office had used the term *appointment* loosely. By the time they got in to see the doctor, got blood tests, a CAT scan and filled her prescription, they were both exhausted. And there was no way he could make the meeting.

Bree had probably been thrilled by his absence.

Liam pulled behind his car, his face etched with concern. "You made it back. Everything all right?"

"Things have been better." Wes forced a weak smile and rubbed his hand over his head. That's when he noticed Bree sitting in the passenger seat of Liam's car. Their eyes met briefly. She forced a quick smile and nodded, then turned away.

"You look like hell. Want to talk about it?" Liam asked, before he could acknowledge the olive branch Bree had extended.

Liam was his best friend. They kept few secrets from each other. But for now, he preferred to keep the news of his mother's illness to himself. As if not talking about it made it less real. A bad dream from which he'd awaken. Besides, he didn't want to discuss it in front of Bree.

"Maybe later."

"Over golf tomorrow? Ten o'clock?"

Wes shook his head and laughed. There were few things in life Liam enjoyed as much as beating his ass in a round of golf. "Yeah, sure."

"Great. I'll pick you up then," Liam said before turning to Bree and thanking her for lunch.

He should've headed inside. After two nights in that too-little bed, he was desperate to sleep in a bed that could accommodate someone taller than a leprechaun.

Instead, he remained rooted to his spot, his feet refusing to budge, as he watched Bree exit the car. When Liam waved and pulled away, Wes didn't respond. He was focused on Bree. She looked stunning, and she seemed fully aware of it.

She strutted toward him in mile-high patent-leather heels that gleamed in the sunlight and made her legs look even longer than he remembered. The white wrap blouse hugged her full breasts, revealing a hint of cleavage. The black pencil skirt grazed the top of her knee. Each step she made offered a generous glimpse of her thigh through a slit positioned over the center of her right leg. She came to a stop in front of him. The same exotic scent she'd worn the night they met at The Alley wafted around her. Fruity and floral. He hadn't been able to get enough of that scent as he held her that night.

"Hello, Brianna." His voice came out softer than he'd intended. Wes cleared his throat and elevated the bass in his voice. "How'd the meeting go?"

"Very well. Sorry you weren't able to make it. Looks like you've been busy the past couple of days." She assessed his clothing. Same jacket and pants he'd worn during their initial meeting. Only more wrinkled.

He could only imagine what she was thinking. No point in trying to dissuade her. Besides, he didn't owe her an explanation. Wes ran a hand over his head. "Yeah, I have. It'll be good to sleep in my own bed tonight."

Her cheeks turned crimson. She bit the corner of her lip. The deep red lip color highlighted how kissable her lips were. A fact to which he could attest. "Can we talk?"

"Sure." He reached into the backseat of the car and pulled out two grocery bags. "But I have to get these groceries in the fridge. Mind stepping inside while I put them away?"

Her hair wasn't pulled back into the severe bun she'd worn earlier in the week. Loose curls cascaded over her right shoulder. She shook her head, and the curls bounced. He balled his fingers into a fist at his side at the thought of fisting a handful of her luxurious hair and taking her from behind. He swallowed, his mouth dry.

"You cook?"

He laughed. "A guy's gotta eat, right?"

"Our meals are being comped." He could hear the click of her heels against the concrete as she followed him up the path to his door.

"I know, but I felt like throwing a steak on the grill."

"In February?"

"When a February day is as beautiful as this one, why not?"

Bree followed him into the kitchen and stood beside the counter making idle chitchat as he put away the groceries. Apologizing was the right thing to do. She believed that. So why was it so difficult to say the words? The words of apology had been lodged in her throat since she noticed he was wearing the same clothes from earlier in the week. He smelled like soap. The utilitarian kind you bought in bulk. A familiar scent. It was all her family could afford when she was growing up. So he'd showered, but he'd been too preoccupied to return here for a change of clothing.

The thought of him spending the past two nights in someone else's bed caused a tightness in her chest that made it hard to breathe deeply. Which was silly. Why should it matter what Wesley Adams did in his spare time and with whom? Her only concern was his actions relating to the event. As long as he nailed this event, he could bang the entire eastern seaboard for all she cared.

The sound of Wes shutting the refrigerator door broke in to her thoughts. He gestured for her to take a seat in the living room. She sank into the cushion of the blue checkered sofa and crossed her legs.

She followed his gaze, which traveled the length of her long legs. His tongue darted out to quickly wet his lips before he dragged his gaze back to hers. "You wanted to talk?"

Her pulse quickened and she smiled inwardly. He still found her attractive. A small vindication.

Bree clasped her hands in her lap, looking down at them for a moment before raising her eyes to his. "I wanted to apologize for how I came off the other day. It was childish and petty. This project is important to both of us. If we're going to work together, I don't want things to be weird between us. So I wanted to clear the air by saying I'm sorry."

Wes seemed pleasantly surprised by her apology. He scooted forward on the couch and gave her a sheepish smile. "I accept your apology, but only if you'll accept mine. I wanted to call, I just…" He sighed, then scooted back on the couch again. His tone turned more serious. "Didn't seem like it was the right time for me."

"Oh." She hadn't meant to say it out loud. Especially not in that sad, wounded-puppy whimper that changed his expression from contrition to pity. When he felt remorse, she had the upper hand. Now that he seemed to pity her, the power had shifted back to him. Bree shot to her feet. "No apology necessary, but thanks. I'll let myself out."

"What prompted the change of heart?"

Her hand was nearly on the doorknob, but his question grabbed her by the shoulders and yanked her back into the room. She turned back to him and shrugged. "For the sake of the project."

He took a few steps toward her. "Why were you so upset about that night?"

"Why does it matter?"

"Curious, I guess." He shoved his hands in his pockets, drawing her attention to the strain the gesture placed on the placard covering his zipper.

"I overreacted. I get cranky when I'm jet-lagged." The space between them was closing too rapidly. She took a few steps backward toward the door.

His self-assured smile suggested that her answer had told him everything he needed to know.

Her cheeks flamed and she swiveled on her heels, but before she could escape, he'd gently caught her by the hand. A familiar heat traveled from his large hand into hers, up her arm and into her chest. She raised her eyes to his.

"Look, I bought more than enough food to share. I'm going to marinate the steaks then get a few hours of sleep. But I should have the steaks on the grill at say—" Wes flipped his wrist and glanced at his watch "—seven thirty. Why don't you join me for dinner? You can assess my cooking abilities for yourself."

His wide grin and close proximity were doing

things to her she wasn't proud of. Wesley Adams wasn't a man she should be flirting with. Nor were they friends. He was a means to an end.

Bree glanced down at his hand on her arm and he dropped it to his side and took a step backward. "Thank you for the offer, but I'm pretty tired, too. I should probably just order in and get some rest."

"The invitation is open, if you change your mind."

Bree had turned and run out of there like her hair was on fire. If it hadn't wounded his pride, he would've found it funny.

Wes closed the door behind her and returned to the kitchen. He seasoned the steaks and put them into the fridge.

You invited her to dinner, genius? Really?

They were forced to work together over the course of the next six months. Like Bree said, they needed to play nice. He appreciated that she'd come to that conclusion. That she had no plans to make the next six months a living hell for both of them.

Being cordial was crucial to the success of the project. Getting to know each other, up close and personal, could only lead to trouble. Yet, he couldn't stop himself. His brain had taken a coffee break and the head on his shoulders was no longer in control.

He'd been dying for another excuse to touch her warm, soft skin. The memory of their night together in London blazed brightly in the back of his mind, like an image from an old-fashioned projector. His skin tingled with the sensation of her body pressed to his on the dance floor. Of his mouth on her lips, her neck, her bare shoulder. The unfinished business between them.

It was good Bree had turned down his invitation. Better for the both of them.

Chapter 4

For the past three hours, Bree had tried to take a nap. Instead, she tossed and turned. Thinking of him. And of that damn kiss. The one that had haunted her for more than a year.

Get your head together. It's not like you've never been kissed.

True. But she'd never been so thoroughly kissed. Kissed in a way that made every nerve in her body raw and frayed. Deeply relaxed, yet ready to spring into action. A kiss that made her want him in the worst way. Body and soul.

In that instant, she'd set aside her plan to make Wesley Adams hers for the night. She'd wanted something deeper with the guy who'd been sweet, funny and incredibly sexy. To be kissed like that for more than just one night. So she'd politely refused his invitation to go back to his place.

She'd regretted it ever since.

Given the chance again, she would've accepted his invitation. If only to ease the tension and stress that had her body strung tighter than a new volleyball net.

Bree slipped on yoga pants, a T-shirt and a hooded sweater, then went downstairs to order from one of the resort restaurants. She grabbed a bottle of water from the fridge and took a sip. A mouthwatering scent had infiltrated the kitchen.

Grilled meat.

Her belly churned. She could almost taste the steak. The one with her name on it.

Bree stepped through the double doors and onto the back deck, following the scent.

"Hey." Wes grinned. He stood over the grill on his deck in a black sleeveless shirt that showcased the gun show he called biceps. His right arm was covered with a tribal tattoo. A pair of lived-in jeans highlighted his assets.

It was colder outside than she thought. Her nipples beaded, pressing against the fabric of her bra. Bree offered a half-hearted wave, then pulled her sweater tight against her body. "Hey."

"You eat yet?" His grin widened when she shook her head. "Got your steak on the grill. C'mon over."

No. No. Tell him no.

Her brain was clear on what to do. Her belly objected, rumbling in response to the delectable aroma. "I'm ordering pizza tonight."

"Or you could have a home-cooked meal with me." His voice indicated that his option was clearly the better choice. Her roiling stomach agreed. "Besides, you're on the road a lot. Home-cooked meals must be a rarity."

"You're assuming I don't cook."

Wes raised an eyebrow, his dark eyes lit with amusement. "Do you?"

She didn't, but that wasn't the point. "It's getting late."

"You're a California girl. It's still afternoon there. Besides, it's just a meal. You can leave as soon as we're done. If that's what you'd like." He'd paused before adding that last bit.

Her jet-lagged brain struggled to manufacture another excuse. Nothing came to her. "Okay. I'll be over in a sec." She headed toward the door.

"Or you can hop the banister now." He closed the lid on the grill and held out a hand to her.

Bree chewed her lower lip as she surveyed the banister between their decks. There were wooden benches on either side of the railing. The banister was only a few feet high. She could easily jump it. Still...

She blew out a breath and stepped up onto the bench. Placing her hand in his, she stepped up onto the railing, then down onto the bench on his side. Before she could jump down, Wes planted his hands on her waist and lowered her to the floor. Taken by surprise, she gasped, drawing in his scent—clean man with a hint of juniper and sandalwood.

Bree fought the desire to lean in, her nose pressed to his freshly scrubbed skin, and inhale deeply. She tried not to muse about how delicious it felt to be back in his arms. So close that heat radiated from his brown skin. She stepped beyond his grasp, shaking her head to clear it of thoughts that would only lead to trouble. "So what's for dinner?"

Wes grinned. "Rib eyes, grilled corn, baked potatoes and grilled onions and peppers. Sound good?"

"Sounds perfect. You went all out tonight."

"Just a little something I threw together." He smiled. "Can I get you a beer or a glass of wine?"

"Red or white?"

"Pink." A wide smile spread across his face. "Sampled a great wine at the grocery store today that'll complement the steak nicely. It's chilling in the fridge now."

"I'll take the wine with dinner." If she was going to be alone with Wesley Adams for the next hour, she'd better do it mostly sober. "Can I help with anything?"

The buzzer sounded in the kitchen. "Potatoes are done. Can you take them out of the oven and plate them? Oven mitts and plates are on the counter."

She slipped inside the kitchen and did as he asked, glad to put space between them.

Bree's eyes twinkled with an excitement she seemed eager to hide as she surveyed her carefully loaded plate. She picked up her utensils. "Everything smells so good."

"Tastes even better. Dig in. Don't be shy." He couldn't peel his gaze from her face long enough to carve his own steak, afraid to miss her reaction.

Bree took a bite. An appreciative moan signaled her approval. The deeply erotic, guttural sound triggered an involuntary twitch below his belt. "This is probably the best steak I've ever had. Where'd you learn to cook like this?"

"My mom is an amazing cook. Taught me every-thing I know." He took a bite of the steak. It was ten-der and succulent. Seasoned to perfection. His mother would be proud.

"It's good she taught you to be self-sufficient. It's no picnic being with someone who isn't." Her brows knitted, as if a bad memory flashed through her brain.

"Something you know from experience, I gather." Wes sipped of his beer. He didn't want to delve deeper into her obvious pain. Yet a part of him was curious.

Bree took a generous gulp from her wineglass. "It was a long time ago."

He took the hint and changed the subject. "So how's Rebecca's shoulder? I read somewhere she'd be side-lined for at least four months."

"Could be a little longer. She's going stir-crazy, but her physical therapy is coming along."

"Good." He put butter and sour cream on his po-tato. "Dealing with an injury can be tough. Especially late in an athlete's career."

"Were you a soccer player, like Liam?" She dug in to her potato, already smothered in butter and sour cream.

"No, rugby was my sport."

"Amateur or professional?"

"I played at university, then on a lower tier regional league. Definitely wasn't in it for the money." He took another swig of his beer.

"Is rugby as rough as they say?"

"Worse. Got half a dozen injuries to prove it."

"Were you hurt badly?"

Wes winced inwardly at the memory of his last

injury, but shrugged nonchalantly. "Sprains and broken bones. Typical injuries in a high-contact sport."

"Is that why you quit?" She took another sip of her wine, her expressive brown eyes trained on him.

"Never really had a passion for the game. It was something to do in university and I was good at it. Mostly, it was a great way to blow off steam."

"Let me guess, you were the misunderstood rebel type." She speared a piece of steak and pointed her fork at him, then put the morsel in her mouth. His eyes followed the motion. He envied that morsel of beef as she savored it, her full lips pursed as she chewed.

"What gave it away?" He chuckled as she eyed the tattoo sleeve on his right arm, part of a large tribal tattoo that also encompassed the right side of his chest and back. "I didn't consider myself a rebel. Too cliché. On the surface, I was a pretty affable guy. Had a lot of anger pent up inside. Rugby seemed like the best way to release it."

Wes cut into his steak and took another bite, chastising himself. He'd invited Bree to dinner to repair the damage he'd caused and build a working relationship. Not to tell her his entire life story.

He seldom discussed his past with the women he dated. And never with the women with whom he did business. He preferred to stick to the casual overview. Fish-out-of-water Southern boy raised in London was usually enough.

So why had he cracked open the door to his past to Bree?

Because there was something about her that put him at ease. Made him feel like he could let down his guard. It was the thing he remembered most about that night. He was attracted to her, of course. She was Bree Evans. Tall. Gorgeous. Miles of smooth, glistening skin the shade of brown sugar. Provocative, yet sweet. She was laid-back and genuine with a smile that could convince an Eskimo to buy a truckload of ice. No wonder sponsors fell all over themselves to get her to endorse their products. Lip gloss, facial cleanser, breakfast cereal and workout contraptions.

Keep your head in the game, buddy. This isn't a date. You're only trying to create some goodwill.

She broke in to his thoughts with a tentative question. "What was it you were so angry about?"

"Life, I guess. The guys I attended boarding school with had the perfect life handed to them on a silver platter. I didn't." He shrugged. "It bugged me."

"Me, too." She was quiet, contemplative. "I was the scholarship kid at an elite private school." She winced, as if the memory caused her physical pain. "Took three buses to get there every morning, but I got an incredible education and a full ride to college because of it. Most importantly, that's where I fell in love with volleyball. That school changed my life, and I'm grateful for it."

"But…" There was something she wasn't saying. The unspoken words were so heavy and dense, they practically hung in the air between them. He should've ignored them, but the word tripped out of his mouth before he could stop it.

"It was hard being thrust into a completely different world. Especially for a gangly girl who wasn't quite sure where she fit in. Who wanted to be liked."

"How could anyone not like Bree Evans, the quintessential girl next door?" He smiled.

Bree glowered at him, then dug in to her potato. "You'd be surprised," she muttered.

Dammit. He walked right into that one. He wanted to make her forget what an ass he'd been. Now they'd come full circle right back to that night. His gut churned from the hurt in her brown eyes, when she raised them to his again.

"Look, about that night—"

Bree waved his words off as she shook her head. "It wasn't the right time for you. I know. I'd rather not talk about it."

Fine. It wasn't like the conversation was his idea of a good time, either. If she didn't want to talk about it, he sure as hell didn't.

They ate in silence for a few minutes. Then Bree engaged him in small talk about the surprisingly mild weather and her lunch with Liam and few of the locals. He nodded politely and responded appropriately. But he couldn't ignore the pain in her eyes, knowing he'd caused it.

He was his own worst enemy. Always had been.

"The time wasn't right because, for me, it never is. Not for anything serious. I'm focused on expanding my business, so I don't get seriously involved with anyone. Ever."

He studied her face, gauging her reaction and whether he should go further. Her lips were pressed into a straight line, her expression devoid of emotion.

Wes pressed his fingertips to his forehead. "When the night began, it seemed we were on the same page, but then... I don't know. It felt like you wanted more. That's not something I can give you. That's why I didn't call. Not because I don't like you. Because I like you too much to start something I can't finish."

Bree drained what was left of her second glass of wine. "Thank you for being so honest and for being so very considerate of my feelings. But I'm a big girl. I can take care of myself." She stood. "Thank you for dinner, but it's getting late. I'd better get back."

"Brianna, don't go. We were having a lovely dinner. I didn't mean to spoil the mood, but I don't want you to feel as if I rejected you. That wasn't it at all."

"I think I'm still a bit jet-lagged." Bree was a terrible liar, but he applauded her effort to remain civil. She took her dishes to the kitchen.

"I'll get it." Wes trailed her to the kitchen and stacked his plate on hers.

"Dinner was delicious. The least I can do is help with the dishes." Bree scraped his plate, then hers, and loaded the dishes into the dishwasher.

He leaned against the refrigerator, arms folded over his chest, as she put away the dirty dishes. She seemed to be processing his words as she rinsed the pots and pans.

Wes held his tongue. After all, how many times could a guy say he was sorry before the words became hollow and meaningless? More importantly, he kept his hands to himself, balled in tight fists beneath his arms.

He ignored the persistent desire to touch her. To taste her mouth and softly caress the skin at the nape of her neck, exposed by her high ponytail. To finish what they'd started that night in London.

He shifted his weight, camouflaging his body's reaction to the tactile memory and the current vision of

Bree bent over the dishwasher—her pert, round ass highlighted by a pair of snug, navy yoga pants.

Maybe they should call it a night, before he did something they'd both regret.

"I've got this. Really." He stepped toward her as she turned suddenly, nearly colliding with him. She planted her hands on his chest to brace herself from the impact. He grabbed her arms to steady her. When their eyes met, her cheeks turned crimson. She dropped her hands and stepped backward.

"Then I'll go." She headed toward the patio door.

"Wait, I'll help you over the—" Before he could get through the doors she'd planted her hands on the railing and vaulted over to the other side.

She was practically a blur as she hurried inside, tossing a final "thanks and good night" over her shoulder.

He ran a hand over his head and sighed.

Way to go, Wes.

Bree retreated to her bed. Her heart rate and breathing were still elevated from her vault over the banister and sprint up the stairs. Knees drawn to her chest, she rested her chin on them and hugged her legs.

The grown-ass woman equivalent of hiding in a corner, hugging her teddy bear.

So much for playing it cool.

She'd accepted his dinner invitation, determined to prove the past was behind them. They'd be able to forge a business relationship that was profitable for everyone involved. She needed to prove it to herself, as much as she needed to prove it to him.

Bex was counting on her to remain calm and stick

with the plan. She promised her friend she would. After all, her future was riding on this event being a success, too.

Bree groaned as she recounted the evening's events. Her plan went off the rails long before they sat down to eat. It was the moment he'd taken her hand in his, then grabbed hold of her waist. Instantly, she'd been transported to that night in London. Her attraction to him was as palpable now as it was then.

Still, she managed to pull it together and get through an hour of dinner conversation. Civilly. Without staring at his strong biceps or focusing on the rise and fall of his well-defined pecs as he laughed.

Okay, that last part had been a monumental failure. He caught her checking him out more than once.

No wonder he felt compelled to outline exactly where things stood between them. He wasn't interested in starting a relationship. A statement that was in direct opposition to the starry-eyed schoolgirl fantasy she couldn't seem to let go of.

His words made her want to crawl under a chair and hide.

He'd seen straight through her ruse, much as he had the night they first met. She'd walked into that club determined to be witty, flirtatious and cosmopolitan. All the things she wasn't. She'd been able to maintain the illusion most of the night. Until she met Wes. He was charming and funny, and he'd made her so comfortable she'd dropped the pretense and slipped back into her own skin, like a comfy pair of pj's. The facade quickly faded away, as did her illusions of being satisfied with something temporary and meaningless. She'd wanted more.

That night, for the first time in a long time, she'd been hopeful she could have it.

She'd been wrong.

Maybe she was just as wrong to think she could work with Wes and not be affected by his smile. His charm. His incredible body.

Bree shut her eyes and tried not to think of it. Or the way his hard muscles felt beneath her fingertips, both times she ended up in his arms tonight.

Stretching her legs, she reached for the remote and turned on the television.

Focus on the plan, not the man. She silently repeated the words her high-school volleyball coach would recite to her when she got too caught up with the opponent on the other side of the net.

Don't be fooled by his good looks and charm. Wesley Adams is the enemy.

A frenemy, at the very least. She'd dealt with plenty of those in her career. Had even partnered up with a couple.

Bree closed her eyes and visualized herself facing off against Wes on the volleyball court. As long as she held onto that image, she'd be good. In control of her thoughts and emotions. Her body's response.

Everything will be fine. She headed back down to the kitchen, repeating the words to herself.

She could do this. But first she needed a bottle of wine. No glass required.

Chapter 5

Wes slipped into the passenger seat of Liam's BMW a few minutes before ten and mumbled his greeting. Despite the comfortable mattress and room-darkening curtains, he would've gotten just as much sleep had he slept on a slab of cold concrete below a bustling railroad bridge. At five in the morning he gave up the pointless battle and went for a run on the beach. But his lack of sleep was catching up to him.

"You're all sunshine and roses this morning, I see." Liam grinned as he turned out of the parking lot and onto the main road. "Why do I feel there's a story involving Bree behind your obvious lack of sleep."

True. Though not in the way his friend was imagining. He'd lain awake last night, his words to Bree and her reaction to them replaying in his head on an endless loop. That was twice he tried to do the right thing where Brianna was concerned, only to have it blow up in his face. A vivid reminder of why he avoided serious relationships. He had a special gift for messing them up. It was a trait he'd gotten from his old man.

When he hadn't been thinking of Bree, he'd been worried about his mother. When sleep finally came, he dreamed of Bree's soft, warm, shapely curves stretching those poor yoga pants to their limit. A shiver ran down his spine now thinking of them.

Still, there was no way he'd give his friend the satisfaction of thinking he was right. Sliding his shades down the bridge of his nose, he peered at Liam. "So you admit that inviting Brianna and I both to work on this project was a harebrained attempt at matchmaking?"

"I'll admit nothing of the sort." His friend's voice was insistent, though the edges of his mouth quirked into an involuntary smirk. He cleared his throat and straightened his expression. "You and Bree are the best people for this project. If something more becomes of it—"

"It won't."

"Fine." Liam kept his eyes on the road ahead, another grin sliding across his mouth. "Though some might say the man doth protest too much."

"Save the Shakespeare bullshit. I'm serious." Wes sighed, softening his voice as he ran his hands through his hair. "Look, I know you see love and happy endings everywhere you look, now that you and Maya are about to get married. But I'm fine with things the way they are."

"I used to think that, too." His friend sported a self-satisfied grin. As if he was in possession of all of the universe's answers about love. If Wes wasn't so damn happy for the guy, he'd slap him on the back of his head, Three Stooges-style, and tell him to get a grip.

"I'm not just saying it." Wes stretched his long legs out and leaned into the headrest, his arms folded over his abdomen. "Not everyone is in search of love. Or even believes it exists." He muttered the last part under his breath and closed his eyes.

Liam chuckled. "I used to think that, too."

Wes brushed crumbs from his navy slacks and pushed the sleeves of his heather gray sweater up his forearms. Though it was mid-February, it was nearly seventy degrees. They had breakfast at the club before hitting the golf course. Despite Liam's reminder to bring his clubs, Wes left them back in London, hoping they'd skip the links. But Liam was two steps ahead of him. He'd purchased himself a new set of clubs and loaned Wes his old ones.

Now, he stood at the seventh green trying to line up his shot and cut in to the lead Liam was quickly building. Wes widened his stance, squared his shoulders, drew the nine-iron back above his shoulders and swung hard. He stood back and watched the ball's ascent.

Liam chuckled as the ball sailed, beautifully, but headed for the pond. It landed with an unceremonious plop, water shooting in the air. A handful of birds flapped their wings in protest to the intrusion. "Impatient as ever, I see. I've told you a million times, you can't rush the shot. Gotta let it come to you. It's a lesson that works in love, too, my friend."

Wes cursed under his breath at the wicked angle

the ball took, then groaned at Liam's brotherly advice. "Is that why we're here today? For Liam Westbrook's lessons in love?"

Liam laughed. "I don't plan to lecture you, if that's what you mean. But what kind of mate would I be if I didn't state the obvious?"

"That I'm being a general ass where Bree's concerned?" No point in beating around the bush.

"I'd have put it a bit more delicately." Liam held back a grin as he climbed behind the wheel of the golf cart. Neither of them were the kind of guys who relished sitting in the passenger seat. But the agreement was the winner of their last round drove the next time. It was a sucker bet. Liam was a far better player. Still, his pride wouldn't allow him to concede or stop believing he'd win next time. So here he was riding shotgun again.

"Bree's a great girl, Liam. You know I think the world of her. But I'm not interested in a relationship. A policy we once shared." He gave his friend a side eye, trying to rein in the green-eyed monster that gave him mixed emotions about his friend's engagement. He was happy for Liam. They were best friends. Had been since they were thirteen years old.

They trusted each other with their lives. Told each other the truth, whether they wanted to hear it or not. And if they couldn't tell each other the truth, they'd both learned to avoid the subject altogether.

Like he'd been trying to do now. Not that his friend was picking up on the hint.

"Come on. You act like I betrayed the bro code or something." Liam pulled alongside the tree and parked in the vicinity of where the ball had crossed over into the water hazard.

Liam was right. He was acting like an overgrown child whose best friend had become friends with the kid next door.

"I didn't mean it like that. I just meant, you once understood that philosophy. Lived by it faithfully. You were the one person I could count on to never give me grief about it being time for me to settle down." Wes shrugged. "I miss that luxury."

"Never thought of that." Liam folded his arms over the steering wheel. His expression was apologetic.

After a few moments of silence between them, he continued. "Back when I shared your philosophy on relationships, I truly believed we were the smartest guys around. But when I fell for Maya I discovered the truth about myself. I wasn't being brave all those years, I was afraid of being hurt again. Too cowardly to take the risk."

Wes climbed out of the cart with his club in hand and dropped his ball. Liam's revelation didn't come as a surprise. He remembered how devastated his friend had been when he discovered his off-and-on girlfriend, Meredith, had fallen for his brother, Hunter. Still, it was unsettling to hear Liam admit it.

Wes turned his back to Liam and concentrated on the game. He took his time and drove the ball again. This time it landed closer to the hole than his friend's had. He slid his club back in the bag and hopped inside the cart.

"Well played, mate." Liam's raised eyebrows knitted together, despite his compliment.

Wes laughed. "Look, I appreciate your concern. I

do. And you know I couldn't be happier for you. Maya
and the girls are amazing. You're a lucky guy. So I
get that you want to see me happy, too. But you're assuming I'm not. That my life is somehow incomplete."

Liam didn't respond. His silence said more than
his words ever could.

Wes couldn't argue. He was content with his life the
way it was, but he couldn't deny that there were nights
when his bed felt cold and empty. Even on nights on
the town, in a room brimming with people, he occasionally felt alone. But he'd been content to ignore
those moments. To fill the empty space with a warm
body or a night of laughter. "I'm focused on growing
Adams Promotions and making the Pleasure Cove
volleyball tournament a success. Don't have time for
distractions. Got it?"

After a long pause, Liam nodded. "All right. Now,
you were going to tell me why you looked so awful
yesterday. What's going on? You sure as hell didn't
look content then."

Wes lowered his eyes, his jaw clenching painfully.
"It's my mom. She's sick."

Liam parked the cart and turned his body in the seat
toward him. "Maya, the girls, and I had lunch with
your mum a couple of months ago. She seemed fine."

"She's done her best to hide it." He swallowed the
lump that formed in his throat. "She was diagnosed
with Parkinson's six months ago."

"Did you know before you went to visit her?" His
friend could understand the anger and frustration he
felt. Liam's father hadn't told him about his battle with
prostate cancer until he was already through his treat-
ments and in remission.

Wes shook his head and shifted in his seat to alleviate the hole that burned in his gut whenever the inevitable thoughts of what was ahead for his mother came to mind. Increased difficulty with balance and movements. Not to mention the involuntary movements that were side effects of the most common medication given for Parkinson's. If the disease continued to progress at its current rate, she would require constant care in a few years. "She didn't want me to worry. Or to feel obligated to return to America. And she didn't want Drake to give up his career."

Liam squeezed his shoulder, forcing Wes to meet his gaze. His friend's knowing smile eased the suffocating pain in his chest. "Sounds like Ms. Lena. She's strong-willed and independent. And she loves you and your brother more than anything in the world."

"But not enough to tell us about her diagnosis." The reality of those words struck him hard. His mother had always been stubborn and determined. She'd made incredible sacrifices to give him and his brother the best life possible, regardless of the cost to her. Yet, now that she needed him, she wouldn't ask for his help. She didn't want to impose on his life. Had he made her feel that way? That she was a bother to him? Wes slumped in his seat, his gaze lowered again. He sure as hell wouldn't be winning any son-of-the-year awards.

Liam patted his friend on the back, then eased his foot onto the gas pedal, setting the cart in motion. "You know how protective your mother is of you two. Like you said, she didn't want you to worry. Besides, not telling you was probably also her way of retaining her dignity and independence. An illness like that forces us to face our own mortality. Even if it's only for a moment. It was hard for my dad. Must be pretty hard for your mum, too."

Mortality.

That word sent a chill down his spine that settled into his gut, twisting it. His mother had given him everything she possibly could. All he'd done was bring her grief. Her marriage ended because of him, and so did her dream career. It killed him that even now she was making sacrifices. She'd already done so much for them. They could never repay her, but he'd do whatever it took to try. Even if that meant moving back to North Carolina.

"Does Drake know?"

"We called him the same day I found out."

"I know how tough this must be for you and Drake. Anything you or your mum need…just say the word."

His friend's words dragged him out of his daze. Wes sat taller in his seat and nodded.

"You've already helped. If you hadn't invited me onto this project…" He shuddered inwardly, wondering how long his mother would've kept the diagnosis to herself. "I appreciate the opportunity and the generous housing offer while we work on the project. I'd only intended to stay for the weeks of our planned meetings, but things have changed. Despite what she thinks, my mother needs me."

"Will you move here permanently?" Liam couldn't hide the excitement in his voice, though he made a valiant effort.

A grin turned up one corner of Wesley's mouth. It was comforting that his best friend was eager to have him move closer. They'd been separated by an ocean most of the past five years. "I'm not ready to sell my

flat in London, but I'm escalating my timeline to expand my business here in the US."

"Let me know how I can help."

"Actually, I do need one more favor." Wes hated
asking his friend for special treatment. This was a
business deal, and he always treated them as such.
But regardless of whom he was working with, he had
to act in his mother's best interest. As she'd always
done for him. "I need to miss our next meeting. I'm
returning to London to set the wheels in motion. Unless some emergency happens with my mother, I don't
anticipate missing another."

"I understand. Of course. We'll get you the meeting notes and bring you up to speed. Communicate
via email until you return."

Wes breathed a sigh of relief. "Thanks for understanding."

"Does that mean you're willing to overlook my
meddling in your love life?" The smile returned to
Liam's face, easing the tension they were both feeling.

Wes laughed and shook his head. "You know, after
that first meeting, I'd planned to turn down the project.
Bree was mad as hell about me leaving her hanging. I
didn't think it was possible for us to work together."

Lines spanned Liam's forehead as he parked the
cart. "And now?"

Wes stepped out of the cart and grabbed his putter.
He shrugged. "Now I need to make this work. Seems
she does, too. We've called a truce. She apologized
for how she reacted after the meeting. I apologized
for being an ass back then. I even invited her over for
dinner last night."

Liam hopped out of the cart, grabbed his putter and

followed his friend onto the green. A huge grin spread across his face. "And after dinner?"

"I grilled steaks. We chatted. Everything was going well until…" Wes rubbed his neck and sighed.

"Until?" Liam raised an eyebrow.

"I wanted Bree to understand why things didn't work out between us. That it was because of me. Not because of anything she did or didn't do."

"Wait, you gave her the bloody it's-not-you-it's-me speech?" Liam scrubbed his hand down his face and shook his head. "Aww, bloody hell. What were you thinking?"

"She looked so hurt about what happened between us. I couldn't stand seeing that wounded look on her face. I had to do something to fix things between us."

"And did it?"

Wes blew out a breath, exasperated with himself. "She bolted out of the door like her hair was on fire and I was holding a can of gasoline."

Liam rubbed his forehead and took a deep breath. "Okay, so dinner didn't go so well. Next time…"

"There isn't going to be a next time." Wes turned to face his friend, needing him to understand how serious he was about this. "Bree and I came to an understanding. We both need this project, and we want it to be the absolute best it can be. But there isn't going to be a romance, maybe not even a friendship. Just a good, productive working relationship. We're both okay with that. I need you to be, too." Wes pointed a finger at his friend.

Liam snapped his mouth closed and lowered his gaze. He grunted, shoving one hand into his pocket.

He gripped his club and assumed his stance. "If that's what you want, fine. I won't interfere."

Liam's agreement was hardly convincing, but he would respect his wishes. He was sure of it. Liam struck the ball and they watched it roll, landing within a few feet of the seventh hole.

It was his turn.

Wes stood over the ball, lining up his shot. He inhaled deeply. *Focus, man. Get the ball in the cup. Simple as that.* He released his breath, drew back the club and smacked the ball, hitting it long.

Too long.

He bit back a curse and climbed back into the cart. If he could keep his foot out of his mouth and his golf ball on the green, maybe he would survive this project.

Chapter 6

It'd been three weeks since the disastrous dinner with Wesley. She hadn't seen him since. There had only been one meeting during the past few weeks, but Wes had skipped it. Probably because of her reaction to his confession that night.

The time wasn't right because, for me, it never is. Not for anything serious.

God, she felt like an idiot. She hadn't accepted his dinner invitation with the hopes of starting something between them. Still, those hopes had lingered in the back of her mind. Despite her desperate attempts to stamp them out.

There is nothing between us. Not now. Not ever.

She repeated the words in her head over and over as she jogged along the beach. Her pace quickened with each repetition, as if she was trying to outrun the words. Or maybe her feelings for him.

He's attractive. Charming. So what? I can think of half a dozen guys who are, too. Guys who are actually interested in me.

Bree came to a halt, as if she'd run into a solid brick wall. The phone calls from her ex that she hadn't returned, along with a text message she'd left unanswered, were vivid in her mind. She could practically hear Alex Hunt's voice, low and gravelly, uttering the words he'd typed that morning.

Been calling you. You're not at your place. Where are you? I'll only be in town for a few more days. We need to talk.

A knot tightened in her stomach. Her muscles tensed and her palms felt clammy, despite the cool breeze blowing across the water onto the beach. Bree calmed her breath and stood tall, stretching her arms toward the sky for a beat before resuming her run.

She was in control. Not Alex. It'd been more than three years since she'd ended their relationship. They were over and there was no way she was going back to him. Ever.

Still, she couldn't deny the unease she felt at his words. How did he know she wasn't at her place? And why, after three years, would he suddenly call? Had he conveniently forgotten how things had ended between them? With her threatening to get a restraining order.

Alex had taken a job in Kansas City not long afterward. She hadn't seen or heard from him since then.

Her threats of filing a complaint against him had obviously worked. So why was he contacting her now?

The truth was, she didn't care and had no desire to find out. She wasn't afraid of Alex. She'd taken defense classes. She could take care of herself if she needed to. Yet, she'd scrapped her plans to return to California and opted to stay at the resort instead. Liam had comped their housing through the wrap-up meeting following the volleyball tournament, not long after Labor Day. She hadn't intended to take him up on it. But when she heard Alex's voice mail, her blood had run cold. She'd canceled her flight home and hired a trainer to work with her in Pleasure Cove.

Bree came to a stop, hands on her hips, sweat running down the side of her face. She checked her pulse. Good, but not great. Breathing heavily, she plopped down into the sand and pulled her cell phone out of her armband and checked her email. Her sporting-goods sponsor was making the final decision on a new line of volleyball attire branded with her name. She needed to review the designs and give her input on which pieces should make the final cut.

No email from the sponsor yet. There was an email from Lisa Chastain with the subject "Changes to Program." She scanned the email, her heart beating faster.

That jerk.

Wes apparently hadn't liked her idea about making the event a family-friendly one. It wasn't part of the original plan, but it was important to her and Bex. They planned to lead volleyball camps for kids aged eight to seventeen. What better way to build a relationship with her target clients than to involve them in the Pleasure Cove tournament?

Wes clearly didn't agree. Was this his way of getting back at her?

Only one way to find out.

Bree searched the tournament contact list for Wesley's number. She inhaled a deep breath, then clicked on the number. The phone rang several times then went to voice mail.

"Hey, this is Wes. Not available right now, but leave me a message, and I'll get back to you."

The beep sounded and her heart stuck in her throat, leaving her speechless for a moment. "Wesley, this is Brianna Evans. I just saw the email about the changes you're requesting. I'd like to discuss it. Please call me back as soon as you get a moment."

Bree finished her run, determined not to think of Wes or Alex.

Five hours later, Wes hadn't answered her original message or picked up the two times she'd called since then. Maybe her behavior was coming dangerously close to that of a stalker. Bree didn't care. This was important. There was no way Liam would side with her over Wes. Miranda and Lisa were enthusiastic about her idea during the meeting, but she doubted they'd have much sway over their boss if he was backing Wes on this.

She had to go directly to the source. Make Wes understand why the family-friendly component of the tournament was critical.

Bree sat at the kitchen counter, tapping her short nails against the granite. Wes had returned to London for the past few weeks, but she'd seen him arrive the day before. He was right next door, ignoring her calls.

Bree could hear Bex's voice in her head.

Whatever it takes.

She sighed, then hopped down from the stool. Wes wasn't answering his phone. Maybe he would answer the door instead. Bree knocked. No answer. She'd smelled food grilling earlier. Maybe he was out back. Bree headed through her guest house and went outside. She looked over the barrier between their back decks. There he was, lounging on a chaise, eyes closed and earphones plugged in.

Bree called his name, but Wes didn't respond or even move an inch. She called him again. Still, he didn't hear her. Finally, she climbed over the barrier. She reached out to shake his arm, but she paused, taking him in.

God, this man is gorgeous.

The temperature was only in the low seventies, but the sun still shone brightly overhead, making it feel much warmer. He'd taken off his shirt and thrown it across the empty chaise. She studied his inked, brown skin. The tattoo on his right arm was part of a much larger tattoo that covered the entire right half of his torso and disappeared below the waistband of the swim shorts, which hung dangerously low on his hips. Just how far down did that tattoo go?

You're not here to ogle him. Get a grip.

Wes cleared his throat. A smirk curled the edges of his mouth.

Damn. Busted again.

"Hey, I was just… I mean I was…" Bree sucked in a deep breath, willing herself to stop babbling. "You didn't answer any of my calls."

"Exactly how many times did you call?" There was slight tension in his voice.

Yep. He definitely thought she was stalking him.

"A couple times," she lied, clearing her throat. "Were you screening my calls?"

"Phone's in the house. Sometimes I like to unplug." He yawned, then shielded his eyes from the sun as he looked up at her. "You should try it some time."

Bree stepped forward, her back molars grinding and her hands balled into fists at her side. "I'll pass on the life advice, thanks. It's bad enough you're taking over my event."

"*Your* event?" Wes raised an eyebrow in slight amusement as he adjusted the chair into a sitting position. "This is Liam's event. You're the celebrity name with the pretty face they hired to front the operation." A smirk lifted the corner of his mouth. "Didn't expect we'd see you beyond the first meeting."

Wes was enjoying making her crazy. If the racing of her pulse and the tightening of her nipples were any indication, he was making her crazy for him, too.

Bree tore her gaze away from the sexy smirk on his lips and forced it upward to meet his, rather than downward to steal another glance at the hard muscles glistening beneath a slight sheen of sweat.

Her nails dug into her palms as she stepped closer. Her shadow fell across him. "This isn't my first rodeo, cowboy. Contrary to what you might think, I'm *not* just a pretty face. I agreed to join this project because Liam wanted my input."

"I was only teasing. Thought it would lighten the mood." His expression was apologetic. Seemingly sincere. He snatched his shirt off the empty chaise and extended his hand toward it. "Why don't you have a seat?"

"I don't want to sit. I want to know why you've vetoed my idea without the courtesy of an email or a phone call." Bree crossed her arms over her chest, where his eyes had wandered momentarily.

Wes climbed to his feet and stretched, giving her an excellent view of the hard muscles of his chest and abdomen, beneath his smooth brown skin.

The man took good care of himself. From head to toe. No doubt about that.

He walked over to the hot tub near the far corner of the deck. After removing the cover, he folded it and placed it on the bench before slipping inside. He closed his eyes as he sank deeper into the bubbling water. The tension seemed to disappear from his shoulders.

Finally, he acknowledged her again, though he didn't open his eyes. "If you want to discuss the idea now, I suggest you grab a swimsuit. Because for the next hour or so, this is where I'll be taking my meetings."

Bree's cheeks flamed and her heart beat so loudly Wes could probably hear it. Her hands tightened into fists at her side, itching with a desire to smack that self-satisfied grin off his handsome face. "I am *not* getting into that hot tub."

"Then I guess we'll talk about this when I return in a week."

"Wesley Adams—"

He gestured that he couldn't hear her, then slipped lower in the water.

Bree gritted her teeth, climbed back over the divider and headed up to her bedroom. If he thought he could drive her off that easily, he was in for a rude awakening.

Wes shut his eyes and allowed the heated water and full-blast jet streams to melt the tension. For as long as he could remember, any stress he was feeling had gone straight to his shoulders. He could still hear his teacher, Ms. Lively, scolding him for hunching his shoulders around his ears, like they were a pair of earrings.

He'd been a sensitive kid. Always in tune with the feelings of others. Particularly his mother and grandmother. His mother had always put on a brave face and tried to hide her anxiety. But she didn't fool him. Not for a minute. Not even when he was twelve.

Over the years he'd learned to control it. To dial back his reaction to other people's feelings. He reserved that kind of investment for the people who really mattered to him.

Lena Adams was at the top of that list.

Despite the brave face she'd put on, she was scared. Afraid of what the future held when her body no longer complied. The pain that simmered beneath her brave smile nestled in his gut like a five-hundred-pound boulder. He hadn't been able to shake it.

The trip back to London hadn't helped. His event manager, Nadia, wasn't happy about his decision to make Pleasure Cove the new home base of the company. She was aware that he'd planned to expand to the US, but she'd expected him to continue living and working in London for the majority of the year. He had, too. His mother's illness changed his plans.

He wouldn't move to New Bern, where his mother lived. She'd feel he was encroaching on her independence. Instead, he'd make Pleasure Cove his home base, keeping him within an easy two-hour drive of his mother. Besides, with Pleasure Cove as his base he could easily work with Westbrook International Luxury Resorts on future projects, while slowly expanding his reach along the East Coast. It wasn't the fancy, New York office he'd planned, but he'd make it work.

"Looks like you're deep in thought. Hope you're thinking about why my family-friendly tournament is the better option."

His eyes fluttered open. Wes blinked. Twice.

Bree stepped down from the bench in a sexy, black one-piece swimsuit that caused all of the tension that had drained from his shoulders to settle below his waist. He swallowed hard as she walked toward him. The asymmetrical swimsuit had one strap, across her left shoulder. Just below her full breasts, a cut-out veered in, nearly to her navel, then dipped back out again at her waist, revealing the smooth, brown skin on the left side of her torso. Her hair was pulled up in a loose ponytail, high at the back of her head.

She was gorgeous. From the sway of her generous hips and the sly turn at the corners of her pouty lips, she damn well knew it.

The gloves were off, and Bree was prepared to play dirty. There was no way in hell he could concentrate on business while she was standing there in…*that*.

His appreciative assessment of the swim attire clinging for dear life to her undulating curves hadn't gone unnoticed. Bree tried to swallow a grin as she inched closer, then slid out of her sandals.

Wes extended his hand to her, but didn't stand. If he did, his appreciation for her choice of swimwear would become painfully obvious. "You took me up on the offer. Didn't think you would."

"Don't underestimate me. I don't give up so easily." She settled into the seat across from his.

He nodded, his gaze settling on her fiercely determined one. Bree was ready for a battle. "I know. Watched you play for years. I've seen you dig out of some tough spots. Your refusal to concede, it's what I admire most about you as a player."

"But not as a colleague seated across the boardroom table, I take it." She folded her arms beneath her breasts, inadvertently providing him with a spectacular view of her cleavage. His gaze dropped there momentarily and she immediately realized her mistake. Bree lowered her arms and narrowed her gaze at him, one eyebrow raised.

"I appreciate tenacity, even in an opponent. Regardless of the playing field. Apparently you do, too. You teamed up with one of your fiercest rivals, Bex Jacobs." Wes reached behind him and opened the cooler. "Beer?"

She stared at him for a moment, as if the question was a test, then nodded. "Yes, thank you."

Wes grabbed two beers, opened them both and handed one to her. "So you and Bex…how'd that happen?"

"We became friends during a trip to the Olympics with other partners. A couple years later, we both found ourselves in need of new partners. Teaming up was a no-brainer."

"A lot of pundits felt it was a mistake for you two to team up."

"Reporters and analysts who were afraid that without our rivalry, there would be nothing else in women's volleyball to talk about." She practically snorted. He held back a grin. "They were wrong."

"They were, and so was I. I was one of those people who thought it was a mistake. Glad I was wrong." He sipped his beer.

"But you're not wrong now?" She narrowed her gaze when he gestured that her estimation was correct. Her cheeks turned deep red and she pursed her lips. "You summarily dismissed the idea without giving it any consideration."

"I have considered your proposal. It's admirable you want to make the event welcoming to families, but that isn't what we're going for here."

"Why not? Because you say so?" She crossed her arms again, higher this time, blocking his view of her curves. It was a move he appreciated—he didn't need the distraction.

"Because we want to make as much money on this event as possible the first time out. We won't do that selling cotton candy and ice cream. Alcohol—" he held up his bottle for emphasis "—*that's* where we'll make our money. Throw in a celebrity chef making gourmet meals. Couple that with overpriced drinks with fancy names. Suddenly we're making money hand over fist our first year."

"You act like there isn't money to be made in family entertainment." The pitch of her voice climbed higher. "Ever heard of theme parks?"

"Of course." He smiled inwardly. She was on the

defensive. Not as calm and collected as she'd been when she'd strolled across the deck. "But this ain't a theme park, darlin'. The Pleasure Cove Luxury Resort is geared toward entertainment of the adult variety. I imagine having Junior underfoot would kill Dad's buzz while he's ogling the celebrity volleyball players."

She folded her arms, lifting her breasts again. Then she dropped them and sighed, not responding. He wasn't sure if she was angry with him or herself.

Despite what she seemed to think, he got no joy from raining on her parade. He'd much prefer to see that gorgeous smile of hers. The one that went straight to his chest and made his heart skip a beat.

Wes leaned in, his voice apologetic. "Look, I admire your idea. I'm just not sure there's a market for a family-friendly volleyball tournament. If there is, it's definitely not Pleasure Cove. Besides, our goal is to make this event rival some of the other popular East Coast volleyball tournaments within the next three years. Inviting small children isn't the way to do that."

Her lower lip jutted out a bit. Even her pout was sexy as hell. It made him want to cross to her side and suck on her lower lip. Hear the soft moans that would emanate from her throat when he did. The memory of how she felt in his arms and the taste of those sweet, kissable lips crawled over his skin, unsettling him.

Keep your hands and lips to yourself, man.

Wes set his beer on the hot tub, dragging his gaze back to her eyes. He hated to see her disappointed. Hated being the cause of it. But he was hired to do a job. Not to protect the volleyball princess's feelings.

So why did he feel like shit for killing her idea?

Bree set her beer bottle on the side of the hot tub. "Then we should be more aggressive with our plan. Give it a music festival vibe. Maybe bring in some up-and-coming local bands on rotating stages. That's what they did at the tournament in LA. I played in that tournament a few times. The lure of the bands boosted attendance."

"This isn't LA. We're not exactly known for our music scene."

"Okay, maybe not Pleasure Cove, but we could expand the reach to the rest of the state." She sighed in response to his unconvinced expression. "Are you saying North Carolina doesn't have the talent to pull this off?"

"Not at all. There are a wide range of talented acts here in the state. But it wouldn't have the kind of draw the LA music scene does. We can integrate local acts, maybe have them featured at some of the smaller venues, but we'll need some heavy hitters, including a highly recognizable act to anchor the center stage. I know you're a California girl, but the East Coast has a totally different vibe."

"Well, at the event in New York—"

He shook his head, ignoring the frown tugging at the corners of her mouth. "This isn't New York, either. We're in the Carolinas. Got no illusion we can beat New York or LA at their own game."

Bree folded her arms again. "Then exactly what do you suggest?"

Wes smiled, waving a hand toward the beach. "We create a competitive advantage based on what sets North Carolina apart."

"And exactly what is that?" She stared at him, one eyebrow raised. Ready for battle.

He chuckled. "The fact that you have to ask means a little research is in order."

"You're giving me homework?" The tension in her voice spiraled.

"I'm giving *us* homework." His brain immediately balked at the statement. He was supposed to be creating distance between him and Bree Evans. Not finding a way to spend more time with her. It was a battle his good sense was losing. He raised his chin. "Spend the next week exploring the state with me."

Her mouth opened and her eyes widened, but she didn't speak. She was considering it. That was more than he'd hoped for. So he pressed further.

"We'll spend a couple of days at the beach, a few in the mountains, and a day or two in Raleigh, Chapel Hill and Charlotte. You'll get a sense of what makes the state unique." She narrowed her gaze at him, so he added, "I'm a North Carolina native, but I've lived in London most of my life. The state is growing rapidly, and so much has changed. That's why I need the refresher. What do you say? Do we have a date?"

Wes regretted his word choice nearly the moment he'd uttered it.

This would be a business trip. Plain and simple. He wouldn't spend the next six months fighting her on every decision they had to make about the tournament. Which celebs to invite. The selection of celebrity chefs. Which bands to hire. Themes. The schedule.

Bree knew volleyball tournaments. She'd competed in plenty of them, competitive and exhibition. But if he could give her a better sense of the venue and what he and Liam were trying to accomplish, she might come around and stop fighting him.

Wes tilted his head, taking her in. This might be the worst idea he ever had. Bree was smart and beautiful. Yet, she was a fierce competitor. Everything about this woman made him want her.

He gripped the sides of the hot tub, determined not to move, when what he really wanted was to take her in his arms and kiss her again. Then take her to his bed.

The physical attraction was enough to battle, but what worried him most was his growing need to be in her company. He felt at ease with Brianna. Her company was a welcome antidote to the anxiety he felt over his mother's illness.

If they could get past the awkwardness of what had happened in London, maybe they could be friends.

"C'mon, it'll be fun."

She raised her gaze to his. "And we'll have separate rooms?"

"Of course. I'll be on my best behavior. I promise."

"Fine." Bree stepped out of the hot tub and dried herself off. She wrapped a towel around her body and secured it. "Email me the itinerary."

She didn't wait for his response, so he didn't offer one. He only hoped he wasn't making another huge mistake that would land both of them in hot water.

Chapter 7

"You agreed to do what?" Bex's voice blared through the speaker on Bree's cell phone, which was propped on the bathroom sink as she detangled her shoulder-length, curly hair. It was a task that took far longer than she cared to admit. "Have you lost your freaking mind? You've got a thing for this guy. Or are we still pretending that you're over him?"

"Hey, you're the one who said do whatever it takes to make this work. That's what I'm doing. Or have you forgotten the plan?" Bree responded, her heart racing. Not because she was arguing with her best friend. Because Bex was right, and they both knew it.

"I know what I said, but I also know you. The girl who wears her heart on her sleeve, and who is really attracted to this guy." Bex sighed. "I don't get this guy. First, he tells you he doesn't believe in anything serious. Next, he's inviting you to spend a week with him exploring North Carolina. What the hell? Is this some kind of sick mind game?"

"Doesn't seem like his style. Besides, now that I've had time to think about it, he's right. I need a better understanding of the locale. Maybe I've been approaching this the wrong way."

"See, that right there is what I'm talking about. He's got you doubting yourself. I thought the plan was to see him as a competitor. The enemy." Bex's Yorkshire terrier, Sheba, barked frantically in the background. Her friend was likely pacing the floor and gesturing wildly, working the poor thing up.

"And don't we always say we need to know our enemy in order to defeat him?"

"If you really mean it, it's a good plan," Bex conceded. "But it feels like you're trying to convince yourself. Are you sure this isn't just about spending some alone time with Wesley Adams?"

Bree stared at herself in the mirror for a moment before dropping her gaze to the phone. "I'm sure."

"Then good luck, but you call me the second you feel yourself falling for this guy. I'll knock some sense back into you, even if I have to fly out there." The smile was back in her friend's voice.

They both laughed. "Promise."

"Good. Anything else I should know about?"

Bree's gut churned. Was she that transparent?

She hadn't told Bex about the messages from her ex. Bree knew how her best friend would react. Without knowing some of the uglier details of the breakup three years ago, Bex had been ready to take a bat to Alex's precious car.

It was just a few voicemails and a text message. He'd get bored and give up when she didn't respond. So why get Bex upset for nothing? Besides, she didn't want to talk about Alex. She'd given him three years of her life, and he didn't deserve another moment of it.

"Everything is fine."

"You're a terrible liar, Brianna Evans," Bex said. "But whether it's Wes or something else that's bothering you, I'm here when you're ready to talk."

Bree ended the call and hoped like hell that everything would be all right.

Wes leaned against the hood of the car, his hands shoved into his pockets as he waited for Bree.

An entire week together. Alone.

What had he been thinking when he proposed this trip?

That there was no way in hell Bree would agree to his request. If he'd bet money on it, he'd have lost his flat back in London and everything in it, because Bree called his bluff. Which left him no choice but to go through with it.

Not one of my better ideas.

Nor was it part of some calculated grand plan. He'd planned this trip two weeks ago, only he'd intended to travel solo. After two decades of living abroad, he was out of touch. He needed this research trip as much as Brianna did. Besides, time on the road alone would've given him a chance to clear his head, still spinning from the reality of his mother's illness.

Then there was the dark truth that he didn't dare admit, not even to himself.

He wanted an excuse to spend time with Bree.

A small part of him hoped that the competitive spirit that made Bree Evans a world class athlete would prompt her to accept his challenge.

Wes glanced at his watch. Five minutes past their scheduled departure.

Maybe she planned to leave him waiting—her retribution for how he'd treated her in London.

Served him right. He'd been an ass, even if he'd done it for the right reasons. Then he heard her voice.

"Sorry I'm late. My mom called as I was leaving." Bree pulled a small carry-on bag behind her. Slim, dark-wash jeans hugged her luscious curves. She wore a red-and-white striped blouse with a wide band at the waist.

"Is everything okay?" He opened the trunk.

"She needed to vent. My dad retired late last year, and he's driving her crazy." A tentative smile settled on her glossed lips.

"That all you're bringing? We'll be gone a week, you know?"

"I have everything I need. When you schlep your own luggage as much as I do, you learn to pack light."

Bree eschewed his offer to take her bag. She lifted the small, black bag into the trunk. The band at her waist rose, providing Wes with a glimpse of the tattoo on her lower right side. A vibrant, purple butterfly landing on a lotus blossom rendered in a deep, rich shade of pink. He'd seen dozens of glossy photos of Bree online and in magazines. That tattoo hadn't been in a single one. He would've remembered. So it was a recent addition. Or maybe she'd always had it airbrushed out of her photos.

What does it mean?

Asking was out of the question. Might as well confess he'd been gawking at her. Not a good move at the outset of their strictly business road trip.

"You're traveling light, too." Her voice broke into his thoughts.

"I'm a simple guy." He closed the trunk and resisted the inclination to open her car door. After her insistence on handling her own luggage, he doubted she'd welcome the action. Instead, he gestured toward the car. "Shall we?"

"Sure." An uneasy smile curled the edges of her mouth. The bravado she'd shown earlier was gone, if only for a moment.

It was a feeling he knew well. They weren't on the road yet, and already the tension crept up his spine.

"Have you eaten?" When she indicated that she had, he slid behind the steering wheel and secured his seat belt. She did the same. "Good. We can hit the road right away. Got a long drive to Asheville."

"I've always wanted to visit there." Her smile deepened into one that lifted her cheeks and lit her eyes from within.

There's that smile. The one he remembered so fondly from their night together in London.

"Good, because we're spending two days there." Wes turned the ignition, then headed onto the road.

"I noticed." She waved a copy of the trip itinerary he emailed her because she'd insisted on one. It was pretty vague. Just a list of the cities he planned to visit and the dates they'd be there. "You're not a man of many details, are you?"

Wes laughed. "You'd be surprised to learn that I'm

known for my attention to detail. It's an essential skill in planning and promotions."

"So this list is purposely vague?" She held up the sheet again.

"I was going for Man of Mystery. Apparently, I've failed miserably." He smiled. "So you'll just have to take my word for it."

Bree's laughter warmed his chest. "So, Man of Mystery, what will we be doing in Asheville for two whole days?"

"Everything." He wished he could rescind the word when her shoulder stiffened and her cheeks turned crimson. "I mean, there's a lot to do there. Two days will barely scratch the surface. Got a few activities planned, but I don't want to ruin the surprise."

"Fair enough." Bree stuffed the piece of paper back into her purse, then dropped her bag on the floor. "How long until we're there?"

"It's nearly a six-hour drive."

Her eyes widened in protest. For a moment, he thought she might bolt from the moving vehicle. He held back a chuckle.

"Don't worry, we'll stop for lunch in Raleigh. Give you a chance to stretch your legs out and sample some of the best barbecue in the state."

"Raleigh's in central North Carolina. So will we be having Eastern or Western-style barbecue?"

"Someone's been doing her research."

"You said I didn't know enough about the state." She shrugged. "I decided you were right."

They were silent for a few minutes, then he asked the question that had lingered in his mind from the moment she agreed to the trip.

"So…why'd you change your mind about joining me on this trip?" Liam would accuse him of looking a gift horse in the mouth. Still, he needed to know.

"Other than the fact that you asked me?" She stared out of the passenger window.

He grinned. "Yeah, besides that."

"Partly because you didn't expect me to say yes. Partly because you were right. We can't beat the Miami or LA tourneys at their own game. We must focus on what sets Pleasure Cove apart. I need a better understanding of the location in order to do that."

"Is that why you haven't gone home between the meetings?"

She didn't reply right away, and he nearly regretted asking. What business was it of his if she hadn't returned home? Yet, when Liam mentioned it, in passing, he couldn't help wondering why she'd stayed.

"Sorry, it's none of my business."

"No, it's fine. I just wondered how you… Ahh, Liam."

Shit.

Should've kept his mouth shut. Now she'd think they were a couple of gossiping men. "We talked while I was in London. He mentioned he saw you at lunch."

She nodded thoughtfully, though he wasn't sure if she accepted his explanation or was simply acknowledging that she heard it. "I was able to conduct all of my meetings via phone or email. Since I had no pressing issues back home, I stayed put. It gave me a chance to familiarize myself with the venue and some spots around town."

"And what do you think of Pleasure Cove?" He was

glad to sway the conversation from the fact that he'd been keeping tabs on her.

"The town or the resort?"

"Both."

"The town is idyllic. Charming. There's an eclectic mix of locally owned shops and eateries along the beach and downtown. I admire the fact that they've kept the big-box stores and chains at bay. A lot of those small, quaint shops couldn't stay afloat if they had to compete with them."

"You have been getting to know the locals. And what you say is true. But their reluctance to change also left the town outdated, almost losing its relevance except with the handful of tourists who've been coming here for years, many of them since they were kids. A lot of the old guard fear the evils of commercialization, but the town and its economy needed the shot in the arm that infusion of cash brought."

"I've heard a few debates about it in town. So I understand the careful balancing act we have to do. We have to find a way to bring in the masses without pissing off the locals. That's why I thought a family-friendly event would work best. It's something everyone in town could enjoy."

It was too early in the trip to get into a heated debate about the format of the tournament again. Bree took the hint and changed direction.

"That reminds me, I think we should source goods and services for the event locally. It won't be feasible in every instance, but it may buy us some goodwill with the locals. Besides, it's just the decent thing to do."

"Great idea. My go-to vendors are all in the UK. I

need to build a database of stateside vendors anyway. I'd love to patronize local shops."

"Good to know you don't disagree with all of my ideas."

Don't take the bait, man.

An uncomfortable silence settled over the car. Wes turned on the radio and focused on the road.

Maybe their trip wasn't off to a stellar start, but he had seven days to convince Bree they were on the same side.

Chapter 8

By the time they arrived in Raleigh, Bree was restless. Their conversation had been cordial, but thankfully there hadn't been much of it during the two-hour drive up I-40W. She'd taken a series of business calls.

Wes probably thought she was being rude. If he did, she couldn't blame him. Under normal circumstances, she would've waited until she arrived to take the calls in private. However, the creative department for her biggest sponsor—a major athletic-wear line—was in a panic.

Already three weeks behind schedule getting to production, her latest sportswear line hit another snag. The team was in crisis mode.

"We're here." Wes pulled into a recently vacated parking space on the street.

"Perfect timing." Bree hit Send on the follow-up

email to the call that had lasted nearly an hour. She shoved her tablet in her bag. "I'm done with work and I'm starving."

"Me, too." Wes stepped out of the car and came around to open her door. A wide smile lifted the corners of his sensuous mouth as he extended his hand to her.

Bree slipped her hand into his. A slight shiver trailed up her arm and his scent enveloped her.

She'd been aware of his masculine scent as they rode in the car, but it was subtle. Standing toe-to-toe with him, she was enraptured by the scent. She inhaled the notes of lavender, orange and patchouli, her eyes fluttering closed for the briefest moment. Bree withdrew her hand from his and stepped away, hitching her purse on her shoulder.

Wesley's gaze dropped to the stretch of skin the movement left exposed at her waist. His eyes traced her tattoo. A butterfly alighting on a lotus blossom. Warmth filled her cheeks.

"Sorry, I didn't mean to stare. It's a beautiful tattoo. The colors are exceptionally vibrant, and it fits you."

"Thanks." She tugged down her blouse.

You are not attracted to him. You are not attracted to him. You are not...

Who was she kidding?

Of course she was attracted to Wesley Adams. He was tall, dark, handsome and incredibly fit. A fact not hidden by the gray, lightweight sweater he wore over a pale blue button-down shirt. His dark eyes, framed by neat, thick brows, seemed to stare right through her, exposing her every thought and emotion.

Bree folded her arms and nodded toward a redbrick-

and-glass building that looked like a converted warehouse. "This the place?"

A stupid question, but she needed to say something. *Anything.*

"You bet." Wes placed a hand low on her back as he steered her out of the way of a group of people who'd spilled out of the restaurant and onto the sidewalk. "Just wait until you try the chopped barbecue and fried okra."

Bree tried to ignore the heat seeping into her skin and the way her body reacted to his touch.

"Not a fan of okra. It's so…slimy. Human food should not be slimy."

The laughter that rumbled in his chest vibrated against her shoulder. "I don't disagree. In fact, the only way I'll eat it is fried." He ushered her inside.

"I'm not eating anyone's okra." Her tone was definitive.

"That'd be a shame, 'cause our okra is awful good." A gorgeous blonde with sparkling blue eyes flashed her brilliant teeth in a good-natured smile.

"I'm sure it is." Bree tucked her hair behind her ear. "It's just not my thing."

"We got a menu full of options. You'll have plenty to choose from."

They settled into their booth and Bree scanned the menu.

"We can order whenever you're ready." Wes sipped his water.

"You haven't touched your menu."

Wes grinned. "Don't need it. I know exactly what I want."

* * *

He hadn't intended to, but as Bree studied the options, her gaze buried in the menu, Wes took the opportunity to study her.

For a moment, why he'd chosen not to call her escaped him.

Right. Because he didn't want to be the asshole who broke the heart of America's volleyball sweetheart.

Being the good guy didn't always pay off.

Bree tugged her full, lower lip between her teeth as she studied the menu.

Sensory memories of that night in London flooded his brain. The flavor of Bree's lip gloss. The warm, sweet taste of her mouth. How her body—with its perfect mix of lean muscles and sexy curves—pressed against his. His pulse raced and heat crawled up his neck.

I'm a bloody masochist.

No other way to explain why he'd torture himself by inviting Bree Evans on this trip.

"I've heard about this place." Excitement lit her brown eyes. "It's supposed to be really good."

"One of the best around. I come here whenever I'm in town."

"You've been living in London. How often do you get to Raleigh?"

"Whenever I visit my mother, we make it a point to come here at least once." He drummed his fingers on the table. "Truthfully? Not often enough. I usually fly Mom out to visit me. I haven't been too keen on returning home."

"Why?" Her intent gaze penetrated him.

He opened his mouth to deliver his usual excuse,

that he had been busy, but there was something about Bree. He didn't want to bullshit her. Still, there was no need to relive his entire life story.

Wes rearranged the salt and pepper shakers. "Running from bad memories, I guess."

"Sorry." Bree lowered her gaze. "I shouldn't have pried. I didn't mean to dredge up bad memories."

"No need to apologize. You couldn't have known." He forced a smile, hoping to set her mind at ease. "You know, I haven't thought of New Bern as home in years. I spent most of my life in London and it's felt like home for the past twenty years, but…"

"But this trip home feels different?" Her wide, brown eyes were like a truth elixir.

Wes nodded. "Yeah. When I first got off that plane last month, it was the first time since I was a kid that I felt some sense of nostalgia. Maybe even a little bit of homesickness."

"So will you be coming home more often now?"

"Actually, I decided to move back to the US. I've always known that one day I wanted to establish my event-and-promo business here." Wes dropped his gaze from hers. He wouldn't lie to her, but she wasn't entitled to know everything about him or his family. "Now feels like the time to do that."

"Your mother must be happy."

"Haven't told her yet. I wanted to wait and see how things worked out with the tournament."

"You mean whether you could stand to work with me for an entire six months." She laughed when his eyes widened. "Relax, I'm not offended. I considered backing out, too."

"I'm glad you didn't." His gaze held hers. His pulse

quickened in response to the slow smile that spread across her face.

"Glad you didn't, either." Bree tucked her hair behind her ear. "I think we have the potential to be an incredible team that delivers on everything Liam is hoping for, but that means we need to function like a team. No surprises."

"Fair enough," Wes conceded, thankful the server stepped in to take their order.

Once their orders were complete, she checked her email again.

"Everything okay with your sponsor?" Wes sipped his sweet tea. "I couldn't help overhearing some of your conversation in the car."

"The usual production drama." She shrugged, putting her phone on the table. "Seems there's some sort of drama whenever we roll out a new line. I've learned to roll with it. What about you? Seems like you had some business drama of your own."

"Got a big corporate event coming up. I'll be there for the event and the days leading up to it, but I'm letting my team take the lead on this one. I've been dealing with this client for a while. He's having a bloody meltdown, as he's wont to do during these events."

"But you weren't speaking to him. You were speaking to a woman."

"How'd you…?"

"You turn up that Southern-boy charm when you're speaking to a woman." The corner of her mouth curved in the sexiest smirk he'd ever seen as she swirled her straw inside her glass. "Even if you're not attracted to her."

Wes didn't acknowledge her assessment as he

leaned back against the booth. What she'd said was true, though not something he did intentionally.

"I was talking to my event manager, Nadia. She's second-in-command. She's bright and capable, but she's nervous about taking over the reins."

"Oh." She seemed relieved by his answer. "I liked how you handled the conversation. You conveyed your confidence in her in a way that felt warm and genuine. It seemed to calm her down. I couldn't hear *what* she was saying, but I noticed the shift in her tone," she added when he gave her a puzzled look.

"That charm of yours is dangerously effective." Bree folded her arms on the table and leaned forward. "Because I still can't believe you talked me in to this trip."

"I'm still stunned by that one myself." Wes chuckled. "But I'm glad you agreed to join me. The trip wouldn't be nearly as fun solo."

Bree's mouth twisted in a reluctant smile. "Now that I'm here, I would think I've earned at least a preview of what to expect over this next week."

"All right." Wes leaned forward, holding back a grin. "We're having dinner tonight and we're going hiking in the morning."

"But where are we—"

"That's all I'm giving you." He held up a hand as the server approached their table with the sampler of appetizers he'd ordered. "I want you to be surprised, especially in Asheville. So you're going to have to give me a little leeway here."

Bree opened her mouth to object, but a genuine smile lit her eyes as she turned her attention to the chicken wings, fried green tomatoes and potato fritters.

"I shouldn't be eating any of this." She grabbed a saucer and unwrapped her silverware. "But that won't stop me from sampling every bit of it."

Wes grinned, reminding himself of all the reasons he shouldn't be attracted to her. His brain agreed, but his body and heart had gone rogue.

He wanted to spend more time with Bree. To learn everything there was to know about her. He couldn't stop the visions of her in his bed, calling his name.

Wes sighed softly. Giving himself the keep-it-in-your-pants speech wouldn't be enough. Brianna Evans had burrowed under his skin and was working her way into his heart.

Chapter 9

Bree stood in front of the mirror in her hotel room and smoothed down her skirt. So maybe the little black dress was sexier than anything she'd normally wear to a business meeting. And maybe she had made a real effort with her makeup tonight.

It wasn't as if she'd flirted with him.

Okay, maybe she had, but only a little. It was certainly nothing serious.

Her phone rang. It was a video call from Bex. Bree cringed. For a moment, she considered not answering, but that would've worried Bex more.

"Hey. You caught me on the way out to dinner." Bree tried to sound nonchalant.

"Obviously, you're not going for pizza and a beer down at the pub." Bex's expression grew wary, as did her tone. "Let me see what you're wearing."

Bree breathed out a long sigh and extended her arm, holding the phone up so Bex could take in the entire outfit—cleavage and all.

"So this is a date." Bex's tone had gone from wary to alarmed.

"It isn't a date." The objection felt weak, even to Bree. "There's a restaurant in our hotel, and it happens to have a dress code."

"Does that dress code require cleavage? The girls are looking pretty spectacular tonight."

Bree's cheeks stung with heat. She smoothed a hand down the clingy, black draped jersey dress. "You're the one who's always saying I don't show off my assets enough."

"And today is the day you decide to listen?" Bex sucked in a deep breath. "Look, Bree, we both know you *really* like this guy. Hell, I like the guy. In any other circumstance, I'd tell you to go for it. Have a little fun. But there are three really important things for you to remember. Wes doesn't want anything serious, you do and this guy is the one standing between us getting what we want out of the tournament. Don't forget any of that."

"You think I'm too naive to hold my own with Wes."

"It isn't that, and this isn't me scolding you or saying in any way that you should change who you are. You see the good in everyone and you wear your heart on your sleeve. I love those things about you. It's why we make such a good team. You balance out my craziness, and I need that." Bex smiled into the camera. "But for you, *nothing* is strictly business. I doubt Wes shares your philosophy."

Bex wasn't wrong. Bree was playing with fire and she knew it. Still, she was drawn to Wes in a way she couldn't explain. Like they were meant to be together. If not as lovers, at least as friends.

There was a knock at her hotel-room door. A knot tightened in her belly.

"I have to go." Bree lowered her voice. "But I'll remember what you've said. Promise."

"Fine. Have fun." Bex's exasperated tone indicated she knew her advice had fallen on deaf ears. "Just be careful. I don't want to have to come out there and kick his ass."

"'Bye, Bex." Bree ended the call and dropped the phone in her clutch. She surveyed herself in the mirror one last time.

This is business. Relax. Have fun.

It was a hollow claim, because the closer she got to the door, the faster her heart beat.

Bree opened the door. "You're early."

"And you...look amazing." Wes jammed his hands in his pockets and leaned against the doorway.

"You sound surprised." There was a nervous lilt to her laughter. "I'd like to think I cleaned up pretty well the night we met."

"You did, but tonight..." He sucked in a deep breath as he surveyed her from head to toe. "Let's just say you've turned it up a notch."

Brianna looked stunning in a form-fitting little black dress that was ultra-feminine and incredibly flattering on her body. The draped neckline drew his attention to her full breasts. The bow-tie belt detail highlighted her small waist and the clingy fabric hugged every single curve.

He cleared his throat as he took a cream-colored cashmere cardigan from her and helped her into it.

She tied the sash at her waist, grabbed her bag and stepped into the hall.

Wes followed her to the elevator, his eyes drawn to how the fabric hugged her curvy bottom. He dragged his eyes away and punched the down button for the elevator.

"You're going to love this restaurant." Wes stared at the elevator doors rather than looking at her. "And this is one of my favorite places to stay whenever I come here."

"It's a beautiful hotel, and it's right across the street from the Biltmore Estate." Bree ran her fingers through her shoulder-length curls. "Almost makes me wish we were going to be here a bit longer, so I'd have time to visit."

"Careful." He grinned inwardly, determined not to ruin the surprise he had planned for her the next day. "Almost sounds like you're enjoying your time with me."

"Don't get too cocky." She laughed. "It's too early to make that call, but so far…yes. I am enjoying the trip."

"Fair enough." He stepped off the elevator and offered his arm to her. She reluctantly slipped her arm through his and fell in step beside him.

They entered the restaurant, greeted by the enticing scent of savory, grilled meat. The gentle strains of live guitar music filled the air.

"It's like an upscale hunting lodge." Bree surveyed

the brown-and-red leather seating and the antler chandeliers hanging overhead. "I honestly wouldn't have thought that was possible."

Wes chuckled. "Wait until you taste the food."

"I've already studied the menu, so I know exactly what I want."

His gaze raked over Bree, his heart beating a little faster. He knew exactly what he wanted, too. But it would be better for both of them if he showed restraint.

They were shown to a table, then placed their orders, falling into an easy conversation about Asheville and some of the activities he enjoyed here.

"Tomorrow morning, I'll take you on a walking tour of downtown. It's called the Urban Trail." Wes sipped his beer.

"You've probably done the trail at least a half a dozen times."

"Actually, I've only done it once with my mother and aunt. Normally, when I come to town I prefer something a little more challenging. Like a brisk hike."

Bree raised an eyebrow, as if she'd been challenged. "Then let's do that instead."

"The hike takes about four hours."

"Then we should get started early."

"The trail can be pretty muddy and it's challenging for a beginner."

"Who says I'm a beginner?" Bree asked incredulously. "You do know I make my living as an athlete, right?"

"Fine." Wes raised his hands, giving in. Bree was determined to go hiking with him. Maybe they'd take the city walking tour later. "Then we'd better make it an early night."

He was disappointed by the prospect.

"Not necessarily." She shrugged. "I'm not in training right now. I can handle staying up past my bedtime. Unless you're the one who can't function without eight hours of beauty sleep."

"I'll manage. Got hiking clothes and shoes?"

"I do."

Bree for the win.

The server brought out his fried calamari and her roasted pear salad. The look of satisfaction on Bree's face after she took the first bite of her salad did things to him.

"Anything else I need to know about tomorrow?"

Wes dug in to his calamari and tried to shift his mind to something that didn't get him so hot and bothered. Like cold showers and sewer drains.

"We'll be on a tight schedule, and you'll want to wear comfortable and casual clothing and footwear for tomorrow afternoon."

"Okay." The expression on Bree's face indicated that the wheels in her head were turning. "Anything else?"

"No." Wes enjoyed keeping her in suspense. Something about her frustrated little pout made him want to kiss her. He wasn't sure who was torturing whom.

Later, as he dined on grass-fed filet mignon and she ate her pan-roasted duck breast, butternut squash risotto and bacon-braised greens, their conversation fell into a comfortable rhythm.

"You didn't mention what took your family to London." Bree sipped her wine.

"My mother was the house manager for a wealthy family that relocated to London," Wes said, then sighed. "Actually, that's what gave us the opportunity to move to London. The reason we moved is because my mother wanted a fresh start for all of us."

Bree's eyes were sympathetic and kind, like a warm hug from a dear friend. He could tell she wanted to delve deeper, but seemed unsure if she should.

"My parents divorced when my brother and I were kids. He was a jazz saxophonist who headlined his own band. He and my mom met when he hired her as the band's female vocalist."

"Your parents were musicians? They must've lived an exciting life." She sliced into her duck and took a bite.

"They did," Wes said. "Which is why the old man didn't adjust too well to family life and working in a factory. He stuck it out eight or nine years, but then he became restless.

"He got the band back together and snagged a few local gigs. At first, that was enough. But then he wanted to hit the road and tour again." Wes drained his beer, then signaled for another. "My mother didn't want to drag us all over the world, and she refused to leave us behind. She didn't want anyone else raising her kids—not even my grandmother."

"Is that when they split?"

"Not at first. He hired a new vocalist and his band toured the States, then Europe. His calls and postcards became less frequent. Eventually he sent a letter saying that he loved us, but that this was something he needed to do for himself. The divorce papers showed up not long afterward."

"Wes, I'm sorry." There was comfort and compassion in her voice, rather than pity. "I understand the betrayal you feel when a parent walks away from you like that…it's indescribable."

"I thought your parents were still together."

Bree seemed to carefully debate her next words. "I'm adopted."

Wes straightened in his seat, the hair lifting on the back of his neck. "You're adopted?"

"Yes." She seemed surprised by his reaction.

"I didn't mean for it to sound as if…" He took a breath. *Get it together, man.* "It's just that I've seen some of your interviews and pictures of your family. You resemble your mother quite a bit. I guess we see what we expect to see."

Nice save.

Bree's shoulders relaxed. "My adoptive mother is my biological great aunt. My bio mom had me when she was really young. Her aunt and uncle weren't able to conceive and they couldn't afford in vitro. So when they learned my bio mom was pregnant and didn't want the baby, they talked her out of termination and offered to adopt me. I got lucky twice."

"It's good you were able to stay with family." He assessed her carefully before asking his next question. Her open expression seemed to give him permission. "If you don't mind me asking, what's your relationship with your birth mom?"

"We don't have one," Bree responded matter-of-factly, but the light in her eyes dimmed and her smile lost its radiance.

Wes glided his hand across the table, wanting to touch hers. He wanted to give her the same comfort her smile had given him earlier. He froze, his fingers a few inches from Bree's.

Keep it strictly business. Maintain your distance.

"Sorry to hear that, Bree." He gripped his beer glass instead. "That must be hard."

"It's not that I don't see her. I do. At every family function. She went on with her life and became a successful lawyer. Got married. Had kids of her own." Bree forced a laugh. "And me, I'm this big family secret that everyone except her husband and kids know about."

Something deep in his chest bubbled, like hot lava threatening to spill out of a volcano. How could Bree's mother sit next to her at barbecues and family weddings, pretending they didn't share the strongest human bond? Didn't the woman have any idea how that must make Bree feel?

Wes tried to curb the anger building toward a woman he'd never even met. He'd always known how lucky he was to have his mother. She'd given up everything for him. Put all of her dreams aside to give him and his brother the best life she could. For that, he couldn't thank her enough.

But it was more than just Bree's situation that bothered him. Her revelation that she was adopted set all those wheels turning in his head. The ones that kept him awake at night.

Adopted children usually went to good homes. Better situations. What about the ones who didn't? Even when everything looked good from the outside, who could know what was happening behind closed doors?

Wes didn't realize neither of them had spoken in several minutes until her voice, soft and apologetic, broke through the jumble of thoughts that wrapped themselves around his skull and squeezed like a vise.

"I didn't mean to put a downer on this lovely meal. I'm not even sure why I told you that. I shouldn't have. Only a handful of people outside of my family know the truth. So, please don't tell anyone."

"Not my business to tell." He shrugged. "But I'm glad you felt comfortable enough to tell me."

Bree squirmed. Something in her eyes indicated that the ease she felt with him was a source of concern for her.

They had that in common, too.

As they finished dinner and shared a generous slice of pecan carrot cake, Wes tried to reassure himself that getting to know Bree was simply a team-building exercise designed to fortify their working relationship. But the truth gnawed at him.

He liked Bree. *A lot.*

He wanted her friendship, and a rogue part of his anatomy wanted something more.

Trying to strike the perfect balance between building an amicable, working relationship with Bree and keeping a safe emotional distance was a dangerous game. A lot was at stake. For him. For Bree. For Westbrook International.

He couldn't afford to screw this up.

Yet, when he walked her back to her room, he wasn't prepared to say good-night.

"Thank you for dinner." Bree leaned in, one hand pressed to his chest, and kissed his cheek. Her soft scent and body heat surrounded him.

He hadn't expected the innocent kiss or that he'd be overwhelmed by her nearness.

Bree's mouth lingered near his as she pulled away so slowly he could hear every microsecond ticking in his head. He willed himself to stay in control. To keep his hands shoved in his pockets, where they wouldn't get him into trouble.

"You're welcome." The words came out much quieter than he'd intended. He dropped his gaze to her sensual lips and she smiled.

"I'd ask you in for an after-dinner drink, but like you said, we've got an early morning." Her voice was soft and captivating, an unspoken invitation.

Wes wet his lower lip and tried to tear his attention away from her mouth and her soft gaze. Tried with every fiber of his being to ignore the fact that he wanted her desperately.

He couldn't.

Slipping his arms around her waist, he pulled her closer. His mouth inched toward hers. Bree's eyes drifted closed as she leaned in, closing the space that remained between them.

His lips were nearly on hers when laughter erupted from a loud group exiting the elevator. Startled, her eyes opened and she stepped beyond his grip.

Her cheeks were crimson and she somehow managed to look both surprised and disappointed.

Feelings he shared.

Still, another part of him was thankful. This was a business trip, not a love connection. Something they'd both do well to remember.

"Bree, I'm sorry, I—"

"Saved by the bell." She forced a smile, then dug her hotel key card out and bid him good-night before closing her door.

Wes dragged a hand through his hair and let out an exasperated sigh. He needed to pull it together or he and the project were in serious trouble.

Chapter 10

Bree hoisted on her backpack and made her way toward the sign that declared their arrival at the Looking Glass Rock Trail head in the Pisgah National Forest.

The forty-five-minute drive to the park had been filled with awkward silence over their near kiss the night before, something neither of them seemed willing to discuss.

She zipped her black jacket up to her neck to ward against the cool, brisk morning air. Bree secured her silk-lined knit hat, tugged on a pair of black gloves and wound a scarf around her neck.

The sun was up and the temperature was rising. By the time they'd hiked to the summit, she'd likely need to shed a few layers. But for now, her breath rose as a visible, steamy cloud in the air.

"Sure you're up for this?" Wes set the car alarm,

then zipped the keys in a backpack he'd stuffed with fruit, protein bars and several bottles of water. "The downtown walking tour is still an option."

"And miss climbing to the top of this…what did you call it again?" They'd seen the view of the commanding rock cliff from the other side. It was a rock climber's dream.

"Looking Glass Rock is a pluton monolith. It was formed when hot magma tried to push its way to the surface, but got stuck underground."

"How could it have been formed underground when it's nearly four thousand feet high?" She fastened the backpack straps that intersected her chest.

"A mountain once shielded the rock." Wes nodded toward the trail. "Over time, it wore away, leaving the igneous rock exposed."

Bree grinned. "Wouldn't have pegged you for a science nerd."

"I'm not." A pained look briefly marred Wesley's handsome face. He flashed an uneasy smile. "We'd better stretch, then get going. Got a full day ahead."

They stretched, then followed some steps. The trail opened onto a forest dominated by the towering trunks of dead hemlock trees. Because of the unseasonably warm weather, many of the newer species of trees that had taken root were in bloom, despite it being late winter.

The ground was dry and the gradual elevation of the trail made for a fairly easy hike. They climbed uphill beside a small stream, then the trail took a right and crossed the creek on a footbridge.

About a mile in, the ground changed from dirt to exposed rock.

Bree squatted down to touch the cool surface. "Can you believe this was once hot, molten liquid?"

"Pretty amazing when you think about it. This could've been an active volcano, spewing hot lava." Wes stepped closer, held out his hand and pulled Bree to her feet.

"Thanks." Bree's cheeks heated as her eyes met his. She tugged her hand free, then went ahead of him on the trail. Her pulse accelerated even more than it had from the exertion of the climb.

The trail rose in a series of hairpin turns, which made it possible to see the trail ahead and below. Switchbacks, Wes had called them. The switchbacks kept the trail from getting too steep.

Bree was thankful for the gradual increase. Despite being a runner and regular strength training, her thigh muscles burned in protest.

Along the way, Wes pointed out the flora and fauna. They'd seen cardinals, blue jays and ruby-throated hummingbirds, whose wings moved so rapidly they were a blur. Suddenly, a streak of white fur dashed across the trail.

"Was that a white squirrel?" Bree tried to pull out her phone and snap a picture, but the squirrel had zero interest in his fifteen minutes of fame.

"White squirrels are the unofficial mascot here in Brevard." Wes grinned. "There's a White Squirrel Festival here on Memorial Day weekend."

Bree scanned the forest, looking for the adorable little furry creature, hoping to snap a shot of it. It would look nice beside the photo of black squirrels she'd taken while visiting Toronto years earlier.

Wes handed her a bottle of water, and she accepted

it gratefully. Bree finished nearly half the bottle as she surveyed the area around them. It was peaceful and beautiful, despite the time of year.

"I see why you love coming here." Bree capped the bottle and stuffed it in her backpack.

"Not yet." He finished his bottle. "But you will. C'mon, we'd better keep moving."

Wes went ahead on the trail and she followed. Finally, they reached a helipad used to airlift injured climbers.

"Is this it?" She looked around. "There's no view here."

"Patience, grasshopper," he called over his shoulder, continuing ahead on a slightly downhill trail. Suddenly, the brush opened onto a rocky platform that offered a view of the valley below. "*This* is the money shot."

"It's incredible." She ventured forward carefully. There was no railing. Just a sheer rock cliff at the edge. "Is it safe?"

Wes tested the surface. "There's no ice and it's dry today, so it shouldn't be slippery. Stay on the flatter area bordering the forest and don't venture too close to the edge. It's a long way down."

Bree inched out farther, enjoying the gentle breeze and the sunshine, and she studied the remarkable view below.

"The view must be stunning when the trees are all green during summer, or in the fall when the leaves are changing colors."

"It is." There was a sadness behind Wes's smile that made her heart ache. "Maybe we'll get a chance to come back here when the tournament is over. Sort of a celebration climb."

"I like that idea." Bree returned her attention to the view, not wanting Wes to see how happy the thought made her. She snapped a few shots of the view with her phone, then pointed to a mountain in the distance. "What's that?"

"Black Balsam Knob and that's Pisgah Mountain." Wes pointed to a ridge with a succession of peaks.

Bree moved forward, taking photos, then suddenly lost her footing. She dropped her phone, but Wes caught it and her before either hit the ground.

"I've got you. You're okay." His voice was calm and reassuring as he steadied her. "You just slipped on a patch of algae."

"But if I'd… I mean, if you hadn't…" Her heart raced as she imagined what could've happened if Wes hadn't been there. She hugged him. "Thank you."

"I'd love to take credit for being the hero, but if you'd fallen, you would've only sustained a few cuts and bruises. I doubt you'd have sailed off the cliff. It's pretty flat here." He held her in his arms. "I'd never put you in jeopardy."

Bree leaned back and met his gaze. "Seriously, Wes, I appreciate what you did."

"I'm letting you go now, so watch your step." His smile reassured her. "Stand over there and I'll get a few shots of you with the mountains in the background."

He took a few photos with her phone, then handed it back to her, and she took a few of him in silly poses that made them both laugh and put her at ease.

"If you aren't a science geek, how do you know so

much about pluton monoliths and the kinds of trees up here?" Bree studied his face as a stormy cloud seemed to settle over him, making her regret the question.

"My dad." Wes frowned as he sat down and removed his backpack. He rummaged inside and pulled out an apple. He handed it to her before getting another for himself.

Bree took off her backpack and sat on the ground beside Wes. She nibbled on the apple, hoping Wes would tell her more, but not wanting to push him. The subject of his father was obviously a sensitive one.

"My dad had been on the road traveling with his band for several months. When he finally came home, I'd asked him to stay with us rather than going back out on the road." Wes chewed a bite of his apple.

"He didn't answer, but a couple days later, he brought me up here and showed me this incredible view." Wes looked around, staring off into the distance. "He said there was so much out there, and that he wanted to experience all of it. And he wanted the same for me, even if that took us on different paths."

Bree placed a hand on Wes's arm before she could stop herself. He seemed to find comfort in the gesture.

"Wes, I'm sorry about your dad." She lowered her voice, not wanting the hikers who'd joined them on the rocky cliff to overhear her. "Do you and your dad keep in touch?"

"Barely, but I'm fine with things the way they are." His expression belied his forceful statement, but Bree didn't press.

"What about your younger brother?"

"Drake sees our father as this larger-than-life heroic figure. He followed his footsteps and became a musician."

"Another sax player in the family?" Bree smiled, trying to lighten the mood.

"A drummer. He practiced on an old set of drums dad left behind."

"Your mom must've been a very patient woman."

"She was." Wes flashed a genuine smile that made her heart soar. "Guess it paid off. Drake's pretty good. He's been working as a session musician mostly, hoping to eventually start his own jazz trio."

"Excuse me," one of the hikers said. "Would you mind taking a group photo of our family?"

Wes obliged, climbing to his feet and accepting the young brunette's cell phone. He took a series of photos of their family of four before handing it back to her.

"Thanks." The girl beamed. "I'd be happy to take a few shots of you and your girl... Oh my God. Look, Mom! It's Bree Evans. It's so great to meet you. I'm a huge fan."

"Thank you so much. It's a pleasure to meet you, too." Bree grinned, hoping she didn't look like a sweaty, hot mess. "And thank you for offering to take our photo, but—"

"Yes," Wes interrupted. "We'd love for you to take some pictures of us."

Bree handed the girl her phone and she and Wes stood together on the rocky cliff with the trees in early bloom spread out behind them.

The girl frowned after taking the photo. "You both look uncomfortable in this one. Maybe we should try again. Stand a little closer and maybe try smiling."

Wes and Bree looked at each other and laughed,

stepping a little closer. He wrapped an arm around her and they smiled.

"Much better." The girl took a few more shots and smiled. She returned the phone and asked that Wes take photos of her and her family with Bree. After Bree autographed the girl's backpack, she and her family began their descent back down the trail.

"We'd better go, too." He picked up both backpacks and handed Bree hers. "There's one more thing I want to show you before we head back to the hotel."

Bree turned and looked one last time at the incredible view, wishing they could stay longer. Or maybe it was just her time with Wes that she didn't want to end.

Chapter 11

Wesley tapped softly on Bree's hotel-room door. She didn't answer right away.

He wouldn't blame her if she'd fallen asleep. After climbing Looking Glass Rock Trail and a quick drive to Looking Glass Falls, they'd grabbed fast food and returned to their respective rooms for a quick shower and change before heading out again.

Wes knocked again, louder this time.

"I'm ready." Bree rushed out of the door, filling the space between them with the scent of fresh summer peaches. Her hair, still wet from the shower, was pulled into a high ponytail.

She wore a casual dress in a bold handkerchief-style print. The vivid orange with accents of pink and teal suited Bree well. A nude leather belt cinched her waist. A tan jacket and nude ballet flats with an ankle strap completed the look.

Casual, but sexy. Funky, but not over the top.

"Something wrong?" Bree's gaze dropped to her feet. She flexed her leg, showing off a sexy, heart-shaped calf.

"Everything's good." Wes steered her down the hallway to the elevator.

The valet brought the car and they went just a little way up the street before he turned onto Biltmore Estate Drive.

"We're going to tour the house?" Bree's eyes lit up. She was clearly thrilled.

"Couldn't bring you to Asheville without taking you for a tour of the largest private residence and the most visited winery in America." Wes chuckled.

They parked and he opened her car door. His gaze instantly followed her mile-long legs to the hem of her dress, which ended well above her knees. Wes extended his hand to her, helping her out of the car. They made their way to the main house.

Wes had toured Biltmore before. But Bree's amazement as they toured the home, with its beautiful atrium, lavish furniture, extensive library and impressive grounds, made him feel he was seeing it all for the first time. There was something about her wide-eyed wonder and pure fascination with the estate that reminded him how genuine she was and how much he enjoyed being with her.

Maybe he wasn't a science nerd, but he was fascinated by history. It was the reason he'd visited the historic property, and several others all over the world, whenever his schedule permitted.

Bree squeezed his arm as she related her enchantment with the estate's incredible library of more than twenty-two thousand volumes.

"Relax, Belle," he teased. "There's a lot more to see."

His *Beauty and the Beast* reference wasn't lost on her. Bree pursed her lips and propped a fist on her hip.

"I happen to love that movie, and I know every single word to every single song. Call me Belle again and I'll start singing to the top of my lungs about the simplicity of this provincial life." She cocked an eyebrow that dared him to try her.

"You win." He couldn't help but grin. "Still, you can't deny the similari—"

Bree spread her arms and opened her mouth, preparing to go into song, when he wrapped his arms around her and pulled her closer.

They both dissolved into a fit of laughter that caused the people around them to give them odd looks.

"You were really going to do it, weren't you?" Wes asked, after they'd regained their composure and rejoined the tour.

"Would've been worth it to see the panicked look on your face." Bree wiped away tears from laughter. "Besides, I need to keep you on your toes. Can't be too predictable."

Wes chuckled. "Mission accomplished."

They toured the remainder of the house and the grounds together. After a tour of the winery, they sampled a variety of wines at the subsequent wine tasting, and purchased their favorites.

"Today was incredible." Bree's face practically

shone once they were in the car and heading down the long road that led off the Biltmore property. "Thank you."

"Glad you enjoyed it, but the night's not over. Got someplace special in mind for dinner. You'll love it."

"Let me pay this time," she said. "I know these are business expenses, but still... I should pick up the tab for something."

"You can pay when we get to Charlotte tomorrow." This wasn't a lovers' getaway, it was a business trip. Still, he didn't feel comfortable allowing Bree to pick up the tab for dinner tonight or any night.

"Deal," she conceded. "Where are we going?"

"You'll have to wait and see."

Bree agreed to his terms begrudgingly.

She should be annoyed with his little game. Yet, she'd been delighted by every one of his surprises. No reason to believe he'd disappoint her now.

Bree's belly tightened in a knot. Her anticipation over their mysterious dinner destination rose, along with a growing fondness for Wes.

They were working together as a team on a project that was equally important to their careers. They needed to get along so they could work together seamlessly.

Didn't her fondness for Wes make working together easier?

Bree focused on the scenery as they drove through the streets of the charming mountain town. She could keep telling herself this trip was strictly business. But her attraction to Wesley Adams was blooming like a pretty, but unwanted, weed.

She glanced at Wes. Was it possible he was growing more handsome as the day went on?

Bree wanted him. There was no doubt about that. He wanted her, too. She was equally sure of that. But did he see the potential for more between them? Did he want it the way she did?

"Everything okay? You've gotten really quiet."

"I'm thinking, that's all."

"Anything you want to talk about?"

"Not really."

"Fair enough." Wes was quiet for a moment, as if contemplating his next question. He seemed to ask despite his better judgment. "Then let me ask why making the tournament a family event is such a focal point for you?"

Discussing the tournament was exactly what she needed right now. After all, that was the point of the trip.

"The truth?" She turned to him. "Bex and I want to elevate the game. Pass our expertise on to the next generation of players. We're planning to put on volleyball clinics for kids eight to seventeen years old. Gearing the tournament toward families will allow us to tap in to our market."

"I see." He mulled over her revelation in silence for a moment. "It's a solid business idea. Who wouldn't want their kids to learn the sport from two of its most successful athletes? But in terms of the tournament, your target market doesn't align with the resort's."

"Pleasure Cove Luxury Resort isn't an adults-only destination," she countered.

"It isn't a family-friendly one, either. It's the kind

of place parents go to get away from their kids for a week."

"That's awful." She couldn't help laughing.

"It's also true." He chuckled, seemingly relieved the mood in the car had lightened. "That doesn't make them bad people. Let's face it, being a parent is one of the toughest jobs in the world. Sometimes you need to take a break and reset."

"You sound like a man who speaks from experience. Are there any little Wesleys out there I don't know about?" She grinned.

His shoulders seemed to stiffen and his smile vanished for a moment. He pulled up to the valet stand in front of a huge, pink stone building.

"No one out there is calling me Dad, I assure you." He forced a smile, but his eyes seemed sadder than she'd ever seen them. He nodded toward the building. "We're here."

A valet at the Omni Grove Park Inn opened the door and helped her out of the car. Wes handed him the keys.

"Shall we?" Wes waved a hand toward the entrance of the building.

"This building is amazing." Bree surveyed the open front hall, which had two massive stone fireplaces blazing. Most of the furniture was art deco. "How long has this place been here?"

"Over a hundred years. The exterior was hewn out of native granite. The roof is comprised of red clay tiles. Some of the original furniture is still on display throughout the hotel."

Wes led her to the Sunset Terrace—a steak-and-seafood restaurant situated on a large, covered outdoor terrace with an incredible mountain view. The server seated them.

"It's stunning." Bree was mesmerized by the incredible view of the mountains as the sun began to set. "A perfect end to a perfect day."

"I wanted your final night here to be memorable." Wes smiled sheepishly. He added quickly, "To give you a sense of the area."

"Then why do I feel like I'm on a date?" Bree couldn't help the smirk that slowly spread across her face.

His eyes widened and he coughed. Wes took a deep drink of his water without response.

"Or maybe I just need to get out more." She sipped her water then returned the glass to the table. "Because the last time I had this much fun was the night we spent together in London."

Wes seemed relieved when the server appeared and took their orders. By the time the man left, he'd gathered himself.

"Bree…" He said her name as if it'd taken every ounce of his energy to utter it. "I like you. A lot. And maybe you're right. This was supposed to be a simple business trip, but I've turned it into what feels like something *more*. It wasn't intentional."

"So we stumbled into a romantic getaway?" One eyebrow raised, she sipped her water.

"Maybe I allowed my attraction to you to shape my choices." Wes sighed heavily. "But the fact remains that we'll be working together, and we need to keep things professional."

"Not to mention that you're not in the market for

anything serious. *Ever.*" She buried her hurt behind a teasing tone and forced smile.

"Then there's that." Wes seemed saddened by the concession. He thanked the server for bringing their bread and decanting their wine. "I wish the circumstances were different."

"What makes you think I'm looking for more?" She traced the bottom of her wineglass, her gaze on her fingertips.

"Because you can't even look me in the eye when you ask the question." He was clearly amused. "Before I met you, I thought the good girl thing was an act to garner sponsorships. It isn't. That's who you genuinely are. That isn't a bad thing, Bree. But I don't want to be known as the scoundrel who broke the heart of America's volleyball sweetheart."

Bree met his gaze, resenting that he knew her so well. Maybe it was the beautiful, romantic setting, but she wasn't prepared to back down.

That night in London she'd been sure they'd connected. That there'd been the potential for something meaningful between them. The past two days had reinforced that belief.

Something was definitely there. Every moment they spent together indicated Wes felt the same.

What is he so afraid of?

They were attracted to each other. So why couldn't they just be adults about it?

Regardless of what happened between them personally, they could simply agree to maintain a professional working relationship.

Bree formulated a proposal in her head.

Sound confident, not desperate.

When she returned her gaze to his, he was carefully assessing her. There was a distance in his gaze that wasn't there moments before.

She lost her nerve, panic gripping her. What if Wes turned her down? Bree couldn't deal with another humiliating rejection.

"So about the tournament..." Wes leaned back in his chair. "I think we agree now that family-friendly isn't the way to go. But I promise to promote your volleyball clinics any way I can. After all, it's the kids' parents who'll be paying for it."

"True." He'd given her a small concession, likely out of pity. Still, she couldn't afford to turn down his offer. "We'd appreciate that."

"You'll need to have your camp dates, website, organization and promo in place by the time we start printing marketing materials. Think you can handle that?" He'd slipped back into business mode, as if their earlier conversation hadn't occurred.

If only Bree could be so pragmatic and detached.

"We'll be ready," she said resolutely. "Bex is restless. She'll be glad to have a project to take on."

"If you need help with the planning and promo—"

"You'd take on a project as small as ours?"

"For high-profile clients like you and Bex? Sure. But I'm not suggesting you hire me. I'm talking about helping as a friend."

"Friends...is that what we are, Wes?" The stunned expression on his face made her regret her words. Wes hadn't done anything wrong. Hadn't promised her anything more than this...whatever this may be. "Sorry. I shouldn't have said that. Your offer is generous. Thank you. I'll talk it over with Bex."

"The sun is setting." Wes pointed in the distance. He seemed anxious to change the subject.

The sky was streaked with lovely shades of purple and orange. The entire scene glowed like a luminescent oil painting.

"It's beautiful. I could sit here staring at it all day."

"Me, too." Wes wasn't looking at the sky. His gaze met hers for a moment that felt like an eternity before he finally turned to survey the mountain range in the distance.

Heart racing and hands trembling, Bree did the same, determined to ignore the mixed signals Wesley Adams was sending.

"Dinner was amazing. Thank you again for such a lovely evening." Bree stopped in front of her hotel-room door.

"It was a good day," Wes said softly, leaning against the door frame. His eyes met hers, and were filled with the same longing, desire and frustration she felt.

And those feelings were heightened, as they'd dined on a tower of lobster, shrimp, crab and oysters.

Bree sank her teeth into her lower lip, her heart racing. The idea had been brewing in her head all night, and she'd been emboldened by the longing in his eyes and the gruffness of his voice.

Even now, she could feel the gentle tug between them. So why couldn't she just say what they were obviously both thinking?

"Wes…" Bree reached out to straighten his tie. "I'm not ready for our night to end."

"We could grab dessert. Maybe go dancing—"

"No." She stepped closer, their eyes meeting. Her

heart beat faster. "I want you. Here. With me. I know you want that, too."

"I do." He sighed heavily. "But we've been over all the reasons this is a terrible idea. Nothing's changed." He pushed a few strands of hair from her face. "I don't want to hurt you, Bree. And I don't want to jeopardize the friendship we've been building."

"Neither do I." Her eyes met his, her voice soft. "And we won't." *Stay calm. Sound confident, not desperate.* "I don't expect anything more than tonight. No promises, no obligations. Just…us."

Bree slipped her arms around his waist, her gaze trained on his as she tried to read him, hoping he'd say yes.

Chapter 12

Wes was trying to do what was in Bree's best interest, but she wasn't making it easy.

Then again, neither had he. Dinner overlooking the sunset? What the hell was he thinking?

This trip was supposed to be about getting better acquainted with the State of North Carolina. Instead, they'd been reminded of all of the reasons they'd gotten on so well together that night in London. The reasons they seemed perfect together.

"I want you, Bree. You know that, but—"

"You're not looking for anything serious." Her tone was sexy, teasing. She leaned in closer. Her soft, sweet scent teased his nostrils. The heat radiating from her body raised his temperature. "Neither am I."

It was a lie, and they both knew it. A lie he wanted desperately to believe.

Wes gripped her shoulders, drowning in her soft gaze. Thoughts of Bree occupied every available space in his brain. Distracted him from what he should be focused on right now—the tournament.

And yet…he wanted this. He wanted her.

The thud of Wes's heartbeat grew louder, his desire for Bree building. He leaned down and slipped his fingers into her hair as his mouth met hers.

A soft sigh escaped her mouth as she pressed her hands to his back and pulled him closer, melding the warmth of her body to his. He pinned her against the door as he captured her mouth in an intense kiss that made him ache for her.

His tongue delved inside her warm mouth. She welcomed it. Glided her own tongue along his as she gripped his shirt.

The voice in his head that was screaming at him not to do this was drowned out by the thud of his heart, his raging pulse and his feverish desire for her.

The elevator dinged, interrupting them as it had the night before. Wes pulled himself away, his eyes studying hers. This time, he couldn't walk away. He extended his palm, his eyes not leaving hers.

Bree dug out her key card and placed it in his palm. There was a hardened edge to her expression, belied by the slight trembling of her hands and her shallow breathing. Wes ushered them inside her room and wrapped one arm around Bree's waist, tugging her body against his.

He trailed kisses down her neck, inhaling her enticing scent. He pressed a soft kiss to her earlobe, then whispered in her ear, "Mixing business and pleasure is always a risky move."

Bree slid one hand up his chest. Her eyes blazed with passion, desire and a bit of defiance. She had no intention of backing down. At this point, neither did he. "Don't worry. I'm worth it."

The edge of his mouth curled. It wasn't the response he'd expected, but it was a sentiment he shared.

She captured his mouth in a greedy kiss that allayed any doubts about whether this was what she truly wanted. About whether she could accept his terms for engagement.

Good. No more Mr. Nice Guy.

Wes lowered his hands to the swell of her curvy bottom, swallowing her soft murmur in response. His body ached with his need for her. A need that'd been simmering since the night they met in London. But now it was at a full-blown boil.

Bree was responsive to his touch as his hands glided along her body—a perfect blend of feminine curves and athletic muscle. Her desire was a living, breathing, palpable thing that demanded satisfaction. He wanted nothing more than to give it to her.

Though the past two days indicated otherwise, this wasn't a fairy-tale romance. Tonight was about passion and desire, mind-blowing sex and pure satisfaction. Then they would both move on.

Wes turned Bree around and nestled her bottom against him as he trailed kisses down her neck. He slipped her dress slightly off her shoulder, and continued kissing his way down it.

She grabbed the hem of her dress and lifted it, but he stopped her.

"Don't take it off." He growled, his lips brushing her ear. He palmed her breast, tracing the tight bud with his thumb. Wes glided his other hand down her side, then up the inside of her thigh. "All night I've imagined what it'd be like to bend you over in this little dress and take you from behind."

Wes slid his fingertips along the crease of her hip, then across the waistband of her silky underwear. Her nipple beaded as he slipped his hand beneath the elastic band and over the narrow patch of curls. Bree gasped when he stroked the stiff bundle of nerves.

"Damn, you're wet." He breathed in her ear, running his tongue along its outer shell. Wes flicked his finger over the nub, enjoying her small gasp and the way her belly tightened in response. "Been thinking about me, haven't you?"

"No longer than you've been thinking about me." The statement began with defiance, but ended with a sensual murmur that did things to him.

"You're right." Wes chuckled, pulling her tighter against his growing shaft. "Because I've been wanting to do this since the night we met."

Wes splayed two fingers and slipped them back and forth over the hardened nub. Bree sucked in a deep breath and looped an arm around his neck, her hips moving against his hand.

He slipped his other hand beneath her dress and gripped her waist, pulling her tight against him. His eyes drifted closed as he reveled in the delicious sensation of her moving against his shaft.

His mouth pressed to her ear, Wes whispered sweet, filthy nothings in it. She rode his hand, her movement growing frenzied as he related every dirty deed he had planned for their night together. Including how he planned to worship that world-champion body of hers with his tongue.

What was it about Bree Evans that made him crazy with want?

"Oh, my God, Wes." Bree was close. Her knees trembled. Her breath came in short, hard exhalations that made his already taut member hard as steel.

He'd wanted to take her from behind. Keep it impersonal. Like two strangers in the dark. But there was something about the way she said his name. Something about how she felt in his arms. He wanted to see every inch of her. To stare in her eyes while she shattered, his name on her tongue.

He gathered her in his arms and carried her to bed.

Bree's heart raced as Wesley set her on her feet beside the bed and started to remove his shirt, one painstaking button at a time.

"Thought we were keeping it quick and dirty." She'd been disappointed that he'd wanted to make their first time together feel impersonal. Transactional. But she thought she'd done a relatively good job of hiding it. After all, that's what she'd agreed to. A no-strings fling.

"Changed my mind." He tossed his shirt and removed his pants without offering further explanation, then growled in her ear, "Now take that dress off before I do."

"Sounds like fun." Bree couldn't help the grin that curled the edges of her mouth at the thought.

Even in the limited light of her darkened hotel room, she could see that she'd surprised him again.

She squealed when he lifted her and tossed her onto

the bed. Suddenly, the dress was off, he'd removed her bra and they were both down to their underwear. Wes trailed kisses down her chest and belly before slowly dragging her panties down her legs.

Before she could react, he'd pressed his open mouth between her legs, his tongue lapping at her sensitive clit. Bree moaned with pleasure at the incredible sensation, calling his name before she could stop herself.

He slid his large palms beneath her hips, gripping them and pulling her closer to his mouth as he pleasured her with his tongue. She writhed as the warm sensation of ecstasy built at her center and her legs started to shake.

Wes pulled away and rummaged on the floor, then she could hear the tearing of the foil packet and make out the silhouette of Wes sheathing himself in the dark. He gripped the base of his length and slowly glided inside of her.

Bree sank her teeth into her lower lip, reveling in the sensation of Wes entering her, inch by inch, until he was fully seated. She cursed, her fingertips pressed to the strong muscles of his back, her fingernails digging into his skin.

Wes held her gaze as he moved his hips. Slowly. Precisely. The friction he created with each thrust of his hips was both torturous and delicious. She arched her back, desperate to heighten the sensation.

Her breathing was rapid and shallow as the pleasure building rose to a crescendo. She came hard, her muscles tensing and her legs shaking as she dug her heels into the mattress and her fingernails into his skin.

The hard muscles of his back tensed as she called his name, her body writhing in ecstasy. His gaze intensified as he moved his hips harder and faster until he'd reached his own edge. Wes's body stiffened and he cursed, his breathing labored. He tumbled on the bed beside her, both of them struggling to catch their breath.

Neither of them spoke.

Finally, Bree turned on her side, facing him. This was her idea, so she should be the one to break the awkward silence.

"Wes, that was…" She pressed a hand to his warm chest as she forced her eyes to meet his. "Incredible."

The edge of his mouth curled in a soft smile as he cupped her cheek. "No, you were incredible." He pressed a kiss to her mouth.

Her racing heart slowed just a bit and her shoulders relaxed. His compliment seemed genuine. Maybe he had enjoyed it as much as she had. Wanted her with the same intensity with which she wanted him.

"I know you're worried that I can't handle casual, but I can."

"Have you ever been in a casual relationship before?" He gave her a knowing smile that indicated he already knew the answer to his question.

"No." Her cheeks heated as she remembered how he'd teased her earlier about being a good girl. "That doesn't mean I'm incapable of being in one. I just hadn't encountered the right opportunity…until now."

Wes pushed a strand of hair off her face. "I want to believe you."

"You can." She kissed his mouth, then trailed kisses down his chest. *Convey strength and confidence.* She looked up at him and smiled in a manner she hoped was seductive. "But by the time I'm done with you, you won't want to walk away from me."

"Maybe you're right." He stroked her hair. "But I will walk away, and I need to know that you'll be okay with that."

Bree swallowed her disappointment and forced a big smile. "Don't worry. I'm a big girl. I'll be fine."

She resumed kissing her way down his hard chest and his tight abs, reminding herself that they were only having a little fun. Enjoying each other's company. That she shouldn't be falling for Wesley Adams. And ignoring the fact that she already was.

Chapter 13

Bree studied Wesley's handsome face as he rubbed his stubbled chin. They sat at a little table by the window. The sunshine warmed them as they chatted over their lavish breakfast, ordered via room service.

Neither of them had wanted to leave her room. They'd barely wanted to leave her bed.

"This is good." Wes took a bite of his eggs Benedict. He cut and speared another bite and held it out to Bree. "You have to try it."

She smiled, but was still shy about what felt like such an intimate gesture. Even after everything they'd done last night.

Her eyes not meeting his, Bree tucked her hair behind her ear and leaned forward, allowing him to slip the forkful of food into her mouth.

"Mmm…" The rich, flavorful hollandaise sauce

melded with the flavors of the forest ham, spinach and tomato. Her eyes drifted closed as she savored the food. "That is good."

His eyes were dark and hooded when her gaze met his. As if he was reliving the sights and sounds of their night together.

Her cheeks filled with heat at the possibility. She tried to push the vision of them together in bed from her head.

"Try my fruit cup." She speared pieces of strawberry, blueberry and banana on her fork and held it out to him.

Wes accepted the offering, his gaze still on her, as if he was waiting for her to say something.

"So, about last night." She dragged the words out slowly as she surveyed his expression.

"Last night was amazing." He sipped his double espresso, his gaze locked with hers.

"It was," Bree agreed, her cheeks stinging. She dropped her gaze as she sipped her decadent mocha cafe. "And I know you planned this spectacular trip for us, but I'd love it if we just…spent the day here in bed."

She laughed nervously in response to his stunned expression. "Don't worry, I'm not suggesting that this means anything. I'm just saying that I enjoyed our night together and I can't think of a better way to spend the day."

Wes set his mug on the table and shifted in his seat. He tilted his head slightly. "Sounds fantastic, but—"

"The rules we established last night still apply." Bree forced a grin, burying the hurt that simmered in her chest. Last night hadn't changed his feelings. "You made that crystal clear."

It was unlike her to be so forward. She'd been the shy wallflower who spent most of her school dances hovering in the corner, hoping not to be noticed. But there was something about Wesley Adams that eased her inhibitions.

Something deeper brewed between them, whether Wes acknowledged it or not.

"Now that that's all settled…" Bree strolled over to Wes and straddled his lap, her arms wrapped around his neck.

Wes chuckled as he wrapped his arms around her waist. "Who knew that America's volleyball sweetheart is a tempting seductress?"

"Not my usual MO." She shrugged. "But then my life usually doesn't leave much time for…this."

"Then I guess that makes me special." There was an uneasiness beneath his smile.

"Don't flatter yourself, playboy." She forced a grin. "I just happen to have some time on my hands."

Wes laughed heartily. He seemed to relax for the first time since they'd begun this conversation. "Then I guess I'm just lucky. Like the night we met."

Something about his statement—that he was lucky to have met her—warmed her chest and made her feel things she shouldn't about Wesley Adams. Feelings she should best ignore.

She kissed him and concentrated on all of the things she should be feeling. His hardened shaft pressed to her sensitive clit. The tightening of her beaded nipples, pressed against the hard muscles of his chest. The graze of his whiskers against her skin. The heat rising between them and the electricity that danced along her spine.

Bree wrapped her long legs around his waist as Wes carried her to the bedroom. He made love to her, and she lost herself in the heat and passion between them. In all of the physical sensations that it was safe to allow herself to feel. While ignoring the nagging insistence that, regardless of what either of them claimed, this was the beginning of something more.

Wes strode back to bed and sipped his beer as he watched Brianna sleeping. He should've returned to his own room last night. Maintained some space between them. But he hadn't. And since they'd chosen to stay another day, they'd only reserved one room. So tonight he had no room to which he could retreat.

He turned on the television with the volume low and studied Bree in the flickering television light. Her hair, loosened from the ponytail and still damp from their earlier shower, was everywhere. Mouth open, one foot hanging off the bed, makeup ruined, and still she was adorable. Probably as much a product of his unsettling feelings for her as her natural beauty.

Bree rolled over, throwing an arm across him. Wes sighed softly and slipped his arm beneath her head, cradling her against him. He stared at the ceiling, listening to the sound of her breathing, and hoped this wasn't a mistake they'd both regret in the weeks ahead.

His phone vibrated on the nightstand beside him. *Drake*. It was late for his brother to be calling. After sunset, Drake was usually preoccupied with a gig or a groupie he'd met during said gig.

"Isn't this the time of night vampires usually hunt their prey?" Wes smirked, teasing his younger brother.

"Usually. But we make an exception when our mothers stumble and fall down half a flight of stairs."

"What happened? Is she all right?" Wes slid his arm from beneath Brianna and climbed out of bed, pacing the floor near the window.

"She got tangled up in the bedding she was carrying downstairs to the wash. Damn lucky to have only have fractured her ankle and sprained her wrist." Drake's gravelly voice was that of a man who spent his nights in smoke-filled clubs.

Wes cursed, running a hand over his head. "This happened tonight?"

Drake hesitated before responding. "Last night. We've been trying to reach you, but your phone was off."

"My phone died last night. I've been…preoccupied." Wes glanced back at Bree. "Started charging it about an hour ago."

He'd always been the reliable son. The one who'd drop everything to help out his mother. But he'd failed her when she'd needed him most, a mistake he wouldn't make again.

"Thanks for being there, Drake."

"She's my mother, too." His words were laced with resentment. "Maybe I'm not always there physically, but I do whatever I can for Mom, no matter where I am in the world."

"Didn't mean to imply otherwise. Like I said, I'm just glad you were able to be there." Wes sighed, kneading the tension in his neck. "Is she still at the hospital?"

"Yes. Her doctor wants to hold her one more night for observation, in light of her Parkinson's." His brother cleared his throat. "When do you think you can get here? I'd love to stay, but I have to catch a plane in the morning. The band's got a gig in Germany in a few days."

"I'm in Asheville, but I'll leave first thing in the morning. I'll be there tomorrow afternoon. Is Mama awake? Can I talk to her?"

"She's resting. The pain meds knocked her out. I'll be leaving shortly, but between Aunt May, Dallas and Shay, she's in good hands. So don't worry. And Wes..." Drake's tone had softened, the tension gone.

"Yeah?"

"Don't beat yourself up over this. There's nothing you could've done to prevent this. And no one blames you for taking a little time for yourself. Certainly not Mama."

Wes wouldn't commit to not feeling guilty about allowing himself to be distracted when there was so much on the line professionally and personally. Still, he appreciated his brother's assurance.

Chapter 14

Bree awoke just in time to see Wesley striding out of the bathroom, freshly showered, with a towel slung low across his waist. As he bent over his luggage, the beads of water on his brown skin highlighted the strong muscles of his shoulders and back.

"Good morning." She sat up in bed, pulling the cover up around her.

"You're up. Good." He turned to her, a grave expression tugging down the corners of his mouth. "I'm afraid I have to bail on the rest of our trip. I have a family emergency. I need to be back home in New Bern as soon as possible."

"What happened? Is it your mother?" Panic bloomed in Bree's chest on his behalf. She knew how close they were.

"My mother tripped down the stairs. She fractured

her ankle and sprained her wrist. I know the injuries might seem minor, but I'm afraid it's part of a larger problem." He paused as if there was something more he wanted to say. Something he wasn't comfortable sharing with her. Wes sighed. "She was diagnosed with Parkinson's six months ago. I only learned about the diagnosis when I went to visit her after our first meeting about the tournament."

"That's where you spent the night." Bree's cheeks warmed the moment she blurted out the words.

"I stayed to accompany her to the doctor the next day and to help out around the house." A knowing smirk curled the corner of Wes's mouth.

"Sorry to hear about your mother. About the fall and the diagnosis." Bree forced her eyes to meet his rather than take in the brown skin stretched over his muscles. "I'll jump in the shower so we can get out of here as soon as possible."

"I'd appreciate that." He rummaged in his suitcase and produced a pair of jeans and a T-shirt. "And I hope you don't mind me stopping by the hospital to get my mom and then getting her settled at her place. As soon as I'm done, I'll get you back to Pleasure Cove."

"Of course not." She wasn't Wes's girlfriend, so why did she feel uneasy about meeting his mother? He'd probably introduce her as a friend or a business associate.

In little more than half an hour, she'd showered, dressed and tossed everything back into her suitcase. They ordered breakfast sandwiches to go and piled in the car.

"So your mom fell last night?" Bree asked between bites of her breakfast croissant.

Wes frowned and sipped his coffee, returning it to the cup holder before responding. "She fell the night before. My phone was off. My brother was finally able to reach me last night, after you'd gone to sleep."

"Oh." She nibbled on more of her sandwich. "So that's why you're...distant this morning. I'm the reason you missed the call about your mother."

"It's my fault. No one else's. Between my mother and the tournament... I should've made sure my phone was on. That I was available." Wesley narrowed his gaze, his eyes focused on the road and his jaw tight. She'd definitely struck a nerve.

"So maybe it isn't my fault directly, but it was me that distracted you." Bree echoed the sentiment clearly written on Wesley's face and implied by his words. "I'm sorry about that. If I'd known your mother was ill—"

"It wasn't your business to know. I only told you because..." He sighed, then muttered under his breath. "Don't really know why I told you. So I'd appreciate it if you wouldn't mention it to her when you meet her."

"Of course." Bree nodded, staring out the window. Hoping to hide the deep flush in her cheeks.

Wes was silent for a moment, his tone lower and softer when he spoke again. "Just so we're clear, I'll be introducing you as my friend and business associate."

"That's accurate. The business-associate part, I mean. The friendship...that's still a work-in-progress."

Wes chuckled. "I guess it is."

Bree clutched a vase of flowers as she approached Mrs. Adams's hospital room. She'd suggested that Wes go up ahead of her and make sure his mother was up to meeting someone new. She tapped on the partially open door, her heart racing. Bree stepped inside when a voice called for her to come inside.

"You must be Brianna." A wide grin spread across the woman's face. She was a beautiful older woman who seemed far too young to be Wesley's mother. "I'm Lena Adams. Wes stepped out to talk to someone about finally letting me out of this place. He told me to expect you. He didn't say you'd be bearing gifts."

Bree sighed in relief. The woman's warm, welcoming demeanor put her at ease. "I walked past the gift shop and they were so beautiful. I couldn't resist. I hope you like them."

"Like them? Honey, this bouquet is stunning. How thoughtful. Thank you." She accepted the crystal vase and inhaled the flowers before setting them on the nightstand beside her bed. She indicated a nearby chair. "Please, have a seat."

Bree sat in the chair, suddenly conscious of whether Mrs. Adams would think her blouse was cut too low or her jeans were too tight.

Relax. You're not his girlfriend.

"Speaking of beauty, you're even more stunning in person." Mrs. Adams grinned.

"Thank you." Bree's cheeks warmed. "Do you follow beach volleyball, Mrs. Adams?"

"Only during the Olympics. But I've seen you in at least a dozen commercials over the years." Excitement lit the older woman's eyes. "And call me Lena, please."

"Someone will be along shortly to complete your discharge." Wesley's tall frame filled the doorway. His eyes met Bree's for a moment before he turned them back to his mother. "I see you've met Bree."

"I have. You didn't tell me that she was as sweet as she is beautiful. Look what she brought me." Lena nodded toward the flowers.

"Thank you, Bree." Wes studied the expensive flower arrangement, then turned toward her. His expression was a mixture of gratitude and suspicion. "They're lovely."

Bree clasped her hands, her eyes roaming anywhere in the room except Wesley or his mother. The elegant bouquet of red roses and orange Asiatic lilies was an expensive gift to a woman she'd never met. But they were beautiful and Wes had said how much his mother enjoyed gardening. So she thought Lena would appreciate them. She hadn't given any thought to the message her gift was sending...until now.

"Yes, they are." Lena emphasized the words as she eyed her son sternly. She returned her warm grin to Bree. "I hope you'll join us at the house for lunch, Brianna. It won't take me long to throw something together. We'll just need to make a quick stop at the grocery store." She turned to Wes.

He frowned, his arms crossed. "The doctor made it very clear that you should get some rest and stay off your feet as much as possible."

"Relax. It'll be fine." She squeezed his arm, then turned to her. "Brianna?"

"I'd love to join you for lunch, but Wes is right. You should be resting. So why don't you let me fix lunch for you?"

Lena's eyes lit up and her smile widened. "That's so thoughtful, Brianna. But I can imagine how busy you must be. I don't want to be any trouble."

"It's no trouble at all. It'd be my pleasure."

"Then we have a date."

The attendant arrived and helped Lena into a wheelchair. They followed the attendant down the hall as he pushed Wes's mother and they chatted.

"Look, Bree, I appreciate your willingness to come here and the flowers...but you don't have to fix lunch. I can pick up something that's already prepared." His voice was hushed.

"Are you afraid to eat my cooking?" Bree teased, hoping to lighten his mood.

Wes held back a smirk. "Should I be?"

"Probably." Bree smiled. "Actual cooking isn't my gift. But, I can assemble a mean chicken salad. Don't worry. I'll pick up a rotisserie at the grocery store."

"Bree." He grabbed her arm, stopping her, so that their eyes met. Wes sighed. "I just want to make sure you understand that nothing has changed between us. We're still just business associates and friends—"

"With benefits." Bree narrowed her gaze, her chin tipped so her eyes met his. "You were crystal clear about that. I'm not an idiot, and I'm not trying to get to you through your mother—if that's what you're thinking."

Wes's stare signaled that he didn't buy her story.

"I got the flowers because they were pretty. I thought your mother would like them. I offered to make lunch because it was clear that if I didn't, she was going to insist on making lunch for us. And because she seems sweet. And I like her. But if you don't want me to have lunch with your mother, fine. I'll rent a car and head back."

"No. Don't. I'm sorry. I'm usually not so ungrateful. I swear." Wes rubbed the back of his neck. "Thank you

for the flowers and for offering to make lunch. Maybe
you can distract her while I move her bed downstairs.
Otherwise, she'd insist on helping me."

Bree nodded and fell back in step with Wes as they
caught up with the attendant and his mother.

Her cheeks flamed and a knot tightened in her gut.
She hadn't been completely honest with Wesley. She
wasn't actively pursuing Wes through his mother, but
she wanted very much for Lena Adams to like her.

Wes finished the last bite of his second helping
of Bree's cranberry-walnut chicken salad served on
warm, fresh, buttery croissants from the local bakery.
So maybe Bree couldn't cook, but she could *assemble*
a damn tasty meal.

He'd wanted to get started on rearranging the house
while Bree fixed lunch, but his mother had insisted
he sit down with them until his cousin Dallas could
come over and give him a hand with moving her bed.
Though she didn't much like the idea of moving her
bed downstairs, even temporarily.

"I know you're worried, son, but I still think you're
making too big of a deal about this. I fell. Accidents
happen. I'll be more careful from now on."

"You can't trudge up and down those steps in an air
cast." He lowered his voice. "Not in your condition."

"I was recently diagnosed with Parkinson's," his
mother explained to Bree, then turned her attention
back to him. "There's a banister. Besides, it's not as
if I can't put any pressure on the foot. And I need
my stuff. You don't plan to bring my entire bedroom
down, do you?"

Bree excused herself and left the kitchen as he and

his mother continued to debate the topic. It was one argument Lena Adams wouldn't win. She was going to sleep on the ground floor, whether she liked it or not.

"Excuse me." Bree returned a few minutes later, smiling. "But I think I might have a solution that'll satisfy you both."

"I'm all ears." His mother gave Bree her attention.

"By all means." Wes gestured for her to continue.

She asked them to follow her to the front of the house.

"Your kitchen has ample eating space, but you also have a formal dining room, which it seems you don't use much." Bree indicated the piles of papers and books that had accumulated on his mother's table again since his last cleaning.

"Point taken." His mother chuckled. "Go on."

"Well, it's such a lovely space. It's a shame you don't get more use out of it. The room is spacious and the pretty bay window faces that lovely little park across the street."

His mother nodded thoughtfully. "It's a sizable room and it does have a beautiful view. But it doesn't have a door and it's right at the entrance. Visitors will have full view of my bedroom."

"That's a simple fix." Bree's eyes lit up. "You could add a wall here and put in a door."

"What happens if she decides to sell the house? Not everyone will want a first-floor bedroom in lieu of a formal dining room." Wes appreciated what Bree was trying to do, but he had to be practical. He wanted his mother to be comfortable, but they couldn't ruin the resale value of the house.

"A valid point." Bree tilted her head, her chin resting on her fist for a moment. She snapped her fingers. "Add a pretty set of French doors instead of a traditional door."

"Guests would still be able to see into my bedroom."

"Not if you mount thick curtains on the door." Bree's gaze shifted from his mother, then to him, and back again.

A wide smile spread across his mother's face, her eyes dancing. "That's a brilliant idea, Brianna. My nephew Dallas is a contractor. He mentioned yesterday that the job they were supposed to work on for the next few days got rescheduled. Maybe he can squeeze me in. He'll be here soon, but I'm going to call him now, so he can give his crew plenty of notice. Besides, I don't want him to give someone else my spot."

"You object?" Bree asked when his mother left the room.

"No. Seems you have everything figured out."

"Why do I have the feeling we're not talking about the plans to relocate your mother's bedroom anymore?" Bree stepped closer.

Her sweet, citrusy scent—like mandarin oranges and orange blossoms—filled his nostrils. The two nights they'd spent together in Asheville rushed to mind with a vivid clarity. A knot tightened low in his belly. His heartbeat quickened and his temperature rose as he recalled the way her brown skin glowed in the moonlight. It took every ounce of willpower he could muster to refrain from leaning down and kissing her soft, glossy lips.

Bree seemed to relish her power over him, and the

fact that with his mother just a few feet away, he was forced to keep his hands to himself.

Pure torture.

"Dallas says he can have his crew here in the morning." His mother returned, saving him from the need to respond to Bree's statement. "He'll be here soon to take measurements. The job should only take a couple of days."

"We still need to move your bed downstairs for now." Wes folded his arms.

"Not necessary. I can sleep right here." His mother patted the sofa she was seated on.

"That thing is hard as a rock. I know." Wes clutched his back as he remembered the last time he'd crammed his long frame onto the uncomfortable pull-out sofa.

"I'm half a foot shorter than you, so I think I'll be all right." She held up her open hand when Wes objected. "This is my compromise. Take it or leave it."

"Fine." Wes blew out an exasperated breath. "But don't complain when your back muscles are as stiff as bricks."

"Deal." She indicated that he should kiss her on the cheek.

He did, then sat beside her, draping an arm over her shoulder. "You've eaten and Dallas will be here shortly. This is a good time for me to take Bree back to Pleasure Cove."

"What a shame." His mother frowned. "I was hoping she'd be here to see the finished result of her idea. Besides, I could use her help decorating the new room."

"Bree's a busy woman. She doesn't have time to

hang out here and play interior decorator." Wesley's shoulders tensed.

"Actually, since the rest of our trip is canceled, I don't have anything planned for the next couple of days." Bree smiled at his mother, her eyes not meeting his. "I'd love to help."

Wes turned to his mother, who was as excited as a kid at Christmas. If it made his mom happy and Bree didn't object, why should he?

They'd shared a bed for two nights. Surely he could deal with her being at his mother's house for two days.

"You sure about this?" Wes gave Bree one last out.

"Positive." Bree grinned. "This will be fun."

Between his mother and Bree, Wes didn't stand a chance.

Chapter 15

Lena Adams was an indomitable spitfire who wouldn't allow minor inconveniences like a fractured ankle or a sprained wrist to keep her from cooking a full meal for her guests. Bree was sure that if she hadn't insisted on helping the woman, Lena would've soldiered through the entire process herself.

She admired Lena's drive and determination, traits her son had obviously inherited.

In the course of an afternoon helping Lena prepare a three-course meal, Bree had doubled her cooking repertoire.

Bree stole another glance out of the kitchen window at Wes working in his mother's backyard. It was the end of winter, yet the North Carolina sunshine beat down overhead, making the already mild temperature feel considerably warmer. Wes had stripped off his T-shirt. The deep brown skin of his bare back and chest glistened with sweat. His black athletic shorts hung low on his hips.

Bree swallowed hard, then sunk her teeth into her lower lip. Her cheeks warmed and a sudden burst of heat crept down her torso and sank low in her belly.

Lena chuckled.

Shaken from her temporary haze, Bree returned to her work of dicing more potatoes for the potato salad.

"Business associates, eh?" The woman could hardly hold back her laughter. "Is that what they're calling it these days?"

Bree froze for a moment, unsure how to answer her.

"Don't know whether you two are trying to pull the wool over my eyes or your own, but in either case, it ain't working."

"I hate to disappoint you, Ms. Lena." Bree emptied the rest of the diced potatoes in a pot of water on the stove, then washed her hands. "But we really are business associates and friends."

"I hope that isn't true." Lena had a sad smile as she poured two icy glasses of syrupy sweet tea. She handed them to Bree. "It's obvious to anyone with one eye and half a brain that you two are into each other."

"Wes isn't looking for a relationship. He's made that abundantly clear." Bree's gaze drifted back to Wes outside. "Neither am I."

"Sometimes we don't know what we want until the situation presents itself." Lena nodded toward Wes. "My boys mean everything to me. But before Wes came along, I was set on a very different life. One that didn't include children or a stable home. I was terribly wrong because being their mother is the best thing that's ever happened to me."

Bree's chest ached and tears stung her eyes. It was clear why Wes loved his mother so much.

"I wish my birth mother felt the same way about me." Bree said the words before she could stop herself.

Her adoptive mother loved her with all her heart. She was grateful for that. Still, she couldn't shake the deep-rooted pain over her birth mother's inability to muster the slightest maternal affection toward her. The woman had two other children, whom she doted on, so clearly she possessed the capacity for maternal feelings. Evidently, Bree wasn't worthy of them.

"If she doesn't, she's either misguided or a fool." Lena squeezed Bree's arm. The woman's words were filled with indignation, but her tone and expression were filled with compassion. "Any woman would be grateful to have a daughter as kind and thoughtful as you."

Bree blinked back tears as she forced a smile. "Thanks."

Lena glanced out at Wes again. "He's probably dehydrated and doesn't even realize it. He gets so focused on the task ahead of him that he sometimes forgets how important it is to stop and take care of himself."

She dipped a towel into a bowl of icy water, wrung it, then draped the cool cloth over Bree's arm. Lena propped open the screen door and nodded toward Wes.

Bree made her way to the garden, where Wes had been working for the past few hours.

"Your mom thought you might like these." She handed him a glass of sweet tea and the cool towel.

He thanked her, then mopped his brow with the towel before hanging it around his neck and nearly draining the glass of tea.

"Your mom was worried you might be getting dehydrated. I can get another glass, if you'd like." She turned to go back to the house, but Wes caught her elbow.

"Thank you. For everything." He stared at her with a heated gaze that lit a flame inside of her and caused her breath to come in quick, shallow bursts. "I know you have better things to do with your time, but you've been great with my mom. I can't tell you how much I appreciate that."

"I'm enjoying my time with her. Besides, she's taught me a lot today." Bree glanced over her shoulder toward the house and saw the kitchen curtains stir. She eased her arm from his grip and took a step back.

"What's wrong?" Wes narrowed his gaze.

"Your mom is convinced there's something going on between us. I don't want to add fuel to the fire." She took a sip of her tea.

"I'll bet." Wes chuckled. "My mother seems genuinely taken with you, and she isn't an easy woman to impress."

"She doesn't strike me as a volleyball fan."

"It's not about what you do. If she's impressed, it's because of who you are. For her, it's all about character. The person you are when no one else is around." Wes frowned, his voice fading at the end.

Bree wanted to ask him if he was all right, but before she could he'd thrust his empty glass into her outstretched hand.

"It was kind of you to offer to stay tonight, but I

really don't mind taking you back to Pleasure Cove. And don't worry about my mother, she'll understand. I promise."

"No." Bree shook her head, then smiled. "I'm enjoying my time with her. And you." Her eyes met his heated stare. "I want to stay. Unless it's uncomfortable for you. My being here, I mean."

Wes leaned against the metal rake, still sizing her up, but not responding right away. The awkward silence stretched on between them for what felt like forever before he finally shrugged. "It's...different. Been a while since I brought a girl home. For any reason. So I'm not surprised that my mother is trying to make something bigger out of this. I hope she hasn't made you uncomfortable."

"No, of course not." Bree forced a smile, not wanting to reveal her discomfort at Wesley's words.

Wes tried to ignore the sound of the shower running in the Jack-and-Jill bathroom between his room and the guest room Bree would be sleeping in. Tried to ignore the vision of water sluicing down Bree's back, between her firm breasts and into the valley between her long legs.

He tried, but failed miserably. His body ached with want and left him with an unsettled feeling in his chest.

He wanted her. In a way that made it clear that what he craved was more than just her body. No matter how many times he tried to tell himself otherwise.

"Wes?" There was a knock at the bathroom door that led to his room.

He cleared his throat and edged closer to the door.

"I hate to bother you, but I can't find another towel."

"Sorry about that." Wes groaned. He meant to re-stock the towels after he'd taken his shower earlier. "I'll get you one."

Wes retrieved some towels from the hallway linen closet and returned to the door. He took a deep breath before he knocked. "Got them."

Bree cracked open the door slightly. The room was still filled with steam and her hair hung in wet curls that clung to her face.

"Thank you." She reached one arm out while shielding her body with the door. "I'll be out in a second, if you need to get in here."

"All I want is you." His gaze held hers. "Naked. In my bed."

Her eyes widened with surprise. She closed the door and bustled around the bathroom, but still hadn't answered him.

Wes groaned, his forehead pressed to the bathroom door. Brianna had gotten under his skin in a way no other woman had. Maybe it was good she hadn't accepted his proposition. She was saving him from himself.

Suddenly, the door opened and she stood before him in one of the fuzzy, cream-colored towels he'd just given her. She gave him a shy smile, but heat raged in her brown eyes.

"I believe you invited me to your room. Does the offer still stand?" Bree seemed to enjoy the stunned look on his face.

He didn't speak. Didn't nod. Instead, he leaned down, cradled her head and pressed his mouth to hers.

Slipped his tongue inside her warm, minty mouth. Pressed his body against hers.

Bree wrapped her arms around him, her hands pressed to his back as she murmured softly, her head tilted.

Her skin was soft and warm and she smelled sweet and sensual. He wanted to taste every inch of her heated skin. Make love to her until they were both sweaty, exhausted and fully satisfied.

Wes slid his hands to her back, then down to her bottom, pulling her against him. He let out a soft sigh at the intense pleasure of her wet heat pressed against him there. He slid his hands beneath the towel, gripped her naked flesh before he lifted her into his arms and carried her to his bed.

Bree's smile was hesitant. Filled with want and need. And something more. Something that tugged at his chest and felt oddly familiar.

He didn't have time to ruminate over it. She took his face into her hands and pulled his mouth down to hers. Kissed him slow and sweet in a way that revved up his body and ignited a flame deep in his chest. It was a feeling that could only mean trouble for both of them.

Wes stripped Bree of her towel and shed his T-shirt and boxers. He trailed kisses from her neck to her center, wet and glistening. Tasted her there. Lapped at her with his tongue while teasing her with his fingers. Until she shattered, her knees trembling and her lips pressed together to muffle her whimpers.

He kissed his way back up to her belly. Laved her hardened, beaded nipples as he slid inside her and rocked them both into a delicious abandon that made him want to forget everything but her.

"You're an incredible woman, Brianna Evans. In every way." Wes kissed her damp forehead and held her tight against him. "Thank you."

Bree was silent for a moment before she pressed a hand to his chest and lifted her head so her eyes met his. "Thank you for what?"

"For being here with me." Wes pulled the damp, curly strands of hair back and tucked them behind her ear so he could study her elegant features in the moonlight. He kissed her cheek. "For being so kind and thoughtful to my mother."

She smiled softly. "Thank you for letting me meet her. I know that isn't something you usually do."

He chuckled. "Try never."

"Why?" Bree hesitated before continuing. "Most guys who feel that way…to be honest, they're probably doing womankind a favor by not getting deeply involved with anyone. But you aren't like that. You're a genuinely good man. You deserve to be happy. To have a full life. So why are you so dead set against getting involved?"

Wes sighed heavily, folding one arm behind his head as he stared at the ceiling. "The men in my family haven't had a very good track record of being good mates."

"My mother gave me up at birth and hasn't wanted anything to do with me since." Bree shrugged, resting her chin on his chest. "Doesn't mean I'd do the same to my kid. Besides, we aren't our parents, Wes. Who we are is based on the decisions we make every single day. Like you making the choice to be there for your mother as she battles her illness. That's why this tournament is so important to you, isn't it?"

"Yes." He traced her bare shoulder with his calloused fingertips. "And I'm not basing my decision on parental history alone."

"We all make mistakes, Wes." Bree was quiet for a moment when he didn't respond. "Doesn't mean that's who we are or that we don't deserve happiness. What matters is that we try to rectify our mistakes and that we learn from them."

"A caged bird escaping its gilded cage." Her gaze dropped to the tattoo on the left side of his chest. The bird was designed of sheets of musical notes. The door it escaped looked like facing capital letter Gs. She traced the ink lightly with her fingertips. "Is that you?"

"No. Got it not long after I graduated university as sort of a tribute to my mother."

"You hoped your mother would go after her dreams again, once you and your brother were no longer her responsibility. That's sweet. *You're* sweet." She leaned in and kissed his mouth.

"But you shouldn't feel guilty about your mom missing out on the life she might've had. You should see the glow on her face when she talks about you and your brother. She doesn't seem to regret a moment of her life. I can't imagine she'd want you lugging around this burden of guilt on her behalf." Bree studied his face, waiting for his reaction.

It was a weight he'd been carrying for years. One not easily budged. He met her gaze. "This is who I am, Bree. It's who I've been most of my life. Sorry if that's not what you wanted to hear."

"I'm sorry, too." She sighed softly, the corner of her

mouth tugged down in a slight frown. "Good night, Wesley."

Bree climbed out of bed, gathered her towel and wrapped it around her again.

"Are you angry with me?" He sat up in bed, pulling the sheet up around his waist.

"No, of course not." There was pity and sadness in her voice. "I just think it's better if I sleep in my room. In case your mother comes looking for one of us in the morning."

Her excuse wasn't very convincing to either of them.

"I don't expect her to hobble up the steps. That was the whole point of moving her downstairs. If anything, she'll call upstairs." Wes kept his voice even. It needed to sound as if he was stating a fact, rather than the passionate plea it was.

He liked the idea of waking up to Bree in his arms.

Bree didn't acknowledge his statement. "See you at breakfast."

She exited through the bathroom door. He groaned when the distinct click of the door locking on the other side of the bathroom indicated she had no intention of returning.

Wes groaned, one arm folded behind his head. He should be glad Bree was honoring his request to keep their relationship casual. Instead, he was pouting like a child whose favorite toy had just been taken away.

Chapter 16

"Another trip with Wes, huh?" Bex's observation was more than a passing interest.

"Uh-huh." Bree turned away from Bex. They were using the video messaging app on her phone, which was propped on the nightstand. She stuffed her makeup bag into her luggage and zipped it. When she finally turned back to the phone, her friend had her arms crossed and one eye cocked. "What?"

"You know what. This isn't just business anymore, and it's obviously escalated beyond banging-buddy status. I'm worried about you. I don't want to see you get hurt." Bex's tone had shifted from exasperation to genuine concern.

"I won't." Her statement lacked conviction.

"Even you don't believe that."

It'd been more than a month since she and Wes had

taken their trip to Asheville. They'd continued their affair in secret, not even telling their best friends. But Bex knew her too well. She'd threatened to hop the next plane to Pleasure Cove if Bree didn't level with her.

So she'd told Bex the truth. She and Wes were friends who just happened to also enjoy sleeping together. A lot. But they were not a couple. Nor would they become one, because that wasn't what either of them wanted right now.

That part was a lie. One Bex saw right through. It was the reason she was so concerned.

Though she tried to allay her friend's concerns, they both knew the truth. In the recesses of her heart, Bree quietly believed Wes to be The Trifecta. The elusive man who would satisfy her body, heart and mind.

Each moment spent with Wesley Adams convinced her that he was the man with whom she could happily spend the rest of her life.

Though their no-strings agreement still stood, Bree was sure Wes cared for her more than he was willing to let on.

It was in his kiss. In his touch. In his voice when he whispered in her ear in the wee hours of the morning. It was in the depths of his dark eyes when he made love to her. In his stolen glances at her when he thought no one else was looking.

What they shared was more than sex or even friendship.

Bree wouldn't call it love, but it was deeper than lust or affection. Still, if Wes wasn't willing to explore his feelings for her, what did it matter? The end of summer would bring the volleyball tournament they'd both worked so hard on, and eventually, the end of their relationship. He'd stay in Pleasure Cove and she'd return to California, as if what they'd shared over the summer meant nothing.

The thought made her chest heavy with grief.

"I can handle whatever happens between us this time." Bree hoped her tone was more convincing.

"Then go to London and have a good time with your *friend*." An uneasy smile curled the edges of Bex's mouth. "How's his mom?"

"She's doing well." A wide smile tightened Bree's cheeks when she thought of Lena. Wes had hired an aide to help his mother around the house. Still, he'd visited Lena each week and Bree had accompanied him twice—at Lena's insistence. She went gladly, because she genuinely enjoyed Lena's company. "The air cast came off yesterday and she's getting around well. Still, I hate that neither of us will be here."

"You sound like a dutiful daughter-in-law." Bex peered into the camera, one eyebrow raised.

"She's an amazing woman. Funny and interesting. I can't help but adore her."

"Just don't get too attached. Walking away from Wes at the end of the summer means walking away from his mother, too."

The doorbell rang and Bree said goodbye to her friend, glad not to have to respond to Bex's very salient point.

It was too late. She'd already fallen for Wes and his mom.

A noise startled Wes awake. According to his mobile, it was a little after three in the morning. Yet,

Bree was no longer in bed. He followed the sound to his sitting room.

The lights were off, but he could make out Bree's form as she stood in front of the large windows that had enticed him into purchasing the flat. She stared into the distance at London's skyline.

"Is everything okay?"

"Everything is fine." She turned toward him, her face barely visible in the light streaming through the window. "Sorry, I didn't mean to wake you. I couldn't sleep. Figured it was a good time to take in this beautiful view."

"I fell for this place the moment I saw that view." He studied her silhouette in the moonlight. Wearing the sheer white lingerie he'd surprised her with, she managed to look naughty and angelic all at once.

"You look amazing." He stood behind her, slipped his arms around her waist and planted soft kisses on her warm neck. Inhaled her scent. Her soft murmur vibrated against his chest, making him want her more. Wes pressed his body to hers as he slipped the white fabric from her shoulder and trailed kisses there. "And as much as I love seeing you in this, what I'd really like is to see you out of it again."

Bree blushed in the moonlight, the corner of her mouth curling in an adorable grin that warmed him.

He couldn't resist smiling in response.

They'd been carrying on their affair for more than a month. Bree had initiated things that night in Asheville. Yet, at her core she was demure and, at times, bashful. He loved that she could be both a wily, determined temptress and the sweet, blushing girl next door.

"You have a big meeting this morning, remember?"

"It's this afternoon," he whispered in her ear, his lips brushing her skin. "Gives me plenty of time to spend with you."

"I like the sound of that." Bree turned around, her gaze meeting his as she slid one hand down his chest and beneath his waistband, taking him in her palm.

Wes sucked in a deep breath as she palmed his heated flesh. Her cool hand warmed as it glided up and down his shaft.

Her nostrils flared and the corner of her mouth curled with satisfaction. She seemed to enjoy the power she had over him as she stroked him, bringing him closer to the edge.

He cradled her face and claimed her mouth in a frantic kiss. Bree had him teetering on the edge. But he was desperate to be inside her again. To stare into those brown eyes, her bare, sweat-slickened skin pressed to his, as he erupted with pleasure.

Wes scooped her in his arms and she squealed, looping her arms around his neck so she wouldn't fall. He carried her to his bed, each of them shedding their clothing. He settled between her thighs and trailed kisses down her neck and between her breasts.

"You do realize I wasn't finished in there."

"But I nearly was, and we couldn't have that."

Scraping one beaded tip between his teeth, he gently teased it with his tongue. Bree squirmed beneath him. Her soft, sensual murmur stoked the fire building inside him.

Wes hated that he'd pulled the heavy curtains shut. He wanted the satisfaction of seeing Bree's lovely face as she called his name in the throes of her climax. A delight he never tired of.

He sheathed himself, then entered her slowly, groaning with pleasure as her snug heat welcomed him.

They moved together, heat building between them and a light sheen of sweat clinging to their skin. Bree's murmurs grew louder. Her breath came faster. She repositioned her legs and pressed her bare feet to his shoulders, allowing him to penetrate deeper.

She clutched the sheets, her back arched as she called his name, riding the wave of her orgasm. Nearly there, he continued his thrusts until his spine stiffened and he shuddered, cursing and moaning. Calling her name.

Breathless and sweaty, he gathered her in his arms and kissed her damp hair.

Bree Evans was the first woman who'd made him question the wisdom of his commitment to remaining unattached. She made him want to believe he was capable of giving her the things she wanted.

Love. Marriage. A family.

More and more, he'd allowed himself to imagine what it would be like to have those things with her. And it didn't feel stifling or confining. The images in his head filled him with warmth and contentment.

He could get used to having Bree in his bed every night, but he wouldn't delude himself by believing he could become something he wasn't. He'd already ruined one woman's life and caused them both irrevocable harm. He wouldn't do that to Bree. No matter how much he wanted her.

Chapter 17

"He's a pretty spectacular fellow, isn't he?"

The woman's voice startled Bree from what she often found herself doing these days—stealing loving glances at Wesley Adams when she thought no one was looking. His event manager, Nadia, obviously was.

The woman had done a poor job of hiding her disbelief when Wes had introduced her as a friend. Standing in the corner, staring at Wes like a lovelorn fool, didn't help.

"He is...very good at what he does, I mean," Bree clarified as she sipped her champagne. Wes and his team were working the party. So they weren't drinking. She had no such constraints. "I've learned a lot from him since we started working on the project together."

"I'll bet." Nadia was barely able to hold back her

grin. "He's taught me quite a lot about the event-planning and promotions business. Still, I've a lot to learn before I'll be anywhere near as gifted as he is."

"Well, he's certainly confident in you," Bree reassured the woman with a smile. "He'd never have entrusted his business to you if he wasn't."

"Thank you." Nadia beamed. "And if you don't mind me saying so, I've known him long enough to realize that what he feels for you is special." She looked over at Wes, who stood on the other side of the room staring at Bree. "I've never seen him light up the way he does when he looks at you. He's completely smitten and it scares him half to death."

A soft smile curved the edge of Bree's mouth and her cheeks warmed as she returned his affectionate gaze. Bree wanted to believe that what Nadia was saying was true. That Wes reciprocated her growing feelings for him.

The warmth she'd felt moments earlier gave way to a dull ache in her chest and a knot in her belly.

She returned her attention to Nadia. "It's not what you think."

"Maybe. Or maybe I'm right and you two are both wrong about what this is." Nadia squeezed her arm and disappeared into the crowd.

Bree released a long, slow breath, her heart beating quickly. They'd grown closer during their two weeks in London. Each day together had felt more intimate, but now their trip was coming to an end.

They'd fallen into an easy rhythm. Making love in the mornings and chatting over breakfast. Dinner together and nights that ended in the same manner they began. In each other's arms.

While Wes worked with his small team to hire more staff and finalize plans for a huge corporate party, Bree worked on the tournament and her own projects. She'd had video and phone conferences with Bex and the marketing consultant they'd hired to help them plan and promote their volleyball camps the following year.

Still, Wes had insisted on taking her to see all of the tourist attractions she hadn't been able to squeeze into her previous working trips to London. Visits to the Tower of London, Kensington Palace and Westminster Abbey. A turn on the London Eye—the giant Ferris wheel on the south bank of the River Thames. A romantic evening stroll across London Bridge and a view of the city from the hauntingly beautiful attached skyscraper—the Shard.

She'd been incredibly happy, and it seemed that Wes was, too. So why did he seem so terrified by the prospect of exploring the feelings they had for each other?

It was a question she'd revisited time and again. Yet, she hadn't wanted to broach the subject with him. She'd willingly agreed to a secret, no-strings-attached fling with Wes. Insisted that she was cosmopolitan enough to handle such an affair. So she'd grin and bear the pain that knotted her belly whenever she considered what would happen once the tournament had ended and they went their separate ways.

"Enjoying the party?" Wes stood beside her.

"Yes." Bree finished her glass of champagne and set it on the tray of a server walking by. "But I think I'll head back to your place. I feel like I'm a distraction to you. Besides, I need to call my mother and yours."

"You're a pleasant distraction. My favorite kind." He smiled warmly. "And as for my mom, I'm grateful you've been so patient with her, but if she's become a nuisance, I'll talk to her."

"Don't you dare. I enjoy spending time with her. I promise." She double-checked that the spare key Wes gave her was in her clutch, then snapped it shut. "See you back at the flat?"

"At least let me hail a taxi for you." Wes frowned.

"I'll be fine." Bree made her way to the exit, hoping that Nadia was right. And that Wes missed her as much as she was already missing him.

Despite all of the noise and movement swirling around him, Wes was focused on one thing—Brianna Evans walking away from him. A thought that had occupied a growing space in his brain.

He shouldn't worry about what would happen at the project's end. He should just enjoy every moment they had together. Stop worrying about the future and commiserating over his past. Live in the now.

Yet, losing her was all he could think of.

Though he couldn't rightly claim to be losing her when they'd be parting ways at his insistence.

"She's even nicer in person." Nadia had a way of sneaking up on him. "I see why you fancy her so."

Wes didn't respond to Nadia's attempt to gauge his relationship with Bree. It was safer to talk business instead.

"How are the two potential new hires doing?" His gaze swept the room, in search of any small details that might have fallen through the cracks.

"Smashing. It's too bad we can only afford to bring one of them onboard. Don't know how we'll choose."

"Maybe we won't have to." Wes held back a grin when Nadia's eyes widened. He'd been so preoccupied with business and Bree that he hadn't told her the news. "I've been talking with the Westbrooks over the past few weeks. They'd like to make us the official event-planning professionals for their London headquarters."

Nadia squeezed his arm and mimicked a silent squeal. "I thought you were determined to do this without them."

"I love and admire the Westbrooks, but I didn't want to feel beholden to them. I went against everyone's advice in starting this business—including Liam and his father. I needed to show them I could make it a success without their family's power and wealth behind me." He shrugged. "I've done that here."

"And in the US? I know your best mate begged you to help him out on short notice, but I get the sense there's more to it than that. Was working with Brianna the carrot that finally won you over?" Nadia grinned.

"Didn't realize she was involved when I agreed to it," he reminded her. An involuntary smile tightened his cheeks. "But working with her has turned out to be a highlight."

"I knew it. You're completely gaga over her, aren't you?" Nadia could barely contain her excitement.

"How is it you're more excited about this than my news about Westbrook International?" He raised a brow. "Especially since I'm promoting you to president of UK operations by the end of the year if everything works out in the US."

This time Nadia's squeal wasn't silent. With the ruckus going on around them, few people noticed. She hugged him.

"I can't believe it. Thank you for your faith in me. I was sure you'd bring some heavy hitter in to head things up here if the project went well across the pond."

"You've been with me since the beginning. Back when we were working out of that mangy old flat. You were there every day and worked solely on commission. How could you think I'd trust anyone else to head up the business here?"

"You're making me blush." Nadia swiped a finger beneath the corner of her eye and sniffled. "Don't expect this to put a stop to me meddling in your love life."

"I don't have a love life."

"Precisely. But you deserve to be happy with someone like Brianna. I quite like her. So don't you dare let her get away." Nadia elbowed him playfully, but then her voice turned somber. "If you care for her the way it seems you do, you'll never forgive yourself if you let her go."

Wes massaged the knot that had formed at the back of his neck.

If only it was that easy.

Chapter 18

Brianna stood at the window taking a mental picture of the view from Wesley's flat. She was trying to memorize it and everything about their past two weeks together in London.

The soft strains of Duke Ellington and John Coltrane's version of "In a Sentimental Mood" drifted from the multi-room audio wired throughout his flat. She'd been listening to the song on repeat. It was Wesley's favorite classic jazz standard. She'd heard it often in the weeks they'd been together, each time with more appreciation than the time before.

On their final night in London together, the song captured her mood brilliantly. Ellington's ethereal piano notes combined with Coltrane's smooth, somber sax made for a brooding, introspective piece reflective of both joy and sadness.

Exactly what she was feeling now.

Her chest filled with warmth as she reflected on the two weeks they'd spent together in London. Yet, a pervasive sense of sadness made her heart ache.

They'd never be in London together again. The city that had originally brought them together.

She inhaled the unbuttoned blue oxford shirt she wore over her bra and panties. The same shirt he'd been wearing before they'd stripped each other naked and made love.

"I'm officially packed and ready for our early morning departure. I'm surprised you're not asleep." Wes joined her at the window.

"Committing this remarkable view to memory." Bree fiddled with the collar of the shirt, hoping Wesley hadn't caught her sniffing its scent moments earlier. They'd shared so many special moments in London. Moments in which they'd grown closer.

London was now inextricably linked with Wesley Adams.

"It isn't as if you'll never return. To London, I mean." His gaze drifted from hers. They were silent for a moment before he shifted the topic. "I've obviously convinced you of the many virtues of 'In a Sentimental Mood.'"

"It's brilliant. Evocative of so many powerful emotions."

"Come here." Wes moved toward the center of the room and extended his hand. When Bree joined him, he took her hand in his and looped an arm around her waist. "Dance with me."

His soft, intimate plea filled her body with heat. A charge of electricity ran along her skin.

She swayed with Wes, her ear pressed to his chest, listening to the thud of his heart as it beat against his strong chest. Her eyes drifted closed for a moment as they swayed and turned about the room ever so slightly with each step.

His chin propped on her head, Wes cradled her closer, neither of them speaking.

The connection they shared was more than sex. More than friendship.

So why was Wes so determined to walk away from the very thing they both seemed to want and need? What was Wes really afraid of?

Bree wanted to ask, but the words wouldn't come. To quiet the pervasive questions that danced in her head, she shifted attention back to the song.

"You said Miles Davis and Thelonious Monk are your favorite jazz artists. So why is a collaboration between Ellington and Coltrane your favorite jazz song?"

"Aside from the brilliance of the collaboration and the complexity of the piece?" Wes's voice rumbled against her ear. "Got my own sentimental connection to the song." He paused so long it seemed he'd decided against divulging it. "My favorite memory of my parents is them dancing to this song."

"That's beautiful." Something about his admission made tears instantly well in her eyes. Bree wasn't sure if she was moved by the poignancy of the story, or by his willingness to share it with her.

"Your mom showed me some old family pictures." Bree hadn't mentioned it before because Wes wasn't inclined to reminisce about his dad. But tonight, he seemed open to it. "Lena is gorgeous now, but she looked like a glamorous movie star in all her photos. And you guys all look so happy."

"In the beginning, my mom was, and I think my dad wanted to be. But his passion was music, being on the road traveling. Maybe he really did love us. But he loved music and life on the road more."

"Wes, I'm sorry." She squeezed him tightly. Bree understood the pain and rejection Wes felt. It was a pain that could only truly be understood by someone who'd endured it, too.

"Don't be." Wes slid his hands beneath the shirt she wore. His rough hands glided along her warm skin. He traced a scar from an old surgery with his thumb.

Bree tensed, self-conscious about the ugly scar. She'd had it incorporated into the tattoo on her side to camouflage the imperfection.

"Does it hurt?" His soft, warm gaze met hers.

"No, and neither does this one." She slipped the shirt from her shoulder enough to reveal a scar that remained from her shoulder surgery a few years ago. "But they've ruined my bikini game." She tried to keep her breathing even as she maintained his heated gaze.

"I assure you that nothing could possibly mar the sight of you in a bikini. Besides, with a one-piece like the one you wore in my hot tub that day…who needs one?" He gripped her bare waist and pulled her closer to him again as he leaned in and whispered in her ear. "By the way, that swimsuit…you weren't playing fair. A man with less willpower would've caved."

"Your concept for the tournament was best, so it's good you were strong enough to resist my charms." She glided a hand up his bare chest. "But I won when it really counted."

"I assume you're talking about when I gave in on other aspects of the tournament—like the stage layout and the celebrities we invited." His sexy mouth curved in a knowing grin that did wicked things to her. Made her want to do wicked things to him.

"Then, too." Bree's cheeks tightened as she tried to hold back a smirk.

Wes kissed her, tightening his grip on her waist as one hand drifted down to squeeze her bottom, pulling her hard against the ridge beneath the fly of his jeans.

She parted her lips and he slipped his warm tongue inside her mouth. Her heart beat faster and her temperature rose as he kissed her hard and deep, with a passion that made her dizzy with want.

Wes turned her around and slipped the shirt from her shoulders. He loosened her bra and let it drift to the floor. When he teased her hardened nipples, her spine stiffened and she sucked in a breath.

He turned her head, capturing her mouth in a bruising kiss that made her core pulse. Wes trailed a hand down her belly, slipping it inside her panties, damp with her desire for him. He teased the bundle of nerves as she moved against his hand. Her heart beat faster as pleasure built in her core. When he pulled his hand away, she released an involuntary whimper, desperate for release.

His eyes met hers, his chest heaving. What she saw there made her weak with want. Wes's gaze radiated heat, passion and raw emotion.

His gaze mirrored everything she'd been feeling. An emotion she hadn't wanted to name. One that felt a lot like love. And looked like what she saw reflected in Wesley's eyes.

Wes took her to his bed and made love to her. It was intensely passionate, but also deeply emotional, in a way it hadn't been before. Things had shifted between them.

Body trembling and her climax building as he held her gaze, something suddenly became very clear.

She wanted to be his. Now and always.

He seemed to want it, to ache for it, too.

Bree blurted out the thing that was on her heart. The one thing she hadn't wanted to say aloud.

"Wes, I love you."

Wes, still recovering from his own release, seemed stunned by Bree's admission.

She'd read him wrong. Had seen what she so desperately wanted to see.

Wes lay beside her, awkward silence stretching between them, making the seconds feel like minutes. Finally, he turned on his side, his head propped on his fist. "Bree, I—I…"

"It's okay." Bree sat up abruptly, her words accompanied by a nervous laugh that only seemed to make him pity her. She dragged her fingers through her hair. "I shouldn't have said that. I was just…you know." She swiped a finger beneath her eye. "Let's talk about something else while I pretend not to be embarrassed that I just said that."

"You have nothing to be embarrassed about, Bree." He stroked her arm. "It isn't you, I swear. I just can't—"

"Please…don't." She inhaled deeply, then forced a painful smile as tears sprung from her eyes. She quickly wiped them away. "Let's talk about something else. Anything. Please."

"Okay." He sat up, too. "Can I get you a glass of wine or something?"

"Wine would be great. Thank you."

While he moved about the kitchen, Bree turned on the bedside lamp, retrieved her underwear and slipped on a T-shirt and a pair of his boxers, since her pajamas were already packed in her luggage. She sat in one of the chairs near the window in his bedroom.

"The French Bordeaux Sauternes we bought at Borough Market." He handed her a glass.

Her hand trembled slightly as she accepted the glass. She took a long sip. Concentrated on the balance of sweetness and acidity. The flavor notes of apricot and honey. *Anything* but the fact that she'd just admitted to Wes that she loved him.

Wes joined her in the sitting area by the window, the space where he often sat and read in the mornings before he would start his day.

He swallowed hard. The words he wanted to say lodged painfully in his throat.

I love you, too.

He had no business saying them. Wouldn't give her false hope.

"You wanted to talk about something else." He set his glass on the small, shabby chic table between them. A salvaged piece he'd held onto from his college days because it was the first piece of furniture his mother had ever refinished. "So tell me, what's next in your career?"

Bree narrowed her gaze at him. It was another loaded topic. He'd known that before he asked her.

She'd been playing volleyball professionally for

well over a decade. With each passing year and each new injury, speculation about the end of her career swirled. Something it seemed Bex was experiencing as she fought to come back from her latest injury.

Still, he really wanted to know. Since they both seemed prone to deep introspection and spontaneous confession tonight, it seemed the perfect time to inquire.

"I hope to play a few more years. So now's the time for me to begin the transition from professional volleyball player to whatever comes next."

"And what is that?" Wes wasn't satisfied with her non-answer. "Will the volleyball camps be your full-time pursuit once you've retired?"

"That's what Bex wants."

"But what does Brianna want?" His voice softened.

"I'm not sure." She shrugged. "Volleyball has been my entire life since I was in middle school. I've sacrificed so much to be the best at what I do. I'm not completely sure where I go from there. Professionally speaking."

They were both silent for a moment, then he asked, "In your heart of hearts, what is it you'd like to be doing, more than anything, outside of playing volleyball?"

"I don't know…"

"I think you do." He swapped his untouched wineglass with her empty one, then sat back in his chair and surveyed her. "Maybe you're reluctant to share it with me, but—"

"What I'm doing now," she said quickly, picking up her wineglass and taking a sip. "Not *this*, obviously." She held up the wineglass and they both laughed.

A little of the tension between them eased. "I mean being a spokesperson for important causes. Helping people. Making a difference." A genuine smile lifted her cheeks and lit her eyes. "Going to visit with sick children at hospitals. Talking to high-risk children at inner-city schools and at boys' and girls' clubs. Helping them see that they matter. That no matter how big their dreams are, they're attainable. They just need to believe in themselves and be willing to work for it. But a good support system helps. And I'd like to be that for those kids."

Bree caught Wes staring at her and her cheeks flushed. She took another sip of her wine as she gazed out of the window. "I sound like a corny do-gooder, right?"

"Look at me, Bree." He shifted forward in his seat as her gaze met his. "Never apologize for who you are. Every character trait, every physical scar...they all make you the remarkable warrior goddess you are. So don't apologize for any of it. Got it?"

She was silent for a moment, then nodded.

"Good." He smiled and her shoulders relaxed. "If that's what you really want to do, do it. Kids like us, who came from nothing, they desperately need someone to believe in them. To support their dreams and give them opportunities they wouldn't have had otherwise."

Bree took another sip of her wine. "The trouble is, if I don't keep playing, in some capacity, I'm no longer relevant, and I won't get opportunities like this."

"Make your own. Start your own organization."

"It's not that simple."

"Isn't it? It's not like you'd have to do everything

yourself. A charity is like any other business. Hire the best people to run it for you."

Bree seemed unconvinced.

"Seems you've given this some thought, but something about the idea scares you. What is it?"

"It seems overwhelming, to say the least. Besides, it's such an important task. I can't let them down. What if I fail?"

"What if you succeed? Think of how many lives you could change?"

"Have you always been this confident?" She crooked an eyebrow as she studied him.

For a moment, he was sure she could see right through him to the scared little boy wearing hand-me-downs at a boarding school filled with children of the rich and famous. "I had to learn. Survival of the fittest, you know?"

She nodded. "I was one of only a handful of minority kids at my entire private school. The only one there on scholarship. So, I worked hard to prove that I was this perfect little girl. That I belonged there as much as anyone else. Still, there's always this part of me that wonders deep down if I'm really good enough." Bree stood quickly and swiped dampness from the corner of her eyes. "It's late. I need to get ready for bed."

Wes sighed as she disappeared behind the bathroom door. If only he could tell Bree the truth. It was him who wasn't good enough for her.

Wes lay awake, more than an hour after they'd gone to bed, watching Bree as she slept. He cared for her more than any woman he'd ever known. And he wanted to believe he deserved her. That they could be happy together forever.

He turned onto his back and stared at the ceiling, trying to quiet the voice that implored him to trust her with the truth.

That he wanted her, and only her.

He had his rules. Rules designed to keep him from ever needlessly hurting anyone again. He was determined not to break those rules by falling for her.

And yet…he already had.

He'd tried to pretend that what they shared was a symbiotic fusion of sex and friendship. One they could both easily walk away from.

But Bree had changed the game.

She'd shown him how gratifying it was to forge a deep connection with someone who knew him in ways no one else did.

But if he truly cared for her, he'd stick to the plan.

He wouldn't take a chance on disappointing her the way his father had disappointed his mother. Or the way he'd once disappointed someone who'd loved him more than he deserved.

Wes glanced at Bree again. They'd had an incredible time in London. It would be hard to return to this flat without thinking of her in his home, in his bed and in his life. And how happy it made him.

But he'd been playing a dangerous game with Bree's heart. Fooling himself into thinking they could do this without either of them getting hurt.

He did love Bree. And because he loved her, he would let her go.

He'd never hurt anyone that way again. The price was far too steep.

Chapter 19

Brianna had broken the rules of their little game, and now Wes was making her pay.

They'd both downplayed her misstep the previous night. However, the next morning, he was polite, but withdrawn. At the very least, distracted. Though they'd both slept during much of it, their nonstop flight home had been uncharacteristically quiet.

Bree silently cursed herself again for saying those three little words their final night in London. It was the perfect way to ruin a sublime trip and kill the mood with her no-strings-attached lover.

Wes put the last of her luggage upstairs and returned to the living room, where she sifted through a stack of mail and a few postcards. He shoved his hands into his pockets, his gaze not quite meeting hers.

"Look, I know you must be tired. Why don't I stay at my place tonight?"

A stab in the heart would've been less painful.

"Of course. I'll see you… I'll guess you'll let me know when."

She put down the mail and went to the kitchen. Bree opened the fridge, pulled over the trash can and tossed spoiled and expired food into it.

"Bree, I don't want to hurt you. You know that. But maybe this was a mistake." Wes made his way to the kitchen.

"I know we agreed not to let things get serious, and I'm the one at fault here. I made the mistake of thinking you had, you know…feelings. Like a regular human." Bree poured the remainder of a half gallon of milk down the drain, rinsed the bottle and tossed it in the recycle bin.

"You think I'm saying this because I *don't* have feelings? You couldn't be more wrong."

"Then level with me. What's this really about?"

"I am leveling with you, but you won't believe me."

Bree closed the fridge. She struggled to be calm and mature about this. After all, what was the difference between her and her stalkerish ex if she couldn't accept that it was over?

"If you've tired of me and you're ready to move on…fine. And maybe I'm wrong, but I don't think that's it. You act as if you don't want intimacy or a real relationship, but I know that isn't true. I see the truth in your eyes whenever we're together. What I can't figure out is what you're so afraid of?"

He narrowed his gaze, as if she'd struck a nerve, but he didn't respond.

"Talk to me, Wes. Whatever it is, just say it." She stepped closer to him, stopping short of touching him. "Is there someone else?"

"Bree, there's no one in the world I'd rather be with. But I'm not prepared to make the kind of promises you're looking for."

"What the hell does that even mean?" Bree stood tall, her arms folded, despite wanting to dissolve into tears. She refused to give him the satisfaction of knowing how deeply his rejection cut.

"I'm trying to be completely honest with you, Bree. I won't be like my old man, making promises he couldn't keep. I won't do that to you. To us. I need to be sure."

"Of what? That no one better will come along?" She glared at him. "And what am I supposed to do? Warm your bed, fingers crossed, hoping one day you'll be ready? No thank you."

"It's not like that. Believe me."

"I don't. And I don't believe this is just about your dad walking out on you. People get divorced. Parents leave. And yeah, we both got saddled with a shitty parent. But we don't have to be them. I'm certainly not going to just lie down and die because I'm afraid I'll be like mine."

Wesley's eyes widened, his mouth falling open. She'd stunned him with a strike to the jugular.

Maybe it wasn't fair for her to bring up his dad, but Wes had opened the door to it when he'd used his old man as an excuse.

Bree sighed, no longer able to take the silence between them.

"I think maybe you're right. This was a mistake. I

take full responsibility. You were very clear from the beginning. I should've taken your word for it instead of pushing you."

"I'm not saying we can't be friends."

"Nor am I." Bree held her head high. "But right now, let's just focus on putting on a kick-ass tournament. Okay?"

Wes's eyes reflected every bit of the pain it caused her to utter those words. He didn't move or speak.

"So that's it?" Wes cleared his throat, his hands shoved in his pockets.

"I think it has to be. But we'll always have London, right?" She forced a smile, not allowing the tears that stung her eyes to fall.

"Always." He cradled her face and kissed her goodbye.

She waited for the click of the door closing behind Wes before she crumbled onto the sofa, tears streaming down her face.

She'd gambled and lost.

Maybe she'd played her hand too soon. Or perhaps the real mistake had been that she'd dared to play the game at all.

Wes straightened his collar and closed his eyes briefly as he exhaled a long, slow breath. It was exactly two weeks before his best friend's wedding and nearly three weeks since he and Bree had ended their affair.

He'd been in Las Vegas for two days with Liam and around twenty of their friends. But it hadn't been enough to lift the testy mood he'd been in since last he'd seen Bree. She'd returned to California the day after they'd ended things, and she'd attended the last two meetings about the volleyball tournament via video conference.

Yet, she'd kept her promise. She'd kept things civil and pleasant between them. As if nothing at all had happened. He'd called her directly a week prior to get her opinion on a change to the celebrity-chef lineup. Brianna answered the phone and had been as syrupy sweet as the sweet tea his mother made. With the issue resolved, he'd tried to make small talk, but she'd politely excused herself to take another call.

She'd saved him from himself. Had he spoken to her at any length, he'd have confessed to missing her every single day.

It was best that Bree was there in California and he was in Vegas celebrating his best friend's impending nuptials.

Wes had expended a tremendous amount of effort the past two days trying to be a proper best man. Immersing himself in the celebratory spirit. But he'd spent most of the weekend attempting to mask the cavernous hole Bree's absence left in his heart.

Wes knocked on the door of Liam's hotel suite. His friend answered the door in the midst of a video chat with his fiancée's daughters, the two little girls he adored as if they were his own.

"Say hello to Uncle Wes." Liam turned the phone toward him.

Sofia and Gabriella waved at him. "Hi, Uncle Wes!"

His mouth curled in an involuntary smile. His first genuine smile of the day. Since he'd been living in Pleasure Cove he'd gotten to know the girls and he now understood why Liam adored them.

He chatted with Sofie and Ella briefly before Liam finished his conversation and promised the girls he'd see them soon.

"Go ahead and say it, mate. They've got me wrapped around their little fingers." Liam grinned.

"That's like saying the earth is round. It's already an established fact." Wes sat on the huge sectional sofa, avoiding the cushion that reeked of beer. Liam's brother, Hunter, had spilled some on it the night before. "Besides, I'm happy for you. You know that."

"I do." Liam poured each of them two fingers of Scotch, then handed him one. He sat in a nearby chair. "I also know you thought I'd gone off my trolley for giving up my confirmed bachelorhood to become an instant dad."

"Also an established fact." Wes chuckled softly, taking a sip of the premium Scotch—Liam's preferred drink. "But I'm man enough to admit when I'm wrong."

"I should expect an apology, should I?" Liam raised an eyebrow incredulously. "Well, for goodness sake, man, get on with it."

"I honestly believed you'd be sacrificing your way of life and your independence when you took on Maya and her daughters. I was wrong. You weren't giving up your life, you were gaining a fuller, richer life. One that's made you happier than I've ever known you to be."

"That's saying a lot since we've known each other since we were thirteen." Liam grinned. "I used to hear chaps say that some woman or other was the best thing that ever happened to them, and I'd think to myself they must have lived sad and dreary lives before marriage. But now I understand, because Maya and the girls are truly the best thing to ever happen to me."

"No cold feet, then? Not even a little?"

"Not even the tiniest little bit." A broad smile lit Liam's eyes. "We already have such a wonderful life together. I look forward to making it official."

"I envy you, my friend."

"I'd much prefer you find your own." Liam tilted his head as he assessed him. "Tell me this foul mood you've been in for the past few weeks has nothing to do with Bree returning to California."

"Why would it?" Not a lie, simply a question.

"You tell me." Liam wore a supremely smug expression.

"I know it's your stag party weekend, but that doesn't mean you get a pass on being a nosy, obnoxious bastard." Wes finished his Scotch and set the glass on the table.

"No? Why should it be different from any other day?"

"Don't tempt me to launch a lamp or something at that big head of yours." Wes picked up a pillow and flung it at his friend and he tossed it back.

The lock clicked and Hunter stepped into the room along with Liam's two brothers-in-law to-be, Nate Johnston and Dash Williams.

"Don't remember seeing a pillow fight on the agenda for the weekend." Hunter put two cases of bitter on the bar and plopped down on the sofa. "Are you two going to braid each other's hair next?"

Wes and Liam picked up pillows and tossed them at Hunter simultaneously.

"Guess that makes us the only two grown-ups in

the room," Nate said to Dash, as he put a case of imported beer on the bar and sat on a bar stool.

"Then we've definitely moved up in the world. The girls will be glad to hear it." Dash chuckled.

Wes checked his watch and stood. "The party limo will be here in ten. Where is Maya's brother Cole?"

Liam scrolled through the messages on his phone. "Cole will meet us at the limo."

"Then we'd better head downstairs. Everyone else is meeting us at the limo, too."

They loaded the beer onto a luggage cart and headed out into the hallway. Dash pushed the cart onto the partially full elevator. Nate and Hunter got on, too. Wes was about to join them when Liam grabbed his arm.

"You go on. We'll catch the next lift." Liam turned to him as the elevator doors closed.

"Look, I know we were joking around in there, but Bree really is phenomenal. If you're this miserable because she's gone, that should tell you something, mate."

"I like her, okay?" Wes looked away from his friend. "I maybe even love her. But what if I'm wrong? What if in six months or two years I feel differently?"

"Love is a gamble, my friend. None of us knows what will happen tomorrow or next year. But if you truly care for her, tell her how you feel and why."

"What if I tell her the truth and she hates me for it?"

"Then you'll know she's not the one for you."

Wesley's chest felt hollow at the thought of peering into his favorite brown eyes and seeing genuine contempt.

Still, in light of the pain her absence had caused him, it was worth the risk.

Chapter 20

Bree stood on her back deck watering her poor, neglected flowers and enjoying the California sun. She put down the watering can and sat at the patio table with Bex, who was reviewing samples for the camp logo.

"Another cup of coffee?" Bree offered.

"No thanks." Bex studied her for a moment, then sighed. "Look, I'm just going to say this. I was wrong about you and Wesley."

"No, you weren't. You were exactly right. You said I would get hurt and I did. I should've listened."

"But you were so happy. You practically glowed on video chat." Bex closed her laptop. "It was annoying."

"Then you should be happy I'm…" Bree sighed, not wanting to finish the sentence.

"Miserable?" Bex squeezed her arm. "I could never be happy about that."

Bree checked her phone. No calls or text messages from Wes.

"He hasn't contacted me, so obviously he doesn't feel the same."

"Maybe that's because you cut him off so abruptly last time he called." Bex had been there when she'd taken the call.

"It doesn't matter. He doesn't want a relationship, and I do. So there's really nothing for us to talk about."

"Start there. Wes doesn't seem like the typical guy who just can't be bothered to keep it in his pants. Something's got this guy spooked about being in a relationship. You need to find out what it is."

"I can't make him tell me."

"Then ask his mother. She adores you."

"I won't pry into his life behind his back. When he's ready to tell me, he will."

Bex pulled up a photo Bree had sent her. It was her and Wesley at the top of the Shard. She scrolled to another of them atop Looking Glass Rock.

"See what I mean? You never looked that happy when you were with that jerk Alex. Not even in the beginning. Can you believe he had the audacity to email me about you?"

Bree dropped her gaze, sinking her teeth into her lower lip.

"What aren't you telling me, Bree? Has Alex been bothering you?"

"He's left messages. I haven't answered any of them, but he keeps calling. And while I was in London, he sent a postcard to me in Pleasure Cove."

"He's stalking you?" Bex's nostrils flared. Her fore-head and cheeks reddened.

"I wouldn't call it that. He's just having a really tough time taking no for an answer. Something I can relate to."

"You were *not* a stalker. A determined seductress? Yes. A stalker? Definitely not."

Bex picked up Bree's phone and handed it to her.

"You want me to call him?"

"No, I want you to call the police."

"Let's just take a minute and breathe, Bex. Alex will eventually get the message or he'll find some-one new to harass."

"So you admit he's harassing you?"

"Yes… I mean, no. Look, I don't want to end up on some tacky gossip show, and that's exactly what's going to happen if I make that call." Bree tried to rea-son with her friend. Bex knew from experience how persistent the paparazzi could be.

"I don't know, Bree. Alex sounds a little unhinged right now. What if his behavior escalates?" Bex folded her arms, her eyebrows drawn together.

"If things get worse, I swear you'll be the first to know."

"What time does your flight leave tomorrow?"

"Ten."

"You should, at least, tell Wes about this guy." Bex frowned.

"It isn't his problem. It's mine. It'll be okay. I prom-ise. Now, let's see those logo samples."

Bree opened Bex's laptop and studied the artwork proofs as if they were the only worry she had in the world.

* * *

Wes stepped outside his door as Bree descended her front stairs.

"Good morning, Wesley." She offered a polite wave.

Her willingness to speak first was a good sign, despite the formal address and schoolteacher tone.

"Hi." He caught up with her and fell in step as she walked toward the main building, where the meeting was being held. "Wasn't sure you'd be here in person for today's meeting."

"It's the last one before Liam goes on his honeymoon. So I thought I should be here."

"I'm glad you're here, Bree. I've missed you."

Bree didn't break her stride or in any way acknowledge his words.

Maybe Bree had found someone else. Someone who wasn't afraid to commit. Someone with less egregious sins in his past.

"I'm sorry about before. I was an ass—"

"On that we can agree." Bree gave him a quick glance.

"But not for the reasons you might think," Wes said quickly. "It's just that when you said...well, what you said, I panicked. Relationships aren't my usual MO. I wasn't sure how to respond."

She stopped and turned to him. "You seemed sure about it being a mistake for us to have gotten involved."

When Wes lowered his gaze, Bree walked away.

"Bree, I'm trying to explain how I felt...how I feel."

She stopped again and glared up at him. "I'll admit, maybe I said it too soon. But the fact that you seem incapable of saying the words doesn't bode well for us."

Bree checked the time on her phone.

"Look, if you want to talk about what went wrong with us…fine. But let's do it after the meeting. I need to have a clear head right now and this isn't helping."

"I'll throw some steaks on the grill, and we can talk over dinner." That would give him time to get his thoughts together. He couldn't afford a repeat performance of his blabbering-idiot show.

She shrugged her agreement.

It wasn't an enthusiastic acceptance, but at least she hadn't turned him down.

Chapter 21

Bree kicked off her heels and unzipped her skirt. It'd been a long, but productive meeting. They'd sold out of the majority of their sponsorships and were at nearly three quarters of their registration capacity.

They'd gotten the local shop owners onboard by opening the vendor opportunities up to them first at a special rate. Everything was organized and running smoothly and many of the local townsfolk had signed up to serve as volunteers for the event. They were in excellent shape.

Bree changed into shorts and a tank, then grabbed her phone to respond to a few emails before dinner. She opened the patio door and let the cool breeze drift in. The smell of charcoal indicated that Wes had already fired up the grill.

She opened the front door to get a nice cross breeze in the guest house.

"Hello, Brianna."

Bree froze, a chill running down her spine. Her hands trembled and her heart raced. She didn't need to look in those icy blue eyes to know whose voice it was.

"Alex, what are you doing here?"

His toothy smile quickly dissolved into an equally disturbing frown. "I've been trying to reach you for months. You haven't responded to any of my messages."

She stood taller, narrowing her gaze. "Then you should've taken the hint."

The frown morphed into a scowl. "I understand why you're treating me this way, Bree. But I just want to talk."

"There is *nothing* for us to talk about. Not now. Not ever." She stuffed her hands in her pockets, hoping he couldn't see how badly they were shaking.

"I've come all this way to talk to you. The least you could do is let me take you out to dinner, so I can explain. I know I wasn't the best person back then, but I'm different now. I just want to show you that I'm not that man anymore."

"Maybe you are different now. If so, that's great. But you put your hands on me, Alex. I can never trust you again."

"It was one time, and I told you how sorry I was. That I didn't mean to do it. I was so stressed out back then, you know?"

"That's not an acceptable excuse for how you treated me. I should've left you long before I did."

"I told you, I'm not that guy anymore." A vein bulged in his forehead. "If you can't go to dinner, we can talk now. I only need ten minutes. Let me come in. We can sit down and hash this out."

"I don't want to hash things out. I don't miss you or us or the way things were. I don't want any of it, and I don't want you. Please, just go away." She scanned the room for something she could use as a weapon if he tried to force his way inside the door. "I don't want to get the police involved, but I will if I have to."

Bree recognized the signs of rage building. The muscles of his neck corded, his pale skin was mottled and his nostrils flared.

"I'm simply asking for a chance to explain myself, and you're threatening to call the cops on me?" he practically shouted as he dragged his fingernails through his dirty blond hair.

Bree didn't flinch, determined not to show any fear. It was fear that fed the monster.

"I'd do it in an instant and happily watch them drag your ass to jail. That probably wouldn't go over too well with that investment bank of yours."

"You wouldn't."

"Try me." She stood her ground. Her chest heaved and her breath came in noisy pants as her own anger overtook any fear she might have had facing him again.

"Everything all right, babe?" Wes was suddenly behind her. He wrapped his arms around her waist possessively.

"Peachy." She wasn't sure when Wes had entered through her patio door, but she was grateful he was there.

"Who is this?" Alex's gaze shifted from Bree to Wes and back again.

"The man who plans to marry her. And the owner of an aluminum bat with your name on it if you don't turn around right now and walk your happy ass outta here. While you still can." Wes's voice was calm and his tone icy as he dropped his hand from her waist and stepped in front of her.

Alex huffed, his jaw clenched. "You're as crazy as she is. Who needs this? You two deserve each other."

He turned and stomped down the stairs to his Mercedes-Benz parked outside. Neither of them moved until he drove away.

When Alex's car left the lot, Bree released a noisy breath, her hands to her mouth.

"Are you okay, baby?" He gripped her shoulders gently. When she nodded, he pulled her into his arms and held her. Wes closed and locked the front door. "Here, come sit down."

He got her a bottle of water and sat on the sofa beside her.

She took a sip, her hands still shaking. "I can't believe he showed up here."

"Tell me everything you know about this guy."

"The short answer? Biggest mistake of my life. That's what happens when you don't listen to your gut," she added under her breath.

"Go on." He leaned forward intently.

Bree brought Wes up to speed on her history with Alex Hunt, and his persistent attempts to contact her over the past few months.

She drank more of her water. "That line about the bat…that was good. Sounds like something your mother would say."

"Who do you think gave me the bat?" Wes walked

over to the window and looked out of it again. "I don't trust this guy to act in his own best interest. You're staying with me tonight."

"Wes, I appreciate what you did. I really do. But I'm fine. Alex won't be back."

"Didn't seem like he was too good at taking a hint or following instructions." Wes crossed his arms, his expression grave. "Guys like that are unpredictable. You never know how far they'll take things. Do you have a restraining order against this guy?"

She shook her head. "No."

"Then get one."

"I don't want the negative publicity, especially with the tournament coming up. Nor do I want to be seen as a victim." She paced the floor. "That would tank my endorsement stock ten times faster than a male athlete being convicted of an actual crime."

"You don't want to be seen as a victim. I get that, but I'm far more concerned about you actually becoming one." A deep frown made his brows appear as angry slashes. "This isn't something to play with."

"And it isn't fair. I never asked for this."

Wes cupped her cheek and spoke softly, his eyes filled with concern. "I know it isn't, honey. But the priority is to keep you safe. You believe that taking action against this guy will make you look weak, but it will empower you. You, in turn, can empower other women dealing with the same bullshit. You want to help people? This is a way to do it."

"Okay." Bree nodded begrudgingly. "I promised Bex I'd get the police involved if the situation escalated."

"You should've told me about this guy earlier. We could've put a halt to this before it got this far."

"I know that we're friends, and you want to help, but I'm not looking for a man to save me. And I don't need a knight in shining armor who walks away the first time he gets freaked out or things get tough."

"Fair enough." Wes wiped his palms on his black basketball shorts. "Now, about why I have trouble saying…" He sighed, then stood again. "It'll be easier if I show you."

Wes led Bree through the patio door and over to his place. He went to his bedroom and retrieved the most precious thing he owned. A black leather photo album with gold lettering on front.

His heart hammered in his chest as he handed the photo album to Bree.

What would she think of him once she knew the truth?

He didn't doubt her discretion. But would she look at him differently? See him as the monster he saw in the mirror?

Bree seemed as nervous as he was. She opened the book reverently. As if it was an artifact that needed to be handled with care.

She studied the pictures on the first two pages. Pictures of the same little boy at various ages from newborn to about twelve years old.

"He's your son." She nearly whispered the words, her fingers delicately tracing the boy's nose and mouth. Mirror images of his own.

"Yes." Wes nodded, taking the seat across from her. "His name is Gray Grammerson."

Her eyes lit with recognition. "The facing capital

*G*s that form the door of the cage on your tattoo. That's for your son."

Wes didn't answer. He didn't need to.

She turned more pages. "Most of these photos were taken from a distance. So you obviously don't share custody of him."

"Right again."

"So he lives with his mother?" Bree stopped turning the pages.

"Not his bio mom. She gave him up for adoption without ever telling me. In fact, I'd never have known about my son had it not been for a mutual friend from university."

"That's awful. Why would she do that?"

"Probably because she didn't think I was worthy of being a father to our child. We weren't together by the time she learned about the pregnancy. I think she also wanted to punish me for hurting her."

Bree raised an eyebrow. "What did you do to make her hate you?"

"I was young and selfish. My life was about meaningless hookups. I wanted her, and she didn't want to be with someone who didn't love her. So I told her I did." He swallowed hard. "We were together a few weeks. Maybe a month. When I was ready to move on, she was devastated."

Bree's eyes were misty. Her expression relayed both disappointment and compassion. "What happened to her?"

"She was an American expat, too. She returned to America. At the time, I was a selfish little prick. I thought, good riddance. I had no idea…" He winced, his eyes not meeting hers. "I had no idea she was pregnant with my son. A few years later, a fellow class-mate contacted me. She'd run in to my ex, who told her about the baby. Our baby. She'd given him up without notifying me. I was devastated."

"Where's his mother now?"

"She's an international-aid worker stationed at one of the largest refugee camps in Uganda."

"Have you talked to her since you learned about your son?"

Wes's jaw clenched involuntarily at the thought of confronting Janine. He shook his head. "It's a conversation I can't imagine going well."

Bree studied a photo of Gray being pushed on a swing by his adoptive mother. "How'd you find him?"

"It's one of the few times I readily accepted help from the Westbrooks. Liam helped me find a detective, who tracked down my son. When I found him, he was in a loving, wonderful family with good parents. I didn't have the heart to disrupt their lives."

"So how'd you get the pictures? The detective?"

"He dug up everything he could find at the outset. A lot of the pictures were on his adoptive parents' social-media pages. I have him do a checkup twice a year, just to make sure everything is okay with my son."

"He's so handsome. Just like his father." Bree smiled faintly as she thumbed through the book, and Wes felt as if she'd given him a lifeline.

She hadn't condemned him or walked out in disgust at the pig he'd been back then. When she reached the end of the book she closed it carefully and set it on the coffee table. She stood in front of him, opened her arms and embraced him.

He hugged her tightly, overwhelmed with a sense of relief and gratitude.

"I'm so sorry." She kissed his head. "It makes sense now, how you feel. But, honey, you can't punish yourself for the rest of your life. What you did was wrong, but you're *not* the one who gave your son away. And look at the effort you put into finding him and into making sure he's safe."

Wes didn't speak. Pain, shame and regret swirled inside him, along with a deep affection for her. Bree's warmth and compassion soothed his soul.

Made him feel human again.

"You aren't the person you were then, Wes. Let go of the guilt and forgive yourself. I know your son wouldn't want you to torture yourself this way."

"What makes you believe that?"

"Because I'd give anything for my bio mother to love me even half as much as you love your son." Her voice broke, tears running down her cheeks.

Wes pulled her onto his lap and kissed her. A kiss that started off tender and sweet. Two people comforting one another over their loss and grief. It slowly heated up. Her kiss became hungrier. His hands searched her familiar curves. Her firm, taut breasts filled his hands.

His tongue danced with hers, the temperature between them rising. He'd missed the feel of her. The taste of her warm, sweet skin. He wanted to lose himself in the comfort of their intense passion. But not before he'd told her everything.

He pulled his mouth from hers, their eyes meeting. "There's something you need to know."

Bree stared at him, her chest heaving, her face filled with apprehension. "All right."

"I love you, Bree. And I'm not just telling you that because you said it first. I'm saying it because it's true. I've waited my entire life to feel like this about someone. I've been miserable without you. I'm afraid I was an awful best man during Liam's stag weekend."

Bree grinned.

"What's so funny?"

"I've been miserable without you, too."

Wesley closed the vent on the grill and locked the patio door. He took Bree upstairs and made love to her, in the fullest sense of the words.

Dinner would have to wait.

Chapter 22

Brianna smoothed down the hem of her skirt, her heart beating rapidly. "Are you sure you want to do this tonight?"

Wesley squeezed her hand and grinned. "The way I see it, this is long overdue."

He pressed a warm, lingering kiss to her lips, one strong hand cradling her face.

Bree leaned into his touch and angled her head, allowing Wes to deepen the kiss. His tongue slid between her lips and glided along hers. He released her hand and planted his on the small of her back, pulling her in tighter against him.

She should pull away. Show a little self-control. After all, though they'd declared their love to each other, they'd yet to tell their family and friends.

Kissing openly outside the resort wasn't very discreet. Still, she couldn't pull herself away, reluctant to allow a single inch of space to separate her from the man she loved madly.

They'd spent the majority of their first three days as a bona fide couple in Wesley's bed. Talking, eating, making love. Taking small steps toward planning for a future together.

The prospect of slowly building a life together was exhilarating and terrifying. And she couldn't think of anything that would challenge her more or make her happier.

Wes pulled his mouth from hers reluctantly and groaned. "We'd better not be late. Liam will never let me hear the end of it."

They rounded the corner and entered the pathway that led to the outdoor patio where Liam and Maya's rehearsal dinner was being held. They were greeted by teasing woots and loud kissing noises.

Bree pressed a hand to her open mouth, her cheeks stinging with heat.

"Guess the secret's out." Wes squeezed her hand.

"No matter. It was just about the worst kept secret in the history of secrets." Liam met them on the path and grinned. "And I should know a thing or two about clandestine relationships."

Wes grinned. "Well, I'm glad you and Maya aren't a secret anymore. I'm excited for you both, Liam. I know you'll continue to be very happy together."

"I'm thrilled for you, mate." Liam's self-congratulatory smile could light the entire Eastern seaboard. He held his arms open and hugged them both. "I knew you two were absolutely perfect for each other."

"Does this mean you're confessing to being a meddling matchmaker?" One corner of Wesley's mouth curved, as he tried to hold back a smirk.

"Now that it's worked? Absolutely." Liam chuckled. "Now, if my best mate has had his fill of snogging this lovely young lady—for the time being—I say we get on with this rehearsal. I'm quite in a hurry to marry a lovely young lady of my own."

Liam's eyes practically glowed as he looked at Maya Alvarez. The woman he would stand beside on the Pleasure Cove Beach and make his wife in less than twenty-four hours.

A table of children squealed with joy, and everyone laughed.

"Those are Maya's daughters—Sofia and Gabriella. That's Kai—the bride's nephew. That's Madison—the bride's niece. The little one is Liam's niece Emma and that's her older brother, Max." Wesley gave Bree a breakdown of all the children in attendance.

"Bree, I'm so glad you're here." Lena's eyes sparkled as she approached, gathering them both in a hug. "You two belong together. I've known it since the day I met you. Saw the love he had for you in his eyes. Saw the same in yours."

Bree smiled, her eyes misty with tears as she glanced up at Wes. "You're a very wise woman, Ms. Lena. And you've raised a truly wonderful man."

Wes leaned in and gave Bree a quick kiss on the lips before deftly moving her through the group of family and friends.

They congratulated Maya, whom Bree had met at a previous business dinner. Wes introduced her to the matron-of-honor, Kendra, and her husband Nathan Johnston, a pro football player. Next, he introduced her to Kendra's and Maya's brother Dash Williams and his fiancée Mikayla.

She met a variety of additional relatives. Liam's father, Nigel, and Mrs. Hanson—the woman who had been Liam and Hunter's nanny since they were boys, but now seemed to enjoy a much more personal relationship with their father. The groom's brother, Hunter, and his wife, Meredith. Kendra and Dash's mother, Ms. Anna. The Johnston family, comprised of Nate's parents and several of his siblings, including his fraternal twin sister Vi. Maya's parents—Curtis and Alita Williams, and her brother Cole.

The rehearsal was lovely. Filled with laughter and tears of joy. During the delicious meal that followed, there was more of the same.

Bree felt at home, like she was among family and old friends. She'd been nervous about the prospect of uprooting her life and moving to Pleasure Cove so that she and Wes could be together and close to his mother. But there was so much love, friendship and good-natured teasing here. And they'd gone out of their way to make her feel like she was part of their extended family.

At the end of the night, she and Wes said their goodbyes, saw Lena to her room at the resort, and strolled along the beach hand-in-hand.

London would always be special for them. It was the place where they'd first met and where they'd both realized they'd fallen in love. But here on the sandy beaches of Pleasure Cove among friends who were already beginning to feel like family...this somehow felt like home.

Not his home or her home, but *theirs*. The place where they could make a life together.

Epilogue

Wes was head over heels in love with the girl who was in his arms. She'd stolen his heart in a way he hadn't thought possible.

He wanted to give her the entire world wrapped in a neat little bow. He'd do anything for her.

The edge of her mouth curled as she slept, mimicking a smile. She seemed to know instinctually that she was safe in his arms. That he'd do everything in his power to protect her and provide for her.

He stroked her soft, downy hair and kissed her forehead.

"Mackenzie Alena Adams," he whispered softly. His lips brushed her warm skin as he inhaled her scent. "Do you have any idea how much you mean to me?"

Mackenzie yawned and stretched, her dark eyes opening for a moment before she closed them again and pressed her fist to her lips in a failed attempt to suck it.

"Hungry again, baby girl?" Wes secured the blanket around his daughter, only a few hours old.

Bree grinned as she stroked their daughter's cheek. "She's beautiful, Wes."

"Just like her mama." Wes pressed a soft, lingering kiss to Bree's lips.

He sat on the edge of Bree's bed and wrapped an arm around her as he cradled their daughter in his arms.

They'd been together for two years and were already engaged when Bree had shown him the positive pregnancy test. With the help of their family and friends, they'd managed to coordinate a simple, but elegant ceremony on Pleasure Cove Beach. The same place they'd witnessed Maya and Liam taking their vows two years earlier. They'd both stood barefoot in the sand, the soft sea air rustling her hair, and declared their commitment to each other.

Even now, he got choked up thinking of how beautiful she'd been in her wedding dress. A sleeveless, cream-colored ball gown with a sweetheart neckline that showcased her breasts, enlarged by the pregnancy.

Wes hadn't thought he could be any happier than he was the day Bree stood there on that beach in front of the world and agreed to be his wife.

He'd been wrong.

Witnessing the birth of their daughter had been even more touching, eliciting tears from both of them.

As a husband and a father, his life had taken on new meaning. Bree had given him the life he'd convinced himself he hadn't wanted. Yet he was happier than he ever imagined possible.

"Would you like to hold your baby sister?" Wes beamed at the handsome boy who was nearly fifteen with a face that looked so much like his own.

The boy who'd washed his hands and had been waiting patiently bobbed his head and took the newborn in his arms.

Wesley's heart felt as if it would burst. *His son.* It still didn't feel real. But Bree had made it happen. She'd written letters to Gray's adoptive parents for more than a year before she'd finally gotten a response.

Gray had learned he was adopted and he wanted to meet his biological parents. He'd been angry with Wes at first, but they'd slowly built a relationship over the past year. And four months ago, Gray had finally met his biological mother—Janine.

Wes had been nervous to see her again. He was uncertain of how he'd react to the woman who'd given away their son without telling him. But when he'd laid eyes on Janine and seen the pain and fear on her face, they both had tears of regret in their eyes.

He and Bree had sat and talked with Janine for an hour before Gray arrived with his adoptive parents. And when they parted ways, he managed to hug his son's mother and wish her well. Something that was only possible because of the love and grace he'd learned from his mother and from being with Bree.

They'd been through a lot. Marriage, a growing family and the expansion of two successful businesses. Bree had become a vocal activist for organizations that raised money to battle his mother's illness and those that protected women from boyfriends and exes like

Alex Hunt—whom they hadn't heard from since Bree filed a restraining order against him.

A wide smile spread across Gray's face. "I think she just smiled at me in her sleep."

"She knows she's safe. That her big brother will always be there to protect her." Bree wore a white-and-green hospital gown with a crusty, baby-puke stain on one shoulder. Her curls were secured in a messy topknot.

She looked happy, but exhausted. Still, she was the most beautiful woman he'd ever seen.

The love of his life.

Maybe he didn't deserve Bree, the kids, or the life they were building together, but he was damn grateful for it. And he'd never, ever let any of them go.

* * * * *

HIS ILLEGITIMATE HEIR

SARAH M. ANDERSON

To Lisa Marie Perry, who never ceases
to shock and amaze me. We'll always
have Jesse Williams!

One

"You ready for this?" Jamal asked from the front seat of the limo.

Zeb Richards felt a smile pull at the corner of his mouth. "I was born ready."

It wasn't an exaggeration. Finally, after all these years, Zeb was coming home to claim what was rightfully his. The Beaumont Brewery had—until very recently—been owned and operated by the Beaumont family. There were a hundred twenty-five years of family history in this building—history that Zeb had been deprived of.

He was a Beaumont by blood. Hardwick Beaumont was Zeb's father.

But he was illegitimate. As far as he knew, outside

of the payoff money Hardwick had given his mother, Emily, shortly after Zeb's birth, no one in the Beaumont family had ever acknowledged his existence.

He was tired of being ignored. More than that, he was tired of being denied his rightful place in the Beaumont family.

So he was finally taking what was rightfully his. After years of careful planning and sheer luck, the Beaumont Brewery now belonged to him.

Jamal snorted, which made Zeb look at him. Jamal Hitchens was Zeb's right-hand man, filling out the roles of chauffeur and bodyguard—plus, he baked a damn fine chocolate chip cookie. Jamal had worked for Zeb ever since he'd blown out his knees his senior year as linebacker at the University of Georgia, but the two of them went back much farther than that.

"You sure about this?" Jamal asked. "I still think I should go in with you."

Zeb shook his head. "No offense, but you'd just scare the hell out of them. I want my new employees intimidated, not terrified."

Jamal met Zeb's gaze in the rearview mirror and an unspoken understanding passed between the two men. Zeb could pull off intimidating all by himself.

With a sigh of resignation, Jamal parked in front of the corporate headquarters and came around to open Zeb's door. Starting right now, Zeb was a Beaumont in every way that counted.

Jamal looked around as Zeb stood and straightened the cuffs on his bespoke suit. "Last chance for backup."

"You're not nervous, are you?" Zeb wasn't. There was such a sense of rightness about this that he couldn't be nervous, so he simply wasn't.

Jamal gave him a look. "You realize you're not going to be hailed as a hero, right? You didn't exactly get this company in a way that most people might call *ethical*."

Zeb notched an eyebrow at his oldest friend. With Jamal at his back, Zeb had gone from being the son of a hairdresser to being the sole owner of ZOLA, a private equity firm that he'd founded. He'd made his millions without a single offer of assistance from the Beaumonts.

More than that, he had proven that he was better than they were. He'd outmaneuvered and outflanked them and taken their precious brewery away from them.

But taking over the family business was something he had to do himself. "Your concern is duly noted. I'll text you if I need backup. Otherwise, you'll be viewing the properties?"

They needed a place to live now that they would be based in Denver. ZOLA, Zeb's company, was still headquartered in New York—a hedge just in case his ownership of the Beaumont Brewery backfired. But buying a house here would signal to everyone that Zeb Richards wasn't going anywhere anytime soon.

Jamal realized he wasn't going to win this fight.

Zeb could tell by the way he straightened his shoulders. "Right, boss. Finest money can buy?"

"Always." It didn't really matter what the house looked like or how many bathrooms it had. All that mattered was that it was better than anyone else's. Specifically, better than any of the other Beaumonts'. "But make sure it's got a nice kitchen."

Jamal smirked at that bone of friendship Zeb threw him. "Good luck."

Zeb slid a sideways glance at Jamal. "Good luck happens when you work for it." And Zeb? He *always* worked for it.

With a sense of purpose, he strode into the corporate headquarters of the Beaumont Brewery. He hadn't called to announce his impending arrival, because he wanted to see what the employees looked like when they weren't ready to be inspected by their new CEO.

However, he was fully aware that he was an unfamiliar African American man walking into a building as if he owned it—which he did. Surely the employees knew that Zebadiah Richards was their new boss. But how many of them would recognize him?

True to form, he got plenty of double takes as he walked through the building. One woman put her hand on her phone as he passed, as if she was going to call security. But then someone else whispered something over the edge of her cubicle wall and the woman's eyes got very wide. Zeb notched an eyebrow at her and she pulled her hand away from her phone like it had burned her.

Silence trailed in his wake as he made his way toward the executive office. Zeb fought hard to keep a smile off his face. So they did know who he was. He appreciated employees who were up-to-date on their corporate leadership. If they recognized him, then they had also probably read the rumors about him.

Zebadiah Richards and his private equity firm bought failing companies, restructured them and sold them for profit. ZOLA had made him rich—and earned him a reputation for ruthlessness.

He would need that reputation here. Contrary to some of the rumors, he was not actually heartless. And he understood that the employees at this brewery had undergone the ouster of not one but two CEOs in less than a year. From his reports on the company's filings, he understood that most people still missed Chadwick Beaumont, the last Beaumont to run the brewery.

Zeb had not gotten Chadwick removed—but he had taken advantage of the turmoil that the sale of the brewery to the conglomerate AllBev had caused. And when Chadwick's temporary replacement, Ethan Logan, had failed to turn the company around fast enough, Zeb had agitated for AllBev to sell the company.

To him, of course.

But what that really meant was that he now owned a company full of employees who were scared and desperate. Employee turnover was at an all-time high. A significant percentage of top-level management had followed Chadwick Beaumont to his new company, Percheron Drafts. Many others had taken early retirement.

The employees who had survived this long were holding on by the skin of their teeth and probably had nothing left to lose. Which made them dangerous. He'd seen it before in other failing companies. Change was a constant in his world but most people hated it and if they fought against it hard enough, they could doom an entire company. When that happened, Zeb shrugged and broke the business up to be sold for its base parts. Normally, he didn't care if that happened—so long as he made a profit, he was happy.

But like he told Jamal, he was here to stay. He was a Beaumont and this was his brewery. He cared about this place and its history because it was his history, acknowledged or not. Not that he'd wanted anyone to know that this was personal—he'd kept his quest to take what was rightfully his quiet for years. That way, no one could preempt his strikes or lock him out.

But now that he was here, he had the overwhelming urge to shout, "Look at me!" He was done being ignored by the Beaumonts and he was done pretending he wasn't one of them.

Whispers of his arrival must have made it to the executive suite because when he rounded the corner, a plump older woman sitting behind a desk in front of what he assumed was the CEO's office stood and swallowed nervously. "Mr. Richards," she said in a crackly voice. "We weren't expecting you today."

Zeb nodded his head in acknowledgment. He didn't explain his sudden appearance and he didn't try to reassure her. "And you are?"

"Delores Hahn," she said. "I'm the executive assistant to the—to you." Her hands twisted nervously in front of her before she caught herself and stilled them. "Welcome to the Beaumont Brewery."

Zeb almost grinned in sympathy. His assistant was in a tough spot, but she was putting on a good face. "Thank you."

Delores cleared her throat. "Would you like a tour of the facilities?" Her voice was still a bit shaky, but she was holding it together. Zeb decided he liked Delores.

Not that he wanted her to know that right away. He was not here to make friends. He was here to run a business. "I will—after I get settled in." Then he headed for his office.

Once inside, he shut the door behind him and leaned against it. This was really happening. After years of plotting and watching and waiting, he had the Beaumont Brewery—his birthright.

He felt like laughing at the wonder of it all. But he didn't. For all he knew, Delores had her ear to the door, listening for any hint of what her new boss was like. Maniacal laughter was not a good first impression, no matter how justified it might be.

Instead, he pushed away from the door and surveyed his office. "Begin as you mean to go on," Zeb reminded himself.

He'd read about this room, studied pictures of it. But he hadn't been prepared for what it would actually feel like to walk into a piece of his family's history—to know that he belonged here, that this was his rightful place.

The building had been constructed in the 1940s by Zeb's grandfather John, soon after Prohibition had ended. The walls were mahogany panels that had been oiled until they gleamed. A built-in bar with a huge mirror took up the whole interior wall—and, if Zeb wasn't mistaken, the beer was on tap.

The exterior wall was lined with windows, hung with heavy gray velvet drapes and crowned with elaborately hand-carved woodwork that told the story of the Beaumont Brewery. His grandfather had had the conference table built in the office because it was so large and the desk was built to match.

Tucked in the far corner was a grouping of two leather club chairs and a matching leather love seat. The wagon-wheel coffee table in front of the chairs was supposed to be a wheel from the wagon that his great-great-grandfather Phillipe Beaumont had driven across the Great Plains on his way to Denver to found the brewery back in the 1880s.

The whole room screamed opulence and wealth

and history. Zeb's history. This was who he was and he would be damned if he let anyone tell him it wasn't his.

He crossed to the desk and turned on the computer—top-of-the-line, of course. Beaumonts never did anything by halves. That was one family trait they all shared.

He sat down in the leather office chair. From as far back as he could remember, his mother, Emily Richards, had told him this belonged to him. Zeb was only four months younger than Chadwick Beaumont. He should have been here, learning the business at his father's knee, instead of standing next to his mother's hairdressing chair.

But Hardwick had never married his mother—despite the fact that Hardwick had married several of his mistresses. But not Emily Richards—and for one simple reason.

Emily was black. Which made her son black.

Which meant Zeb didn't exist in the eyes of the Beaumonts.

For so long, he had been shut out of half of his heritage. And now he had the one thing that the Beaumonts had valued above all else—the Beaumont Brewery.

God, it felt good to come home.

He got himself under control. Taking possession of the brewery was a victory—but it was just the first step in making sure the Beaumonts paid for excluding him.

He was not the only Beaumont bastard Hardwick had left behind. It was time to start doing things his way. He grinned. The Beaumonts weren't going to see this coming.

He pressed the button on an antique-looking intercom. It buzzed to life and Delores said, "Yes, sir?"

"I want you to arrange a press conference for this Friday. I'm going to be announcing my plans for the brewery."

There was a pause. "Yes, sir," she said in a way that had an edge to it. "I assume you want the conference here?" Already Zeb could tell she was getting over her nervousness at his unannounced arrival.

If he had to guess, he'd say that someone like Delores Hahn had probably made the last CEO's life miserable. "Yes, on the front steps of the brewery. Oh, and Delores?"

"Yes?"

"Write a memo. Every employee needs to have an updated résumé on my desk by end of business tomorrow."

There was another pause—this one was longer. Zeb could only imagine the glare she was giving the intercom right about now. "Why? I mean—of course I'll get right on it. But is there a reason?"

"Of course there is, Delores. There is a reason behind every single thing I do. And the reason for the memo is simple. Every employee needs to reapply for their own job." He exhaled slowly, letting the tension build. "Including you."

* * *

"Boss?"

Casey Johnson jerked her head toward the sound of Larry's voice—which meant she smacked her forehead against the bottom of tank number fifteen. "Ow, dammit." She pushed herself out from under the tank, rubbing her head. "What?"

Larry Kaczynski was a middle-aged man with a beer gut, which was appropriate considering he brewed beer for a living. Normally, he was full of bluster and the latest stats on his fantasy football team. But today he looked worried. Specifically, he looked worried about the piece of paper in his hand. "The new guy... He's here."

"Well, good for him," Casey said, turning her attention back to her tank. This was the second new CEO in less than a year and, given recent history, he probably wouldn't make it past a couple of months. All Casey had to do was outlast him.

That, of course, was the challenge. Beer did not brew itself—although, given the attitude of the last CEO, some people thought it did.

Tank fifteen was her priority right now. Being a brewmaster was about brewing beer—but it was also about making sure the equipment was clean and functional. And right now tank fifteen wasn't either of those things.

"You don't understand," Larry sputtered before she'd rolled back under the tank. "He's been on the property for less than an hour and he's already sent this memo..."

"Larry," she said, her voice echoing against the body of the tank, "are you going to get to the point today?"

"We have to reapply for our jobs," Larry said in a rush. "By the end of the day tomorrow. I don't— Casey, you know me. I don't even have a résumé. I've worked here for the last thirty years."

Oh, for the love of everything holy... Casey pushed herself out from under the tank again and sat up. "Okay," she said in a much softer voice as she got to her feet. "Start from the beginning. What does the memo say?" Because Larry was like a canary in a coal mine. If he kept calm, the staff she was left with would also keep calm. But if Larry panicked...

Larry looked down at the paper in his hands again. He swallowed hard and Casey got the strangest sensation he was trying not to crack.

Crap. They were screwed. "It just says that by end of business tomorrow, every Beaumont Brewery employee needs to have an updated résumé on the new CEO's desk so he can decide if they get to keep their job or not."

Son of a... "Let me see."

Larry handed over the paper as if he'd suddenly discovered it was contagious, and he stepped back. "What am I going to do, boss?"

Casey scanned the memo and saw that Larry had

pretty much read verbatim. Every employee, no exceptions.

She did not have time for this. She was responsible for brewing about seven thousand gallons of beer every single day of the year on a skeleton staff of seventeen people. Two years ago, forty people had been responsible for that level of production. But two years ago, the company hadn't been in the middle of the never-ending string of upstart CEOs.

And now the latest CEO was rolling up into *her* brewery and scaring the hell out of *her* employees? This new guy thought he would tell her she had to apply for her job—the job she'd earned?

She didn't know much about this Zebadiah Richards—but he was going to get one thing straight if he thought he was going to run this company.

The Beaumont Brewery brewed beer. No beer, no brewery. And no brewmaster, no beer.

She turned to Larry, who was pale and possibly shaking. She understood why he was scared—Larry was not the brightest bulb and he knew it. That was the reason he hadn't left when Chadwick lost the company or when Ethan Logan tried to right the sinking ship.

That was why Casey had been promoted over him to brewmaster, even though Larry had almost twenty years of experience on her. He liked his job, he liked beer and as long as he got regular cost-of-living increases in his salary and a year-end bonus, he was perfectly content to spend the rest of his life right where he was. He hadn't wanted the responsibility of management.

Frankly, Casey was starting to wonder why she had. "I'll take care of this," she told him.

Surprisingly, this announcement made Larry look even more nervous. Apparently, he didn't put a lot of faith in her ability to keep her temper. "What are you going to do?"

His reaction made it clear that he was afraid she'd get fired—and then he'd be in charge. "This Richards guy and I are going to have words."

Larry fretted. "Are you sure that's the smart thing to do?"

"Probably not," she agreed. "But what's he going to do—fire the brewmaster? I don't think so, Larry." She patted him on the shoulder. "Don't worry, okay?"

Larry gave her a weak smile, but he nodded resolutely.

Casey hurried to her office and stripped off her hairnet. She knew she was no great beauty, but nobody wanted to confront a new boss in a hairnet. She grabbed her Beaumont Brewery hat and slid her ponytail through the back. And she was off, yelling over her shoulder to Larry, "See if you can get that drainage tube off—and if you can, see if you can get it flushed again. I'll be back in a bit."

She did *not* have time for this. She was already working ten- to twelve-hour days—six or seven days a week—just to keep the equipment clean and the beer flowing. If she lost more of her staff…

It wouldn't come to that. She wouldn't let it. And if it did…

Okay, so she'd promised Larry she wouldn't get fired. But what if she did? Her options weren't great, but at least she had some. Unlike Larry, she did have an updated résumé that she kept on file just in case. She didn't want to use it. She wanted to stay right here at the Beaumont Brewery and brew her favorite beer for the rest of her life.

Or at least, she had. No, if she was being honest, what she really wanted was to be the brewmaster at the old Beaumont Brewery, the one she'd worked at for the previous twelve years—the one that the Beaumont family had run. Back then the brewery had been a family business and the owners had been personally invested in their employees.

They'd even given a wide-eyed college girl the chance to do something no one else had—brew beer.

But the memo in her hand reminded her that this wasn't the same brewery. The Beaumonts no longer ran things and the company was suffering.

She was suffering. She couldn't remember the last time she'd strung together more than twenty-four hours of free time. She was doing the job of three people and, thanks to the hiring freeze the last CEO implemented, there was no relief in sight. And now this. She could not afford to lose another single person.

She was a thirty-two-year-old brewmaster—and a woman, at that. She'd come so far so fast. But not one of her predecessors in the illustrious history of the Beaumont Brewery had put up with quite this much crap. They'd been left to brew beer in relative peace.

She stormed to the CEO suite. Delores was behind the desk. When she saw Casey coming, the older woman jumped to her feet with surprising agility. "Casey—wait. You don't—"

"Oh, yes, I do," she said, blowing past Delores and shoving open the door to the CEO's office. "Just who the hell do you think you…are?"

Two

Casey came to a stumbling stop. Where was he? The desk was vacant and no one was sitting on the leather couches.

But then a movement off to her left caught her eye and she turned and gasped in surprise.

A man stood by the windows, looking out over the brewery campus. He had his hands in his pockets and his back turned to her—but despite that, everything about him screamed power and money. The cut of his suit fit him like a second skin and he stood with his feet shoulder-width apart, as if he were master of all he saw.

A shiver went through her. She was not the kind of girl who went for power suits or the men who wore them but something about this man—this man who was threatening her job—took her breath away. Was it the broad shoulders? Or the raw power wafting off him like the finest cologne?

And then he turned to face her and all she could see were his eyes—*green* eyes. Good Lord, those eyes—they held her gaze like a magnet and she knew her breath was gone for good.

He was, hands down, the most handsome man she'd ever seen. Everything—the power suit, the broad shoulders, the close-cropped hair and most especially the eyes—it was a potent blend that she felt powerless to resist. And this was her new boss? The man who'd sent out the memo?

He notched an eyebrow at her and let his gaze travel over her body. And any admiration she had for a good suit and nice eyes died on the vine because she knew exactly what he saw. Underneath her lab coat, she had on a men's small polo shirt with Beaumont Brewery embroidered over the chest—and she'd sweat through it because the brew room was always hot. Her face was probably red from the heat and also from the anger, and she no doubt smelled like mash and wort.

She must look like a madwoman.

A conclusion he no doubt reached on his own, because by the time he looked her in the eyes, one corner of his mouth had curved up into the kind of smile that said exactly one thing.

He thought she was a joke.

Well, he'd soon learn this was no laughing matter.

"Congratulations," he said in a voice that bordered on cold. "You're first." He lifted his wrist and looked down at a watch that, even at this distance, Casey could tell was expensive. "Thirty-five minutes. I'm impressed."

His imperious attitude poured cold water on the heat that had almost swamped her. She wasn't here to gawk at a gorgeous man. She was here to protect her workers. "Are you Richards?"

"Zebadiah Richards, yes. Your new boss," he added in a menacing tone, as if he thought he could intimidate her. Didn't he know she had so very little left to lose? "And you are?"

She'd worked in a male-dominated industry for twelve years. She couldn't be intimidated. "I'm Casey Johnson—your brewmaster." What kind of name was Zebadiah? Was that biblical? "What's the meaning of this?" She held up the memo.

Richards's eyes widened in surprise—but only for a second before he once again looked ice-cold. "Forgive me," he said in a smooth voice when Casey glared at him. "I must say that you are not what I was expecting."

Casey rolled her eyes and made no attempt to hide it. Few people expected women to like beer. Even fewer people expected women to brew beer. And with a name like Casey, everyone just assumed she was a man—and usually, they assumed she was a man like Larry. Middle-aged, beer gut—the whole nine yards. "It's not my problem if you made a set of erroneous assumptions."

The moment she said it, she realized she'd also made some erroneous assumptions herself. Because she had not anticipated that the new CEO would look quite like him. Oh, sure—the power suit was par for the course. But his hair was close-cropped to his head and his eyes... Damn, she just couldn't get past them.

He grinned—oh, Lord, that was not good. Well, it was—but in a bad way because that grin took everything hard and cold about him and warmed him up. She was certainly about to break out in another sweat.

"Indeed. Well, since you're the first person to barge into my office, I'll tell you the meaning of that memo, Ms. Johnson—although I'd hope the employees here at the brewery would be able to figure it out on their own. Everyone has to reapply for their jobs."

She welcomed his condescending tone because it pushed her from falling into the heat of his eyes and kept her focused on her task. "Is that a fact? Where'd you learn that management technique? Management 'R' Us?"

Something that almost looked like amusement flickered over his gaze and she was tempted to smile. A lot of people found her abrasive and yeah, she could rub people the wrong way. She didn't pull her punches and she wasn't about to sit down and shut up just because she was a girl and men didn't like to have their authority challenged.

What was rarer was for someone to get her sense of humor. Could this Richards actually be a real man who smiled? God, she wanted to work for a man she wouldn't have to fight every step of the way. Maybe they could get along. Maybe...

But as quickly as it had appeared, the humor was gone. His eyes narrowed and Casey thought, *You're not the only one who can be condescending.*

"The purpose is twofold, Ms. Johnson. One, I'd like to see what skill sets my employees possess. And two, I want to see if they can follow basic instructions."

So much for a sense of humor. Men as hot as he was probably weren't allowed to laugh at a joke. Pity. On the other hand, if he smiled, it might kill her with handsomeness and the only thing worse than a CEO she couldn't work with would be a CEO she lusted after.

No lusting allowed. And he was making that easier with every single thing he said.

"Let me assure you, Mr. Richards, that this company did not spring fully formed from your forehead yesterday. We've been brewing beer here for—"

"For over one hundred and thirty years—I know." He tilted his head to the side and gave her a long look. "And you've only been doing it for less than a year—is that correct?"

If she weren't so pissed at him, she'd have been

terrified, because that was most definitely a threat to her job. But she didn't have time for unproductive emotions and anger was vastly more useful than fear.

"I have—and I earned that job. But before you question how a woman my age can have possibly surpassed all the good ol' boys who normally brew beer, let me tell you that it's also because all the more experienced brewers have already left the company. If you want to maintain a quality product line, you're stuck with me for the foreseeable future." She waved the memo in front of her. "And I don't have time to deal with this crap."

But instead of doing anything any normal boss would do when basically yelled at by an employee— like firing her on the spot—Richards tilted his head to one side and looked at her again and she absolutely did not shiver when he did it. "Why not?"

"Why not what?"

"Why don't you have time to respond to a simple administrative task?"

Casey didn't want to betray any sign of weakness but a trickle of sweat rolled out from under her hat and into her eye. Dammit. He better not think she was crying. She wiped her eyes with the palm of her hand. "Because I'm operating with a bare-bones staff—I have been for the last nine months. I'm doing the work of three people—we all are. We're under-staffed, overworked and—"

"And you don't have time for this 'crap,' as you so eloquently put it," he murmured.

Was that a note of sympathy? Or was he mocking her? She couldn't read him that well.

Not yet, a teasing voice in the back of her mind whispered. But she pushed that voice away. She wasn't interested in reading him better. "Not if you want to fulfill production orders."

"So just hire more people."

Now she gaped at him. "What?"

He shrugged, which was an impossibly smooth gesture on him. Men should not be that smooth. It wasn't good for them, she decided. And it definitely wasn't good for her. This would be so much easier if he were at least 70 percent less attractive. "Hire more people. But I want to see their résumés, too. Why let the new people off easy, right?"

This guy didn't know anything, did he? They were screwed, then. This was the beginning of the end. Now she would have to help Larry write a résumé.

"But...there's been a hiring freeze," she told him. "For the last eight months. Until we can show a profit."

Richards stepped forward and traced a finger over the top of the conference table. It was an oddly intimate motion—a caress, almost. Watching his hand move over the wood...

She broke out in goose bumps.

"Tell me, Ms. Johnson, was it Chadwick Beaumont who put on the hiring freeze? Or Ethan Logan?"

There was something about his voice that matched his caress of the conference table. Casey studied him.

She had the oddest feeling that he looked familiar but she was sure she would remember seeing him before. Who could forget those eyes? Those…everything?

"Logan did."

"Ah," he said, shifting so he wasn't silhouetted against the window anymore. More light fell on him and Casey was startled to realize that the green eyes were set against skin that wasn't light but wasn't exactly deep brown, either. His skin was warm, almost tan, and she realized he was at least partly African American. Why hadn't she seen that right away?

Well, she knew why. First off, she was mad and when she was mad, she didn't exactly pay attention to the bigger picture. She hadn't noticed the fullness to his frowning lips or the slight flare of his nostrils. Second off, his eyes had demanded her total attention. They were striking, so gorgeous, and even… familiar?

His hand was still on top of the conference table. "So what you're telling me is that the only non-Beaumont to run this company instituted a series of policies designed to cut costs and, in the process, hamstrung the operations and production?"

"Yes." There was something about the way he said *the only non-Beaumont* that threw her for a loop.

And then—maybe because now she was paying more attention—it hit her like a ton of bricks.

This guy—this Zeb Richards who wasn't quite black and wasn't quite white—he looked vaguely familiar. Something in the nose, the chin…those eyes…

He looked a little bit like Chadwick Beaumont.

Sweet merciful heavens. He *was* a Beaumont, too.

Her knees gave in to the weight of the revelation and she lurched forward to lean on the coffee table. "Oh, my God," she asked, staring at him. "You're one of them, aren't you?"

Richards snatched his hand back and put it in his pocket like he was trying to hide something. "I can neither confirm nor deny that—at least, not until the press conference on Friday." He moved away from the conference table and toward his desk.

If he was trying to intimidate her, it wasn't working. Casey followed him. He sat behind the desk— the same place she had seen Chadwick Beaumont too many times to count and, at least three times, Hardwick Beaumont. The resemblance was unmistakable.

"My God," she repeated again. "You're one of the bastards."

He leaned back in his chair and steepled his fingers. Everything about him had shut down. No traces of humor, no hints of warmth. She was staring at the coldest man she'd ever seen. "The bastards?"

"Beaumont's bastards—there were always rumors that Hardwick had a bunch of illegitimate children." She blinked. It all made sense, in a way. The Beaumonts were a notoriously good-looking group of men and women—far too handsome for their own good. And this man… He was gorgeous. But not the same kind of blond handsomeness that had marked Chadwick and Matthew Beaumont. She knew he would stand out in a crowd of Beaumonts. Hell, he would stand out in *any* crowd. "He was your father, wasn't he?"

Richards stared at her for a long time and she got the feeling he was making some sort of decision. She didn't know what—he hadn't fired her yet but the day wasn't over.

Her mind felt like it was fizzing with information. Zeb Richards—the mysterious man who was rumored to have single-handedly driven down the brewery's stock price so he could force AllBev to sell off the company—was a Beaumont? Did Chadwick know? Was he in on it or was this something else?

One word whispered across her mind. *Revenge.*

Because up until about thirty-seven seconds ago, Beaumont's bastards had never been anything but a rumor. And now one of them had the company.

She had no idea if this was a good thing or a very, *very* bad thing.

Suddenly, Richards leaned forward and made a minute adjustment to something on his desk. "We've gotten off track. Your primary reason for barging into my office unannounced was about résumés."

She felt like a bottle of beer that had been shaken but hadn't been opened. At any second, she might explode from the pressure. "Right," she agreed, collapsing into the chair in front of his desk. "The problem is, some of my employees have been here for twenty, thirty years and they don't have a résumé ready to go. Producing one on short notice is going to cause nothing but panic. They aren't the kind of guys who look good on paper. What matters is that they do good work for me and we produce a quality product." She took a deep breath, trying to sound managerial. "Are you familiar with our product line?"

The corner of Richard's mouth twitched. "It's beer, right?"

She rolled her eyes at him, which, surprisingly, made him grin even more. Oh, that was a bad idea, making him smile like that, because when he did, all the hard, cold edges fell away from his face. He was the kind of handsome that wasn't fair to the rest of humanity.

Sinful. That was what he was. And she had been too well behaved for too long.

She shivered. She wasn't sure if it had anything to do with the smile on his face or the fact that she was cooling off and her sweat-soaked shirt was now sticking to her skin. "That's correct. We brew beer here. I appreciate you giving me the go-ahead to hire more workers but that's a process that will take weeks. Training will also take time. Placing additional paperwork demands on my staff runs the risk of compromising the quality of our beer."

Richards didn't say anything. Casey cleared her throat. "You *are* interested in the beer, right?"

He gave her another one of those measured looks.

Casey sighed. She really wasn't so complicated that he had to stare at her.

"I'm interested in the beer," he finally said. "This is a family company and I'd like to keep it that way. I must say," he went on before Casey could ask about that whole "family" thing, "I certainly appreciate your willingness to defend your staff. However, I'd like to be reassured that the employees who work for this brewery not only are able to follow basic instructions," he added with a notch of his eyebrow that made Casey want to pound on something, "but have the skills to take this company in a new direction."

"A new direction? We're...still going to brew beer, right? We're not getting into electronics or apps or anything?"

"Oh, we'll be getting into apps," he said. "But I need to know if there's anyone on staff who can handle that or if I'm going to need to bring in an outside developer—you see my point, don't you? The Beaumont Brewery has been losing market share. You brew seven thousand gallons a day—but it was eleven thousand years ago. The popularity of craft breweries—and I'm including Percheron Drafts in that—has slowly eroded our sales."

Our sales? He was serious, she realized. He was here to run this company.

"While I understand Logan's cost-cutting measures," he went on, oblivious to the way her mouth had dropped open, "what we need to do at this point is not to hunker down and hope for the best, but invest heavily in research and development—new products. And part of that is connecting with our audience." His gaze traveled around the room and Casey thought there was something about him that seemed...hopeful, almost.

She wanted to like her job. She wanted to like working for Zeb Richards. And if he was really talking about launching new products—new beers—well, then she might like her job again. The feeling that blossomed in her chest was so unfamiliar that it took a second to realize what it was—hope. Hope that this might actually work out.

"Part of what made the Beaumont Brewery a success was its long family traditions," Richards went on in a quiet voice. "That's why Logan failed. The employees liked Chadwick—any idiot knows that. And his brother Phillip? Phillip was the brewery's connection with our target market. When we lost both Phillip and Chadwick, the brewery lost its way."

Everything he said made sense. Because Casey had spent the last year not only feeling lost but knowing they were lost. They lost ground, they lost employees, they lost friends—they lost the knowledge and the tradition that had made them great. She was only one woman—one woman who liked to make beer. She couldn't save the company all by herself but she was doing her damnedest to save the beer.

Still, Richards had been on the job for about two hours now—maybe less. He was talking a hell of a good game, but at this point, that was all it was—

talk. All talk and sinful handsomeness, with a hearty dollop of mystery.

But action was what this company needed. His mesmerizing eyes wouldn't right this ship all by themselves.

Still, if Richards really was a Beaumont by birth—bastard or not—he just might be able to do it. She'd long ago learned to never underestimate the Beaumonts.

"So you're going to be the one to light the path?"

He stared her in the eyes, one eyebrow gently lifted. God, if she wasn't careful, she could get lost in his gaze. "I have a plan, Ms. Johnson. You let me worry about the company and you worry about the beer."

"Sounds good to me," she muttered.

She stood because it seemed like a final sort of statement. But Richards stopped her. "How many workers do you need to hire?"

"At least ten. What I need most right now is maintenance staff. I don't know how much you know about beer, but most of what I do is automated. It's making sure to push the right button at the right time and checking to make sure that things come together the right way. It doesn't take a lot of know-how to brew beer, honestly, once you have the recipes." At this statement, both of his eyebrows lifted. "But keeping equipment running is another matter. It's hot, messy work and I need at least eight people who can take a tank apart and put it back together in less than an hour."

He thought about that for a moment. "I don't mean to be rude, but is that what you were doing before you came in here?"

She rolled her eyes again. "What gave it away?"

He grinned. Casey took another step back from the desk—away from Zeb Richards smiling at her. She tried to take comfort in the fact that he probably knew exactly how lethal his grin could be. Men as gorgeous as he was didn't get through life without knowing exactly what kind of effect they had on women—and it usually made them jerks. Which was fine. Gorgeous jerks never went for women like her and she didn't bother with them, either.

But there was something in the way he was looking at her that felt like a warning.

"I'll compromise with you, Ms. Johnson. You and your staff will be excused from submitting résumés."

That didn't sound like a compromise. That sounded like she was getting everything she asked for. Which meant the other shoe was about to drop. "And?"

"Instead…" He paused and shot her another grin. This one wasn't warm and fuzzy—this one was the sharp smile of a man who'd somehow bought a company out from under the Beaumonts. Out from under his own family. "…you and your team will produce a selection of new beers for me to choose from."

That was one hell of a shoe—and it had landed right on her. "I'm sorry?"

"Your point that the skills of some of your employees won't readily translate into bullet points on a résumé is well taken. So I'd like to see their skills demonstrated in action."

She knew her mouth was open, but she didn't think she could get it closed. She gave it a shot—nope, it was still open. "I can't just…"

"You do know how to brew beer, don't you?"

He was needling her—and it was working, dammit. "Of course I know how to brew beer. I've been brewing Beaumont beer for twelve years."

"Then what's the problem?"

It was probably bad form to strangle your boss on his first day on the job. Tempting, though. "I can't just produce beer by snapping my fingers. I have to test new recipes—and some of them are not going to work—and then there's the brewing time, and I won't be able to do any of that until I get more staff hired."

"How long will it take?"

She grasped at the first number that popped into her mind. "Two months. At least. Maybe three."

"Fine. Three months to hire the workers and test some new recipes." He sat forward in his chair and dropped his gaze to the desk, as if they were done.

"It isn't that simple," she told him. "We need to get Marketing to provide us with guidance on what's currently popular and two—"

"I don't care what Marketing says." He cut her off. "This is my company and I want it to brew beers that I like."

"But I don't even know what you like." The moment the words left her mouth, she wished she could take them back. But it was too late. He fixed those eyes on her. Heat flushed down her back, warming her from the inside out. "I mean, when it comes to beer," she quickly corrected. "We've got everything on tap..." she added, trying not to blush as she motioned to the bar that ran along one side of the wall.

Richards leaned forward on his elbows as his gaze raked up and down her body again. Damn it all, he was a jerk. He only confirmed it when he opened his mouth and said, "I'd be more than happy to take some time after work and show you exactly what I like."

Well. If that was how it was going to be, he was making it a lot easier *not* to develop a crush on him. Because she had not gotten this job by sleeping her way to the top. He might be the most beautiful man she'd ever seen and those green eyes were the stuff of fantasy—but none of it mattered if he used his power as CEO to take advantage of his employees. She was good at what she did and she wouldn't let anyone take that away from her.

"Mr. Richards, you're going to have to decide what kind of Beaumont you are going to be—*if* you really are one." His eyes hardened, but she didn't back down. "Because if you're going to be a predator like your father instead of a businessman like your brother, you're going to need a new brewmaster."

Head held high, she walked out of his office and back to her own.

Then she updated her résumé.

Three

Zeb did not have time to think about his new brew-master's parting shot. It was, however, difficult not to think about *her*.

He'd known full well there would be pushback against the memo. He hadn't lied when he'd told her he wanted to see who could follow directions—but he also wanted to see who wouldn't and why. Because the fact was, having the entire company divert work hours to producing résumés was not an efficient use of time. And the workers who already had up-to-date résumés ready to go—well, that was because they were a flight risk.

He couldn't say he was surprised when the brew-master was the first person to call him on it.

But he still couldn't believe the brewmaster was a young woman with fire in her eyes and a fierce instinct to protect her employees. A woman who didn't look at him like he was ripe for the picking. A woman who took one look at him—okay, maybe more than one—and saw the truth.

A young woman with a hell of a mouth on her.

Zeb pushed Casey Johnson from his mind and picked up his phone. He started scrolling through his contacts until he came to one name in particular—Daniel Lee. He dialed and waited.

"Hello?"

"Daniel—it's Zeb. Are you still in?"

There was a pause on the other end of the line. Daniel Lee was a former political operative who'd worked behind the scenes to get several incumbents defeated. He could manipulate public perception and he could drill down into data. But that wasn't why Zeb called him.

Daniel—much like Zeb—was one of *them*. Beaumont's bastards.

"Where are you?" Daniel asked, and Zeb didn't miss the way he neatly avoided the question.

"Sitting in the CEO's office of the Beaumont Brewery. I scheduled a press conference for Friday— I'd like you to be there. I want to show the whole world that they can't ignore us anymore."

There was another pause. On one level, Zeb appreciated that Daniel was methodical. Everything he did was well thought-out and carefully researched, with the data to back it up.

But on the other hand, Zeb didn't want his relationship with his brother to be one based solely on how the numbers played out. He didn't know Daniel very well—they'd met only two months ago, after Zeb had spent almost a year and thousands upon thousands of dollars tracking down two of his half brothers. But he and Daniel were family all the same and when Zeb announced to the world that he was a Beaumont and this was his brewery, he wanted his brothers by his side.

"What about CJ?" Daniel asked.

Zeb exhaled. "He's out." Zeb had tracked down two illegitimate brothers; all three of them had been born within five years of each other. Daniel was three years younger than Zeb and half-Korean.

The other brother he'd found was Carlos Julián Santino—although he now went by CJ Wesley. Unlike Zeb and Daniel, CJ was a rancher. He didn't seem to have inherited the Beaumont drive for business.

Two months ago, when the men had all met for the first time over dinner and Zeb had laid out his plan for taking control of the brewery and finally taking what was rightfully theirs, Daniel politely agreed to look at the numbers and weigh the outcomes. But CJ had said he wasn't interested. Unlike Zeb's mother, CJ's mother had married and he'd been adopted by her husband. CJ did not consider Hardwick Beau-

mont to be his father. He'd made his position clear—
he wanted nothing to do with the Beaumonts or the
brewery.

He wanted nothing to do with his brothers.

"That's unfortunate," Daniel said. "I had hoped..."

Yeah, Zeb had hoped, too. But he wasn't going to
dwell on his failures. Not when success was within
his grasp. "I need you by my side, Daniel. This is
our time. I won't be swept under the rug any longer.
We are both Beaumonts. It's not enough that I've
taken their company away from them—I need it to
do better than it did under them. And that means I
need you. This is the dawn of a new era."

Daniel chuckled. "You can stop with the hard
sell—I'm in. But I get to be the chief marketing officer, right?"

"I wouldn't have it any other way."

There was another long pause. "This had better
work," Daniel said in a menacing voice.

Which made Zeb grin. "It already has."

It was late afternoon before Zeb was able to get
a tour of the facilities. Delores, tablet in hand, alter-
nated between leading the way and falling behind
him. Zeb couldn't tell if she was humoring him or
if she really was that intimidated.

The tour moved slowly because in every department, Zeb stopped and talked with the staff. He was
pleased when several managers asked to speak to him
privately and then questioned the need to have a ré-

sumé for every single person on staff—wouldn't it be better if they just turned in a report on head count? It was heartening, really. Those managers were willing to risk their necks to protect their people—while they still looked for a way to do what Zeb told them.

However, Zeb didn't want to be seen as a weak leader who changed his mind. He allowed the managers to submit a report by the deadline, but he still wanted to see résumés. He informed everyone that the hiring freeze was over but he needed to know what he had before he began to fill the empty cubicles.

As he'd anticipated after his conversation with Casey, the news that the hiring freeze was over— coupled with the announcement that he would prefer not to see his staff working ten- to twelve-hour days—bought him a considerable amount of goodwill. That was not to say people weren't still wary—they were—but the overwhelming emotion was relief. It was obvious Casey wasn't the only one doing the job of two or three people.

The brewhouse was the last stop on their tour. Zeb wasn't sure if that was because it was the logical conclusion or because Delores was trying to delay another confrontation with Casey.

Unsurprisingly, the brewhouse was warm, and emptier than he expected. He saw now what Casey had meant when she said most of the process was automated. The few men he did see wore white lab coats and hairnets, along with safety goggles. They held tablets and when Zeb and Delores passed them, they paused and looked up.

"The staffing levels two years ago?" Zeb asked again.

He'd asked that question at least five times already. Two years ago, the company had been in the capable hands of Chadwick Beaumont. They'd been turning a consistent profit and their market share was stable. That hadn't been enough for some of their board members, though. Leon Harper had agitated for the company's sale, which made him hundreds of millions of dollars. From everything Zeb had read about Harper, the man was a foul piece of humanity. But there was no way Zeb ever could've gotten control of the company without him.

Delores tapped her tablet as they walked along. The room was oddly silent—there was the low hum of machinery, but it wasn't enough to dampen the echoes from their footfalls. The noise bounced off the huge tanks that reached at least twenty feet high. The only other noise was a regular hammering that got louder the farther they went into the room.

"Forty-two," she said after several minutes. "That was when we were at peak capacity. Ah, here we are."

Delores pointed at the floor and he looked down and saw two pairs of jeans-clad legs jutting out from underneath the tank.

Delores gave him a cautious smile and turned her attention back to the legs. "Casey?"

Zeb had to wonder what Delores had thought of Casey bursting into his office earlier—and whether or not Casey had said anything on her way out. He still hadn't decided what he thought of the young woman. Because she did seem impossibly young to be in charge. But what she might have lacked in maturity she made up for with sheer grit.

She probably didn't realize it, but there were very few people in this world who would dare burst into his office and dress him down. And those who would try would rarely be able to withstand the force of his disdain.

But she had. Easily. But more than that, she'd rebuffed his exploratory offer. No, that wasn't a strong enough word for how she'd destroyed him with her parting shot.

So many women looked at him as their golden ticket. He was rich and attractive and single—he knew that. But he didn't want to be anyone's ticket anywhere.

Casey Johnson hadn't treated him like that. She'd matched him verbal barb for barb and *then* bested him, all while looking like a hot mess.

He'd be lying if he said he wasn't intrigued.

"…try it again," came a muffled voice from underneath the tank. This was immediately followed by more hammering, which, at this close range, was deafening.

Zeb fought the urge to cover his ears and Delores winced. When there was a break in the hammering, she gently tapped one of the two pairs of shoes with her toe. "Casey—Mr. Richards is here."

The person whose shoe she'd nudged started—which was followed by a dull *thunk* and someone going, "Ow, dammit. What?"

And then she slid out from under the tank. She was in a white lab coat, a hairnet and safety goggles, just like everyone else. "Hello again, Ms. Johnson."

Her eyes widened. She was not what one might call a conventional beauty—especially not in the hairnet. She had a small spiderweb scar on one cheek that was more noticeable when she was red in the face—and Zeb hadn't yet seen her *not* red in the face. It was an imperfection, but it drew his eyes to her. She was maybe four inches shorter than he was and he thought her eyes were light brown. He wasn't even sure what color her hair was—it had been under the hat in his office.

But she was passionate about beer and Zeb appreciated that.

"You again," she said in a tone that sounded intentionally bored. "Back for more?"

He almost laughed—but he didn't. He was Zeb Richards, CEO of the Beaumont Brewery. And he was not going to snicker when his brewmaster copped an attitude. Still, her manner was refreshing after a day of people bowing and scraping.

Once again, he found himself running through her parting shot. Was he like his father or like his brother? He didn't know much about either of them.

He knew his father had a lot of children—and ignored some of them—and he knew his half brother had successfully run the company for about ten years. But that was common knowledge anyone with an internet connection could find out.

Almost everyone else here—including one prone brewmaster with an attitude problem—would have known what she meant by that. But he didn't.

Not yet, anyway.

Delores looked shocked. "Casey," she hissed in warning. "I'm giving Mr. Richards a tour of the facilities. Would you like to show him around the tanks?"

For a moment, Casey looked contrite in the face of Delores's scolding and Zeb got the feeling Delores had held the company together longer than anyone else.

But the moment was short. "Can't. The damned tank won't cooperate. I'm busy. Come back tomorrow." And with that, she slid right back under the tank. Before either he or Delores could say anything else, that infernal hammering picked up again. This time, he was sure it was even louder.

Delores turned to him, looking stricken. "I apologize, Mr. Richards. I—"

Zeb held up a hand to cut her off. Then he nudged the shoes again. This time, both people slid out. The other person was a man in his midfifties. He looked panic-stricken. Casey glared up at Zeb. *"What."*

"You and I need to schedule a time to go over the product line and discuss ideas for new launches."

She rolled her eyes, which made Delores gasp in horror. "Can't you get someone from Sales to go over the beer with you?"

"No, I can't," he said coldly. It was one thing to let her get the better of him in the privacy of his office but another thing entirely to let her run unchallenged in front of staff. "It has to be you, Ms. Johnson. If you want to brew a new beer that matches my tastes, you should actually know what my tastes are. When can this tank be back up and running?"

She gave him a dull look. "It's hard to tell, what with all the constant interruptions." But then she notched an eyebrow at him, the corner of her mouth curving into a delicate grin, as if they shared a private joke.

He did some quick mental calculating. They didn't have to meet before Friday—getting the press conference organized had to be his first priority. But by next week he needed to be working toward a new product line.

However, he was also aware that the press conference was going to create waves. It would be best to leave Monday open. "Lunch, Tuesday. Plan accordingly."

For just one second, he thought she would argue with him. Her mouth opened and she looked like she was spoiling for a fight. But then she changed her mind. "Fine. Tuesday. Now if you'll excuse me," she added, sliding back out of view.

"I'm so sorry," Delores repeated as they hurried away from the hammering. "Casey is…"

Zeb didn't rush into the gap. He was curious what the rest of the company thought of her.

He was surprised to realize *he* admired her. It couldn't be easy keeping the beer flowing—especially not as a young woman. She had to be at least twenty years younger than nearly every other man he'd seen in the brewhouse. But she hadn't let that stop her.

Because she was, most likely, unstoppable.

He hoped the employees thought highly of her. He needed people like her who cared for the company and the beer. People who weren't constrained by what they were or were not supposed to be.

Just like he wasn't.

"She's young," Delores finished.

Zeb snorted. Compared to his assistant, almost everyone would be.

"But she's very good," Delores said with finality.

"Good." He had no doubt that Casey Johnson would fight him at every step. "Make sure HR fast-tracks her hires. I want her to have all the help she needs."

He was looking forward to this.

Four

"Thank you all for joining me today," Zeb said, looking out at the worried faces of his chief officers, vice presidents and departmental heads. They were all crammed around the conference table in his office. They had twenty minutes until the press conference was scheduled to start and Zeb thought it was best to give his employees a little warning.

Everyone looked anxious. He couldn't blame them. He'd made everyone surrender their cell phones when they'd come into the office and a few people looked as if they were going through withdrawal. But he wasn't about to run the risk of someone preempting his announcement.

Only one person in the room looked like she knew

what was coming next—Casey Johnson. Today she also looked like a member of the managerial team, Zeb noted with an inward smile. Her hair was slicked back into a neat bun and she wore a pale purple blouse and a pair of slacks. The change from the woman who'd stormed into his office was so big that if it hadn't been for the faint spiderweb scar on her cheek, Zeb wouldn't have recognized her.

"I'm going to tell you the same thing that I'm going to tell the press in twenty minutes," Zeb said. "I wanted to give you advance warning. When I make my announcement, I expect each and every one of you to look supportive. We're going to present a unified force. Not only is the Beaumont Brewery back, but it's going to be better than ever." He glanced at Casey. She notched an eyebrow at him and made a little motion with her hands that Zeb took to mean *Get on with it.*

So he did. "Hardwick Beaumont was my father."

As expected, the entire room shuddered with a gasp, followed by a rumbling murmur of disbelief. With amusement, Zeb noted that Casey stared around the room as if everyone else should have already realized the truth.

She didn't understand how unusual she was. No one had ever looked at him and seen the Beaumont in him. All they could see was a black man from Atlanta. Very few people ever bothered to look past that, even when he'd started making serious money.

But she had.

Some of the senior employees looked grim but not surprised. Everyone else seemed nothing but shocked. And the day wasn't over yet. When the murmur had subsided, Zeb pressed on.

"Some of you have met Daniel Lee," Zeb said, motioning to Daniel, who stood near the door. "In addition to being our new chief marketing officer, Daniel is also one of Hardwick's sons. So when I tell the reporters," he went on, ignoring the second round of shocked murmurs, "that the Beaumont Brewery is back in Beaumont hands, I want to know that I have your full support. I've spent the last week getting to know you and your teams. I know that Chadwick Beaumont, my half brother," he added, proud of the way he kept his voice level, "ran this company with a sense of pride and family honor and I'm making this promise to you, here, in this room—we will restore the Beaumont pride and we will restore the honor to this company. My last name may not be Beaumont, but I am one nonetheless. Do I have your support?"

Again, his eyes found Casey's. She was looking at him and then Daniel—no doubt looking for the family resemblance that lurked beneath their unique racial heritages.

Murmurs continued to rumble around the room, like thunder before a storm. Zeb waited. He wasn't going to ask a second time, because that would denote weakness and he was never weak.

"Does Chadwick know what you're doing?"

Zeb didn't see who asked the question, but from

the voice, he guessed it was one of the older people in the room. Maybe even someone who had once worked not only for Chadwick but for Hardwick, as well. "He will shortly. At this time, Chadwick is a competitor. I wish him well, as I'm sure we all do, but he's not coming back. This is my company now. Not only do I want to get us back to where we were when he was in charge of things, but I want to get us ahead of where we were. I'll be laying out the details at the press conference, but I promise you this. We will have new beers," he said, nodding to Casey, "and new marketing strategies, thanks to Daniel and his extensive experience."

He could tell he didn't have them. The ones standing were shuffling their feet and the ones sitting were looking anywhere but at him. If this had been a normal business negotiation, he'd have let the silence stretch. But it wasn't. "This was once a great place to work and I want to make it that place again. As I discussed with some of you, I've lifted the hiring freeze. The bottom line is and will continue to be important, but so is the beer."

An older man in the back stepped forward. "The last guy tried to run us into the ground."

"The last guy wasn't a Beaumont," Zeb shot back. He could see the doubt in their eyes. He didn't look the part that he was trying to sell them on.

Then Casey stood, acting far more respectable— and respectful—than the last time he had seen her. "I don't know about everyone else, but I just want to make beer. And if you say we're going to keep making beer, then I'm in."

Zeb acknowledged her with a nod of his head and looked around this room. He'd wager that there'd be one or two resignations on his desk by Monday morning. Maybe more. But Casey fixed them with a stern look and most of his employees stood up.

"All right," the older man who had spoken earlier repeated. Zeb was going to have to learn his name soon, because he clearly commanded a great deal of respect. "What do we have to do?"

"Daniel has arranged this press conference. Think of it as a political rally." Which was what Daniel knew best. The similarities were not coincidences. "I'd like everyone to look supportive and encouraging of the new plan."

"Try to smile," Daniel said, and Zeb saw nearly everyone jump in surprise. It was the first time Daniel had spoken. "I'm going to line you up and then we're going to walk out onto the front steps of the building. I'm going to group you accordingly. You are all the face of the Beaumont Brewery, each and every one of you. Try to remember that when the cameras are rolling."

Spoken like a true political consultant.

"Mr. Richards," Delores said, poking her head in the room, "it's almost time."

Daniel began arranging everyone in line as he wanted them and people went along with it. Zeb went back to his private bathroom to splash water on his face. Did he have enough support to put on a good show?

Probably.

He stared at the mirror. He *was* a Beaumont. For almost his entire life, that fact had been a secret that only three people knew—him and his parents. If his mother had so much as breathed a word about his true parentage, Hardwick would've come after her with pitchforks and torches. He would've burned her to the ground.

But Hardwick was dead and Zeb no longer had to keep his father's secrets. Now the whole world was going to know who he really was.

He walked out to find one person still in the conference room. He couldn't even be surprised when he saw it was Casey Johnson. For some reason, something in his chest unclenched.

"How did I do?" The moment the words left his mouth, he started. He didn't need her approval. He didn't even want it. But he'd asked for it anyway.

She tilted her head to one side and studied him. "Not bad," she finally allowed. "You may lose the entire marketing department."

Zeb's eyebrows jumped up. Was it because of him or because he brought in Daniel, another outsider? "You think so?"

She nodded and then sighed. "Are you sure you know what you're doing?"

"Can you keep a secret?"

"If I say yes, is that your cue to say, 'So can I'?"

Zeb would never admit to being nervous. But if he *had* been, a little verbal sparring with Ms. Johnson would have been just the thing to distract him. He gave her a measured look. "I'll take that as a no, you can't keep a secret. Nevertheless," he went on before she could protest, "I am putting the fate of this company in the hands of a young woman with an attitude problem, when any other sane owner would turn toward an older, more experienced brewmaster. I have faith in you, Ms. Johnson. Try to have a little in me."

She clearly did not win a lot of poker games. One second, she looked like she wanted to tear him a new one for daring to suggest she might have an attitude problem. But then the compliment registered and the oddest thing happened.

She blushed. Not the overheated red that he'd seen on her several times now. This was a delicate coloring of her cheeks, a kiss of light pink along her skin. "You have faith in me?"

"I had a beer last night. Since you've been in charge of brewing for the last year, I feel it's a reasonable assumption that you brewed it. So yes, I have faith in your abilities." Her lips parted. She sucked in a little gasp and Zeb was nearly overcome with the urge to lean forward and kiss her. Because she looked utterly kissable right now.

But the moment the thought occurred to him, he pushed it away. What the hell was wrong with him today? He was about to go out and face a bloodthirsty pack of reporters. Kissing anyone—least of all his brewmaster—should have been the farthest thing from his mind. Especially considering the setdown she'd given him a few days ago.

Was he like his father or his brother?

Still, he couldn't fight the urge to lean forward. Her eyes widened and her pupils darkened.

"Don't let me down," he said in a low voice.

He wasn't sure what she would say. But then the door swung open again and Daniel poked his head in.

"Ah, Ms... Johnson, is it? We're waiting on you." He looked over her head to Zeb. "Two minutes."

Ms. Johnson turned, but at the doorway, she paused and looked back. "Don't let the company down," she told him.

He hoped he wouldn't.

Casey knew she should be paying more attention to whatever Zeb was saying. Because he was certainly saying a lot of things, some of them passionately. She caught phrases like *quality beer* and *family company* but for the most part, she tuned out.

He had faith in her? That was so disconcerting that she didn't have a good response. But the thing that had really blown her mind was that she had been—and this was by her own estimation—a royal bitch during the two times they'd met previous to today.

It wasn't that no one respected her. The guys she'd worked with for the last twelve years respected her. Because she had earned it. She had shown up, day in and day out. She had taken their crap and given as good as she got. She had taken every single job they threw at her, even the really awful ones like scrubbing out the tanks. Guys like Larry respected her because they knew her.

Aside from those two conversations, Zeb Richards didn't know her at all.

Maybe what he'd said was a load of crap. After all, a guy as good-looking as he was didn't get to be where he was in life without learning how to say the right thing at the right time to a woman. And he'd already hit on her once, on that first day when she'd burst into his office. So it was entirely possible that he'd figured out the one thing she needed to hear and then said it to soften her up.

Even though she wasn't paying attention, she still knew the moment he dropped his big bomb. She felt the tension ripple among her coworkers—but that wasn't it. No, the entire corps of reporters recoiled in shock. Seconds later, they were all shouting questions.

"Can you prove that Hardwick Beaumont was your father?"

"How many more bastards are there?"

"Did you plan the takeover with Chadwick Beaumont?"

"What are your plans for the brewery now that the Beaumonts are back in charge?"

Casey studied Richards. The reporters had jumped out of their chairs and were now crowding the stage, as if being first in line meant their questions would be answered first. Even though they weren't shouting at her, she still had the urge to flee in horror.

But not Richards. He stood behind his podium and stared down at the reporters as if they were nothing more than gnats bothering him on a summer day. After a moment, the reporters quieted down. Richards waited until they returned to their seats before ignoring the questions completely and moving on with his prepared remarks.

Well, that was impressive. She glanced at the one person who had thrown her for a loop this morning—Daniel Lee. The two men stood nearly shoulder to shoulder, with Daniel just a step behind and to the right of Richards. Richards had two inches on his half brother and maybe forty pounds of what appeared to be pure muscle. The two men shouldn't have looked anything alike. Lee was clearly Asian American and Richards wasn't definitively one ethnicity or another. But despite those differences—and despite the fact that they had apparently not been raised together, like the other Beaumonts had been—there was something similar about them. The way they held their heads, their chins—not that Casey had met all of the Beaumont siblings, but apparently, they all shared the same jaw.

As Richards continued to talk about his plans for restoring the Beaumont family honor, Casey wondered where she fit in all of this.

In her time, when she'd been a young intern fresh

out of college and desperate to get her foot in the door, Hardwick Beaumont had been...well, not an old man, but an older man. He'd had a sharp eye and wandering hands. Wally Winking, the old brewmaster, whose voice still held a faint hint of a German accent even though he'd been at the brewery for over fifty years, had told her she reminded him of his granddaughter. Then he'd told her never to be alone with Hardwick. She hadn't had to ask why.

Three days ago, Richards had made a pass at her. That was something his father would have done. But today?

Today, when they'd been alone together, he'd had faith in her abilities. He made it sound like he respected her—both as a person and as a brewmaster.

And that was what made him sound like his brother Chadwick.

Oh, her father was going to have a field day with this. And then he was going to be mad at her that she hadn't warned him in advance. To say that Carl Johnson was heavily invested in her career would be like saying that NASA sometimes thought about Mars. He constantly worried that she was on the verge of losing her job—a sentiment that had only gotten stronger over the last year. Her dad was protective of his little girl, which was both sweet and irritating.

What was she going to tell her father? She hadn't told him about her confrontational first meeting with Richards—or the second one, for that matter. But she was pretty sure she would be on the news to-night, one face in a human backdrop behind Zeb Richards as he completely blew up everything people thought they knew about the Beaumont family and the brewery.

Well, there was only one thing to do. As soon as Daniel Lee gave her phone back, she had to text her dad.

Oh, the reporters were shouting again. Richards picked up his tablet to walk off the platform. Daniel motioned to the people in front of her as they were beginning to walk back up the front steps. The press conference was apparently over. Thank God for that.

Richards appeared to be ignoring the reporters but that only made the reporters shout louder. He'd almost made it to the door when Natalie Baker—the beautiful blonde woman who trafficked in local Denver gossip on her show, *A Good Morning with Natalie Baker*—physically blocked Zeb's way with her body. And her breasts. They were really nice ones, the kind that Casey had never had and never would.

Natalie Baker all but purred a question at Richards. "Are there more like you?" she asked, her gaze sweeping to include Daniel in the question.

It must've been the breasts, because for the first time, Richards went off script. "I've located one more brother, but he's not part of this venture. Now if you'll excuse me."

Baker looked thrilled and the rest of the crowd started shouting questions again. *That was a dumb thing to do*, Casey thought. Now everyone would have to know who the third one was and why he wasn't on the stage with Richards and Lee.

Men. A nice rack and they lost their little minds.

She didn't get a chance to talk to Richards again. And even if she had, what would she have said? *Nice press conference that I didn't pay attention to?* No, even she knew that was not the way to go about things.

Besides, she had her own brand of damage control to deal with. She needed to text her dad, warning him that the company would be in the news again but he shouldn't panic—her boss had faith in her. Then she had to go back and warn her crew. No, it was probably too late for that. She had to reassure them that they were going to keep making beer. Then she had to start the hiring process for some new employees and she had to make sure that tank fifteen was actually working properly today...

And she had to get ready for Tuesday. She was having lunch and beer with the boss.

Which boss would show up?

Five

Frankly, he could use a beer.

"Did you contact CJ?" Daniel asked. "He needs to be warned."

Here, in the privacy of his own office with no one but Daniel around, Zeb allowed himself to lean forward and pinch the bridge of his nose. Make that several beers.

"I did. He didn't seem concerned. As long as we keep his name and whereabouts out of it, he thinks he's unfindable."

Daniel snorted. "You found him."

"A fact of which I reminded him." Zeb knew that CJ's refusal to be a part of Zeb's vision for the brothers wasn't personal. Still, it bugged him. "I think it's safe to say that he's a little more laid-back than we are."

That made Daniel grin. "He'll come around. Eventually. Has there been any other…contact?"

"No." It wasn't that he expected the acknowledged members of the Beaumont family to storm the brewery gates and engage in a battle for the heart and soul of the family business. But while the rest of the world was engaged in furious rounds of questions and speculation, there had been radio silence from the Beaumonts themselves. Not even a *No comment*. Just…nothing.

Not that Zeb expected any of them to fall over themselves to welcome him and Daniel into the family. He didn't.

He checked his watch.

"Do you have a hot date?" Daniel asked in an offhand way.

"I'm having lunch with the brewmaster, Casey Johnson."

That got Daniel's attention. He sat up straighter. "And?"

And she asked me if I was like my father or my brother and I didn't have an answer.

But that wasn't what he said. In fact, he didn't say anything. Yes, he and Daniel were in this together, and yes, they were technically brothers. But there were some things he still didn't want to share. Daniel was too smart and he knew how to bend the truth to suit his purposes.

Zeb had no desire to be bent to anyone's purposes but his own. "We're going over the product line. It's hard to believe that a woman so young is the brewmaster in charge of all of our beer and I want to make sure she knows her stuff."

His phone rang. He winced inwardly—it was his mother. "I've got to take this. We'll talk later?"

Daniel nodded. "One last thing. I had four resignations in the marketing department."

Casey had not been wrong about that, either. She had a certain brashness to her, but she knew this business. "Hire whoever you want," Zeb said as he answered the call. "Hello, Mom."

"I shouldn't have to call you," his mother said, the steel in her voice sounding extra sharp today.

How much beer could one man reasonably drink at work? Zeb was going to have to test that limit today, because if there was one thing he didn't want to deal with right now, it was his mother.

"But I'm glad you did," he replied easily. "How's the salon?"

"Humph." Emily Richards ran a chain of successful hair salons in Georgia. Thanks to his careful management, Doo-Wop and Pop! had gone from being six chairs in a strip-mall storefront to fifteen locations scattered throughout Georgia and a small but successful line of hair weaves and braid accessories targeted toward the affluent African American buyer.

Zeb had done that for his mother. He'd taken her

from lower middle class, where the two of them got by on $30,000 a year, to upper class. Doo-Wop and Pop! had made Emily Richards rich and was on track to make even more profit this year.

But that *humph* told Zeb everything he needed to know. It didn't matter that he had taken his mother's idea and turned it into a hugely successful woman-owned business. All that really mattered to Emily Richards was getting revenge on the man she claimed had ruined her life.

A fact she drove home with her next statement. "Well? Did you finally take what's yours?"

It always came back to the brewery. And the way she said *finally* grated on his nerves like a steel file. Still, she was his mother. "It's really mine, Mom."

Those words should have filled him with satisfaction. He had done what he had set out to do. The Beaumont Brewery was his now.

So why did he feel so odd?

He shook it off. It had been an exceptionally long weekend, after all. As expected, his press conference had created not just waves but tsunamis that had to be dealt with. His one mistake—revealing that there was a third Beaumont bastard, unnamed and unknown—had threatened to undermine his triumphant ascension to power.

"They'll come for you," his mother intoned ominously. "Those Beaumonts can't let it rest. You watch your back."

Not for the first time, Zeb wondered if his mother

was a touch paranoid. He understood now what he hadn't when he was little—that his father had bought her silence. But more and more, she acted like his siblings would go to extreme measures to enforce that silence.

His father, maybe. But none of the research he'd done on any of his siblings had turned up any proclivities for violence.

Still, he knew he couldn't convince his mother. So he let it go.

There was a knock on the door and before he could say anything, it popped open. In walked Jamal, boxes stacked in his hands. When he saw that Zeb was on the phone, he nodded his head in greeting and moved quietly to the conference table. There he began unpacking lunch.

"I will," Zeb promised his mother. And it wasn't even one of those little white lies he told her to keep her happy. He had stirred up several hornets' nests over the last few days. It only made good sense to watch his back.

"They deserve to pay for what they did to me. And you," she added as an afterthought.

But wasn't that the thing? None of the Beaumonts who were living today had ever done anything to Zeb. They'd just…ignored him.

"I've got to go, Mom. I have a meeting that starts in a few minutes." He didn't miss the way his Southern accent was stronger. Hearing it roll off Mom's tongue made his show up in force.

"Humph," she repeated. "Love you, baby boy."

"Love you, too, Mom." He hung up.

"Let me guess," Jamal said as he spread out the four-course meal he had prepared. "She's still not happy."

"Let it go, man." But something about the conversation with his mother was bugging him.

For a long time, his mother had spoken of what the Beaumonts owed *him*. They had taken what rightfully belonged to him and it was his duty to get it back. And if they wouldn't give it to him legitimately, he would just have to take it by force.

But that was all she'd ever told him about the Beaumont family. She'd never told him anything about his father or his father's family. She'd told him practically nothing about her time in Denver—he wasn't all that sure what she had done for Hardwick back in the '70s. Every time he asked, she refused to answer and instead launched into another rant about how they'd cut him out of what was rightfully his.

He had so many questions and not enough answers. He was missing something and he knew it. It was a feeling he did not enjoy, because in his business, answers made money.

His intercom buzzed. "Mr. Richards, Ms. Johnson is here."

Jamal shot him a funny look. "I thought you said you were having lunch with your brewmaster."

Before Zeb could explain, the door opened and Casey walked in. "Good morning. I spoke with the

cook in the cafeteria. She said she hadn't been asked
to prepare any— Oh. Hello," she said cautiously
when she caught sight of Jamal plating up what
smelled like his famous salt-crusted beef tenderloin.

Zeb noted with amusement that today she was
back in the unisex lab coat with Beaumont Brewery
embroidered on the lapel—but she wasn't bright red
or sweating buckets. Her hair was still in a ponytail,
though. She was, on the whole, one of the least feminine women he'd ever met. He couldn't even begin
to imagine her in a dress but somehow that made her
all the more intriguing.

No, he was not going to be intrigued by her. Especially not with Jamal watching. "Ms. Johnson, this
is Jamal—"

"Jamal Hitchens?"

Now it was Jamal's turn to take a step back and
look at Casey with caution. "Yeah… You recognize
me?" He shot a funny look over to Zeb, but he just
shrugged.

He was learning what Zeb had already figured
out. There was no way to predict what Casey Johnson would do or say.

"Of course I recognize you," she gushed. "You
played for the University of Georgia—you were in
the running for the Heisman, weren't you? I mean,
until you blew your knees out. Sorry about that," she
added, wincing.

Jamal was gaping down at her as if she'd peeled

off her skin to reveal an alien in disguise. "You know who I am?"

"Ms. Johnson is a woman of many talents," Zeb said, not even bothering to fight the grin. Jamal would've gone pro if it hadn't been for his knees. But it was rare that anyone remembered a distant runner-up for the Heisman who hadn't played ball in years. "I've learned it's best not to underestimate her. Ms. Johnson is my brewmaster."

It was hard to get the drop on Jamal, but one small woman in a lab coat clearly had. "What are you doing here?" Casey sniffed the air. "God, that smells good."

Honest to God, Jamal blushed. "Oh. Thank you." He glanced nervously at Zeb.

"Jamal is my oldest friend," Zeb explained. He almost added, *He's the closest thing I have to a brother*—but then he stopped himself. Even if it was true, the whole point of this endeavor with the Beaumont Brewery was to prove that he had a family whether they wanted him or not. "He is my right-hand man. One of his many talents is cooking. I asked him to prepare some of my favorites today to accompany our tasting." He turned to Jamal, whose mouth was still flopped open in shock. "What did you bring?" Zeb prodded.

"What? Oh, right. The food." It was so unusual to hear Jamal sound unsure of himself that Zeb had to stare. "It's a tasting menu," he began, sounding embarrassed about it. It was rare that Jamal's past life in sports ever intersected with his current life. Actually, Zeb couldn't remember a time when someone who hadn't played football recognized him.

Jamal ran through the menu—in addition to the salt-crusted beef tenderloin, which had been paired with new potatoes, there was a spaghetti Bolognese, a vichyssoise soup and Jamal's famous fried chicken. Dessert was flourless chocolate cupcakes dusted with powdered sugar—Zeb's favorite.

Casey surveyed the feast before her, and Zeb got the feeling that she didn't approve. He couldn't say why he thought that, because she was perfectly polite to Jamal at all times. In fact, when he tried to leave, she insisted on getting a picture with him so she could send it to her father—apparently, her father was a huge sports fan and would also know who Jamal was.

So Zeb took the photo for her and then Jamal hurried away, somewhere between flattered and uncomfortable.

And then Zeb and Casey were alone.

She didn't move. "So Jamal Hitchens is an old friend of yours?"

"Yes."

"And he's your…personal chef?"

Zeb settled into his seat at the head of the conference table. "Among other things, yes." He didn't offer up any other information.

"You don't really strike me as a sports guy," she replied.

"Come, now, Ms. Johnson. Surely you've researched me by now?"

Her cheeks colored again. He liked that delicate blush on her. He shouldn't, but he did. "I don't remember reading about you owning a sports franchise."

Zeb lifted one shoulder. "Who knows. Maybe I'll buy a team and make Jamal the general manager. After all, what goes together better than sports and beer?"

She was still standing near the door, as if he were an alligator that looked hungry. Finally, she asked, "Have you decided, then?"

"About what?"

He saw her swallow, but it was the only betrayal of her nerves. Well, that and the fact that she wasn't smart-mouthing him. Actually, that she wasn't saying whatever came to mind was unusual.

"About what kind of Beaumont you're going to be."

He involuntarily tensed and then let out a breath slowly. Like his father or his brother? He had no idea.

He wanted to ask what she knew—was it the same as the public image of the company? Or was there something else he didn't know? Maybe his father had secretly been the kindest man on earth. Or maybe Chadwick was just as bad as Hardwick had been. He didn't know.

What he did know was that the last time he'd seen her, he'd had the urge to kiss her. It'd been nerves, he'd decided. He'd been concerned about the press conference and Casey Johnson was the closest thing to a friendly face here—when she wasn't scowling at him. That was all that passing desire had been. Reassurance. Comfort.

He didn't feel comfortable now.

"I'm going to be a different kind of Beaumont," he said confidently because it was the only true thing he *could* say. "I'm my own man."

She thought this over. "And what kind of man is that?"

She had guts, he had to admit. Anyone else might have nodded and smiled and said, *Of course.* But not her. "The kind with strong opinions about beer."

"Fair enough." She headed for the bar.

Zeb watched her as she pulled on the tap with a smooth, practiced hand. He needed to stop being surprised at her competency. She was the brewmaster. Of course she knew how to pour beer. Tapping the keg was probably second nature to her. And there wasn't a doubt in his mind that she could also destroy him in a sports trivia contest.

But this was different from watching a bartender fill a pint glass. Watching her hands on the taps was far more interesting than it'd ever been before. She had long fingers and they wrapped around each handle with a firm, sure grip.

Unexpectedly, he found himself wondering what else she'd grip like that. But the moment the thought found its way to his consciousness, he pushed it aside. This wasn't about attraction. This was about beer.

Then she glanced up at him and a soft smile

ghosted across her lips, like she was actually glad to see him, and Zeb forgot about beer. Instead, he openly stared at her. Was she glad he was here? Was she able to look at him and see not just a hidden bastard or a ruthless businessman but…

…him? Did she see *him*?

Zeb cleared his throat and shifted in his seat as Casey gathered up the pint glasses. After a moment's consideration, she set down one pair of glasses in front of the tenderloin and another in front of the pasta. Zeb reached for the closest glass, but she said, "Wait! If we're going to do this right, I have to walk you through the beers."

"Is there a wrong way to drink beer?" he asked, pulling his hand back.

"Mr. Richards," she said, exasperated. "This is a tasting. We're not 'drinking beer.' I don't drink on the job—none of us do. I sample. That's all this is."

She was scolding him, he realized. He was confident that he'd never been scolded by an employee before. The thought made him laugh—which got him some serious side-eye.

"Fine," he said, trying to restrain himself. When had that become difficult to do? He was always restrained. *Always.* "We'll do this your way."

He'd told Jamal the truth. He should never underestimate Casey Johnson.

She went back behind his bar and filled more half-pint glasses, twenty in all. Each pair was placed in front of a different dish. And the whole time, she was quiet.

Silence was a negotiating tactic and, as such, one that never worked on Zeb. Except…he felt himself getting twitchy as he watched her focus on her work. The next thing he knew, he was volunteering information. "Four people in the marketing department have resigned," he announced into the silence. "You were right about that."

She shrugged, as if it were no big deal. "You gave a nice talk about family honor and a bunch of other stuff, but you didn't warn anyone that you were bringing in a new CMO. People were upset."

Was she upset? No, it didn't matter, he told himself. He wasn't in this business for the touchy-feely. He was in it to make money. Well, that and to get revenge against the Beaumonts.

So, with that firmly in mind, he said, "The position was vacant. And Daniel's brilliant when it comes to campaigns. I have no doubt the skills he learned in politics will apply to beer, as well." But even as he said it, he wondered why he felt the need to explain his managerial decisions to her.

Evidently, she wondered the same thing, as she held up her hands in surrender. "Hey, you don't have to justify it to me. Although it might have been a good idea to justify it to the marketing department."

She was probably right—but he didn't want to admit that, so he changed tactics. "How about your department? Anyone there decide I was the final straw?" As he asked it, he realized what he really wanted to know was if *she'd* decided he was the final straw.

What the hell was this? He didn't care what his employees thought about him. He never had. All he cared about was that people knew their jobs and did them well. Results—that was what he cared about. This was business, not a popularity contest.

Or it had been, he thought as Casey smirked at him when she took her seat.

"My people are nervous, but that's to be expected. The ones who've hung in this long don't like change. They keep hoping that things will go back to the way they were," she said, catching his eye. No, that was a hedge. She already *had* his eye because he couldn't stop staring at her. "Or some reasonable facsimile thereof. A new normal, maybe. But no, I haven't had anyone quit on me."

A new normal. He liked that. "Good. I don't want you to be understaffed again."

She paused and then cleared her throat. When she looked up at him again, he felt the ground shift under his feet. She was gazing at him with something he so desperately wanted to think was appreciation. Why did he need her approval so damned bad?

"Thank you," she said softly. "I mean, I get that owning the company is part of your birthright, I guess, but this place…" She looked around as her voice trailed off with something that Zeb recognized—longing.

It was as if he were seeing another woman—one younger, more idealistic. A version of Casey that must have somehow found her way to the Beaumont Brewery years ago. Had she gotten the job through her father or an uncle? An old family friend?

Or had she walked into this company and, in her normal assertive way, simply demanded a job and refused to take no for an answer?

He had a feeling that was it.

He wanted to know what she was doing here— what this place meant to her and why she'd risked so much to defend it. Because they both knew that he could have fired her already. Being without a brewmaster for a day or a week would have been a problem, but problems were what he fixed.

But he hadn't fired her. She'd pushed him and challenged him and...and he liked that. He liked that she wasn't afraid of him. Which didn't make any sense—fear and intimidation were weapons he deployed easily and often to get what he wanted, the way he wanted it. Almost every other employee in this company had backed down in the face of his memos and decrees. But not *this* employee.

Not Casey.

"Okay," she announced in a tone that made it clear she wasn't going to finish her earlier statement. She produced a tablet from her lab-coat pocket and sat to his right. "Let's get started."

They went through each of the ten Beaumont beers, one at a time. "As you taste each one," she said without looking at him, "think about the flavors as they hit your tongue."

He coughed. "The...flavors?"

She handed him a pint glass and picked up the other for herself. "Drinking beer isn't just chugging to get drunk," she said in a voice that made it sound like she was praying, almost. She held her glass up and gazed at the way the light filtered through the beer. Zeb knew he should do the same—but he couldn't. He was watching her.

"Drinking beer fulfills each of the senses. Every detail contributes to the full experience," she said in that voice that was serious yet also...wistful. "How does the color make you feel?" She brought the glass back to her lips—but she didn't drink. Instead, her eyes drifted shut as she inhaled deeply. "What does it smell like—and how do the aromas affect the taste? How does it feel in your mouth?"

Her lips parted and, fascinated, Zeb watched as she tipped the glass back and took a drink. Her eyelashes fluttered in what looked to him like complete and total satisfaction. Once she'd swallowed, she sighed. "So we'll rate each beer on a scale of one to five."

Did she have any idea how sensual she looked right now? Did she look like that when she'd been satisfied in bed? Or was it just the beer that did that to her? If he leaned over and touched his fingertips to her cheek to angle her chin up so he could press his lips against hers, would she let him?

"Mr. Richards?"

"What?" Zeb shook back to himself to find that Casey was staring at him with amusement.

"Ready?"

"Yes," he said because, once again, that was the truth. He'd thought he'd been ready to take over this company—but until right then, he hadn't been sure he was ready for someone like Casey Johnson.

They got to work, sipping each beer and rating it accordingly. Amazingly, Zeb was able to focus on the beer—which was good. He could not keep staring at his brewmaster like some love-struck puppy. He was Zeb Richards, for God's sake.

"I've always preferred the Rocky Top," Zeb told her, pointedly sampling—not drinking—the stalwart of the Beaumont product line. "But the Rocky Top Light tastes like dishwater."

Casey frowned at this and made a note on her tablet. "I'd argue with you, but you're right. However, it remains one of our bestsellers among women aged twenty-one to thirty-five and is one of our top overall sellers."

That was interesting. "It's the beer we target toward women and you don't like it?"

She looked up at him sharply and he could almost hear her snapping, *Women are not interchangeable.* But she didn't. Instead, in as polite a voice as he'd ever heard from her, she said, "People drink beer for different reasons," while she made notes. "I don't want to sacrifice taste for something as arbitrary as calorie count."

"Can you make it better?"

That got her attention. "We've used the same formula for... Well, since the '80s, I think. You'd want to mess with that?"

He didn't lean forward, no matter how much he wanted to. Instead, he kept plenty of space between them. "There's always room for improvement, don't you think? I'm not trapped by the past." But the moment he said it, he wondered how true that was. "Perhaps one of your experiments can be an improved light-beer recipe."

She held his gaze, her lips curved into a slight smile. It was disturbing how much he liked her meeting his challenges straight on like that. "I'll do that."

They went through the rest of the beers and, true to her word, Zeb couldn't have said that he'd drunk enough to even get a slight buzz. Finally, as they'd eaten the last of their cupcakes, he leaned back and said, "So what are we missing?"

She surprised him then. She picked up what was left of her Rocky Top and took a long drink. "Look— here's the thing about our current product line. It's fine. It's...serviceable."

He notched an eyebrow at her. "It gets the job done?"

"Exactly. But when we lost Percheron Drafts, we lost the IPA, the stout—the bigger beers with bolder tastes. We lost seasonal beers—the summer shandy and the fall Oktoberfest beers. What we've got now is basic. I'd love to get us back to having one or two spotlight beers that we could rotate in and out." She got a wistful look on her face. "It's hard to see that here, though."

"What do you mean?"

"I mean, look at this." She swept her hand out, encompassing the remains of their lunch. "*This.* Most people who drink our beer don't do so in the luxury of a private office with a catered four-course meal. They drink a beer at a game or on their couch, with a burger or a brat."

Suddenly, a feeling he'd gotten earlier—that she hadn't approved of the setup—got stronger. "What about you? Where do you drink your beer?"

"Me? Oh. I have season tickets to the Rockies. My dad and I go to every home game we can. Have you done that?" He shook his head. "You should. I've learned a lot about what people like just standing in line to get a beer at the game. I talk with the beer guys—that sort of thing."

"A ball game?" He must have sounded doubtful, because she nodded encouragingly. "I can get a box."

"Really?" She rolled her eyes. "That's not how people drink beer. Here. I'll tell you what—there's a game tomorrow night at seven, against the Braves. My dad can't go. You can use his ticket. Come with me and see what I mean."

He stared at her. It didn't sound like a come-on— but then, he'd never gotten quite so turned on watching another woman drink beer before. Nothing was typical when it came to this woman. "You're serious, aren't you?"

"Of course."

He had a feeling she was right. He'd spent years learning about the corporate workings of the brewery from a distance. If he was going to run this place as his own—and he was—then he needed to understand not just the employees but their customers.

Besides, the Braves were his team. And beyond that, this was a chance to see Casey outside work. Suddenly, that seemed important—vital, even. What was she like when she wasn't wearing a lab coat? He shouldn't have wanted to know. But he did anyway.

"It's a da—" Casey's eyes got huge and her cheeks flushed and Zeb remembered that he wasn't having a drink with a pretty girl at a bar. He was at the brewery and he was the CEO. He had to act like it. "Company outing," he finished, as if that was what he'd meant to say all along.

She cleared her throat. "Covert market research, if you will." Her gaze flickered over his Hugo Boss suit. "And try to blend, maybe?"

He gave her a level stare, but she was unaffected. "Tomorrow at seven."

"Gate C." She gathered up her tablet. "We'll talk then."

He nodded and watched her walk out. Once the door was firmly closed behind her, he allowed himself to grin.

Whether she liked it or not, they had a date.

Six

Casey really didn't know what to expect as she stood near the C gate at Coors Field. She'd told Richards to blend but she was having trouble picturing him in anything other than a perfectly tailored suit.

Not that she was spending a lot of time thinking about him in a perfectly tailored suit. She wasn't. Just because he was the epitome of masculine grace and style, that was no reason at all to think about her boss.

Besides, she didn't even go for guys in suits. She usually went for blue-collar guys, the kind who kicked back on the weekend with a bunch of beer to watch sports. That was what she was comfortable with, anyway. And comfort was good, right?

And anyway, even if she did go for guys in suits—which she did not—she was positive she didn't go for guys like Richards. It wasn't that he was African American. She had looked him up, and one of the few pictures of him on the internet was him standing with a woman named Emily Richards in Atlanta, Georgia, outside a Doo-Wop and Pop! Salon. It was easy to see the resemblance between them—she was clearly his mother.

No, her not going for guys like Richards had nothing to do with race and everything to do with the fact that he was way too intense for her. The way he'd stared at her over the lip of his pint glass during their tasting lunch? Intensity personified, and as thrilling as it had been, it wasn't what she needed on her time off. Really. She had enough intensity at work. That was why she always went for low-key guys—guys who were fun for a weekend but never wanted anything more than that.

Right. So it was settled. She absolutely did not go for someone like Richards in a suit. Good.

"Casey?"

Casey whipped around and found herself staring not at a businessman in a suit—and also not at someone who was blending. Zeb Richards stood before her in a white T-shirt with bright red raglan sleeves. She was vaguely aware that he had on a hat and reasonably certain that he was wearing blue jeans, but she couldn't tear her eyes away from his chest. The

T-shirt molded to his body in a way that his power suit hadn't. Her mouth went dry.

Good God.

That was as far as her brain got, because she tried to drag her eyes away from his chest—and made it exactly as far as his biceps.

Sweet mother of pearl was the last coherent thought she had as she tried to take in the magnitude of those biceps.

And when thinking stopped, she was left with nothing but her physical response. Her nipples tightened and her skin flushed—*flushed*, dammit, like she was an innocent schoolgirl confronted with a man's body for the first time. All that flushing left her shaken and sweaty and completely unable to look away. It took all of her self-control not to lean over and put a hand to that chest and feel what she was looking at. Because she'd be willing to bet a lot of money that he *felt* even better than he looked.

"…Casey?" he said with what she hoped like hell was humor in his voice. "Hello?"

"What?" Crap, she'd been caught gaping at him. "Right. Hi." Dumbly, she held up the tickets.

"Is there something wrong with my shirt?" He asked, looking down. Then he grasped the hem of the shirt and pulled it out so he could see the front, which had a graphic of the Braves' tomahawk on it. But when he did that, the neck of the shirt came down and Casey caught a glimpse of his collarbones.

She had no idea collarbones could be sexy. This

was turning out to be quite an educational evening and it had only just begun. How on earth was she going to get through the rest of it without doing something humiliating, like *drooling* on the man?

Because drooling was off-limits. Everything about him was off-limits.

This was not a date. Nope. He was her boss, for crying out loud.

"Um, no. I mean, I didn't actually figure you would show up in the opposing team's shirt." Finally—and way too late for decency's sake—she managed to look up into his face. He was smiling at her, as if he knew exactly what kind of effect he had on her. Dammit. This was the other reason she didn't go for men like him. They were too cocky for their own good.

"That's all," she went on. "You don't exactly blend." She was pretty sure she was babbling.

"I'm from Atlanta, you know." He smirked at her and suddenly there it was—a luscious Southern accent that threatened to melt her. "Who did you think I was going to root for?" His gaze swept over her and Casey felt each and every hair on her body stand at attention. "I don't have anything purple," he went on when his gaze made it back to her face with something that looked a heck of a lot like approval.

She fought the urge to stand up straighter. She would not pose for him. This was not a date. She didn't care what he thought of her appearance. "We could fix that," she told him, waving at the T-shirt sellers hawking all sorts of Rockies gear. He scrunched his nose at her. "Or not," she said with a melodramatic sigh, trying to get her wits about her. "It's still better than a suit. Come on. We need to get in if we want to grab a beer before the game starts."

He looked around. People in purple hats and T-shirts were making their way inside and he was already getting a few funny looks. "This is literally your home turf. Lead on."

She headed toward the turnstiles. Zeb made a move toward one with a shorter line, but Casey put her hand on his arm. "This one," she told him, guiding him toward Joel's line.

"Why?"

"You'll see." At this cryptic statement, Zeb gave her a hard look. Oddly enough, it didn't carry as much weight as it might have if he'd been in a tie, surrounded by all the brewery history in his office. Instead, he looked almost…adorable.

Crap, this was bad. She absolutely couldn't be thinking of Zebadiah Richards as adorable. Or hot. Or…anything.

There might have been some grumbling following that statement, but Casey decided that she probably shouldn't get into a shouting match with him before they'd even gotten inside the stadium.

The line moved quickly and then Joel said, "Casey! There's my girl."

"Hey, Joel," she said, leaning over to give the old man a quick hug.

"Where's Carl?" Joel asked, eyeing Zeb behind her.

"Union meeting. Who do you think's going to win today?" She and Joel had the same conversation at nearly every game.

"You have to ask? The Braves are weak this season." Then he noticed Richards's shirt behind her and his easy smile twisted into a grimace of disapproval. He leaned over and grabbed two of the special promotion items—bobblehead dolls of the team. "Take one to your dad. I know he collects them."

"Aw, thanks, Joel. And give my best to Martha, okay?"

Joel gave a bobblehead to Richards, as well. "Good luck, fella," he muttered.

When they were several feet away, Richards said, "I see what you mean about blending. Do you want this?" He held out the bobblehead.

"I'm good. Two is my personal limit on these things. Give it to Jamal or something." She led him over to her favorite beer vendor. "Speaking of, where is Jamal? I thought you might bring him."

Honestly, she couldn't decide if she'd wanted Jamal to be here or not. If he had been, then maybe she'd have been able to focus on *not* focusing on Zeb a little better. Three was a crowd, after all.

But still…she was glad Zeb had come alone.

This time, he held back and waited until she picked the beer line. "He's still unpacking."

"Oh?" There were about six people in front of

them. This game was going to be nowhere near a sellout. "So you really did move out here?"

"Of course." He slid her a side glance. "I said that at the press conference, you know."

They moved up a step in line. Casey decided that it was probably best not to admit that she hadn't been paying attention during the press conference. "So where are you guys at?"

"I bought a house over on Cedar Avenue. Jamal picked it out because he liked the kitchen."

Her eyes bugged out of her head. "You bought the mansion by the country club?"

"You know it?" He said it in such a casual way, as if buying the most expensive house in the Denver area were no biggie.

Well, maybe for him, it wasn't. Why was she surprised? She shouldn't have been. She wasn't. Someone like Zeb Richards would definitely plunk down nearly $10 million for a house and not think anything of it. "Yeah. My dad was hired to do some work there a couple years ago. He said it was an amazing house."

"I suppose it is." He didn't sound very convinced about this. But before Casey could ask him what he didn't like about the house, he went on, "What does your dad do? And I'm going to pay you back for his ticket. I'm sorry that I'm using it in his place."

She waved this away. "Don't worry about it. He really did have a union meeting tonight. He's an electrician. He does a lot of work in older homes—renovations and upgrading antique wiring. There's still a lot of knob-and-tube wiring in Denver, you know."

One corner of his mouth—not that she was staring at his mouth—curved up into a smile that was positively dangerous.

"What?" she said defensively—because if she didn't defend herself from that sly smile… Well, she didn't know what would happen. But it wouldn't be good.

In fact, it would be bad. The very best kind of bad.

"Nothing. I've just got to stop being surprised by you, that's all." They advanced another place in line. "What are we ordering?"

"Well, seeing as this is Coors Field, we really don't have too many options when it comes to beer. It's—shockingly—Coors."

"No!" he said in surprise. "Do they make beer?"

She stared at him. "Wait—was that a joke? Were you trying to be funny?"

That grin—oh, *hell*. "Depends. Did it work?"

No—well, yes, but *no*. No, she couldn't allow him to be a regular guy. If this "company outing" was going to stay strictly aboveboard, he could not suddenly develop a set of pecs *and* a sense of humor at the same time. She couldn't take it. "Mr. Richards—"

"Really, Casey," he said, cutting her off, "we're about to drink a competitor's beer outside of normal business hours at a game. Call me Zeb."

She was a strong woman. She was. She'd worked at the Beaumont Brewery for twelve years and during that time, she'd never once gotten involved with a coworker. She'd had to negotiate the fine line between "innocent flirting" and "sexual harassment" on too many occasions, but once she'd earned her place at the table, that had fallen away.

But this? Calling Richards by his first name? Buying beer with him at a ball game? Pointedly not staring at the way he filled out an officially licensed T-shirt? Listening to him crack jokes?

She simply wasn't that strong. This wasn't a company outing. It was starting to feel like a date.

They reached the cashier. "Casey!" Marco gave her a high five over the counter.

She could feel Zeb behind her. He wasn't touching her, but he was close enough that her skin was prickling. "Marco—what's the latest?"

"It happened, girl." Marco pointed to a neon sign over his head—one that proudly proclaimed they served Percheron Drafts.

Casey whistled. "You were right."

"I told you," he went on. "They cut a deal. You wanna try something? Their pale ale is good. Or is that not allowed? I heard you had a new boss there—another crazy Beaumont. Two of them, even!" He chuckled and shook his head in disbelief. "You think the Beaumonts knew their brother or half brother or whatever he is took over? I heard it might have been planned..."

It took everything Casey had not to look back over her shoulder at Zeb. Maybe she was reading too much into the situation, but she would put money on the fact that he wasn't grinning anymore. "I bet it was a hell of a surprise," she said, desperate to change the subject. "Give me the pale ale and—"

"Nachos, extra jalapeños?" He winked at her. "I'm on it."

"A *hell* of a surprise," Zeb whispered in her ear. The closeness of his voice was so unexpected that she jumped. But just then Marco came back with her order.

"Gotta say," Marco went on, ringing up her total, "it was good to see a brother up there, though. I mean…he was black, right?"

Behind her, Zeb made a noise that sounded like it was somewhere between a laugh and a choke. "It doesn't really matter," she said honestly as she handed over the cash, "as long as we get the beer right."

"Ah, that's what I like about you, Casey—a woman who knows her beer." He gave her a moony look, as if he were dazzled by beauty they both knew she didn't have. "It's not too late to marry me, you know that?"

Hand to God, Casey thought she heard Zeb growl behind her.

Okay, that was not the kind of noise a boss made when an employee engaged in chitchat with a— Well, Marco sold beer. So with a colleague of sorts. However, it was the sort of noise a man on a date made.

Not a date. *Not* a date.

For the first time, Marco seemed to notice the looming Braves fan behind her. "Come back and see me at the fifth?" Marco pleaded, keeping a cautious eye on Zeb.

"You know I will. And have Kenny bring me a stout in the third, okay?" She and Dad didn't have the super-expensive seats where people took her order and delivered it to her. But Kenny the beer vendor would bring them another beer in the third and again in the seventh—and not the beer he hawked to everyone else.

She got her nachos and her beer and moved off to the side. It was then she noticed that Zeb's eyes hadn't left her.

A shiver of heat went through her because Zeb's gaze was intense. He looked at her like…like she didn't even know what. She wasn't sure she wanted to find out, because what if he could see right through her?

What if he could see how much she was attracted to *him*?

This was a bad idea. She was on a date with her brand-new CEO and he was hot and funny and brooding all at once and they were drinking their chief competitor's product and…

Zeb glanced over at her as he paid for his food and shot another warm grin at her.

And she was in trouble. Big, *big* trouble.

Seven

Zeb followed Casey to the seats. He tried his best to keep his gaze locked on the swinging ponytail that hung out the back of her Rockies hat—and not on her backside.

That was proving to be quite a challenge, though, because her backside was a sight to behold. Her jeans clung to her curves in all the right ways. Why hadn't he noticed that before?

Oh, yeah—the lab coat.

Which hadn't shown him the real woman. But this? A bright young woman with hips and curves who was friends with everyone and completely at home in the male bastion of a baseball stadium?

Who'd said—out loud—that it didn't matter if Zeb was black or not?

She turned suddenly and he snapped his gaze back up to her face. "Here," she said, notching an eyebrow at him and gesturing toward a nearly empty row. "Seats nine and ten."

They were eight rows off the first baseline, right behind the dugout. "Great seats," he told her. "I didn't bring my glove."

She snorted as she worked her way down the row. "Definitely keep your eyes on the ball here. You never know."

He made his way to seat nine. There weren't many people around, but he had a feeling that if there had been, they'd all have known Casey.

"What did you get?" she asked once they were seated.

"The Percheron lager."

"Oh, that's such a nice beer," she said with a wistful sigh.

"Yeah?" He held out his plastic collector's cup to her. "Have a drink."

She looked at him for a long moment and then leaned over and pressed her lips against the rim of his cup. Fascinated, he watched as her mouth opened and she took a sip.

Heat shot through his body, driving his pulse to a sudden pounding in his veins. It only got worse when she leaned back just enough that she could sweep her tongue over her lips, getting every last drop of beer.

Damn. Watching Casey Johnson drink beer was almost a holy experience.

Greedy was not a word he embraced. *Greedy* implied a lack of control—stupid mistakes and rash consequences. He was not a greedy person. He was methodical and detailed and careful. Always.

But right now he wanted. He wanted her lips to drink him in like she'd drunk the beer. He wanted her tongue to sweep over his lips with that slow intensity. God help him, he wanted her to savor him. And if that made him greedy, then so be it.

So, carefully, he turned the cup around and put his lips where hers had been. Her eyes darkened as he drank. "You're right," he said, the taste of the beer and of Casey mixing on his tongue. "It's a beautiful beer."

Her breath caught and her cheeks colored, throwing the spiderweb scar on her cheek into high relief. And then, heaven help him, she leaned toward him. She could have leaned away, turned away—done something to put distance between them. She could have made it clear that she didn't want him at all.

But she didn't. She felt it, too, this connection between them. Her lips parted ever so slightly and she leaned forward, close enough for him to touch. Close enough for him to take a sip.

The crack of a bat and the crowd cheering snapped his attention away. His head was buzzing as if he'd chugged a six-pack.

"Did they score?" Casey asked, shaking off her

confusion. Then she did lean away, settling back into her chair.

Zeb immediately tamped down that rush of lust. They were in public, for God's sake. This wasn't like him. He didn't go for women like Casey—she was the walking embodiment of a tomboy. Women he favored were cultured and refined, elegant and beautiful. They were everything he'd spent his life trying to become.

Accepted. Welcomed. They belonged in the finest social circles.

Women he liked would never sit on the first-base side and hope to catch a fly ball. They wouldn't appreciate the finer points of an IPA or a lager. They wouldn't be proud of a father who was an electrician and they wouldn't be caught dead in a baseball hat—but Casey?

She was rough-and-tumble and there was a decent chance she could best him in an arm-wrestling contest. There shouldn't have been a single thing about her that he found attractive.

So why couldn't he stop staring at her?

Because he couldn't. "Did you want to try mine? I helped develop it."

He leaned close to her and waited until she held the cup up to his lips. He couldn't tear his gaze away from hers, though. He saw when she sucked in a gasp when he ran his tongue over the rim before he reached up and placed his palm on the bottom of the cup, slowly tilting it back. The bitterness of the brew washed over him.

It wasn't like he'd never had an IPA before. But this was different. He could taste the beer, sure. But there was something about the brightness of the hops, the way it danced on his tongue—it tasted like…

Like her.

"It's really good," he told her. "You developed it?"

"I did. Percheron was, um…"

"It's all right," he said, leaning back. "I don't think if you say Chadwick's name three times, he magically appears. I understand the company's history."

"Oh. Okay." Damn, that blush only made her look prettier. "Well, Percheron was Chadwick's pet project and I'd been there for almost ten years by that point and he let me help. I was the assistant brewmaster for Percheron when he…" Her voice trailed off and she turned to face the field. "When he left."

Zeb mulled that over a bit. "Why didn't you go with him?"

"Because the brewmaster did and Chadwick wanted to actually make the beer himself. Percheron is a much smaller company."

He heard the sorrow in her voice. She'd wanted to go with her old boss—that much was clear.

Then she turned a wide smile in his direction. "Plus, if I'd left the brewery, I'd still be an assistant brewmaster. I'm the brewmaster for the third-largest brewery in the country because I outlasted everyone else. Attrition isn't the best way to get a promotion but it was effective nonetheless."

"That's what you wanted?"

She looked smug, the cat that had all the cream to herself. His pulse picked up another notch. "That's what I wanted."

Underneath that beer-drinking, sports-loving exterior, Zeb had to admire the sheer ambition of this woman. Not just anyone would set out to be the first—or youngest—female brewmaster in the country.

But Casey would. And she'd accomplished her goal.

Zeb took a long drink of his lager. It was good, too. "So, Percheron Drafts was your baby?"

"It was Chadwick's, but I was Igor to his Frankenstein."

He laughed—a deep, long sound that shocked him. That kind of laugh wasn't dignified or intimidating. Zeb didn't allow himself to laugh like that, because he was a CEO and he had to instill fear in the hearts of his enemies.

Except…except he was at a ball game, kicking back with a pretty girl and a beer, and his team was at the plate and the weather was warm and it was…

…perfect.

"So I want you to make Percheron—or something like it—your baby again."

Even though he wasn't looking at Casey, he felt the current of tension pass through her. "What?"

"I understand Chadwick started Percheron Drafts to compete with the explosion of craft breweries. And we lost that. I don't want to throw in that particular towel just yet. So, you want to try experimental beers? That's what I want you to do, too."

She turned to face him again, and dammit, she practically glowed. Maybe it was just the setting sun, but he didn't think so. She looked so happy—and he'd put that look on her face.

"Thank you," she said in a voice so quiet that he had to lean forward to hear it. "When you started, I thought…"

He smirked. She'd thought many things, he'd be willing to bet—and precious few of them had been good.

"Can you keep a secret?" he asked.

Her lips twisted in what he hoped was an amused grin. "How many times are you going to ask me that?"

"I'm not such a bad guy," he went on, ignoring her sass. "But don't tell anyone."

She mimed locking her lips and throwing the key over her shoulder.

Somewhere in the background, a ball game was happening. And he loved sports, he really did. But he had questions. He'd learned a little more about what kind of man his half brother was but that was just the tip of the iceberg.

But the spell of the moment had been broken. They settled in and watched the game. Sure enough, by the third inning, a grizzled older man came around with a stout for Casey. Zeb didn't warrant that level of personal service—certainly not in the opposing team's colors. As he sipped the flagship beer of his second-largest competitor, he decided it was...serviceable. Just as Casey had described their own beer.

A fact that was only highlighted when Casey let him sip her stout. "It's going to be tough to beat," he said with a sigh as she took a long drink.

For the first time, he had a doubt about what he was doing. He'd spent years—*years*—plotting and scheming to get his birthright back. He was a Beaumont and he was going to make sure everyone knew it.

But now, sitting here and drinking his half brother's beer...

He was reminded once again what he didn't have. Chadwick had literally decades to learn about the business of the brewery and the craft of beer. And Zeb—well, he knew a hell of a lot about business. But he hadn't learned it at his father's knee. Beer was his birthright—but he couldn't whip up his own batch if his life depended on it.

Casey patted his arm. "We don't have to beat it." She paused and he heard her clear her throat. "Unless..."

"Unless what?"

She looked into her cup. It was half-empty. "Unless you're out to destroy Percheron Drafts."

That was what she said. What she was really asking was, *Are you out to destroy the other Beaumonts?* It was a fair question.

"Because that's kind of a big thing," she went on in a quiet voice, looking anywhere but at him. "I don't know how many people would be supportive of that. At work, I mean." She grimaced. "There might be a lot of resignations."

She wouldn't be supportive of that. She would quit. She'd quit and go elsewhere because even though her first loyalty was to herself and then the beer, the Beaumont family was pretty high on her list.

Again, he wondered how she'd come to this point in her life. The youngest female brewmaster at the third-largest brewery in the country. He might not know the details of her story, but he recognized this one simple truth: she was who she was in large part because the Beaumonts had given her a chance. Because she'd been Igor to Chadwick Beaumont's Frankenstein.

She'd give up her dream job if it came down to a choice between the Beaumont Brewery and Percheron Drafts.

This thought made him more than a little uncomfortable because he could try to explain how it was all business, how this was a battle for market share between two corporations and corporations were not people, but none of that was entirely true.

If he forced her to choose between the Beaumonts and himself, she'd choose them over him.

"There was a time," he said in a quiet voice, "when I wanted to destroy them."

Her head snapped up. "What?"

"I used to hate them. They had everything and I had nothing." Nothing but a bitter mother and a head for business.

"But…" She stared at him, her mouth open wide. "But *look* at you. You're rich and powerful and hot and you did that all on your own." He blinked at her, but she didn't seem to be aware of what she'd just said, because she went on without missing a beat, "Some of those Beaumonts— I mean, don't get me wrong—I like them. But they're more than a little messed up. Trust me. I was around them long enough to see how the public image wasn't reality. Phillip was a hot mess and Chadwick was miserable and Frances… I mean, they had everything handed to them and it didn't make them any happier." She shook her head and slouched back in her seat.

And suddenly, he felt he had to make her understand that this wasn't about his siblings, because he was an adult and he realized now what he hadn't known as a child—that his siblings were younger than he was and probably knew only what the rest of the world did about Hardwick Beaumont.

"Casey," he said. She looked at him and he could see how nervous she was. "I was going to say that I used to hate them—but I don't. How could I? I don't know them and I doubt any of them knew a thing about me before that press conference. I'm not out to destroy them and I'm not out to destroy Percheron Drafts. It's enough that I have the brewery."

She looked at him then—really looked at him. Zeb started to squirm in his seat, because, honestly? He didn't know what she saw. Did she see a man who made sure his mom had a booming business and his best friend had a good-paying job he loved? Did she see a son who'd never know his father?

Or—worse—would she see a boy rejected by his family, a man who wasn't black and wasn't white but who occupied a no-man's-land in the middle? Would she see an impostor who'd decided he was a Beaumont, regardless of how true it might actually be?

He didn't want to know what she saw. Because quite unexpectedly, Casey Johnson's opinion had become important to him and he didn't want to know if she didn't approve of him.

So he quickly changed the subject. "Tell me..." he said, keeping his voice casual as he turned his attention back to the field. He didn't even know what inning it was anymore. There—the scoreboard said fourth. The home team was at the plate and they already had two outs. Almost halfway done with this corporate outing. "Does that happen often?"

"What? Your boss admitting that he's not a total bastard?"

Zeb choked on his beer. "Actually, I meant that guy proposing to you."

"Who, Marco?" She snorted. "He proposes every time I see him. And since I have season tickets…"

"What does your dad think of that?"

That got him a serious side-eye. "First off, Marco's joking. Second off, my father is many things, but he's not my keeper. And third off—why do you care?"

"I don't," he answered quickly. Maybe too quickly. "Just trying to get a fuller picture of the one person responsible for keeping my company afloat."

She snorted as a pop fly ended the inning. "Come on," she said, standing and stretching. "Let's go."

Slowly, they worked their way out of the seats and back to the concession stands. He got a stout for himself and Casey got a porter. Marco flirted shamelessly but this time, Zeb focused on Casey. She smiled and joked, but at no point did she look at the young man the way she'd looked at him earlier. She didn't blush and she didn't lean toward Marco.

There was no heat. She was exactly as she appeared—a friendly tomboy. The difference between this woman and the one who'd blushed so prettily back in the seats, whose eyes had dilated and who'd leaned toward him with desire writ large on her face—that difference was huge.

With more beer and more nachos, they made their way back to their seats. As odd as it was, Zeb was having trouble remembering the last time he'd taken a night off like this. Yeah, they were still talking beer and competitors but…

But he was having fun. He was three beers in and

even though he wasn't drunk—not even close—he was more relaxed than he'd been in a long time. It'd been months of watching and waiting to make sure all the final pieces of the puzzle were in place, and he was pretty sure he hadn't stopped to appreciate all that he'd accomplished.

Well, sort of relaxed. There was something else the beer vendor—Marco—had said that itched at the back of Zeb's mind.

"Did you mean what you said?" he blurted out. Hmm. Maybe he was a little more buzzed than he thought.

There was a longish pause before she said, "About?"

"That it didn't matter if I was black or not." Because it always mattered. *Always.* He was either "exotic" because he had an African American mother and green eyes or he was black and a borderline thug. He never got to be just a businessman. He was always a black businessman.

It was something white people never even thought about. But he always had that extra hurdle to clear. He didn't get to make mistakes, because even one would be proof that he couldn't cut it.

Not that he was complaining. He'd learned his lesson early in life—no one was going to give him a single damned thing. Not his father, not his family, not the world. Everything he wanted out of this life, he had to take. Being a black businessman made him a tougher negotiator, a sharper investor.

He wanted the brewery and the legitimacy that

came with it. He wanted his father's approval and, short of that, he wanted the extended Beaumont family to know who he was.

He was Zebadiah Richards and he would not be ignored.

Not that Casey was ignoring him. She'd turned to look at him again—and for the second time tonight, he thought she was seeing more than he wanted her to.

Dammit, he should have kept his mouth shut.

"You tell me—does it matter?"

"It shouldn't." More than anything, he wanted it to not matter.

She shrugged. "Then it doesn't."

He should let this go. He had his victory—of sorts—and besides, what did it matter if she looked at him and saw a black CEO or just a CEO?

Or even, a small voice in the back of his mind whispered, *something other than a CEO? Something more?*

But he couldn't revel in his small victory. He needed to know—was she serious or was she paying lip service because he was her boss? "So you're saying it doesn't matter that my mother spent the last thirty-seven years doing hair in a black neighborhood in Atlanta? That I went to a historically black college? That people have pulled out of deals with me because no matter how light skinned I am, I'll never be white enough?"

He hadn't meant to say all of that. But the only

thing worse than his skin color being the first—and
sometimes only—thing people used to define him
was when people tried to explain they didn't "see
color." They meant well—he knew that—but the
truth was, it *did* matter. He'd made his first fortune
for his mother, merchandising a line of weave and
braid products for upper-class African American
consumers that had, thanks to millennials, reached
a small level of crossover success in the mainstream
market. When people said they didn't see color, they
effectively erased the blackness from his life.

Being African American wasn't who he was—but
it was a part of him. And for some reason, he needed
her to understand that.

He had her full attention now. Her gaze swept
over him and he felt his muscles tighten, almost as
if he were in fight-or-flight mode. And he didn't run.
He never ran.

"Will our beer suddenly taste black?" she asked.

"Don't be ridiculous. We might broaden our marketing reach, though."

She tilted her head. "All I care about is the beer."

"Seriously?"

She sighed heavily. "Let me ask you this—when
you drink a Rocky Top beer, does it taste feminine?"

"You're being ridiculous."

That got him a hard glare. A glare he probably deserved, but still. "Zeb, I don't know what you want
me to say here. Of course it matters, because that's
your life. That's who you are. But I can't hold that

against you, and anyway, why would I want to? You didn't ask for that. You can't change that, any more than I can change the fact that my mother died in a car accident when I was two and left me with this," she said, pointing to her scarred cheek, "and my father raised me as best he could—and that meant beer and sports and changing my own oil in my car. We both exist in a space that someone else is always going to say we shouldn't—so what? We're here. We like beer." She grinned hugely at him. "Get used to it."

Everything around him went still. He wasn't breathing. He wasn't sure his heart was even beating. He didn't hear the sounds of the game or the chatter of the fans around them.

His entire world narrowed to her. All he could see and hear and feel—because dammit, she was close enough that their forearms kept touching, their knees bumping—was Casey.

It mattered. *He* mattered. No conditions, no exceptions. He mattered just the way he was.

Had anyone ever said as much to him? Even his own mother? No. What had mattered was what he wasn't. He wasn't a Beaumont. He wasn't legitimate. He wasn't white.

Something in his chest unclenched, something he'd never known he was holding tightly. Something that felt like…

…peace.

He dimly heard a loud crack and then Casey jolted and shouted, "Look out!"

Zeb moved without thinking. He was in a weird space—everything happened as if it were in slow motion. His head turned like he was stuck in molasses, like the baseball was coming directly for him at a snail's pace. He reached out slowly and caught the fly ball a few inches from Casey's shoulder.

The pain of the ball smacking into his palm snapped him out of it. "Damn," he hissed, shaking his hand as a smattering of applause broke out from the crowd. "That hurt."

Casey turned her face toward him, her eyes wide. There was an unfamiliar feeling trying to make its way to the forefront of Zeb's mind as he stared into her beautiful light brown eyes, one he couldn't name. He wasn't sure he wanted to.

"You caught the ball bare-handed," she said, her voice breathy. Then, before Zeb could do anything, she looked down to where he was still holding the foul ball. She moved slowly when she pulled the ball out of his palm and stared at his reddening skin. Lightly, so lightly it almost hurt, she traced her fingertip over the palm of his hand. "Did it hurt?"

That unnamed, unfamiliar feeling was immediately buried under something that was much easier to identify—lust. "Not much," he said, and he didn't miss the way his voice dropped. He had a vague sense that he wasn't being entirely honest—it hurt enough to snap him out of his reverie. But with her stroking his skin…

…everything felt just fine.

And it got a whole lot better when she lifted his hand and pressed a kiss against his palm. "Do we need to go and get some ice or…?"

Or? *Or* sounded good. *Or* sounded great. "Only if you want to," he told her, shifting so that he was cupping her cheek in his hand. "Your call."

Because he wasn't talking about ice. Or beer. Or baseball.

He dragged his thumb over the top of her cheek as she leaned into his touch. She lifted her gaze to his face and for a second, he thought he'd taken it too far. He'd misread the signals and she would storm out of the stadium just like she'd stormed out of his office that first day. She would quit and he would deserve it.

Except she didn't. "I live a block away," she said, and he heard the slightest shiver in her voice, felt a matching shiver in her body. "If that's what you need."

What did he need? It should've been a simple question with a simple answer—her. Right now he needed her.

But there was nothing simple about Casey Johnson and everything got much more complicated when she pressed his hand closer to her cheek.

For the first time in a very long time, Zeb was at a loss for words. It wasn't like him. When it came to women, he'd always known what to say, when to say it. Growing up in a hair salon had given him plenty of opportunity to learn what women wanted, what they needed and where those two things met and when they didn't. *Smooth*, more than one of his paramours had called him. And he was. Smooth and cool and…cold. Distant. Reserved.

He didn't feel any of those things right now. All he could feel was the heat that flowed between her skin and his.

"I need to cool down," he told her, only dimly aware that that was not the smoothest line he had ever uttered. But he didn't have anything else right now. His hand was throbbing and his blood was throbbing and his dick—that, especially, was throbbing. Everything about him was hot and hard, and even though he was no innocent wallflower, it all felt strange and new. He felt strange and new because Casey saw him in a way that no one else did.

He didn't know what was going to happen. Even if all she did was take him back to her place and stick some ice on his hand, that was fine, too. He was not going to be *that* guy.

Still, when she said, "Come with me," Zeb hoped that he could do exactly that.

Eight

Was she seriously doing this? Taking Zeb Richards back to her apartment?

Well, obviously, she was. She was holding his not-wounded hand and leading him away from the stadium. So there really wasn't any question about what was happening here.

This was crazy. Absolutely crazy. She shouldn't be taking him back to her apartment, she shouldn't be holding his hand and she most especially shouldn't be thinking about what would happen when they got there.

But she was. She was thinking about peeling that T-shirt off him and running her hands over his muscles and...

His fingers tightened around hers and he pulled her a step closer to him. He was hot in a way that she hadn't anticipated. Heat radiated off his body, so much so that she thought the edges around his skin might waver like a mirage if she looked at him head-on.

She swallowed and tried to think of things she had done that were crazier than this. Walking into the brewery and demanding a job—that had been pretty bold. And there was that summer fling with a rookie on the Rockies—but he'd been traded to Seattle in the off-season and their paths didn't cross anymore. That had been wild and a hell of a lot of fun.

But nothing came close to bringing the new CEO of the Beaumont Brewery home with her. And the thing was, she wasn't entirely sure what had changed. One moment, they'd been talking—okay, flirting. They'd been flirting. But it seemed…innocent, almost.

And then she had told him about her mom dying in a car accident and he caught that ball before it hit her—she still didn't know how the hell he'd managed that—and everything had changed.

And now she was bringing her boss home with her.

Except that wasn't true, either. It was—but it also wasn't. She wasn't bringing home the ice-cold man in a suit who'd had the sheer nerve to call a press conference and announce that he was one of the Beaumont bastards. That man was fascinating—but that wasn't who was holding her hand.

She was bringing Zeb home. The son of a hairdresser who liked baseball and didn't look at her like she was his best friend or, worse, one of the guys.

She was probably going to regret this. But she didn't care right now. Because Zeb was looking at her and she felt beautiful, sensual, desirable and so very feminine. And that was what she wanted, even if it was for only a little while.

They made it back to her apartment. She led him to the elevator. Even standing here, holding his hand, felt off. This was the part she was never any good at. Sitting in front of the game with beers in their hands—yes. Then she could talk and flirt and be herself. But when she wanted to be that beautiful, desirable creature men craved…she froze up. It was not a pleasant sensation.

The elevator doors opened and they stepped inside. Casey hit the button for the fifth floor and the door slid shut. The next thing she knew, Zeb had pressed into the back of the elevator. His body held hers against the wall—but other than that, he didn't touch her and he didn't kiss her.

"Tell me I didn't read you wrong back there," he said, his voice low and husky. It sent a shiver down her spine and one corner of his mouth curved up into a cocky half smile. He lifted one hand and moved as if he were going to touch her face—but didn't. "Casey…"

This was her out—if she wanted it. She could laugh it off and say, *Gosh, how's your hand?* And that'd be that.

"You didn't," she whispered.

Then he did touch her. He cupped her cheek in his hand and tilted her head up. "Do I really matter to you?" he whispered against her skin. "Or are you just here for the beer?"

If Casey allowed herself to admit that she had thought of this moment before right now—and she wasn't necessarily admitting to anything—she hadn't pictured this. She assumed Zeb would pin her against the wall or his desk and seduce her ruthlessly. Not that there was anything wrong with being seduced ruthlessly—it had its place in the world and her fantasies.

But this tenderness? She didn't quite know what to make of it.

"At work tomorrow," she said, squinting her eyes shut because the last thing she wanted to think about was the number of company policies she was about to break, "it's about the beer." She felt Zeb tense and then there was a little bit of space between their bodies as he stepped away from her.

Oh, no. She wasn't going to let him go. Not when she had him right where she wanted him. She locked her arms around his neck and pulled him back into her. "But we're not at work right now, are we?"

"Right," he agreed. Her body molded to his and his to hers. "Nothing at work. But outside of work…"

Then he kissed her. And that? *That* bordered on a ruthless seduction because it wasn't a gentle, tentative touch of two lips meeting and exploring for the first time. No, when he kissed her, he *claimed* her. The heat from his mouth seared her, and suddenly, she was too hot—for the elevator, for her clothes, for any of it.

"Tell me what you want," he said again when his lips trailed over her jaw and down her neck.

This was crazy—but the very best kind of crazy. Carte blanche with someone as strong and hot and masculine as Zeb Richards? Oh, yeah, this was the stuff of fantasies.

She started to say what she always said. "Tell me—"

Just then, the elevator came to a stop and the door opened. Damn. She'd forgotten they weren't actually in her apartment yet.

Zeb pushed back as she fumbled around for her keys. Hopefully, that would be the last interruption for at least the next hour. Quickly, she led him down the hall. "It's not much," she explained, suddenly nervous all over again. Her studio apartment was certainly not one of the grand old mansions of Denver.

She unlocked the door. Zeb followed her in, and once the door was shut behind them, he put his hands on her hips. "Nice place," he said, and she could tell from the tone of his voice that he wasn't looking at her apartment at all. "Beautiful views," he added, and then he was pulling the hem of her shirt, lifting it until he accidentally knocked her hat off her head. The whole thing got hung up on her ponytail and, laughing, she reached around to help untangle it.

"What would you like me to tell you?" As he spoke, his lips were against the base of her neck, his teeth skimming over her sensitive skin.

She couldn't stop the shiver that went through her. "Tell me…" She opened her mouth to explain that she wanted to feel pretty—but stopped because she couldn't figure out how to say it without sounding lame, desperate even. And besides, wanting to feel pretty—it didn't exactly mesh with her fantasy about a ruthless seduction. So she hedged. She always hedged. "…what you're going to do to me."

In the past, that had worked like a charm. Ask for a little dirty talk? The cocky young men she brought home were always ready and willing.

But Zeb wasn't. Instead, he stood behind her, skimming the tips of his fingers over her shoulders and down her bare back. He didn't even wrench her bra off her, for crying out loud. All he did was… touch her.

Not that she was complaining about being touched. Her eyelids fluttered shut and she leaned into his touch.

"You still haven't told me what you want. I'm more than happy to describe it for you, but I need to know what I should be doing in the first place. For instance…" One hand removed itself from her skin. The next thing she knew, he wrapped her ponytail around his hand and pivoted, bringing her against the small countertop in her kitchen. "I could bend you over and take you hard and fast right here." He pulled her hair just enough that she had to lean back. "And I'd make sure you screamed when you came," he growled as he slipped his hand down over the seam of her jeans. With exquisite precision, he pressed against her most sensitive spot.

"Oh," she gasped, writhing against his hand. Her pulse pounded against where he was touching her and he used her ponytail to tilt her head so he could do more than skim his teeth over her neck. He bit down and, with the smallest movement of his hand, almost brought her to her knees. *"Zeb."*

And then the bastard stopped. "But maybe you don't like it rough," he said in the most casual voice she'd ever heard as he pulled his hands away from her ponytail and her pants. What the hell?

Then his hands were tracing the lines of her shoulders again.

"Maybe you want slow, sensual seduction, where I start kissing here…" he murmured against her neck. Then his lips moved down over her shoulder and he slid his hands up her waist to cup her breasts. "And there."

This time, both hands slid over the front of her jeans and maybe it was shameless, but she arched her back and opened for him. "And everywhere," he finished. "Until you can't take it."

And then he stopped *again*.

What was happening here? Because in the past, when she told someone to talk dirty to her, it got crude *fast*. And it wasn't like the sex was bad—it was good. She liked it. But it felt like...

It always felt like that was the best she could hope for. She wasn't pretty and she wasn't soft and she wasn't feminine, and so crude, fast sex was the best she could expect any man to do when faced with her naked.

And suddenly, she realized that wasn't what she wanted. Not anymore. Not from him.

"Maybe you want to be in charge," he went on, his voice so deep but different, too, because now there was that trace of a Southern accent coming through. It sounded like sin on the wind, that voice—honey sweet with just a hint of danger to it. He spun her around so he was leaning back on the counter and she had him boxed in. He dropped his hands and stared at her hungrily with those beautiful eyes. "Maybe I need to step back and let you show me what you want."

It was an intense feeling, being in Zeb Richards's sights.

"So what's it going to be?" But even as he asked it—sounding cool and calm and in complete control—she saw a muscle in his jaw tic and a tremor pass through his body. His gaze dipped down to her breasts, to her lucky purple bra that she wore to every home game, and a growl that she felt in her very center came rumbling out of his chest. He was hanging on to his control by the very thinnest of threads. Because of her.

He was waiting, she realized. It was her move. So that was what she did. She reached up and pulled his hat off his head and launched it somewhere in the middle of her apartment. He leaned toward her but he didn't touch her.

"What about you? What do you want?" she asked.

He shook his head in mock disappointment even as he smiled slyly at her. "I have this rule—if you don't tell me what you want, I won't give it to you. No mixed signals, no mind reading. I'm not going to guess and risk being wrong."

This wasn't working, she decided. At the very least, it wasn't what she was used to. All this... talking. It wasn't what she was good at. It only highlighted how awkward she was at things like seduction and romance, things that came naturally to other women.

She appreciated the fact that he wanted to be sure about her, about this—really, she did. But she didn't want to think. She didn't want each interaction to be a negotiation. She wanted to be swept away so she could pretend, if only for a little while, that she was soft and sultry and beautiful.

And she'd never get to hold on to that fantasy if she had to explain what she wanted, because explaining would only draw attention to what she wasn't.

Which left only one possible conclusion, really. She was done talking.

She leaned forward and grabbed the hem of his shirt. In one swift motion, she pulled it up and over his head and tossed it on the floor. And right about then, she not only stopped talking but stopped thinking.

Because Zeb's chest was a sight to behold. That T-shirt hadn't been lying. *Muscles*, she thought dimly as she reached out to stroke her hand over one of his packs. So many muscles.

"Casey…" He almost moaned when she skimmed her hand over his bare skin and moved lower. As she palmed the rippling muscles of his abs, he sucked in a breath and gripped the countertop so hard she could see his arms shaking. "You're killing me, woman."

That was better, she decided. She couldn't pull off seductive, but there was a lot to be said for raw sexual energy. That, at least, she could handle.

So she decided to handle it. Personally. She hooked her hands into the waistband of his jeans and pulled his hips toward her. As she did so, she started working at the buttons of his fly. His chest promised great, great things and she wanted to see if the rest of him could deliver on that promise.

"What do you want to hear?" he asked in that low, sensual voice that was summer sex on the wind.

Tell me I'm pretty.

But she couldn't say that, because she knew what would happen. She would ask him to tell her she was pretty and he would. He would probably even make it sound so good that she would believe him. After all, she thought as she pushed his jeans down and cupped him through his boxer briefs, what guy wouldn't find a woman who was about to sleep with him pretty?

She'd been here before, too. She might be pretty enough in the heat of the moment but the second the climactic high began to fade, so did any perceived beauty she possessed. Then she'd get her decidedly unfeminine clothes back on and before she knew it, she'd be one of the boys again.

She didn't just want him to tell her she was pretty or beautiful or sensual or any of those things. She wanted him to make her believe it, all of it, today, tomorrow and into next week, at the very least. And *that* was a trick no one had been able to master yet.

So she gave the waistband of his briefs a tug and freed him. He sprang to attention as a low groan issued from Zeb's throat.

Immediately, her jaw dropped. "Oh, Zeb," she breathed as she wrapped one and then the other hand around his girth, one on top of the other. Slowly, she stroked up the length of him and then back down. Then she looked up at him and caught him watching her. "I am *impressed.*"

He thrust in her hands—but even that was controlled. They were standing in her kitchen, both shirtless, and she was stroking him—and he wasn't even touching her. Sure, the look in his eyes was enough to make her shiver with want because she was having an impact. The cords of his neck tightened and his jaw clenched as his length slid in her grip.

But it wasn't enough. She needed more. "Feel free to join in," she told him.

"You're doing a pretty damn good job all by yourself," he ground out through gritted teeth. But even as he said it, he pried one hand off the countertop and gripped the back of her neck, pulling her into his chest. God, he was almost red-hot to the touch and all she wanted to do was be burned.

"Stop holding back." It came out as an order, but what was she supposed to do? If he was holding back out of some sort of sense of chivalry—however misguided—or consent or whatever, then she needed to get that cleared up right now.

She needed to tell him what she wanted—he'd already told her she had to, right? But she couldn't figure out how to say it without sounding sad about it, so instead, she fell back on the tried-and-true. "You've got what I want," she said as she gave him a firm squeeze. "So show me what you can do with it."

There was just a moment's hesitation—the calm before the storm, she realized. Zeb's eyes darkened and his fingers flexed against the back of her neck.

And then he exploded into movement. Casey was spun around and lifted up onto the countertop, her legs parted as he stepped into her. It happened so fast that she was almost dizzy. And *that* was what she needed right now. She needed his lips on her mouth, her neck, her chest. She needed his fingertips smoothly unhooking her lucky bra and she needed to hear the groan of desire when the bra fell to the ground.

"Damn, Casey—look at you," he said in a tone that was almost reverential.

Casey's eyes drifted shut as he stroked his fingertips over the tops of her breasts and then around her nipples.

"Yes," she whispered as he leaned down to take her in his mouth. His teeth scraped over her sensitive skin and then he sucked on her. "Oh, yes," she hissed, holding him to her.

His hand slid around her back and pulled her to the edge of the counter and then he was grinding against her, his erection hard and hot and everything she wanted—well, almost everything. There was the unfortunate matter of her jeans and the barrier they formed between the two of them.

"This is what you want, isn't it?" Zeb thrust against her. "You want me to take you here, on the countertop, because I can't wait long enough to get you into a bed?"

Every word was punctuated by another thrust. And every thrust was punctuated by a low moan that Casey couldn't have held if she'd tried.

"God, yes," she whimpered as her hips shimmied against his. This was better. Zeb was overpowering her senses, hard and fast. She didn't want to think. She just wanted to feel.

"I wonder," he said in a voice that bordered on ruthless, "if I should bite you here," he said as he traced a pattern on her shoulders with his tongue, "or here—" and he kissed the top of her left breast "—or…here." With that, he crouched down and nipped her inner thigh, and even though she could barely feel his teeth through the denim, she still shuddered with anticipation. This was better. This was things going according to script.

"D, all of the above." It was at that point that she discovered a problem. Zeb wore his hair close-cropped—there was nothing for her to thread her fingers through, nothing for her to hold on to as he rubbed along the seam of her jeans, over her very center.

But her hips bucked when he pressed against her. "Look at you," he growled as he came to his feet. "Just look at you."

She sucked in a ragged gasp when his hands moved and then he was undoing the button of her jeans and sliding down the zipper.

"I'd rather look at you," she told him as she lifted one hip and then the other off the countertop so he could work her jeans down. "You are, hands down, the most gorgeous man I've ever seen."

She let her hands skim over his shoulders and down his arms. It wasn't fair—there wasn't an ounce of fat on him. She was going to have to revise her opinion of men in suits, she thought dimly as he peeled her jeans the rest of the way off her legs.

"I can't wait," he growled in her ear, the raw urgency in his voice sending another shiver of desire through her body. He pulled the thin cotton of her panties to one side and then his erection was grinding directly against her. "Are you on something? Do you have something?"

"I'm on the Pill," she told him, her hips flexing to meet his. In that moment, she did feel desirable and wanted. His finger tested her body and she moaned into him. She might not be sensual or gorgeous, but she could still do this to a man—drive him so crazy with need that he couldn't even wait to get her undressed all the way.

"Now," she told him. "Now, Zeb. Please."

She didn't have to ask twice. He positioned himself at her entrance. "You're so ready for me. God, just look at you." But he didn't thrust into her. Instead, it appeared he was actually going to look at her.

She pushed back against her insecurity as he studied her. She knew she couldn't measure up to his other lovers—a man that looked like him? He could have his pick of women. Hell, she wasn't even sure why he was here with her—except for the fact that she was...well, *available*. "Why are you stopping? Don't stop."

"Is that how you want it? Hard and fast?" Even as he asked, he moved, pushing into her inch by agonizing inch.

"Zeb." Even as she wrapped her legs around his hips and tried to draw him in farther. And when that worked only to a point, she wrapped her arms around his waist and dug her fingernails into his back.

That did the trick. With a roar of desire, he thrust forward and sank all the way into her. Oh, *God*. She took him in easily, moaning with desire. "Is that what you want?"

She heard his self-control hanging by a thread.

So she raked her nails up and down his back— not hard enough to break skin, but more than enough that he could feel it. He withdrew and thrust into her again, this time harder and faster.

"Yes," she whimpered. "More." She leaned her head back, lifting her chest up to him. "I need more."

Without breaking rhythm, he bent down and nipped at her breast again.

"More," she demanded because she was already so, so close. She needed just a little something to push her over the edge.

"I love a woman who knows what she wants." He sucked her nipple into his mouth—hard. There was just a hint of pain around the edges of the plea-sure and it shocked her to her very core in the best way possible.

"Oh, God—" But anything else she would've tried to say got lost as his mouth worked on her and he buried himself in her again and again.

The orgasm snapped back on her like a rubber band pulled too tight, so strong she couldn't even cry out. She couldn't breathe—she couldn't think. All she could do was feel. It was everything she wanted and more. Everything she'd wanted since she'd stormed into his office that very first day and seen him. Ruthless seduction and mind-blowing climaxes and want and need all blended together into mindless pleasure.

Zeb relinquished his hold on her breast and buried his face in her neck, driving in harder and harder. She felt his teeth on her again, just as he promised. And then his hands moved between them and his thumb pressed against her sex as he thrust harder, and this time, Casey did scream. The orgasm shook through her and left her rag-doll limp as he thrust one final time and then froze. His shoulders slumped and he pulled her in close.

"God, Casey…" She took it as a source of personal pride that he sounded shaky. "That was *amazing*."

All she could do was sigh. That was enough. She'd take *amazing* every day of the week.

And then he had to go and ruin it.

He leaned back and shot her a surprised smile and said, "I should have guessed a girl like you would want it hard like that."

She didn't allow herself to be disappointed, because, really, what had she expected? She wasn't pretty or beautiful or sensual or sexy, damn it all. She was fun and cool, maybe, and she was definitely available. But beyond that? She was a good time, but that was it.

So she did what she always did. She put on her

good-time smile and pushed him back so he was forced to withdraw from her body.

"Always happy to be a surprise," she said, inwardly cringing. "If you'll excuse me…"

Then she hurried to the bathroom and shut the door.

Nine

Nine

Jesus, what the hell had just happened? What had he just done?

Zeb looked down at Casey, mostly naked and flushed. Sitting on the edge of her kitchen counter. Staring at him as if she didn't know how they had gotten here.

Well, that made two of them. He felt like he was coming out of a fog—one of the thick ones that didn't just turn the world a ghostly white but blotted out the sun almost completely.

He had just taken her on her countertop. Had there even been any seduction? He tried to think but now that his blood was no longer pounding in his veins, he felt sluggish and stupid, a dull headache building in the back of his head. Hungover—that was how he felt. He didn't feel like he was in control anymore.

And he didn't like that.

He never lost control. *Ever.* He enjoyed women and sex, but this?

"If you'll excuse me," Casey said, hopping off the counter. She notched an eyebrow at him in something that looked like a challenge—but hell if he could figure out what the challenge was.

This was bad. As he watched her walk away, her body naked except for a pair of purple panties that might have matched her bra, his pulse tried to pick up the pace again. He was more than a little tempted to follow her back through her apartment, because if sex in the kitchen had been great, how good would sex in a bed be?

He was horrified to realize that he had not just had this thought but had actually taken two steps after her. He stumbled to a stop and realized that his jeans were still hanging off his butt. He tucked back into his boxer briefs and buttoned up, and the whole time, he tried to form a coherent thought.

What the hell was wrong with him? This wasn't like him. For God's sake—he hadn't even worn a condom. He had a dim recollection—she'd said she was on the Pill, right? How much had he had to drink, anyway? Three beers—that was all.

Even so, he'd done something he associated with getting plastered in a bar—he'd gone home with a woman and had wild, crazy, indiscriminate sex with her.

He scrubbed his hand over his face, but it didn't help. So he went to the sink and splashed cold water on his face. His hand—ostensibly the reason they'd come back to her place—throbbed in pain. He let the cold water run over it.

The indiscriminate sex was bad enough. But worse was that he'd just had sex with his brewmaster. An *employee*. An employee at the Beaumont Brewery, the very company he'd worked years to acquire. A company he was striving to turn around and manage productively.

And he…he couldn't even say he'd fallen into bed with Casey. They hadn't made it that far.

He splashed water on his face again. It didn't help.

He needed to think. He'd just done something he'd never done before and he wasn't sure how to handle it. Sure, he knew that employers and employees carried on affairs all the time. It happened. But it also created a ripple effect of problems. Zeb couldn't count the number of companies he'd bought that could trace their disintegration back to an affair between two adults who should have known better. And until this evening, he'd always been above such baser attractions. *Always.*

But that was before he'd met Casey. With her, he hadn't known better. And, apparently, neither had she.

Zeb found the paper towels and dried off his face. Then he scooped up his shirt and shrugged back into it. He had no idea where his hat had gone, but frankly, that was the least of his problems.

He'd lost control and gotten swept up in the moment with an employee.

It couldn't happen again.

That was the only reasonable conclusion. Yes, the sex had been amazing—but Zeb's position in the brewery and the community at large was tenuous at best. He couldn't jeopardize all of his plans for sex.

Hot, dirty, hard sex. Maybe the best sex he'd ever had. Raw and desperate and...

An involuntary shudder worked through his body. Jesus, what was *wrong* with him?

He heard the bathroom door open from somewhere inside the apartment. He could salvage this situation. He was reasonably sure that, before all the clothes had come off, she'd said...something about work. How they weren't going to do *that* at work. If he was remembering that right, then she also understood the tenuous situation they were in.

So he turned away from the sink to face her and explain, in a calm and rational way, that while what they shared had been lovely, it wasn't going to happen again.

He never got that far.

Because what he saw took his breath away and anything calm and rational was drowned out in a roar of blood rushing through his ears.

Casey had a short silk robe belted around her waist. Her hair was no longer pulled back into a ponytail—instead, it was down. Glorious waves brushed her shoulders and Zeb was almost overwhelmed with the urge to wind his fingers into that hair and pull her close to him again.

Last week, he wouldn't have called her beautiful. She still wasn't, not in the classic way. But right now, with the late-evening light filtering through the windows behind her, lighting her up with a glow, she was...

She was simply the most gorgeous woman he'd ever seen.

He was in so much trouble.

It only got worse when she smiled at him. Not the wide, friendly smile she'd aimed at every single person in the ballpark tonight. No, this was a small movement of the lips—something intimate. Something that was for him and him alone.

And then it was gone. "Can you hand me my bra?" she asked in the same voice she'd used when she'd been joking around with that beer guy.

"Sure," he said. This was good, right? This was exactly what he wanted. He didn't need her suddenly deciding she was in love with him or anything.

"Thanks." She scooped up her shirt and her jeans and disappeared again. "Do you want to try and catch the end of the game?" she called out from somewhere deeper in the apartment. Which was *not* an invitation to join her.

Zeb stood there, blinking. What the hell? Okay, so

he didn't want her to go all mushy on him. But she was acting like what had just happened…

…hadn't. Like they hadn't been flirting all night and hadn't just had some of the best sex of his life.

"Uh…" he said because seriously, what was wrong with him? First he lost control. Then he decided that this had to be a one-time-only thing. Then she appeared to be not only agreeing to the one-time thing but beating him to the punch? And that bothered him? It shouldn't have. It really shouldn't have.

But it did.

"I'll probably head back to the stadium," she said, reappearing and looking exactly the way she had when he'd first laid eyes on her this evening. Her hair was tucked back under her ball cap and she had his red cap in her hands.

It was like he hadn't left a mark on her at all.

But then he saw her swallow as she held his hat out to him. "This, um…this won't affect my job performance," she said with mock bravado.

Strangely, that made him feel better, in a perverse sort of way. He'd made an impact after all.

"It changes nothing," he agreed. He wasn't sure if his lie was any smoother than hers had been. "You're still in charge of the beer and I still want you to come up with a new product line."

And I still want you.

But he didn't say that part, because the signals she was sending out were loud and clear—no more touching. No more wanting.

"Okay. Good. Great." She shot him a wide smile that didn't get anywhere near her eyes.

In all his years, he'd never been in a postsex situation that was even half this awkward. Ever.

"I think I'm going to head home," he said, trying to sound just as cool as she did.

As his words hung in the air between them, something in her eyes changed and he knew that he'd hurt her.

Dammit, that wasn't what he wanted. At the very least, there'd been a moment when she'd made him feel things he hadn't thought he was capable of feeling and the sex had been electric. If nothing else, he was appreciative of those gifts she'd given him. So, even though it probably wasn't the best idea, he stepped into her and laced his fingers with hers.

"Thank you," he said in a low whisper. "I know we can't do this again—but I had a really good time tonight."

"You did?" Clearly, she didn't believe him.

"I did. The ball game and the beer and..." he cleared his throat. *And you.* But he didn't say that. "It was great. All of it." He squeezed her fingers and then, reluctantly, let go and stepped back. It was harder to do than he expected it to be. "I trust this will stay between us?"

That wasn't the right thing to say. But the hell of it was, he wasn't sure what, exactly, the right thing would be. There was no good way out of this.

"Of course," she replied stiffly. "I don't kiss and tell."

"I didn't—" He forced himself to exhale slowly. Attempting to bridge the divide between boss and lover wasn't working and he was better at being the boss anyway. "I look forward to seeing what you come up with," he said as he turned toward the door. "At work," he added stupidly.

"Right. See you at work," she said behind him as he walked out and shut the door behind him.

Just as the door closed, he thought he heard her sigh in what sounded like disappointment.

Well. He'd wondered what she'd seen when she'd looked at him.

He wished now he didn't know the answer.

All told, it could have been worse.

Her team had won and she'd gotten a bobblehead doll for Dad. She'd gotten to drink some Percheron Drafts, which were like memories in a cup. She'd gotten permission to do something similar—new, bold beers that would be hers and hers alone. None of that was bad.

Except for the part where she'd kind of, sort of, slept with her boss. And had some of the most intense orgasms of her life. And…and wanted more. She wanted more with him. More beers at the game, more short walks home, more time exploring his body with hers.

That part was not so good, because she was not going to get more.

Casey made sure to avoid the executive wing of the brewery as much as possible. It wasn't that she was avoiding Zeb, necessarily. She was just really focused on her job.

Okay, that was a total lie because she was avoiding him. But it was easy to do—in addition to overseeing the production lines, she was hiring new people and then training new people and resisting the urge to take a sledgehammer to tank fifteen because that damned piece of machinery had it coming and she had the urge to destroy something.

But underneath all of those everyday thoughts lurked two others that kept her constantly occupied. First, she had to come up with some new beers. She already had a porter in the fermenting tanks—she wanted to start with something that wasn't anywhere close to what the Beaumont Brewery currently had.

And then there was Zeb. He to be avoided at all costs. Besides, it wasn't like she wanted to see him again. She didn't. Really.

Okay, so the orgasms had been amazing. And yes, she'd had fun watching the game with him. And all right, he was simply the most gorgeous man she had ever seen, in or out of a suit.

But that didn't mean she wanted to see him again. Why would she? He had been everything she had expected—handsome, charming, great sex—and exactly nothing more than that.

She wanted him to be different. And he was—there was no argument about that. He was more intelligent, more ambitious and vastly wealthier than any other man she had ever even looked at. And that didn't even include the racial differences.

But she wanted him to be different in other ways, too. She felt stupid because she knew that, on at least one level, this was nothing but her own fault. The man had specifically asked her to tell him what she wanted—and she hadn't. Men, in her long and illustrious experience of being surrounded by them, were not mind readers. Never had been, never would be. So for her to have expected that Zeb would somehow magically guess what she needed was to feel gorgeous and beautiful and sultry—without her telling him—was unfair to both of them.

She didn't understand what was wrong with her. Why couldn't she ask for what she wanted? Why was it so hard to say that she wanted to be seduced with sweet nothings whispered in her ear? That instead of rough and dirty sex all the time, she wanted candlelight and silky negligees and—yes—bottles of champagne instead of beer? She wanted beautiful things. She wanted to *be* beautiful.

Well, one thing was clear. She was never going to get it if she didn't ask for it. Let this be a lesson, she decided. Next time a man said, *Tell me what you want*, she was going to tell him. It would be awkward and weird—but then, so was not getting what she wanted.

Next time, then. Not with her boss.

Casey wasn't sure what she expected from Zeb, but he seemed to be keeping his distance, as well. It wasn't that she wanted flowers or even a sweet little note...

Okay, that was another lie—she totally wanted flowers and the kind of love letter that she could hang on to during the long, dark winter nights. But the risk that came with any of those things showing up on her desk at work was too great. No one had ever sent her flowers at work before. If anything even remotely romantic showed up on her desk, the gossip would be vicious. Everyone would know something was up and there were always those few people in the office who wouldn't rest until they knew what they thought was the truth. And she knew damned well that if they couldn't get to the truth, they'd make up their own.

So it was fine that she avoided Zeb and he avoided her and they both apparently pretended that nothing had happened.

It was a week and a half later when she got the first email from him.

Ms. Johnson,
Status report?

Casey couldn't help but stare at her computer, her lips twisted in a grimace of displeasure. She knew she wasn't the kind of girl who got a lot of romance in her life, but really? He hadn't even signed the email, for God's sake. Four simple words that didn't seem very simple at all.

So she wrote back.

Mr. Richards, I've hired six new employees. Please see attached for their résumés. The new test beers are in process. Tank fifteen is still off-line. Further updates as events warrant.

And because she was still apparently mentally twelve, she didn't sign her email, either.

It was another day before Zeb replied.

Timeline on test beers?

Casey frowned at her email for the second time in as many days. Was he on a strict four-word diet or was she imagining things? This time, she hadn't even gotten the courtesy of a salutation.

This was fine, right? This was maintaining a professional distance with no repercussions from their one indiscretion.

Didn't feel any less awkward, though.

Still testing, she wrote back. It's going to be another few weeks before I know if I have anything.

The next day she got an even shorter email from him.

Status report?

Two words. Two stinking words and they drove her nuts. She was half-tempted to ask one of the other department heads if they got the same terse emails every day or so—but she didn't want to draw any attention to her relationship with Zeb, especially if that wasn't how he treated his other employees.

It was clear that he regretted their evening. In all reality, she should have been thankful she still had her job, because so far, she hadn't managed to handle herself as a professional around him yet. She was either yelling at him or throwing herself at him. Neither was good.

So she replied to his two-word emails that came every other day with the briefest summary she could.

Test beers still fermenting. Tank fifteen still not working. Hired a new employee—another woman.

But...

There were days when she looked at those short messages and wondered if maybe he wasn't asking something else. All she ever told him about was the beer. What if he was really asking about her?

What if *Status report?* was his really terrible way of asking, *How are you?*

What if he thought about her like she thought about him? Did he lie awake at night, remembering the feel of her hands on his body, like she remembered his? Did he think about the way he had fit against her, in her? Did he toss and turn until the frustration was too much and he had to take himself in hand—just like she had to stroke herself until a pale imitation of the climax he'd given her took the edge off?

Ridiculous, she decided. Of course he wasn't thinking about her. He'd made his position clear. They'd had a good time together once and once was enough. That was just how this went. She knew that. She was fun for a little while, but she was not the kind of woman men could see themselves in a relationship with. And to think that such a thing might be percolating just under the surface of the world's shortest emails was delusional at best. To convince herself that Zeb might actually care for her was nothing but heartache waiting to happen.

So she kept her mouth shut and went about her job, training her new employees, trying to beat tank fifteen into submission and tinkering with her new recipes. She caught evening games with her dad and added to her bobblehead collection and did her best to forget about one evening of wild abandon in Zeb Richards's arms.

Everything had gone back to normal.

Oh, no.

Casey stared down at the pack of birth control pills with a dawning sense of horror. Something was wrong. She hadn't been paying attention—but she was at the end of this pack. Which meant that five days ago, she should've started her period. What the hell? Why had she skipped her period?

This was *not* normal. She was regular. That was one of the advantages of being on the Pill. No surprises. No missed periods. No heart attacks at six fifty in the morning before she'd even had her coffee, for crying out loud.

In a moment of terror, she tried to recall—she hadn't skipped a dose. She had programmed a reminder into her phone. The reminder went off ten minutes after her alarm so she took a pill at exactly the same time every single day. She hadn't been sick—no antibiotics to screw with her system. Plus, she'd been on this brand for about a year.

Okay, so… She hadn't exactly had a lot of sex in the last year. Actually, now that she thought about it, there hadn't been anyone since that ballplayer a year and a half ago.

Unexpectedly, her stomach rolled and even though she hadn't had breakfast or her coffee, she raced for the bathroom. Which only made her more nervous. Was she barfing because she was panicking or was this morning sickness? Good Lord.

What if this was morning sickness?

Oh, God—what if she was…?

No, she couldn't even think it. Because if she was…

Oh, God.

What was she going to do?

Ten

"Anything else?" Zeb asked Daniel.

Daniel shook his head. "The sooner we know what the new beers are going to be, the sooner we'll be able to get started on the marketing."

Zeb nodded. "I've been getting regular status updates from Casey, but I'll check in with her again."

Which wasn't exactly the truth. He had been asking for regular status updates, and like a good employee, Casey had been replying to him. The emails were short and getting shorter all the time. He was pretty sure that the last one had been two words. Nothing yet. He could almost hear her sneering them. And he could definitely hear her going, *What do you want from me?*

Truthfully, he wasn't sure. Each time he sent her an email asking for a status report, he wondered if maybe he shouldn't do something else. Ask her how she was doing, ask if things were better now that she'd hired new people.

Ask her if she'd been to many more baseball games. If she'd caught any more foul balls.

He wanted to know if she ever thought of him outside the context of beer and the brewery. If he ever drifted through her dreams like she did his.

"Well, let me know. If you thought it would help," Daniel said as he stood and began to gather his things, "I could go talk to her about the production schedule myself."

"No," Zeb said too quickly. Daniel paused and shot him a hard look. "I mean, that won't be necessary. Your time is too valuable."

For a long, painful moment, Daniel didn't say anything. "Is there something I need to know?" he asked in a voice that was too silky for its own good.

God, no. No one needed to know about that moment of insanity that still haunted him. "Absolutely not."

It was clear that Daniel didn't buy this—but he also decided not to press it. "If it becomes something I need to know about, you'll tell me, right?"

Zeb knew that Daniel had been a political consultant, even something of a fixer—more than willing to roll around in the mud if it meant getting his opponent dirty, too. The thought of Daniel doing any digging into Casey's life made Zeb more than a little uncomfortable. Plus, he had no desire to give Daniel anything he could hold over Zeb's head. This was clearly one case where sharing was not caring, brotherly bonds of love be damned.

"Certainly," Zeb said with confidence because he was certain this was not a situation Daniel needed to know anything about. His one moment of indiscretion would remain just that—a moment.

"Right," Daniel said. With that, he turned and walked out of the office.

Zeb did the same thing he'd been doing for weeks now—he sent a short email to Casey asking for a status report.

She was exactly as she had been before their indiscretion. Terse and borderline snippy, but she got the job done and done well. He had been at the brewery for only about five weeks. And in that short amount of time, Casey had already managed to goose production up by another five hundred gallons. Imagine what she could do if she ever figured out the mystery that was apparently tank fifteen.

Then, just like he did every time he thought about Casey and the night that hadn't been a date, he forced himself to stop thinking about her. Really, it shouldn't have been this hard to *not* think about her. Maybe it was the brewery, he reasoned. For so long, taking his rightful place as the CEO of the Beaumont Brewery had occupied his every waking thought. And now he'd achieved that goal. Clearly, his mind was just at…loose ends. That was all.

This did not explain why when his intercom buzzed, he was pricing tickets to the next Rockies home game. The seats directly behind Casey's were available.

"Mr. Richards?" Delores's voice crackled over the old-fashioned speaker.

"Yes?" He quickly closed the browser tab.

"Ms. Johnson is here." There was a bit of mumbling in the background that he didn't understand. "She says she has a status report for you."

Well. This was something new. It had been—what—a little over three weeks since he'd last seen her? And also, she had waited to be announced by Delores? That wasn't like her. The Casey Johnson he knew would have stormed into this office and caught him looking at baseball tickets. She would've known exactly what he was thinking, too.

So something was off. "Send her in." And then he braced for the worst.

Had she gotten another job? And if so…

If she didn't work for him anymore, would it be unethical to ask her out?

He didn't get any further than that in his thinking, because the door opened and she walked in. Zeb stood, but instantly, he could see that something was wrong. Instead of the sweaty hot mess that she frequently was during work hours, she looked pale. Her eyes were huge and for some reason, he thought she looked scared. What the hell was she scared of? Not him, that much he knew. She had never once been scared of him. And it couldn't be the last email he'd sent, either. There hadn't been anything unusual about that—it was the same basic email he'd been sending for weeks now.

"What's wrong?" He said the moment the door shut behind her.

She didn't answer right away.

"Casey?" He came out from around the desk and began to walk to her.

"I have…" Her voice shook and it just worried him all the more. She swallowed and tried again. "I have a status report for you."

She was starting to freak him out. "Is everything okay? Was there an on-the-job accident?" He tried to smile. "Did tank fifteen finally blow up?"

She tried to smile, too. He felt the blood drain out of his face at the sight of that awful grimace.

"No," she said in a voice that was a pale imitation of her normal tone. "That's not what I have a status report about."

Okay. Good. Nothing had happened on the line. "Is this about the beers?"

She shook her head, a small movement. "They're still in process. I think the porter is going to be really good."

"Excellent." He waited because there had to be a reason she was here. "Was there something else?"

Her eyes got even wider. She swallowed again. "I—"

And then the worst thing that could have possibly happened did—she squeezed her eyes shut tight and a single tear trickled down her left cheek.

It was physically painful to watch that tear. He wanted to go to her and pull her into his arms and promise that whatever had happened, he'd take care of it.

But they were at work and Delores was sitting just a few feet away. So he pushed his instincts aside. He was her boss. Nothing more. "Yes?"

The seconds ticked by while he waited. It wasn't like whatever she was trying to tell him was the end of the world, was it?

And then it was.

"I'm pregnant," she said in a shattered voice.

He couldn't even blink as his brain tried to process what she had just said. "Pregnant?" he asked as if he had never heard the word before.

She nodded. "I don't understand… I mean, I'm on the Pill—or I was. I didn't miss any. This isn't supposed to happen." Her chin quivered and another tear spilled over and ran down the side of her face.

Pregnant. She was pregnant. "And I'm the…" He couldn't even say it. *Hell*.

She nodded again. "I hadn't been with anyone in over a year." She looked up at him. "You believe me, right?"

He didn't want to. The entire thing was unbelievable.

What the hell did he know about fatherhood?

Nothing, that's what. Not a single damned thing. He'd been raised by a single mother, by a collective of women in a beauty shop. His male role models had been few and far between.

He wasn't going to be a father. Not on purpose and not by accident.

In that moment, another flash of anger hit him— but not at her. He was furious with himself. He never lost control. He never got so carried away with a woman that he couldn't even make sure that he followed the basic protocols of birth control. Except for one time.

And one time was all it took, apparently.

"You're sure?" Because this was the sort of thing that one needed to be sure about.

She nodded again. "I realized yesterday morning that I was at the end of my month of pills and I hadn't had my…" She blushed. Somehow, in the midst of a discussion about one-night stands and pregnancy, she still had the ability to look innocent. "After work yesterday, I bought a test. It was positive." Her voice cracked on that last, important word.

Positive.

Of all the words in the English language that had the potential to change his life, he had never figured *positive* would be the one to actually do it.

"We…" He cleared his throat. *We.* There was now a *we.* "We can't talk about this. Here." He looked around the office—his father's office. The man who had gotten his mother pregnant and paid her to leave town. "During work hours."

She looked ill. "Right. Sorry. I didn't mean to use work hours for personal business."

Dimly, he was glad to see that she still had her attitude. "We'll…we'll meet. Tonight. I can come to you."

"No," she said quickly.

"Right." She didn't want him back in her apartment, where he'd gotten carried away and gotten her into this mess. He wanted to use a less painful word—*situation*, *predicament*—but this was a straight-up mess. "Come to my place. At seven." She already knew where he lived. Hell, her father had done work in his house at some point.

"I don't… Jamal," she said weakly.

"Come on, Casey. We have to have this conversation somewhere and I'm sure as hell not going to have it in public. Not when you look like you're about to start sobbing and I can't even think straight."

Her eyes narrowed and he instantly regretted his words. "Of course. It's unfortunate that this upsets me," she said in a voice that could freeze fire.

"That's not what I—"

She held up her hand. "Fine. Seven, your place." She gave him a hard look—which was undercut by her scrubbing at her face with the heel of her hand. "All I ask is that you not have Jamal around." She turned and began to walk out of his office.

For some reason, he couldn't let her go. "Casey?"

She paused, her hand on the doorknob. But she didn't turn around. "What?"

"Thank you for telling me. I'm sure we can work something out."

She glanced back at him, disappointment all over her face. "Work something out," she murmured. "Well. I guess we know what kind of Beaumont you are."

Before Zeb could ask her what the hell she meant by that, she was gone.

Eleven

"Hey, baby boy."

At the sound of his mother's voice, something unclenched in Zeb's chest. He'd screwed up—but he knew it'd work out. "Hey, Mom. Sorry to interrupt you."

"You've been quiet out there," she scolded. "Those Beaumonts giving you any trouble?"

"No." The silence had been deafening, almost. But he couldn't think about that other family right now. "It's just been busy. Taking over the company is a massive undertaking." Which was the truth. Taking over the Beaumont Brewery was easily the hardest thing he'd ever done. No, right now he had to focus on his own family. "Mom…"

She was instantly on high alert. "What's wrong?"

There wasn't a good way to have this conversation. "I'm going to be a father."

Emily Richards was hard to stun. She'd heard it all, done it all—but for a long moment, she was shocked into silence. "A baby? I'm going to be a *grandma*?"

"Yeah." Zeb dropped his head into his hands. He hadn't wanted to tell her—but he'd needed to.

This was history repeating itself. "Just like my old man, huh?"

He expected her to go off on Hardwick Beaumont, that lying, cheating bastard who'd left her high and dry. But she didn't. "You gonna buy this girl off?"

"Of course not, Mom. Come on." He didn't know what to do—but he knew what he didn't want to happen. And he didn't want to put Casey aside or buy her off.

"Are you going to take this baby away from her?"

"That's not funny." But he knew she wasn't joking. Hardwick had either paid off his babies' mothers or married and divorced them, always keeping custody.

"Baby boy…" She sighed, a sound that was disappointment and hope all together. "I want to know my grandbaby—and her mother." Zeb couldn't think of what to say. He couldn't think, period. His mother went on, "Be better than your father, Zeb. I think you know what you need to do."

Which was how Zeb wound up at a jewelry store.

He couldn't hope to make sense of what Casey had told him that morning but he knew enough to realize that he hadn't handled himself well.

Actually, no, that was letting himself off easy. In reality, he hadn't handled himself well since...the ball game. If he had realized that her getting pregnant was a legitimate outcome instead of a distant possibility...

He wanted to think that he wouldn't have slept with her. But at the very least, he wouldn't have walked out of her apartment with that disappointed sigh of hers lingering in his ears.

He'd hurt her then. He'd pissed her off today. He might not be an expert in women, but even he knew that the best solution here was diamonds.

The logic was sound. However, the fact that the diamonds he was looking at were set into engagement rings...

He was going to be a father. This thought kept coming back to him over and over again. What did he know about being a father? Nothing.

His own father had paid his mother to make sure that he never had to look at Zeb and acknowledge him as a son. Hardwick Beaumont might have been a brilliant businessman, but there was no way around the obvious fact that he'd been a terrible person. Or maybe he'd been a paragon of virtue in every area of his life except when it came to his mistresses— Emily Richards and Daniel's mother and CJ's and

God only knew how many mothers of other illegitimate children.

"Let me see that one," he said to the clerk behind the counter, pointing to a huge pear-cut diamond with smaller diamonds set in the band.

Because this was where he'd come to in his life. He was going to be a father. He'd made that choice when he'd slept with Casey. Now he had to take responsibility.

He did not want to be a father like Hardwick had been. Zeb didn't want to hide any kid of his away, denying him his birthright. If he had a child, he was going to claim that child. He was going to fight for that child, damn it all, just like his father should have fought for him. His mother wanted to know her grandbaby.

He didn't want to have to fight Casey, though. Because the simplest way to stay in his child's life was to marry the mother.

Because, really, what were the alternatives?

He could struggle through custody agreements and legal arrangements—all of which would be fodder for gossip rags. He could pretend he hadn't slept with his brewmaster and put his own child through the special kind of hell that was a childhood divorced from half his heritage. He could do what Hardwick had done and cut a check to ensure his kid was well cared for—and nothing more.

Or he could ask Casey to marry him. Tonight. It

would be sudden and out of left field and she might very well say no.

Married. He'd never seen himself married. But then, he'd never seen himself as a father, either. One fifteen-minute conversation this afternoon and suddenly he was an entirely different person, one he wasn't sure he recognized. He stared at the engagement ring, but he was seeing a life where he and Casey were tied together both by a child and by law.

No, not just that. By more than that. There was more between them than just a baby. So much more.

He'd spend his days with her watching baseball and discussing beer and—hopefully—having great sex. And the kid—he knew Casey would be good with the kid. She'd be the kind of mom who went to practices and games. She'd be fun, hands-on.

As for Zeb…

Well, he had two different businesses to run. He had to work. He'd made a fortune—but fortunes could be lost as fast as they'd been made. He'd seen it happen. And he couldn't let it happen to him. More than that, he couldn't let it happen to Casey. To their family.

He had to take care of them. Hardwick Beaumont had cut Emily Richards a check and the money had been enough to take care of him when he'd been a baby—but it hadn't lasted forever. His mother had needed to work to make ends meet. She'd worked days, nights, weekends.

There had been times when Zeb wondered if she

was avoiding him. Emily Richards had always been happy to foist child care off on the other stylists and the customers. No one minded, but there'd been times he'd just wanted his mom and she'd been too busy.

He couldn't fault her drive. She was a self-made woman. But she'd put her business ahead of him, her own son. Even now, Zeb had trouble talking to her without feeling like he was imposing upon her time.

He didn't want that for his child. He wanted more for his family. He didn't want his baby's mother to miss out on all the little things that made up a childhood. He didn't want to miss them, either—but not only was the brewery his legacy, it would be his child's, as well. He *couldn't* let the brewery slide.

He'd work hard, as he always had. But he would be there. Part of his child's life. Maybe every once in a while, he'd even make it for a game or a play or whatever kids did in school. And he'd have Casey by his side.

"I'll take it," he said, even though he wasn't sure what he was looking at anymore. But he'd take that life, with Casey and their child.

"It's a beautiful piece." A deep voice came from his side.

Zeb snapped out of his reverie and turned to find himself face-to-face with none other than Chadwick Beaumont. For a long moment, Zeb did nothing but stare. It wasn't like looking in a mirror. Chadwick was white, with sandy blond hair that he wore a little long and floppy. But despite that, there were things Zeb recognized—the jawline and the eyes.

Zeb's green eyes had marked him as different in the African American community. But here? Here, standing with this man he had never seen up close before, his eyes marked him as something else. They marked him as one of the Beaumonts.

Chadwick stuck out his hand. "I'm Chadwick."

"Zeb," he said, operating on autopilot as his hand went out to give Chadwick's a firm shake. "And who's this?" he asked, trying to smile at the little girl Chadwick was holding.

"This is my daughter, Catherine."

Zeb studied the little girl. She couldn't be more than a year and a half old. "Hi there, Catherine," he said softly. He looked at Chadwick. "I didn't realize I was an uncle." The idea seemed so foreign to him that it was almost unrecognizable.

The little girl turned her face away and into Chadwick's neck—then, a second later, she turned back, peeking at Zeb through thick lashes.

"You are—Byron has two children. Technically, Catherine is my wife's daughter from a previous relationship. But I've adopted her." Chadwick patted his daughter on her back. "I found that, when it comes to being a Beaumont, it's best to embrace a flexible definition of the word *family*."

An awkward silence grew between them because Zeb didn't quite know what to say to that. He'd always thought that, at some point, he would confront the Beaumonts. In his mind's eye, the confrontation was not nearly this...polite. There wouldn't be any chitchat. He would revel in what he had done, taking the company away from them and punishing them for failing to acknowledge him and they would...cower or beg for forgiveness. Or something.

There was a part of him that still wanted that—but not in the middle of a high-end jewelry store and not in front of a toddler.

So instead, he didn't say anything. He had no idea what he was even supposed to say as he looked at this man who shared his eyes.

Suddenly, Zeb desperately wanted to know what kind of man this brother of his was. More specifically, he wanted to know what kind of man Casey thought Chadwick was. Because Zeb still didn't know if he was like his father or his brother and he needed to know.

"Who's the lucky woman?" Chadwick asked.

"Excuse me?"

Just then the clerk came back with the small bag that held an engagement ring. Chadwick smiled. "The ring. Anyone I know?"

It took a lot to make Zeb blush, but right then his face got hot. Instead of responding, he went on the offensive. "What about you?"

Chadwick smiled again, but this time it softened everything about his face. Zeb recognized that look—and it only got stronger when Chadwick leaned down and pressed a kiss to the top of his daughter's head. It was the look of love. "My wife is expecting again and the pregnancy has been…tiring. I'm picking her up something because, really, there's nothing else I can do and diamonds tend to make everything better. Wouldn't you agree?"

"Congratulations," Zeb said automatically. But he didn't tell this man that he'd had the exact same thought. He only hoped he wasn't wrong about the diamonds.

"Will there be anything else?" The clerk asked in a super-perky voice.

Zeb and Chadwick turned to see her looking at them with bright eyes and a wide smile. Crap. He needed to have a conversation with Chadwick— even if he wasn't exactly sure what the conversation should be about. But it couldn't happen here. How much longer before someone put two and two together and there were cameras or news crews and reporters or cell-phone-toting gossipmongers crowding them? Zeb didn't want to deal with it himself— he couldn't imagine that Chadwick wanted to put his daughter through it, either.

"No," he said just as another clerk approached and handed a small bag to Chadwick.

"Your necklace, Mr. Beaumont," the second clerk said. She and the first clerk stood elbow to elbow, grinning like loons.

They had to get out of here right now. "Would you like to…" *continue this conversation elsewhere?* But he didn't even get that far before Chadwick gave a quick nod of his head.

Both men picked up their small bags and headed out of the store. When they were safely away from the eager clerks, Zeb bit the bullet and asked first. "Would you like to go get a drink or something?"

"I wish I could," Chadwick said in a regretful voice. "But I don't think any conversation we have should be in public. And besides," he went on, switching his daughter to his other arm, "we probably only have another half an hour before we have a meltdown."

"Sure," Zeb said, trying to keep the disappointment out of his voice.

Chadwick stopped, which made Zeb stop, too. "You want answers." It was not a question.

Yes. "I don't want to intrude on your family time."

Chadwick stared at Zeb for a moment longer and his face cracked with the biggest smile that Zeb had ever seen. "You *are* family, Zeb."

That simple statement made Zeb feel as if someone had just gut-shot him. It took everything he had not to double over. This man considered *him* family? There was such a sense of relief that appeared out of nowhere—

But at the same time, Zeb was angry. If he was family, why hadn't Chadwick seen fit to inform him of that before now? Why had he waited until a chance meeting in a jewelry store, for God's sake?

Chadwick's eyes cut behind Zeb's shoulder. "We

need to keep moving." He began walking again and Zeb had no choice but to follow. They headed out toward the parking lot.

Finally, Zeb asked, "How long have you known? About me, I mean."

"About six years. After my…" He winced. "I mean *our* father—"

Zeb cut him off. "He wasn't my father. Not really."

Chadwick nodded. "After Hardwick died," he went on diplomatically, "it took me a while to stabilize the company and get my bearings. I'd always heard rumors about other children and when I finally got to the point where I had a handle on the situation, I hired an investigator."

"Did you know about Daniel before the press conference?"

Chadwick nodded. "And Carlos."

That brought Zeb up short. CJ was not as unfindable as he liked to think he was. "He prefers CJ."

Chadwick smirked. "Duly noted. And of course, we already knew about Matthew. There was actually a bit of a break after that. I don't know if Hardwick got tired of paying off his mistresses or what."

"Are there more of us? Because I could only find the other two."

Chadwick nodded again. "There are a few that are still kids. The youngest is thirteen. I'm in contact with his mother, but she has decided that she's not interested in introducing her son to the family. I provide a monthly stipend—basically, I pay child support for the other three children." They reached a fancy SUV with darkened windows. "It seems like the least I can do, after everything Hardwick did." He opened up the back door and slid his daughter into the seat.

As he buckled in the little girl, Zeb stared at Chadwick in openmouthed shock. "You...you pay child support? For your half siblings?"

"They are family," Chadwick said simply as he clicked the buckle on the child seat. He straightened and turned to face Zeb. But he didn't add anything else. He just waited.

Family. It was such an odd concept to him. He had a family—his mother and the larger community that had orbited around her salon. He had Jamal. And now, whether she liked it or not, he had Casey, too.

"Why didn't you contact me?" He had so many questions, but that one was first. Chadwick was taking care of the other bastards. Why not him?

"By the time I found you, we were both in our thirties. You'd built up your business on your own, and at the time, I didn't think you wanted anything to do with us." Chadwick shrugged. "I didn't realize until later how wrong I was."

"What kind of man was he?" Zeb asked. And he felt wrong, somehow, asking it—but he needed to know. He was getting a very good idea of what kind of man Chadwick was—loyal, dependable, the kind of man who would pay child support for his siblings because they were family, whether they liked it or not. The kind of man who not only cared about his wife but bought her diamonds because she was tired. The kind of man who knew how to put his own daughter into a safety seat.

Zeb knew he couldn't be like Chadwick, but he was beginning to understand what Casey meant when she asked if Zeb was like his brother.

Chadwick sighed and looked up at the sky. It was getting late, but the sun was still bright. "Why don't you come back to the house? This isn't the sort of thing that we can discuss in a parking lot."

Zeb just stared at the man. His brother. Chadwick had made the offer casually, as if it were truly no big deal. Zeb was family and family should come home and have a beer. Simple.

But it wasn't. Nothing about this was simple.

Zeb held up his small jewelry bag with the engagement ring that he somehow had to convince Casey to wear. "I have something to do at seven." He braced himself for Chadwick to ask about who the lucky woman was again, but the question didn't come.

Instead, Chadwick answered Zeb's earlier question. "Hardwick Beaumont..." He sighed and closed the door, as if he were trying to shield his daughter from the truth. "He was a man of contradictions— but then again, I'm sure we all are." He paused. "He was... For me, he was hard. He was a hard man. He was a perfectionist and when I couldn't give him perfection..." Chadwick grimaced.

"Was he violent?"

"He could be. But I think that was just with me, because I was his heir. He ignored Phillip almost completely, but then Frances—his first daughter— he spoiled her in every sense of the word." Chadwick tried to smile, but it looked like a thing of pain. "You asked me why I hadn't contacted you earlier—well, the truth is, I think I was a little jealous of you."

"What?" Surely, Zeb hadn't heard correctly. Surely, his brother, the heir of the Beaumont fortune, had not just said that he was—

"Jealous," Chadwick confirmed. "I'm not exaggerating when I say that Hardwick screwed us all up. I..." He took a deep breath and stared up at the night sky again. "He was my father, so I couldn't hate him, but I don't think I loved him, either. And I don't think he loved us. Certainly not me. So when I found out about you and the others, how you'd spent your whole lives without Hardwick standing over you, threatening and occasionally hitting you, I was jealous. You managed to make yourself into a respected businessman on your own. You did what you wanted— not what *he* wanted. It's taken me most of my life to separate out what I want from what he demanded."

Zeb was having trouble processing this information. "And I spent years trying to get what you have," he said, feeling numb. Years of believing that he had been cut out of his rightful place next to Hardwick Beaumont. It had never occurred to him that perhaps he didn't want to be next to Hardwick Beaumont.

Because he could see in Chadwick's eyes that this was the truth. His father had been a terrible man. Sure, Zeb had known that—a good man did not buy off his mistress and send her packing. A good man did not pretend like he didn't have multiple children hidden away. A good man took care of his family, no matter what.

Zeb suddenly had no idea if he was a good man or not. He took care of his mother, even when she drove him nuts, and he looked out for Jamal, the closest thing he'd had to a brother growing up.

But the Beaumonts were his family, too. Instead of looking out for them, he'd done everything he could to undermine them.

He realized Chadwick was staring. "I'm sorry," Chadwick said quickly. "You look like him."

Zeb snorted. "I look like my mother."

"I know." Chadwick moved a hand, as if he were going to pat Zeb on the shoulder—but he didn't. Instead, he dropped his arm back to his side. Then he waited. Zeb appreciated the silence while he tried to put his thoughts in order.

He knew he was running out of time. Chadwick's daughter would sit quietly for only so long—either that, or someone with a camera would show up. But he had so many questions. And he wasn't even sure that the answers would make it better.

For the first time in his life, he wasn't sure that knowing more was a good thing.

"I don't know how much of it was PR," Chadwick

suddenly began. "But the press conference was brilliant and I wanted to let you know that we're glad to see that the brewery is back in family hands."

Really? But Zeb didn't let his surprise at this statement show. "We're still competitors," he replied. "Casey is formulating a line of beers to compete directly with Percheron Drafts as we speak."

Chadwick notched an eyebrow at him. "She'll be brilliant at it," he said, but with more caution in his voice. Too late, Zeb realized that he had spoken of her with too much familiarity. "And I expect nothing less—from both of you."

Inside the car, the little girl fussed. "I have to get going," Chadwick said, and this time, he did clap Zeb on the shoulder. "Come to the house sometime. We'll have dinner. Serena would love to meet you."

Zeb assumed that was Chadwick's wife. "What about the rest of your brothers and sisters?"

"You mean *our* brothers and sisters. They're… curious, shall we say. But getting all of us together in one room can be overwhelming. Besides, Serena was my executive assistant at the brewery. She knows almost as much about the place as I do."

Zeb stared at him. "You married your assistant?" Because that seemed odd, somehow. This seemed like something their father would've done. Well, maybe not the marrying part.

Had his brother gotten his assistant pregnant and then married her? Was history repeating itself? Was

it possible for history to repeat itself even if Zeb
hadn't known what that history was?

Chadwick gave him a look that might've intimidated a lesser man. But not Zeb. "I try not to be my
father," he said in a voice that was colder than Zeb
had heard yet. "But it seemed to be a family trait—
falling for our employees. I married my assistant.
Phillip married a horse trainer he hired. Frances married the last CEO of the brewery."

Oh, God. Had he somehow managed to turn into
his father without ever even knowing a single thing
about the man? He had gotten Casey pregnant because when he was around her, he couldn't help himself. She'd taken all of his prized control and blown
it to smithereens, just as if she'd been blowing foam
off a beer.

"Hardwick Beaumont is dead," Chadwick said
with finality. "He doesn't have any more power over
me, over any of us." He looked down at the small
bag Zeb still clutched in his hand. "We are known
for our control—both having it and losing it. But it's
not the control that defines us. It's how we deal with
the consequences."

Inside the car, the toddler started to cry in earnest.
"Come by sometime," Chadwick said as he stuck out
his hand. "I look forward to seeing how you turn the
brewery around."

"I will," Zeb said as they shook hands.

"If you have any other questions, just ask."

Zeb nodded and stood aside as Chadwick got

into his vehicle and drove away—back to the family home, to his assistant and their children. Back to where he could be his own man, without having to prove anything to his father ever again.

Hardwick Beaumont was dead. Suddenly, years of plotting and planning, watching and waiting for an opportunity to take revenge against the Beaumonts—was it all for nothing?

Because Zeb wasn't sure he wanted revenge—not on his brothers. Not anymore. How could he? If they'd known of him for only six years—hell, six years ago, Zeb had been just moving to New York, just taking ZOLA to the next level. What would he have done, six years ago? He wouldn't have given up ZOLA. He would've been suspicious of any overtures that Chadwick might've made. He wouldn't have wanted to put himself in a position where any Beaumont had power over him. And then he wouldn't have been in a position to take the brewery back from the corporation that bought it.

And now? Now Chadwick wanted him to succeed? Even though they were competitors—and nowhere near friends—he hoped that Zeb would turn the brewery around?

It was damned hard to get revenge against a dead man. And Zeb wasn't sure he wanted revenge against the living.

He looked down at the small bag with an engagement ring in it.

What did he want?

Twelve

What did she want?

Casey had been asking herself that exact question for hours now. And the answer hadn't changed much.

She had no idea.

Well, that wasn't entirely the truth. What she wanted was… God, it sounded so silly, even in her head. But she wanted something romantic to happen. The hell of it was, she didn't know exactly what that was. She wanted Zeb to pull her into his arms and promise that everything was going to be all right. And not just the general promise, either. She wanted specific promises. He was going to take care of her and the baby. He was going to be a good father. He was going to be…

Seriously, they didn't have a whole lot of a relationship here. She didn't even know if she wanted to have a relationship—beyond the one that centered around a child, of course. Sometimes she did and sometimes she didn't. He was so gorgeous—too gorgeous. Zeb wasn't the kind of guy she normally went for; he was cool and smooth. Plus, he was a Beaumont. As a collective, they weren't known for being the most faithful of husbands.

That was unfair to Chadwick. But it wasn't unfair enough to Hardwick.

Fidelity aside, she had absolutely no idea if Zeb could be the kind of father she wanted her child to have. It wasn't that her own father, Carl Johnson, was perfect—he wasn't. But he cared. He had *always* cared for Casey, fighting for her and protecting her and encouraging her to do things that other people wouldn't have supported.

That was what she wanted. She wanted to do that for her and for this child.

Based on Zeb's reaction in the office earlier? She didn't have a lot of faith.

Casey had not been the best of friends with Chadwick Beaumont. They had been coworkers who got along well, and he'd never seen her as anything more than one of the guys. Which was fine. But she knew all of the office gossip—he had fallen in love with his assistant just as Serena Chase had gotten pregnant with someone else's baby. He had given up the company for her and adopted the baby girl as his own. Hell, even Ethan Logan—who had not understood a damned thing about beer—had given up the company for Frances Beaumont because they'd fallen in love.

Zeb's entire reason for being in Denver was the brewery.

Besides, she didn't want him to give it up. In fact, she preferred not to give it up, either. She had no idea what the company's maternity-leave policy looked like, though. She didn't know if Larry could handle the production lines while she was away. And after the leave was over, she didn't know how she would be a working mother with a newborn.

She didn't know if she would have to make it work herself or if she'd have help. And she still didn't know what she wanted that help to look like. But she didn't want to give up her job. She'd worked years to earn her place at the brewery's table. She loved being a brewmaster. It was who she was.

She was running a little bit late by the time she made it to the mansion where Zeb had set up shop. As she got out of her car, she realized her hands were shaking. Okay, everything was shaking. Was it too early to start blaming things on hormones? God, she had no idea. She hadn't spent a lot of time around babies and small children growing up. Other girls got jobs as babysitters. She went to work as an electrical assistant for her father. Small children were a mystery to her.

Oh, God. And now she was going to have one.

Stuck in this tornado of thoughts, she rang the bell. She knew she needed to tell Zeb what she wanted. Hadn't she resolved that she was going to do better at that? Okay, that resolution had been specifically about sex—but the concept held. Men were not mind readers. She needed to tell him what she wanted to happen here.

All she had to do in the next thirty seconds was figure out what that was.

It wasn't even thirty seconds before the door opened and there stood Zeb, looking nothing like the CEO she'd seen in the office just a few hours ago. But he didn't look like the sports fan that she'd gone on an almost date with, either. He was something in the middle. His loose-fitting black T-shirt hinted at his muscles, instead of clinging to them. It made him look softer. Easier to be around. God, how she needed him to be easier right now.

"Hi," she croaked. She cleared her throat and tried to smile.

"Come in," he said in a gentle voice. Which was, all things considered, a step up from this morning's reaction.

He shut the door behind her and then led her through the house. It was massive, a maze of rooms and parlors and stairs. He led her to a room that could best be described as a study—floor-to-ceiling bookcases, a plush Persian rug, heavy leather furniture and a fireplace. It was ornate, in a manly sort of way. And, thankfully, it was empty.

Zeb shut the door behind her and then they were alone. She couldn't bring herself to sit—she had too much nervous energy. She forced herself to stand in the middle of the room. "This is nice."

"Jamal can take the credit." Zeb gave her a long look and then he walked toward her. She hadn't actually seen him for several weeks—outside of this morning, of course. Was it possible she had forgotten how intense it was being in Zeb Richards's sights? "How are you?" he asked as he got near.

"Well, I'm pregnant."

He took another step closer and she tensed. Right about now it would be great if she could figure out what she wanted. "I don't mean this to sound callous," he said, lifting his hands in what looked a hell of a lot like surrender, "but I thought you said you were on the Pill?"

"I am. I mean, I was. I diagnosed myself via the internet—these things can…happen. It's something called breakthrough ovulation, apparently." He was another step closer and even though neither of them were making any broad declarations of love, her body was responding to his nearness all the same.

She could feel a prickle of heat starting low on her back and working its way up to her neck. Her cheeks were flushing and, God help her, all she wanted was for him to wrap his arms around her and tell her that everything was going to be all right.

And then, amazingly, that was exactly what happened. Zeb reached her and folded his strong arms around her and pulled her against the muscles of his chest and held her. "These things just happen, huh?"

With a sigh, she sank into his arms. This probably wasn't a good idea. But then, anything involving her touching Zeb Richards was probably a bad idea. Because once she started touching him, it was just too damn hard to stop. "Yeah."

"I'm sorry it happened to you."

She needed to hear that—but what killed her was the sincerity in his voice. Her eyes began to water. Oh, no—she didn't want to cry. She wasn't a crier. Really. She was definitely going to blame that one on the hormones.

"What are we going to do?" she asked. "I haven't seen you in weeks. We had one almost date and everything about it was great except that it ended… awkwardly. And since then…"

"Since then," he said as she could feel his voice rumbling deep out of his chest. It shouldn't have been soothing, dammit. She wanted to keep her wits about her, but he was lulling her into a sense of warmth and security. "Since then I've thought of you constantly. I wanted to see you but I got the feeling you might not have reciprocated that desire."

What? "Is that why you've been sending me emails every day?" She leaned back and looked up at him. "Asking for status reports?"

Oh, God, that blush was going to be the death of her. If there was one thing she knew, it was that an adorable Zeb Richards was an irresistible Zeb Richards. "You said at work that it was all about the beer. So I was trying to keep it professional."

Even as he said it, though, he was backing her up until they reached one of the overstuffed leather couches. Then he was pulling her down onto his lap and curling his arms around her and holding her tight. "But we're not at work right now, are we?"

She sighed into him. "No, we're not. We can't even claim that this is a corporate outing."

He chuckled and ran his hand up and down her back. She leaned into his touch because it was what she wanted. And she hadn't even had to ask for it. She let herself relax into him and wrapped her arms around his neck. "What are we going to do, Zeb?"

His hand kept moving up and down and he began rubbing his other hand along the side of her thigh. "I'm going to take care of you," he said, his voice soft and close to her ear.

God, it was what she needed to hear. She knew she was strong and independent. She lived her life on her own terms. She'd gotten the job she wanted and a nice place close to the ballpark. She paid her bills on time and managed to sock some away for retirement.

But this? Suddenly, her life was not exactly her own anymore and she didn't know how to deal with it.

"There's something between us," Zeb said, his breath caressing her cheek. She turned her face toward him. "I feel it. When I'm around you…" He cupped her face in his hands. "I could fall for you."

Her heart began to pound. "I feel it, too," she whispered, her lips moving against his. "I'm not supposed to go for someone like you. You're my boss and everything about this is wrong. So why can't I help myself?"

"I don't know. But I don't think I want you to."

And then he was kissing her. Unlike the first time, which had been hurried and frantic, this was everything she dreamed a kiss could be. Slowly, his lips moved over hers as he kissed the corner of her mouth and then ran his tongue along her lower lip.

If she'd been able to help herself, she wouldn't have opened her lips for him, wouldn't have drawn his tongue into her mouth, wouldn't have run her hands over his hair. If she'd been able to help herself at all, she wouldn't have moaned into his mouth when he nipped at her lip, her neck, her earlobe.

"I want you in a bed this time," he said when she skimmed her hands over his chest and went to grab the hem of his shirt. "I want to strip you bare and lay you out and I want to show you exactly what I can do for you."

"Yes," she gasped. And then she gasped again when he stood, lifting her in his arms as if she weighed next to nothing.

"Casey," he said as he stood there, holding her. His gaze stroked over her face. "Have I ever told you how beautiful you are?"

Thirteen

Whatever he'd just said, he needed to make sure he said it again. Often.

Because suddenly, Casey was all over him. She kissed him with so much passion he almost had to sit down on the couch again so he could strip her shirt off her and sink into her soft body and…

He slammed on the brakes. That wasn't what he'd promised her. Bed. He needed to get to a bed. And at the rate they were going, he needed to get there quickly.

It would be so tempting to get lost in her body. She had that ability, to make him lose himself. But it was different now. Everything was different. She was carrying his child. This wasn't about mindless pleasure, not anymore.

It wasn't like he wanted to be thinking about Chadwick Beaumont right now, but even as he carried Casey out of the office and up the wide staircase to his suite of rooms, he couldn't stop replaying some of the things his brother had said.

Casey took Zeb's hard-won control and blew it to smithereens, but that wasn't what made him a Beaumont. It was what he did after that.

He could turn her away. He could set her up with a monthly stipend and let her raise their child, just as Chadwick was doing with some of their half siblings.

But that was what his father would do. And Zeb knew now that he did not want to be like that man. And what was more, he didn't *have* to be like his father. He wasn't sure he could be as selfless as his brother was—but he didn't have to be that way, either.

He could be something else. Someone else. Someone who was both a Beaumont *and* a Richards.

A sense of rightness filled him. It was right that he take Casey to bed—a real bed this time. It was right that he make love to her tonight, tomorrow— maybe even for the rest of their lives. It was right that he become a part of the Beaumont family by *making* himself a part of it—both by finally taking his place as the head of the brewery and by starting his own family.

It was right to be here with Casey. To marry her and take care of her and their baby.

He kicked open the door to a suite of rooms and

carried her through. Why was this house so damned big? Because he had to pass through another room and a half before he even got anywhere near his bed and each step was agony. He was rock hard and she was warm and soft against him and all he wanted to do was bury himself in her again and again.

Finally, he made it to his bed. Carefully, he set her down on top of the covers. He was burning for her as he lowered himself down on top of her—gently, this time. He knew that just because she was a few weeks along, didn't mean she was now some impossibly fragile, delicate flower who would snap if he looked at her wrong. But he wanted to treat her with care.

So, carefully, he slipped her T-shirt over her head. He smiled down at her plain beige bra. "No purple today?"

"I didn't wear my lucky bra, because I didn't think I was going to get lucky," she said in a husky voice. This time, when she grabbed at the hem of his shirt, he didn't stop her.

He wanted to take this slow, but when she ran her hands over his chest, her fingernails lightly grazing his nipples, she took what little self-control he had left and blew it away. Suddenly, he was undoing her jeans and yanking them off and she was grabbing his and trying to push them off his hips.

"Zeb…" she said, and he heard the need for him in her voice.

His blood was pounding in his veins—and other places—but he had to prove to her that he could be good for her. So instead of falling into her body, he knelt in front of the bed and, grabbing her by the hips, pulled her to the edge of it.

"I'm going to take care of you," he promised. He had never meant the words more than he did right now.

Last time, he hadn't even gotten her panties off her. Last time, he'd been more than a little selfish. This time, however, it was all about her.

He lowered his mouth to her sex and was rewarded as a ripple of tension moved through her body.

"Oh," she gasped as he spread her wide and kissed her again and again.

With each touch, her body spasmed around him. She ran her hand over his hair, heightening his awareness. Everything was about her. All he could see and taste and touch and smell and hear was her. Her sweetness was on his tongue and her moans were in his ears and her soft skin was under his hands.

Last time, he hadn't done this—taking the time to learn her. But this time? Every touch, every sigh, was a lesson—one he committed to memory.

This was right. The connection he felt with her— because that was what it was, a connection—it was something he'd never had before. He'd spent the last three weeks trying to ignore it, but he was done with that. He wasn't going to lie to himself anymore.

He wanted her. And by God, he was going to have her.

He slipped a finger inside her and her hips came off the bed as she cried out. "Zeb!"

"Let me show you what I can do for you," he murmured against her skin. "God, Casey—you're so beautiful."

"Yes, yes—don't stop!"

So he didn't. He stroked his tongue over her sex and his fingers into her body and told her again and again how beautiful she was, how good she felt around him. And the whole time, he got harder and harder until he wasn't sure he could make it. He needed her to let go so that he could let go.

Finally, he put his teeth against her sex—just a small nip, not a true bite. But that was what it took. Something a little bit raw and a little bit hard in the middle of something slow and sensual. She needed both.

Luckily, he could give her that. He could give her anything she wanted.

Her body tensed around him and her back came off the bed as the orgasm moved through her. Even he couldn't hold himself back anymore. The last of his control snapped and he let it carry him as he surged up onto the bed, between her legs. "You are so beautiful when you come," he said as he joined his body to hers.

Everything else fell away. His messy family history and their jobs, baseball and status reports—none of that mattered. All that mattered was that Casey was here with him and there was something between them and they couldn't fight it. Not anymore.

She cried out again as a second orgasm took her and he couldn't hold back anything else. His own climax took him and he slammed his mouth down over hers. If this was the rest of his life, he could be a happy man.

Suddenly exhausted, he collapsed onto her. She wrapped her arms around his back and held him to her. "Wow, Zeb," she murmured in his ear.

"I forgot to ask about birth control that time." She laughed at that, which made him smile. He managed to prop himself up on his elbows to look down at her. "Casey—" he said, but then he stopped because he suddenly realized he was about to tell her that he thought he was in love with her.

She stroked her fingertips over his cheek. "That…" she said, and he could hear the happiness in her voice. "That was everything I have ever dreamed." There was a pause. "And maybe a few things I hadn't thought of yet."

It was his turn to laugh. "Just think, after we're married, we get to do that every night." He withdrew from her body and rolled to the side, pulling her into his arms.

"What?" She didn't curl up in his arms like he thought she would.

"I'm going to take care of you," he told her again, pulling her into him. "I didn't have the chance to tell you, but I ran into Chadwick this afternoon and talking with him cleared up a couple of things for me."

"It…did?"

"It did. You've asked me if I'm like my father or my brother and I didn't know either of them. I only knew what was public knowledge. I knew that my father was not a good man, because he paid my mother to disappear. And I knew that everyone at the brewery liked Chadwick. But that didn't tell me what I needed to know."

"What did you need to know?" Her voice sounded oddly distant. Maybe she was tired from the sex?

That he could understand. His own eyelids were drifting shut but he forced himself to think for a bit longer. "When you asked me which one I was like, you were really asking me if I could be a good man. And not just a good man—a good man for you. I understand what that means now. You need someone who's loyal, who will take care of you and our child. You need someone who appreciates you the way you are."

Then she did curl into him. She slung her arm around his waist and held him tight. "Yes," she whispered against skin. "Yes, that's what I need."

"And that's what I want to give you." He disentangled himself long enough to reach over the side of the bed and retrieve his pants. He pulled out the small velvet-covered box with the ring inside. "I want to marry you and take care of you and our baby together. You won't have to struggle with being a single mother or worrying about making ends meet—I'll take care of all of that."

She stared at the box. "How do you mean?"

Was it his imagination or did she sound cautious? They were past that. He was all in. This was the right thing to do. He was stepping up and taking care of his own—her and their child.

"Obviously, we can't keep working together and you're going to need to take it easy. And your apartment was cute, but it's not big enough for the three of us." He hugged her. "I know I haven't talked about my childhood a lot—it was fine, but it was rough, too. My mom—she worked all the time and I basically lived at the salon, with a whole gaggle of employees watching over me. All I knew was that my dad didn't want me and my mom was working. And I don't want that kind of life for our baby. I don't want us to pass the baby off to employees or strangers. I want us to do this right."

"But…but I have to work, Zeb."

"No, you don't—don't you see? We'll get married and you can stay home—here. I'll take care of everything. We can be a family. And I can get to know Chadwick and his family—my family, I mean. All of the Beaumonts. I don't have to show them that I'm better than them. Because I think maybe…" He sighed. "Maybe they're going to accept me just the way I am, too."

He still couldn't believe that was possible. His whole life, he'd never felt completely secure in his own skin. He was either too light or too black, stuck in a no-man's-land in between.

But here in Denver? Chadwick wished him well and had invited him to be part of the family. And all Casey cared about was that he accepted her the exact same way he wanted to be accepted.

Finally, he had come home.

He opened the box and took the ring out. "Marry me, Casey. I know it's quick but I think it's the right thing."

She sat up and stared at him. "Wait— I— *Wait.*"

He looked at her, confused. "What?"

A look of dawning horror crossed over her face— a look that was not what any man wanted to see after sex that good and a heartfelt offer of marriage. "You want to marry me so I can stay home and raise our kid?"

"Well…yes. I don't want to be the kind of father my own father was. I want to be part of my kid's life. I want to be part of your life. And I don't want you to struggle like my mom did. You mean too much to me to let that happen."

And then, suddenly, she was moving. She rolled out of the bed and away from him, gathering up her clothes.

"Are you serious?" she said, and he heard a decided note of panic in her voice. "That's not what I want."

"What do you mean, it's not what you want? I

thought we agreed—there was something between us and you're pregnant and this makes sense."

"This does *not* make sense," she said as she angrily jabbed her legs into her jeans. "I am not about to quit my job so I can stay home and raise your baby."

"Casey—wait!" But she was already through the first door. She didn't even have a shirt on yet. She was running away as fast as she could.

Zeb threw himself out of bed, the engagement ring still in his hand. "Casey!" he called after her. "Talk to me, dammit. What is your problem here? I thought this would work. There's something here and I don't want to let that go." Unless…

Something new occurred to him. She had given him every indication that she wanted the baby, even if it was unexpected. But what if…?

What if she didn't? What if she didn't want to read stories at night and teach their kid how to ride a bike or throw a baseball? What if she didn't want to be the hands-on mom he'd imagined, coaching T-ball and playing in the park? The kind of mother he didn't have.

What if she was going to be like his mother— distant and reserved and…*bitter* about an unplanned pregnancy?

She swung around on him, her eyes blazing. "You don't know what you're talking about," she shot at him. The words sliced through the air like bullets out of a gun. "I don't want to quit my job. I've never wanted to be a stay-at-home mom."

"But you can't keep working," he told her, pushing against the rising panic in his chest. "You shouldn't have to."

That was the wrong thing to say. "I don't *have* to do anything I don't want to do. After I have this baby, I'm going to need help. If you think I'm going to give up my job and my life and fit myself into your world just because I'm pregnant with your baby, you've got another think coming."

She spun again and stalked away from him. "Casey!" He sprinted after her and managed to catch up to her—but only because she was trying to get her shirt on. "I'm trying to do the right thing here."

He was horrified to see tears spill over her eyelids. "Is this how it's going to be? Every time we're together, you make me feel so good—and then you ruin it. You just ruin it, Zeb." She scrubbed her hand across her face. "You'll be all perfect and then you'll be a total jerk."

What the hell was she talking about? "I'm trying not to be a jerk. I thought a marriage proposal and a commitment was the right thing to do. Obviously, we can't keep working together, because we can't keep our hands off each other." Her cheeks blushed a furious red. But then again, everything about her was furious right now. "So this is the obvious solution. I'm *not* going to raise a bastard. You *are* going to marry me. We *will* raise our child together and, damn it all, we *will* be a happy family. Unless..." He swallowed. "Unless you don't want me?"

She looked at him like he was stupid. Happiness seemed a long way off. She hadn't even put her bra on—it was hanging from her hand.

"You are trying so hard not to be like your father—but this? Telling me what I want? Telling me what I'm going to do without giving me an option? You're essentially firing me. You're going to put me in this house and make me completely dependent upon you. You're going to hide me away here under the pretense of taking care of me because you somehow think that's going to absolve you of any guilt you feel. And that?" She jabbed at his chest with a finger. "That is *exactly* what your father would've done."

Her words hit him like a sledgehammer to the chest, so hard that he physically stumbled backward.

"I am not trying to hide anyone away. I'm not ashamed of you!" He realized too late he was shouting but he couldn't stop. "I just want my kid to have something I didn't—two loving parents who give a damn about whether he lives or dies!"

Her face softened—but only a little bit. She still looked fierce and when she spoke, it was in a low voice that somehow hurt all the more. "I am your brewmaster and I might be the mother of your child. I care about this baby and I could care very much for you—but not if you're going to spend the rest of our lives ordering me about. I am not your underling, Zeb. You don't get to decide that what you *think* you want is the same thing that I need. Because I'm only going to say this once. I'm sorry you had a miserable childhood. But it had nothing—not a damn thing—to do with the fact that you were raised by a single parent." A tear trickled down the side of her face and she scrubbed it away. "Don't you dare act like you're the only one raised by a single parent who had to work and sacrifice to survive."

"I never said that." But too late, he remembered her telling him how her mother had died in a car accident when she was two.

"Didn't you?" She moved in closer, and for a delusional second, he thought all was forgiven when she leaned in to kiss his cheek. But then she stepped back. "I give a damn, Zeb. Never think I don't. But I won't let your fears dictate my life."

She stepped around him, and this time, he didn't pull her back. He couldn't. Because he had the awful feeling that she might be right.

The door shut behind her, but he just stood there. Numbly, he looked down at the diamond ring in his hand. His father wouldn't have committed to the rest of his life with a woman he had gotten pregnant—he knew that.

But everything else?

He knew so little and the thing was, he wasn't sure he wanted to know more. He didn't know exactly what had happened between his parents. He couldn't be sure what made his mother the most bitter—the fact that Hardwick Beaumont had cast her aside? Or had it been something else? Had he forced her out of the company? Made her leave town and go back to Atlanta?

Why was this even a question? Hardwick had been married to a wealthy and powerful woman in her own right. Zeb was only four months younger than Chadwick. Of course Hardwick would've done everything within his power to hide Emily and Zeb.

And Zeb's mother…had she resented him? He was a living reminder of her great mistake—undeniable with his father's green eyes. Maybe she hadn't been able to love Zeb enough. And maybe—just maybe—that wasn't his fault.

Fourteen

She couldn't do this. Hell, at this point, she wasn't even sure what "this" was.

Could she be with Zeb? Could they have a relationship? Or would it always devolve into awful awkwardness? Could she work with him or was that impossible? If she didn't work at the brewery, what was she going to do?

It was hard enough to be a woman and a brewmaster. It wasn't like there were tons of jobs ripe for the picking at breweries conveniently located near her apartment. Plus, she was kind of pregnant. How was she supposed to interview at companies that might or might not exist and then ask for maternity leave after only a month or two on the job?

The entire situation was ridiculous. And she couldn't even think the whole thing over while drinking a bottle of beer. Somehow, that was the straw that was going to break her back. How was she going to brew beer without testing it?

There was a possible solution—she could go to Chadwick. He'd find a place for her at Percheron Drafts, she was pretty sure. And at least in the past, he had demonstrated a willingness to work around maternity leave. He knew what she was capable of, and frankly, his was the only brewery within the area that wouldn't force her to relocate. Plus...her child would be a Beaumont. Sort of. Chadwick would be her baby's uncle and the man was nothing if not loyal to the family name.

But even just thinking about going to Chadwick felt wrong. She wasn't six, running to her father to tattle. She was a grown woman. She'd gotten herself into this mess and she had to get herself out of it.

The worst part was, Zeb had been right. There *was* something between them. There had been since the very first moment she had walked into his office and locked eyes with him. There was chemistry and raw sexual attraction and the sex was amazing. And when he was doing everything right, he was practically...perfect.

But when he wasn't perfect, he *really* wasn't perfect.

Instead of going back to her apartment, Casey found herself heading toward her father's small ranch house in Brentwood. She'd grown up in this little house, and at one time, it had seemed like a mansion to her. She hadn't ever wanted to live in a real mansion. She didn't need to be surrounded by all the trappings of luxury—and she also did not need a diamond that probably cost more than a year's salary on her finger.

Instead, she wanted what she'd had growing up. A father who doted on her, who taught her how to do things like change a tire and throw a baseball and brew beer. A father who protected her.

She hadn't grown up with all the luxuries that money could buy. But she'd been happy. Was it wrong to want that? Was it wrong to *demand* that?

No. It wasn't. So that wasn't the right question.

The bigger question was, could she demand that of Zeb?

She was happy to see that the lights were on at home. Sometimes a girl needed her father. She walked in the house, feeling a little bit like a teenager who had stayed out past curfew and was about to get in trouble. "Daddy?"

"In the kitchen," he called back.

Casey smiled at that. Any other parent who was in the kitchen might reasonably be expected to be cooking. But not Carl Johnson. She knew without even seeing it that he had something taken apart on the kitchen table—a lamp or doorbell, something.

True to form, a chandelier was sitting in the middle of the table, wires strung everywhere.

The chandelier was a piece of work—cut crystal prisms caught the light and made it look like the room was glowing. It belonged in a mansion like Zeb's. Here, in her father's house, it looked horribly out of place. She knew the feeling.

It was such a comforting thing, sitting at this table while her father tinkered with this or that. Casey slid into her old seat. "How are you doing, Daddy?"

"Pretty good. How are you?" He looked at her and paused. "Honey? Is everything okay?"

No. Things were not all right and she wasn't sure how to fix them. "I think I've made a mistake."

He rested his hand on her shoulder. "Are you in trouble? You know I don't like you living in that apartment by yourself. There's still plenty of room for you here."

She smiled weakly at him. "It's not that. But I… I did something stupid and now I think I've messed everything up."

"Does this have something to do with work?" When Casey didn't reply immediately, her dad pressed on. "This is about your new boss?"

There was no good way to say this. "Yeah, it does. I'm… I'm pregnant."

Her father stiffened, his grip on her shoulder tight before he quickly released her. "Them Beaumonts— I never did trust them. Are you okay? Did he hurt you?"

Casey slumped forward, head in her hands and her elbows on the table. "No, it's not like that, Dad. I *like* him. He likes me. But I'm not sure that that's going to be enough." She looked at her father. He looked skeptical. "He asked me to marry him."

Her father sat straight up. "He did? Well, I guess that's the right thing to do—better than what his old man would've done." There was a long pause during which Casey went back to slumping against her hands. "Do you want to get married? Because you don't have to do anything you don't want to, honey."

"I don't know what to do. When he asked me, he made it clear that he expected me to quit my job and stay home and be a mother full-time." She sighed. It wasn't only that, though.

No, the thing that really bothered her had been the implication that she, Casey Johnson, wasn't good enough to be the mother to his child as she was. Instead, she needed to become someone else. The perfect mother. And what the hell did she know about mothering? Nothing. She'd never had one.

"And that's not what I want. I fought hard to get my job, Dad. And I like brewing beer. I don't want to throw that all away because of one mistake. But if I don't marry him, how am I going to keep working at the brewery?" Her father opened his mouth, but she cut him off. "And no, I don't think asking Chadwick for a job is the best solution, either. I have no desire to be the rope in Beaumont tug-of-war."

They sat quietly for a few moments, but it wasn't long until her father had picked up a few pieces of wire. He began stripping them in an absentminded sort of way. "This guy—"

"Zeb. Zeb Richards."

Another piece of copper shone in the light. "This Zeb—he's one of them Beaumont bastards, right?" Casey nodded. "And he offered to marry you so his kid wouldn't be a bastard like he was?"

"Yeah. I just… I just don't want that to be the only reason. I mean, I can see he's trying to do the right thing, but if I get married, I'd kind of like it to be for love."

Her dad nodded and continued to strip the wire. "I wish your mom were here," he said in an offhand way. "I don't know what to tell you, honey. But I will say this. Your mom and I got married because we had to."

"What?" Casey shot straight up in her chair and stared at him. Her father was blushing. Oh, *Lord*.

"I never told you about this, because it didn't seem right. We'd been dating around and she got pregnant and I asked her to marry me. I hadn't before then, because I wasn't sure I wanted to settle down, but with you on the way, I grew up—fast."

She gaped at him. "I had no idea, Dad."

"I didn't want you to think you were a mistake, honey. Because you are the best thing that's ever happened to me." His eyes shone and he cleared his throat a few times—all while still stripping wire. "Anyway, that first year—that was rough. We had to learn how to talk to each other, how to live together.

But you were born, and suddenly, everything about us just made more sense. And then when the accident came…" He shuddered. "The reason I'm telling you this," he went on in a more serious voice, as if he hadn't just announced that she was a surprise, "is that sometimes love comes a little later. If you guys like each other and you both want this kid, maybe you should think about it." He put down his wire trimmers and rested a hand on hers. "The most important thing is that you two talk to each other."

She felt awful because, well, there hadn't been a lot of talk. She'd gone over to his place tonight to do just that, and instead, they'd fallen into bed.

The one time she had sat down and had a conversation with the man had been at the ball game. She had liked him a great deal then—more than enough to bring him home with her. Maybe they could make this work.

No matter what Zeb had said, they didn't have to get married. Times had changed and her dad wasn't about to bust out a shotgun to escort them down the aisle.

She wasn't opposed to getting married. She didn't have anything against marriage. She just… Well, she didn't want their marriage to be on his terms only.

She knew who she was. She was a woman in her early thirties, unexpectedly pregnant. But she was also a huge sports fan. She could rewire a house. She brewed beer and changed her own oil.

She was never going to be a perfect stay-at-home

mom, baking cookies and wearing pearls and lunching with ladies. That wasn't who she was.

If Zeb wanted to marry her and raise their child as a family, then not only did he have to accept that she was going to do things differently, but he was going to have to support her. Encourage her.

That did not mean taking her job away under the pretext of taking care of her. That meant helping her find a way to work at the job she loved *and* raise a happy, healthy child.

She wanted it all.

And by God, it was all or nothing.

But men—even men as powerful as Zebadiah Richards—were not mind readers. She knew that. Hell, she was *living* that.

She needed to tell him what she wanted. Without falling into bed with him and without it devolving into awkward awfulness.

"I sure am sorry, honey," her dad went on. "I'd love to be a grandfather—but I hate that this has put you in an awkward position." He gave her fingers a squeeze. "You know that, no matter what you decide, I'll be here to back you up."

She leaned in to her dad's shoulder and he wrapped his arms around her and hugged her. "I know, Daddy. I appreciate it."

"Tell you what," Dad said when she straightened up. "Tomorrow's Friday, right? And the Rockies play a game at three. Why don't you play hooky tomorrow? Stay here with me tonight. We'll make a day of it."

She knew that this was not a solution in any way, shape or form. At some point, she was going to have to sit down with Zeb and hash out what, exactly, they were going to do.

Soon. Next week, she'd be an adult again. She would deal with this unexpected pregnancy with maturity and wisdom. Eventually, she needed to talk with Zeb.

But for right now, she needed to be the girl she'd always been.

Sometimes, fathers did know best.

Fifteen

"Where is she?"

The man Zeb had stopped—middle-aged, pot-bellied... He knew that he'd been introduced to this man before. Larry? Lance? Something like that. It wasn't important.

What was important was finding Casey.

"She's not here," the man said, his chins wobbling dangerously.

Zeb supposed he should be thankful that, since Casey was one of exactly two women in the production department, everyone knew which "she" he was talking about.

"Yes, I can see that. What I want to know," he said

slowly and carefully, which caused all the blood to drain out of the guy's face, "is where she is now."

It wasn't fair to terrorize employees like this, but dammit, Zeb needed to talk to Casey. She had stormed out of his house last night and by the time he'd gotten dressed, she had disappeared. She hadn't been at her apartment—the security guy said he hadn't seen her. In desperation, Zeb had even stopped by the brewery, just to make sure she wasn't tinkering with her brews. But the place had been quiet and the night shift swore she hadn't been in.

Her office was just as dark this morning. He didn't know where she was and he was past worrying and headed straight for full-on panic.

Which meant that he was currently scaring the hell out of one of his employees. He stared at the man, willing himself not to shake the guy. "Well?"

"She said she wouldn't be in today."

Zeb took a deep breath and forced himself to remain calm. "Do you have any idea where she might be?"

He must not have been doing a good job at the whole "calm" thing, because his employee backed up another step. "Sometimes she takes off in the afternoon to go to a game. With her dad. But you wouldn't fire her for that, right?" The man straightened his shoulders and approximated a stern look. "I don't think you should."

The game. Of course—why hadn't Zeb thought of that? She had season tickets, right? She'd be at the game. The relief was so strong it almost buckled his knees.

"No, I'm not going to fire her," he assured the guy. "Thanks for the tip, though. And keep up the good work."

On the walk back to his office, he called up the time for the baseball game. Three o'clock—that wasn't her taking the afternoon off. That was her taking the whole day. Had he upset her so much that she couldn't even face him? It wasn't like her to avoid a confrontation, after all.

What a mess. His attempt at a marriage proposal last night had not been his best work. But then, he had no experience proposing marriage while his brain was still fogged over from an amazing climax. He didn't have any experience in proposing marriage at all.

That was the situation he was going to change, though. He couldn't walk away from her. Hell, he hadn't even been able to do that before she had realized she was pregnant. There was something about her that he couldn't ignore. Yes, she was beautiful, and yes, she challenged him. Boy, did she challenge him. But there was more to it than that.

His entire life had been spent trying to prove that he was someone. That he was a Beaumont, that he belonged in the business world—that he mattered, regardless of his humble origins or the color of his skin.

And for all that Casey argued with him, she never

once asked him to be anyone other than himself. She accepted him as who he was—even if who he was happened to be a man who sometimes said the wrong thing at the wrong time.

He had made her a promise that he would take care of her, and by God, he was going to do that.

But this time, he was going to ask her how she wanted him to take care of her. Because he should have known that telling her what to do was a bad idea.

Ah, the seats behind hers were still available for this afternoon's game. Zeb bought the tickets.

He was going to do something he had never done before—he was going to take the afternoon off work.

"You want me to go get you some more nachos, honey?" Dad asked for the third time in a mere two innings.

Casey looked down at the chips covered in gloppy cheese. She was only kind of pregnant—wasn't it too soon for her stomach to be doing this many flips?

"I'm okay." She looked up and saw Dad staring at her. He looked so eager that she knew he needed something to do. "Really. But I could use another Sprite." Frankly, at this point, clear soda was the only thing keeping her stomach settled.

"I'll be right back," Dad said with a relieved smile, as if her problems could all be solved with more food. *Men*, Casey thought with another grin after he was gone.

Whereas she had no idea what she could do to make this better. No, it wasn't the most mature thing in the world to have skipped work today. It was just delaying the inevitable conversation that she would have to have with Zeb at some point or another.

There had been a moment last night—the moment before the kiss—where he'd told her that he was going to take care of her. That had been what she wanted. Hadn't that been why she'd gone to her dad after she had stormed out of Zeb's house? Because she wanted someone to take care of her?

But it wasn't a fair comparison. Her father had known her for her entire life. Of course he would know what she wanted—wasn't that why they were at this game today? It wasn't fair for her to hope and hope and just keep on hoping, dammit, that Zeb would guess correctly. Especially not when he'd gotten so close. There *was* a big part of her that wanted him to take care of her.

There was an equally big part of her that did not want to quit her job and be a stay-at-home mom. What if he couldn't see that? He was a hard-driving businessman who wasn't used to taking no for an answer. What if she couldn't convince him that she would be a better mom if she could keep her job and keep doing what she loved?

She was keeping her eye on the ball when she heard someone shuffling into the seat behind her. By instinct, she leaned forward to avoid any accidental hot dogs down the back of her neck. But as she did so, she startled as a voice came low and close to her ear. "It's a nice afternoon for baseball, isn't it?"

Zeb. She would recognize his voice anywhere— deep and serious, with just a hint of playfulness around the edge.

"Nice enough to skip work, even," he added when she didn't manage to come up with a coherent response.

Okay, now he was teasing her. She settled back in her chair, but she didn't turn around and look at him. She didn't want to see him in the suit and she didn't want to see him in a T-shirt. So she kept her eyes focused on the game in front of her. "How did you find me?"

"I asked Larry. I should've figured it out by myself. You weren't at your apartment and you weren't at work."

"I went home—I mean, my dad's home."

"I upset you. I didn't mean to, but I did." He exhaled and she felt his warmth against the back of her neck. "I shouldn't have assumed you would want to stay home. I know you and I know you're far too ambitious to give up everything you've worked for just because of something like this."

Now she did twist around. Good Lord—he was wearing purple. A Rockies T-shirt and a Rockies hat.

"You blend," she said in surprise. "I didn't think you knew how to do that."

"I can be taught." One corner of his mouth curved up in a small smile—the kind of smile that sent a shiver down her back. "I'm working on doing a better job of listening."

"Really?"

"Really. I have to tell you, I was frantic this morning when I couldn't find you at work. I was afraid you might quit on me and then where would I be?"

"But that's a problem, don't you see? How am I going to do my job? How am I going to brew beer if I can't drink it?"

Zeb settled back in his seat, that half smile still firmly on his face. "One of the things I've learned during my tenure as CEO of the Beaumont Brewery is that my employees do not drink on the job. They may sample in small quantities, but no one is ever drunk while they're at work—a fact which I appreciate. And I've also learned that I have extremely competent employees who care deeply about our brewery."

She stared at him in confusion. "What are you saying?"

He had the nerve to shrug nonchalantly. "I grew up in a hair salon, listening to women talk about pregnancies and babies and children. Obviously, we have to check with a doctor, but I think you taking a small sip every now and then isn't going to hurt anyone. And I don't want that to be the reason why you think you would have to leave a job you love."

She began to get a crick in her lower back. "Why are you here?" Because he was being perfect again and when he was perfect, he was simply irresistible.

"I'm here for you, Casey. I screwed up last night—I didn't ask you what you wanted. So that's what I'm doing now. What do you want to do?"

She was only vaguely aware that she was staring at him, mouth wide-open. But this was *the* moment. If she didn't tell him what she wanted right now, she might never get another chance.

"Come sit by me," she said. Obligingly, Zeb clambered down over the back of Dad's seat and settled in.

For a moment, Casey was silent as she watched the batter line out to right field. Zeb didn't say anything, though. He just waited for her.

"Okay," she said, mentally psyching herself up for this. Why could she defend her beer and her employees—but asking something for herself was such a struggle?

Well, to hell with that. She was doing this. Right now. "It's hard for me to ask for stuff that I want," she admitted. It wasn't a graceful statement, but it was the truth.

Zeb turned and looked at her funny. "You? Didn't you barge into my office and tell me off on my first day?"

"It's different. I defend my job and I defend my workers but for me to sit here and tell you what I want—it's…it's hard, okay? So just humor me."

"I will always listen to you, Casey. I want you to know that."

Her cheeks began to heat and the back of her neck prickled, but she wasn't allowing herself to get lost in the awkwardness of the moment. Instead, she forged ahead.

"The last time we were at a game together... I wanted you to tell me that I was beautiful and sensual and...and gorgeous. But it felt stupid, asking for that, so I didn't, and then after we..." She cleared her throat, hoping against hope that she hadn't turned bright red and knowing it was way too late for that. "Well, afterward, what you said made me feel even less pretty than normal. And so I shut down on you."

Now it was his turn to stare at her, mouth open and eyes wide. "But...do you have any idea how much you turn me on? How gorgeous you are?"

God, she was going to die of embarrassment. "It's not that—okay, maybe it is. But it's that I've always been this tomboy. And when we were together in my kitchen, it was good. Great," she added quickly when he notched an eyebrow at her. "But I don't want that to be all there is. If we're going to have a relationship, I need romance. And most people think I don't, because I drink beer and I watch ball games."

She had not died of mortification yet, which had to count for something.

"Romance," he said, but he didn't sound like he was mocking her. Instead, he sounded...thoughtful.

A small flicker of hope sparked to life underneath the heat of embarrassment. "Yes."

He touched her then, his hand on hers. More heat. There'd always be this heat between them. "Duly noted. What else? Because I will do everything in my power to give you what you want and what you need."

For a moment, she almost got lost in his gaze. God, those green eyes—from the very first moment, they had pulled her in and refused to let her go. "I don't want to give up my job. And I don't want to quit and go someplace else. I've worked hard for my job and I love it. I love everything about making beer and everything about working for the brewery. Even my new CEO, who occasionally sends out mixed signals."

At that, Zeb laughed out loud. "Can you keep a secret?"

"Depends on the secret," she said archly.

"Before I met you, I don't think I ever did anything but work. That's all I've known. It's all my mom did and I thought I had to prove myself to her, to my father—to everyone. I've been so focused on being the boss and on besting the Beaumonts for so long that..." He sighed and looked out at the game. But Casey could tell he wasn't seeing it. "That I've forgotten how to be me. Then I met you. When I'm with you, I don't feel like I have to be something that I'm not. I don't have to prove myself over and over again. I can just be *me*." The look he gave her was tinged with sadness. "It's hard for me to let go of that—of being the CEO. But you make me want to do better."

"Oh, Zeb—there's so much more to you than just this brewery."

He cupped her face. "That goes for you, too—you are more than just a brewmaster to me. You are a passionate, beautiful woman who earned my respect first and my love second."

Tears begin to prick at Casey's eyes. Stupid hormones. "Oh, Zeb…"

"There's something between us and I don't want to screw that up. Any more than I already have," he added, looking sheepish.

"What do you want?" She felt it was only fair to ask him.

"I want to know my child. I want to be a part of his or her life. I don't want my child to be raised as a bastard." He paused and Casey felt a twinge of disappointment. It wasn't like she could disagree with that kind of sentiment—it was a damn noble one.

But was it enough? She wanted to be wanted not just because she was pregnant but because she was… Well, because she was Casey.

But before she could open her mouth to tell Zeb this, he went on, "That's not all."

"It's not?" Her voice came out with a bit of a waver in it.

He leaned in closer. "It's not. I want to be with someone who I respect, who I trust to pull me back to myself when I've forgotten how to be anything but the boss. I want to be with someone who sparks something in me, someone I look forward to coming home to every single night." Casey gasped, but he kept going. "I want to be with someone who's just as committed to her work as I am to mine—but who also knows how to relax and kick back. I want to be with someone who understands the different families I'm a part of now and who loves me because of them, not in spite of them." His lips were now just a breath away from hers. She could feel his warmth and she wanted nothing more than to melt into him again. "But most of all, I want to be with someone who can tell me what she wants—what she needs— and when she needs it. So tell me, Casey—what do you want?"

This was really happening. "I want to know you care, that you'll fight for me and the baby—and for us. That you'll protect us and support us, even if we do things that other people don't think we should."

Oh, God—that grin on him was too much. She couldn't resist him and she was tired of trying. "Like be the youngest female brewmaster in the country?"

He understood. "Yeah, that. If we do this, I want to do this right," she told him. "But I want to meet you in the middle. I don't know if I want to live in the big house and I know we can't live in my tiny apartment."

His eyes warmed. "We can talk about that."

"That's what I want—I want to know that I can talk to you and know that you'll listen. I want to know that everything is going to work out for the best."

He pulled back, just the tiniest bit. "I can't guarantee anything, Casey. But I can promise you this—I will love you and our baby no matter what."

Love. That was the something between them— the thing that neither of them could walk away from.

"That's what I want," she told him. She leaned into him, wrapping her hand around the back of his neck and pulling him in closer. "I love you, too. That's all."

"Then I'm yours. All you have to do is ask." He gave her a crooked grin. "I won't always get it right. I'm not a mind reader, you know."

She couldn't help it—she laughed. "Did the all-powerful Zebadiah Richards just admit there was something he couldn't do?"

"Shh," he teased, his eyes sparkling. "Don't tell anyone. It's a secret." Then he leaned in closer. "Let me give you everything, Casey. We'll run the brewery together and raise our kid. We'll do it our way."

"*Yes.* I want you."

Just as his lips brushed against hers, she heard someone clearing his throat—loudly.

Dad. In all the talk, she'd forgotten that he'd left to fetch a soda for her. She jolted in her seat, but Zeb didn't let her go. Instead, he wrapped his arms around her shoulders.

"Everything okay?" Dad asked as he eyed the two of them suspiciously. "You want me to get rid of him, honey?"

Casey looked up at her dad as she leaned back into Zeb's arms and smiled. "Nope," she said, knowing that this was right. "I want him to stay right here with me."

Everything she'd ever wanted was hers—a family, her job and Zeb. He was all hers.

All she'd had to do was ask for him.

* * * * *

PREGNANT
BY THE CEO

HELENKAY DIMON

One

Ellie Gold had never punched anyone before, but she vowed to end that lifelong streak right now.

Wearing the only cocktail dress she owned, simple

and black, with a matching black lace overlay, and spiky heels that made her arches ache, she stepped into the private dining room on the top floor of the historic Hay-Adams Hotel named, interestingly enough, the Top of the Hay.

For a second the anger choking her brain cleared. Her breath hitched as her gaze wandered around the sparkling space with the fancy chandeliers and cream-colored walls. Only the business people milling around with death grips on their drinks, all looking awkward and out of place in their navy suits, threatened to ruin the fairy-tale moment.

French doors lined the outer walls and vaulted skylights soared above her. She stretched up on tiptoe to peek around more than one set of shoulders to the stunning view of the White House below.

Her balance faltered and she might have landed headfirst in a nearby tray of champagne glasses but fingers wrapped around her elbow and steadied her. She glanced up to say thank-you and saw a face... *his* face.

Derrick Jameson, the oldest son of a vast empire that included everything from commercial real estate in Washington, DC, to a prize-winning horse farm in the Virginia countryside. The guy who excelled at making her life miserable.

Just seeing him made her forget how to spell. She wasn't all that sure she could recite the alphabet if pressed, either. She wanted to blame the fury flowing through her, but even she had to admit that might not be the real reason for her hottie-induced speech lapse.

She'd researched Derrick before tonight, reading online in stories that droned on about his money and

dating life. But seeing him up close? No one had prepared her for that.

The black hair and striking light brown eyes. She'd
read about his family background and picked up on
the subtle hint of Japanese heritage passed on from his
maternal grandmother. The firm chin. Those shoulders.

The features combined into a potent package of
tall, dark and delicious. He gave off a confident vibe.
In control and assessing. But his unspoken determination to destroy her reputation and rip her family apart
marred her appreciation of his pretty face.

"Ms. Gold." He nodded and threw in a little smile
for a group of people walking past him. "I didn't expect to see you at a business function."

Her voice came back to her in a rush. So did the
rage swirling in her gut. "Interesting tactic."

"Excuse me?"

"That charming thing you're doing?" She leaned
in closer and dropped her voice to a whisper, ignoring
how good he smelled. "I'm not buying it."

He continued to hold her arm. Not in a tight grip.
No, his thumb brushed back and forth over her bare
skin in a gentle caress, as if trying to soothe her. The
guy seemed oblivious to the fact that he was the one
causing her stress. Well, him and everyone and everything else in her life.

He might not know it but she hovered right on the
edge and his decisions kept shoving her closer to the
abyss. Her baby brother, Noah, was in a strange emotional downward spiral, all thanks to Derrick and his
claims about Noah stealing from him.

She'd practically raised Noah after their parents

died in a car crash. He wasn't easy, but he wasn't a thief. Her brother had been argumentative and frustrated back then, much more so than other kids. She'd dragged him to a specialist, who diagnosed him with oppositional defiant disorder, something she'd never even heard of before that moment.

She'd scraped together the money for the therapies not covered by insurance. But even now, at times of stress or when he felt cornered, the flashes of anger would come back and he'd buck authority. Something about Derrick had Noah's negative behavior kicking to the surface again.

The worst part was that Noah didn't even see it. She did. She'd watched him make bad choices as a kid, tried to help him to the point where she'd sacrificed her personal life to spend all of her extra time with him. The idea that his issues were resurging now, at twenty, deflated her.

She'd deal with that later. Right now she needed to handle Derrick.

"This is serious." Serious enough for her to track him down through a series of calls to his office.

"Is it?" Amusement filled his voice as he handed her his glass of champagne.

She couldn't think of anything more annoying than that welcoming lilt to his voice. The whole fake-charming scene threw her off. She didn't realize he had shifted and moved them toward the elevators until she looked around the room and saw the space between them and the rest of the party.

She didn't know if this was a rich guy's way of escorting her out of the building or something else. Either way, she was not ready to be dismissed. There was too much at stake for her to give up now. "Mr. Jameson, I—"

"Derrick."

She'd investigated Derrick's business when her baby brother got a job there seven months ago. At first, Noah had talked about Derrick in a nonstop cycle of hero worship. His enthusiasm had rubbed off on her. She'd clicked on every photo of him. Let her mind wander, tried to imagine what it might be like to see that shockingly handsome face close up.

Now she knew.

She worked in human resources up until six weeks ago. She hadn't reached management level yet. The Jameson family was the equivalent of DC royalty. She didn't move in their world. She also possessed a general distrust of people who rolled around in that kind of money. But Noah had been impressed. And, up until that point in his life, almost *nothing* had impressed her brilliant but moody brother.

In theory, Derrick was more mature and reasonable than her brother. But thanks to this gossip site silliness she wasn't totally convinced that was true.

"The *DC Insider* posted a note about us." The comment rolled out of her mouth as if it made any sense. She still couldn't believe she had to confront him about this.

For a second Derrick stared at her, not saying a word, then he nodded. "I know."

Words backed up in her brain until she finally pushed them out. "What kind of response is that?"

"My name is in the social column because I allowed it to be there."

Good grief. "Are you kidding?"

He frowned at her. "No."

"I'm thinking people have let you get away with nonsense for far too long." When he started to pipe in, she talked right over him. "I mean, really. Do you know how condescending you sound?"

This time he studied her. She could feel him assessing and reordering his strategy as they talked.

"I called you *lovely* in that *Insider* quote, if that helps," he said.

It took a second for her brain to catch up again. She silently blamed all the people in suits standing around, staring at them and whispering, but she worried his smooth tone might be the *real* issue with her concentration. "It doesn't, and that's not the point."

"Should I have used a different word?"

His focus on vocabulary made her head pound. She shifted until she put her back to most of the room. Maybe not seeing the gawkers would help. "Stop talking."

He made a sound that came close to a growl. "People don't usually speak to me that way."

"Which is probably part of the problem here." She'd never worked in a classroom but her mother had. Ellie called up that disappointed-fifth-grade-teacher tone without even trying. "Okay, so you're admitting you planted the article?"

"Of course."

The champagne sloshed over the side of her glass. "The one about me?"

Because that was the point. She came there to pry the truth out of him about the planted story, maybe put him on the defensive. He ruined her plans by admitting to spreading the gossip, like it was no big deal.

He slipped the flute out of her fingers and put it on the small table behind him. "Technically, the story is about me."

She inhaled, trying to bring some air into her lungs and refresh her brain cells. She refused to get lost in his words or have a "him" versus "them" fight because she had the very clear sense confusing wordplay was one of the ways he won arguments. "Okay, why do it?"

"To change the public conversation from your brother's false allegations while I figure out what he did with the money that is now missing from my business accounts." Derrick answered without blinking, following their conversation with ease as it bounced around.

She decided to ignore the money part for now. "But you named me as your...well, I guess as the woman you're dating?"

"That's right."

She had no idea what to think about that nonchalant response. "We don't even know each other. Why would you think that's okay?"

"My *business* is the most important thing to me."

She didn't try to hide her wince at his sudden stern tone. "My *brother* is the most important thing to me."

"Wrong answer, Ellie."

Was he really making a tsking sound? "What is wrong with you?"

"I have two brothers, both adults," Derrick explained with all the emotion of someone reading a recipe. "They take care of themselves. I take care of me and the business."

"That's cold...bloodless."

He actually smiled. "Is it possible you're the one with the confused priorities?"

She swallowed a gasp, along with a bit of her anger and possibly some of her dignity. The whole conversation was ridiculous but she could not tear herself away from him...not yet.

"Let me get this straight. A perpetual bachelor and notorious ladies' man who is being trolled on the internet by my little brother in his antibusiness videos is giving me advice on interpersonal relationships?" She wanted to sigh, throw things. "Listen, Mr. Jameson."

"It's still Derrick."

The way he stayed calm made her temper spike even more. The heat rose inside her and flooded her cheeks with every controlled word he uttered. She refused to believe the sudden need for a fan had anything to do with his perfect face or that sexy smile. Not that she found either all that appealing. "Do not mention my name to anyone ever again."

"Now, Ellie." His eyes narrowed. "You don't think that's maybe—just a little—extreme."

Apparently she was not the only one familiar with the teacher tone. He threw it out there and nailed her with it. As if she needed another reason to dislike him. "Leave my brother alone."

"When your brother comes clean and then backs off those videos, I will."

"You're a grown-up."

"So is he." Derrick leaned in close enough for his warm breath to brush her cheek. "My suggestion to you is that you start treating him like one."

"I'm not kidding around."

His eyes traveled over her face, lingering on her mouth. "I can see that."

She fought off the tremor moving through her. "Leave me out of your games."

Before he could say anything else or touch her again, she slipped around him and through the crowd of people heading toward them. Kept going until she got on the elevator and watched the doors close on his smiling face. Getting her breathing to return to normal and the image of his face to disappear from her mind took longer.

An hour later Ellie poured a glass of red wine as she kicked off her stupid heels. Thanks to a bout of storming and muttering, she'd wasted most of her energy and hadn't made it to her apartment. She needed to vent and that meant taking the Metro to her best friend's condo instead.

Vanessa McAllister's one-bedroom place was small but cozy. Light bounced off the bright yellow walls. During the day, the sun beamed in from the large window at the far end of the living room.

A steady beat of background conversation came from the television. Ellie had no idea what show was on and didn't care. Vanessa didn't appear to, either.

Of course, very little ruffled her. Between her navy career father and her French mother, Vanessa had been all over the world. She spoke a ridiculous number of languages that served her well in her job at the museum.

Ellie trusted Vanessa with any secret. They'd met in college and had been best friends ever since. They supported and cheered for each other. And right now, Vanessa was frowning.

She sat on the stool at her kitchen's breakfast bar. She sipped from her almost-empty glass of red wine as she scowled at the laptop screen in front of her. "Tell me again what happened at that fancy cocktail party."

The somewhat distant tone. That wasn't good.

Ellie was almost afraid to answer. She did, anyway. "I met Derrick Jameson and told him to back off."

The explanation sounded good. So strong. Just what Ellie wanted to be. After years of racing around, trying to keep every ball in the air and failing most of the time, Ellie wanted to be in control of her life and not running behind it, trying to catch up.

Vanessa tapped on the keyboard. "Uh-huh."

Yeah, not good. "What does that response mean?"

"Did you happen to see a photographer while you were there?" Vanessa sat straighter and waved her hand in the air. "Forget it. I'll just go ahead and read it to you before you explode."

Ellie dropped the paper napkin she was twisting in her fingers. "Wait, read what?"

"The latest from that *Insider* site."

"No." Ellie's stomach fell. She could have sworn it hit the floor.

"'Derrick Jameson and Ellie Gold made an official appearance together at the swanky Hay-Adams Hotel tonight. No word on whether they got a room, but they did leave the business party one right after the other, making more than one partygoer wonder if Derrick sprang for the presidential suite...'"

Silence screamed through the room. Ellie could feel it hammering in her head as it rumbled through her.

"Okay." Vanessa cleared her throat. "So, that happened."

"It did *not* happen." Ellie reached over and turned the laptop to face her. "We argued. We fought."

She started tapping random keys. Anything to make that now familiar *Insider* website disappear.

"Wait, go back. There's a photo." Vanessa swatted Ellie's hand away then leaned in and pointed at the screen. "Why does it look like you're hanging on his arm?"

As if Ellie could deny it. The evidence, even though it didn't show the whole story, was right there. Her pressing against him, looking up at him. Anyone seeing this would believe they were having an intimate chat.

"That's not… I was just…" The words clogged her throat in the rush to get them out. "I'm going to kill him."

Vanessa winced. "You can't think that he—"

"Of course he planted this. I'm his PR plan." And he wasn't even trying to hide it. He'd been very clear. She just hadn't realized he'd turned it on full-time.

Vanessa made a humming sound. "He really is cute."

"Don't."

"But clearly a gigantic ass." Vanessa's voice sounded harsher that time.

"Better." But still not good enough. Ellie wanted to forget all about his smug face.

"Hating him doesn't fix the Noah situation," Vanessa said, being far too reasonable for the moment.

"Or help with my income issue or get my life under control. Yeah, I know."

Vanessa's shoulders fell as she sighed. "I can give you money, or move in here with me and don't pay rent for a few months. Give yourself a financial break."

"I can't."

"You can." Vanessa made a grumbling sound as she said something under her breath that wasn't quite clear. "I'm thinking about stuffing twenties into your purse while you're not looking."

With that, Ellie felt some of the Derrick-related anger drain away. She reached over and gave her friend's arm a quick squeeze. "You're awesome and I love you, but this is bigger than a short-term money problem. It's like everything is spinning and I can't make it stop." Even now her life choices ran through her head as she questioned each one. "I still can't believe I got fired for something that wasn't my fault."

"So, take it back." Vanessa grabbed the bottle and refilled her glass. "Control, I mean. Start with one thing. You take a small piece, conquer that and then move on."

The advice rolled around in Ellie's head until it took hold. She knew exactly which battle to wage first. "Right. Derrick Jameson."

"Um, no. I was thinking more like you could get a temp job and rebuild." Vanessa topped off Ellie's glass. "A guy like Jameson is not easily managed. Forget him. Handle what *you* need first."

The suggestion made sense but Ellie couldn't survive that way. She'd spent so much of her life fixing things. First, for her father, who had one pipe dream after another, and her mother, who had fought to keep them together as a family. Then for her brother. She didn't have the energy left to tackle straightening out her life, but she would. Later. Once she'd dealt with Derrick and Noah was back on track. "I have to handle these other pieces first."

Vanessa shook her head. "Ellie, you can't fix everything."

"I can fix this. If Derrick Jameson wants a battle, he's going to get one."

Two

The DC Insider: *The hottest romance in town just got more interesting. Ever wonder what happens when the lady in question calls our office to insist there is no romance? Well, we call the gentlemen for his comment. And Derrick Jameson did not disappoint. The usually demanding businessman chuckled and said, "You should listen to Ellie. I enjoy acquiescing to her." These two are never dull.*

She'd been summoned.

The call came at a little after nine the next morning. Ellie debated ignoring it. She wasn't exactly the type to jump when a man ordered, but then Derrick was no ordinary man. He seemed to enjoy ticking her off.

Yet there she was, two hours later, walking along

a long hallway on the fifteenth floor of the Jameson Industries' office building. Pristine white walls surrounded her as her heels clicked against the polished hardwood floors. People moved in and out and around cubicle walls. They carried stacks of papers and shuffled with a sense of urgency.

She missed the energy of a busy office. Insurance underwriting wasn't the most exciting topic but she'd worked in human resources, slowly taking on more responsibility. She loved coming into a pile of files waiting on her desk each morning and solving problems.

Everything went fine until the big boss took an overactive interest in her. She'd done everything she'd been trained to do. Documented his behavior. She'd known how hard it was to report that sort of thing up the chain of command without becoming the subject of gossip. Before her boss made his move she'd set up a system to handle the concerns. Then she got fired before she could implement it.

The attorney she contacted about the firing but could barely afford said she had a good case. But her former boss had the resources to drag the thing out and exhaust her.

She tried not to think about that as two men headed straight for her. She slipped to the side, banging into the wall and knocking the corner of a painting. One that likely cost more than her car. After that, one more turn and she moved into a quieter part of the floor. No one scurried here.

Sleek furniture made of unblemished leather with shiny chrome accents filled the open reception area. That, and a desk covered with piles of files, was all that stood between her and a set of closed double doors. Those and the guy next to her. She couldn't remember her escort's name, wasn't even sure he'd offered it.

Before she could ask, he reached out and knocked on the door to the right in front of them. One brisk thwack then he opened it. Even gestured for her to step inside in front of him.

No, thank you.

Her legs refused to move, anyway. The threshold seemed innocent enough, but the man on the other side was not. Every inch of this place screamed money. Something she'd never had enough of and worked liked crazy to stockpile in case her life hit a bump... just as it had. More like a Himalayan mountain, but still.

She couldn't see Derrick at the moment, but she did have an unrestricted view of his desk. The thing had to be eight feet long. Formidable, like the man who sat at it.

She refused to go one step further. Decided to call out instead. "What do you want?"

"Come inside," the faceless voice said from some hidden corner of the office.

She noted the deep and commanding tone. Yeah, this was going to be a quick meeting.

"I'm fine here," she said.

The security guy put his hand over his mouth to cover what sounded like a fake cough. He hesitated a second before saying anything. "You really should obey him."

Apparently she'd gotten off the elevator and stepped back a century. "Did you use the word *obey*?"

"Don't fight with Jackson. It's me you want," Derrick said, still without making an appearance.

She glanced at the man looming next to her. He stood well over six feet with brown hair and a lean athletic build. Attractive in a liked-to-run-along-the-Potomac sort of way, he looked far too amused by what was happening. "Is Jackson your first name or last?"

Before he could answer, Derrick stepped out of the room off to the side of his office and into the doorway. Hovered right in front of her. He nodded as a small smile played on the corner of his mouth. "Ellie, it's good to see you again."

The warmth in his eyes. That tone. A strange dizziness slammed into her when he got close. No way was she being reeled in by that charm thing he seemed to have flicked on. Nope, she knew better.

She managed a nod. "Mr. Jameson."

"Come inside. Despite our argument last night, we have a lot to discuss." He swept a hand toward the inside of his oversize corner office.

The very real sense she was out of her league slammed into her. "What would you do if I said no?"

He frowned. "Why would you?"

"You have this guy following me around the hallways…no offense." She winced as she glanced at Jackson before looking at Derrick again. "Then there's the part where you ordered me to come here. Today. Right now."

"Ten minutes ago."

"What?"

"I *asked* you to meet with me ten minutes ago. I assumed you being late was some sort of power play.

Unless you have a problem with tardiness. If so, we'll need to work on that."

She glanced at Jackson again. "Is he serious?"

Jackson nodded. "Almost always."

"Ellie." That's it. Derrick just said her name then turned and walked across the room, stopping next to his desk.

"Your manners need some work." She didn't bother mumbling as she followed him. If he wasn't going to be subtle, neither was she.

"So I've been told."

"Then there's the very real sense you're setting me up." Not so much a sense as a fact. If he planted one rumor, he could plant many. And that seemed to be his intent.

"How so?" He had the nerve to look confused.

She refused to believe he was that clueless.

"I complain about a story on the internet about us and suddenly there's a photo of us up there, complete with a new quote from you." An annoying quote. One that didn't say anything yet managed to say a lot. "I called them and denied that we were together and you…actually, I don't know what you were doing when you talked to the *Insider*."

"I was being a gentleman."

She took a few steps. Hovering there in his office gave her confidence. "You mean the I-don't-kiss-and-tell thing? Oh, please. You were toying with them because it amused you."

"Admittedly, I'm not often at a loss for words, but I'm not sure what to say to that comment."

"You could admit you set me up to be featured on

the *Insider*. Again." The sound of a cough and rustling had her turning around.

Jackson stood there with his attention focused on Derrick. "Do you need anything from me, sir?"

"No, but it would be wise to stay close by in the hall in case Ms. Gold brought a weapon."

She had forgotten poor Jackson was still there. Hearing the door click behind her as he left, she tried not to fidget. Now it was the two of them temporarily trapped in a room bigger than her entire apartment.

Rather than retreat, she stepped forward. Followed Derrick's trail until she stood on the opposite side of his desk and watched him slip into his chair. "As if I could have gotten anything through the two rounds of security."

He leaned back. "I find myself a bit more careful these days."

"These days?"

"Since your brother stole from me then turned around a few days later and tried to throw the scent off him by taking public shots at me." Derrick motioned toward the chair next to her.

"So, that's it. The rumors, the photos, the fake social news suggesting we're together." She dumped her purse on the seat but remained on her feet. "You're coming after me to get even. This is some sort of weird revenge."

Derrick nodded. "A fascinating theory."

That really was the only explanation. Even though money had always been tight, Noah wasn't the type to steal.

"I see the dramatic streak runs in the family." Derrick's exhale filled the room. "Lucky me."

Right. I'm the dramatic one. "Says the guy who has a private butler and an office set off from everyone else."

"Security."

Everything inside her froze. "Excuse me?"

"Jackson is my head of security."

She relaxed but not much. Something told her she needed to be on her toes with this guy. He might talk smooth and look like he stepped out of her hottest fantasy, but that didn't change the facts. He was a ruthless jackass. "Do that many people want to kill you?"

"My family has significant business interests. That sort of thing tends to attract trouble."

She'd never been called that before. "Are you referring to me as the trouble?"

He shrugged. "Let's hope not."

She'd taken about all of the put-her-on-the-defensive moves that she could stand. It was time to get to the point so she could run out of there. "Mr. Jame—"

"I believe I asked you to call me Derrick."

That's what she called him in her head… "Do you think that's wise?"

"I'm afraid you've lost me."

"You and my brother are locked in some sort of public pissing match. You're threatening him with lawyers. He's making you look bad on the internet, which has bled over to traditional media." She put her palms on his desk and leaned in. "What I'm saying is that fake rumors or not, we're on opposite sides of this battle."

His gaze skimmed over her. "We don't have to be."

He hadn't moved but the heated words swept over her in a caress that had her shaking her head and standing straight again. She not only needed to be careful with Derrick, she needed body armor.

She blocked out every other thought and concentrated on the guy she'd come to think of as cold-blooded. "Has anyone ever pointed out your cryptic way of speaking?"

"Then let me be clear." Derrick balanced his elbows on the edge of his desk and leaned in toward her. "Your brother took money out of my business accounts and is going to go to jail unless I step in and save him."

"No, that's not—"

Derrick held up a finger. "There's nothing to debate. That's a fact." He let his hand fall again. "But I am willing to help him."

She could almost feel a trap closing over her head. The need to bolt overtook her but she forced her legs to stay still. "Why?"

"Most people would ask how."

She refused to be taken off guard by double-talk. "I'm not like everyone else."

"I'm starting to see that." Derrick watched her for a second. His gaze moved over her face in the silence. After a visible inhale, he began again, his voice louder and more firm. "I will help your brother but he has to do something for me."

"You don't like that he's making you look like a complete jerk, maybe even a bit incompetent." She got that.

Derrick fired Noah eight weeks ago, exactly two weeks before she lost her job. Noah's videos started out as a way to let off steam. Then he gained followers. A lot of them. He even managed to make money off his internet work, but she had no idea how.

He'd become a symbol for the "little man" fighting against the corporate machine. As his following grew, so did his stories about Derrick and the company.

Blame it on Noah's baby face or his sarcasm, but media and online sites had picked up the battle. Then Derrick's lawyers had made contact…and so had the prosecutor's office about the missing funds.

And now Derrick had the *Insider* and its gossip network working for him.

"I have shareholders and business associates," Derrick said.

"So, this is about money."

Derrick's frown deepened. "Isn't everything?"

Not an unexpected answer, but still… "It worries me that you don't know how scary that question is."

"I'm proposing a quid pro quo. I make your brother's legal issues disappear. He shuts down his site and I assist him in finding other more profitable and appropriate ways to channel his technology experience."

That sounded somewhat reasonable, which scared her. "That's the entire deal you're offering?"

"No."

She beat back a wave of disappointment. She'd taken care of her brilliant brother for so long. Tried to keep him occupied and out of trouble. The idea of having someone else handle that job sounded really good to her at the moment. With her life in shambles and the need to find a new job nipping at her, she loved the idea of having one less stress to deal with.

"I haven't told you what I get out of this," Derrick said.

Her heart sank. She held in a groan before it could escape her lips. "You did. He stops running the site."

It might sound easy but it wasn't. Noah didn't have anything else right now except for his anger at Derrick and the attention from his videos. It was the "thing" that kept Noah going. It also provided him with more attention and praise than he'd ever gotten.

"The damage is done. He's lied and caused me what could be irreparable damage," Derrick said.

His words pounded her but she kept her shoulders up and her back straight. "That sounds like a legal term."

"Because it is."

That meant more fighting. More lawyer fees on top of the ones for her employment attorney. "I thought you were worried about the lost money."

"There are bigger issues here."

She couldn't imagine money being a side concern. "Noah is a kid."

"Noah is twenty and a genius." When she opened her mouth to respond, Derrick talked right over her. "You are twenty-nine, which means you're old enough to know he's looking at criminal charges and civil repercussions for the money, which I'm willing to overlook right now."

"I'm going to pretend I know what that means and jump ahead. What is your part of the quid pro quo? Because you don't strike me as a guy who does things to be nice." That wasn't quite true. He'd hired Noah and ignored his lack of a degree and questionable people skills. But he'd also had security escort Noah out of the building months later. Now that she knew how that felt, she had even more sympathy for her brother. "What do you want?"

"You."

A weird, high-pitched ringing filled her ears. She shook her head but it refused to die down. "What?"

"The carefully placed stories about us have been aimed at diffusing some of your brother's damage."

"In other words, you're using me to somehow make yourself look better."

He shrugged. "That's not the way I'd put it."

"Of course not, since you're clearly clueless about women."

That had him sitting straighter. "Excuse me?"

Bull's-eye. The idea that she'd found the one thing sure to grab his attention—questioning his success with women—filled her with relief. "You're letting people believe we're together and—"

"Dating. People are starting to believe we're dating and that your brother doesn't like it and is trying to break us up by launching false charges against me." Derrick looked far too pleased with himself. "Which was exactly my plan."

"That's ridiculous." She could think of a lot of other words to describe it but kept the conversation G-rated.

"I thought so, too, when the PR team suggested it, but I guess the public does like a good love story."

A scream rattled around inside her. "Did you ever think to ask me first?"

"No."

The quick response had her sputtering. "That's really your answer?"

"I called you *lovely* in my interview with the *Insider*, which I think we can agree was a bit of a stretch since you looked ready to punch me the first time we met in person."

"Oh, you picked up on that?" *Good to know.*

"Let's get down to it." He leaned in again. Didn't break eye contact. "We're talking about a business arrangement."

"Who is?"

"You will pose as my girlfriend for an appropriate length of time, short though because the timing is important here. Long enough for us to sell that we've been dating. Then you'll act as my fiancée and—"

"Wait." That ringing in her ears turned into a loud clanging sound.

He stared at her. "I haven't finished explaining the plan."

When his PR team said he'd needed to create a diversion, it made sense in an abstract sort of way. But they could not have meant her. He—they—didn't even know her. And no way did they mean an engagement.

She suspected they'd talked about him finding a life outside the office. She tried to direct him there. "I'm sure there are women in town who would want to date you. It's tough out there and my brother isn't exactly highlighting your good side. But you have money and you're...you know..."

He studied her now, like how he might study something on the bottom of his shoe. "I have no idea what you're trying to say."

"Well, your face is...fine." As in perfect and compelling. Way too kissable.

His eyes widened. *"Fine?"*

Because space seemed like a good idea she stepped away from the desk. Tried to draw enough air into her lungs and head to be able to breathe again. "Don't rich people travel in packs? I'm sure you can hang out at your country club or polo club, or wherever it is you go for fun, and find a nice woman who—"

"I am not hard up for a date." He sounded stunned at the idea.

"Well, there." She almost clapped but decided that was too much. "Good for you."

"I am, however, on the wrong side of your brother's ill-advised rant." He made a face that suggested he thought she should be picking up on his point a bit faster. "I explained this to you at the hotel."

"You said you needed good news to balance out the bad." That made sense, which only made her wariness tick up even higher. "So, hire someone to pretend date you if you don't want an actual girlfriend."

"It needs to be you. You provide a reason for your brother's specific attack." When she tried to stop him, he kept right on talking. Rolled right over her. "We put on a very public show. We get people to see us as a couple, get engaged—not for real, of course—and we neutralize some of the damage your brother has done."

"A fake fiancée." She said the words nice and slow, thinking he'd stop her because he had to be kidding.

Never mind that she could barely stand him. Sure, she'd spun wild daydreams about him. Even imagined what he might look like without that serious suit and the fancy office, but come on.

"Exactly." The phone on his desk rang. He hit a button and the sound cut off. "You've spent a significant part of your life protecting your baby brother and I suspect you will continue to do so now, even though it's misguided."

That hit a bit too close to the comments Vanessa had made last night. "Misguided? I'm confused. Are you arguing for this fake engagement thing or not?"

"People will see us together, which will telegraph the message that I am not the man your brother says I am. You wouldn't date me otherwise. It will be a business arrangement that will benefit you greatly, and it will keep me from going after him for the money." He shrugged. "And, since time is a factor, I went ahead and started the rumors. As you know."

"Because that made sense to you?"

"Because your brother is in serious legal trouble and I can help him. I can also provide some guidance for the future and take the pressure off you. In many ways."

For the first time she noticed his hands. Those long fingers. The strength. The way he rubbed his palms together as if that in-control voice didn't quite match whatever was happening inside him.

But none of that calmed her wariness. Not when every word he uttered carried a note of a threat. "What does that mean?"

"You were recently fired."

Her stomach dropped, and not in a good way. Forget his deep, soothing voice and the sexy confidence that thrummed off him. If he made one wrong comment about her losing her job she would lunge across the desk and strangle him with that blue tie. "Laid off."

"We both know that's not true." Derrick didn't stop talking long enough to let her break in. "It would appear I'm not the only one who has an image to salvage. While you're doing that, I will pay your bills."

That sounded like…well, not good. "No."

"Consider this an acting role of sorts. One for which you should be paid." He picked up the folder in front of him and slid it toward her. "Here."

"What's that?"

"A contract."

The guy was prepared. She had to give him that. "You think I'm going to say yes then sign something?"

"Why wouldn't you?"

"Love, honor, decency." She probably should have thrown in a few more words but her brain refused to reboot. It had been misfiring ever since he'd smiled that first time.

"I'm not sure what any of those have to do with this arrangement." He nodded at the folder. "Take a look. Everyone benefits."

"Mostly you."

"I don't deny I get something out of this, but so do you. More important, so does Noah."

That sounded good but she doubted Derrick would deal fairly with Noah at this point. She couldn't believe the charges against her brother. But the idea that Derrick would waste time going after Noah if he was innocent didn't make much sense, either.

As soon as the doubts crept into her head about her brother, she tried to push them out again. *Be loyal.* "Noah denies the charges."

"He's lying." Derrick didn't even flinch as he talked. Never broke eye contact. Didn't give away any sign that he doubted what he said.

Something about his coolness made her insides shake. "Why should I believe you over my brother?"

"Deep down, you know I'm right."

"I don't think—"

"Yes, it would be better if you didn't, but I'm betting you will study this proposal from every angle." Derrick put his hand on the folder. "You can have until tomorrow morning."

She had to grab on to the chair next to her for balance. The room had started spinning and with each word he said rocked her harder. "For what?"

"To give me your response. As I said, time is of the essence. I am currently holding off the prosecutor but he needs an answer about your brother."

"And he'll do what you say?"

"We went to college together."

"Of course you did." From her experience with the job search she knew powerful people stuck together. But the caress of Derrick's voice, the concern in his tone—it all had her taking another step back. "This bargain or offer or whatever it is...it's ridiculous. You know that, right? I need to know you know that."

But even as she said the words her mind starting working. He could help Noah. She could get her life in order. Derrick offered breathing room and support, and that tempted her even though she knew she couldn't trust him one inch.

"Your brother's actions leave me with little option, and he shows no signs of stopping even if he is arrested. Shareholder discontent is an issue. I also have a reputation in the community."

"One that would suffer if people found out you made an offer for a fake fiancée."

He hadn't been moving but still his body froze. "Is that a threat, Ellie?"

"I'm trying to understand why a man with your money and power would make this offer."

"That's my problem, not yours."

"If I'm going to be your fiancée then—"

He held up a hand. "In name only."

"No sex then?" *Where had that come from?*

His eyebrow lifted. "I am willing to negotiate that point. Very willing."

She could almost feel his fingertips brush over her. "Forget it."

"You have until tomorrow at ten to give me an answer." He broke eye contact and hit a button on his phone. "Not ten after, Ellie. Ten exactly."

It was a dismissal. She heard it, felt it and ignored it. "I wouldn't clear your calendar if I were you."

He didn't look up. "Ten."

Three

Derrick leaned back in his oversize desk chair and blew out a long, haggard breath as the door closed behind Ellie and she left his office. He'd expected anger and a hint of distrust. He would have worried if she'd said yes to his fake engagement offer and jumped in. Eagerness was not a bonus in this type of situation.

No, he'd been prepared for all that. The sucker punch of need that slammed in to his gut the second he saw her again? That one had been a surprise.

She'd walked in with her long brown hair tied up behind her head with those strands hanging down, all sexy and loose. She'd worn a thin black skirt and white shirt and all he could think about was stripping both off her. The tight body. Those legs. The way fire lit her hazel eyes as she argued.

It all worked for him.

His attraction to her had sparked the minute she'd opened her mouth. She was tough and smart, and not easy to throw off or to scare. She met every one of his verbal shots with one of her own.

The woman was hot, no question.

She didn't fit his usual type.

He thought about the women he'd dated over the past few years. All cool, reserved business types. He preferred competent over sparks and heat. Maybe that's why the last three were now some of this favorite business associates. Friends, even.

He didn't believe in the idea of grand love. That struck him as nonsense. He'd grown up in a family that yelled. His father pitted him and his two brothers against each other. At his urging, they'd been racing and competing since the cradle. Every mistake had been dissected and fed back to them in an endless loop by their unforgiving father and then by the press that followed the Jameson boys' every move.

Never mind that Derrick's grandfather was a disgraced congressman or that their father, Eldrick Jameson, a self-made man with three former wives and a new much-younger one, had made his initial millions, before he lost them, by not always playing fair. Derrick and his brothers were magazine and news favorites, and few in the press gave them favorable coverage no matter what they did.

No, Derrick didn't believe much in emotions. But he did believe in this company. He'd rebuilt it from the dust left over from his father's fires and while the old man ran through woman after woman. Derrick labored over every contract and every deal. Gave his life to it. And now he was getting screwed by the old man—again.

His father handed down his requirements for turning the business over, the main one being that Derrick clean up his reputation and resolve "the Noah problem" within ninety days. That meant dealing with Ellie since his PR team thought trying to deal with Noah directly could result in another video.

From the photos he'd seen of her before they met at the party, he'd expected pretty in a girl-next-door kind of way. Quiet. Not someone likely to light his fire. From what he knew about her job situation, he'd expected desperation and a willingness to deal.

He got none of that.

Jackson Richards opened the door and slid inside the office. He wore a stupid grin as he walked across the office and stopped in front of Derrick. "She's not what I expected."

Now there was an understatement. "Me, either. And did you call me *sir* earlier?" That was new and Derrick didn't like it.

Jackson shrugged. "I thought it fit with the mood you were trying to create."

"You can skip the overly deferential act. I have enough people around here who do that."

"Are you engaged yet?" Jackson sounded amused at the idea.

Derrick was happy someone thought the nightmare situation was funny. "She's difficult."

"She sounds perfect for you."

Jackson was one of the few people who could get away with the comment. They'd known each other for years and were about the same age, both in their midthirties. Eldrick had brought Jackson into the company, but Derrick liked him despite that. They'd been friends from the start. With Jackson, Derrick let the firm line between boss and employee blur.

But right now his mind was on the hot brunette with the impressive ass who'd just left his office. "She seems to think I should be able to find a real date."

"Did you tell her about your father's conditions for signing the business over to you and how you have something of an impossible deadline in which to meet them?"

The damn agreement. Leave it to Eldrick to make everything difficult. "You mean selling it to me? For a lot of money he can then spend on my new stepmother? Of course not."

Jackson winced. "It might help your case."

"I doubt Ellie would be sympathetic."

"Not if you keep placing false rumors with the *Insider*." Jackson shook his head. "I warned you that could backfire. Women hate stuff like that, and with good reason."

"Speaking of which, is the photographer waiting outside?" That's why her tardiness mattered. Much later and she would have blown his plans.

"When Ellie figures out you staged this meeting to get a photo of her coming out of your office she's—"

"Going to yell." Derrick knew it. He even felt a twinge of guilt over it—one he could easily ignore. "But we know this is about more than a PR job. This is about saving the company and there's no way I'm letting her know I need her help for something that big. I'm not giving her that power over me."

"Very romantic."

"This is business. According to my father's stipulations, I have to get my brothers in line and in this office, clean up my image and stop Noah Gold's public hit job, all while single-handedly running a commercial real estate company."

After a lifetime of aiming his sons at each other, Derrick's father wanted them to be one big happy family, all working in the office and getting along. And if they didn't, Derrick would lose the business that meant everything to him. His father already had a buyer outside the family interested. A rich old friend with liquidity and the ability to move fast on the sale.

Just thinking about the requirements of his father's stupid business proposal touched off a new wave of fury in Derrick's gut. He literally could forfeit everything because of his father's stupid whims.

Derrick was about to launch into an angry rant about Eldrick when his office door pushed open. Ellie stepped inside again, looking a little flushed and not a bit worried or afraid of him.

He liked her attitude but the security lapse was a concern. Then he thought about the photographer and wondered if the guy had moved too soon. "How did you get in here?"

"I walked."

He guessed he should have expected that answer from her. "You shouldn't be able to wander around the building without an escort."

She waved the concern away as she approached the desk and held out her hand. "You can worry about your over-the-top paranoid protocol later. Give me the agreement."

"What?"

She continued to hold out her hand. "If I'm going to consider this—"

"Are you?" That surprised him when almost nothing did.

"—I want to make sure you didn't add anything weird in here."

Whatever he planned to say left his head. He suddenly wanted to know what her definition of "weird" might be. "Like what?"

"With you?" She snorted. "Who knows? I don't trust you."

Jackson nodded as he grabbed the folder and gave it to her. "A very solid beginning for a relationship."

Her eyes narrowed as her gaze moved from Jackson to Derrick. "Your guy knows about this nonsense fake dating and engagement offer of yours?"

"Yes, and that document in your hand is nonnegotiable." Derrick knew from their combined thirty minutes together so far that she'd be whipping out the red pen and revising if he didn't put a stop to it now.

She shrugged at him as she opened the file and took a peek inside. "Whatever."

He fought back a sigh. "I'm serious, Ellie."

Her head shot up and she glared at him. "You're not going to win every argument."

"I think I am." He rarely lost and had no intention of starting now. "I'll see you at ten tomorrow."

She turned and headed for the door. "You'll get my answer when you get it."

She was gone before Derrick could respond.

Damn, he liked her. The fire and self-assurance were so sexy. She wasn't yet thirty but she'd grown up fast when she'd lost her parents. He understood what it was like to take on responsibility early. It was one of the reasons he thought they'd be able to handle this arrangement. She would get what she needed and he'd get his obstinate father off his back.

Jackson cleared his throat. "You're smiling."

Derrick refused to play this game. "She's...interesting."

"This engagement thing *is* fake, right?"

"Of course."

"Right." Jackson exhaled. "That explains the stupid look on your face whenever you see her."

Four

The DC Insider: *Visits to the prestigious Hay-Adams. Visits to his office. It appears Ms. Ellie Gold has not only snagged our Hottest Ticket in Town's attention but also has him spinning in circles. Well done, Ellie!*

He had to be kidding. That thought kept running through Ellie's mind as she paged through Derrick's ten—no, fourteen-page agreement while sitting on her couch the next morning.

The thing had tiny print, and rules, and footnotes to new rules and references to yet more rules. The list of restrictions seemed endless. She couldn't date anyone else. He had final approval over the people she saw on a friendly basis during the "term of their arrangement" and over any work plans she intended to pursue.

She had to act loving, whatever that meant. He hadn't used the word *obey* but it was implied in almost every line. And that wasn't even the most ridiculous part. He thought they'd live together. *Actually live together*.

She glanced around her small apartment, from one stack of empty boxes to another. She had savings but that would run out if she didn't find a new job and a cheaper place to live soon. That would be easier if her jackass of an ex-boss hadn't launched an offensive strike when she filed her internal complaint and fired her first, insisting she came on to him. As if that would ever happen.

The man's wife had left town to watch over a sick aunt and he'd had his hands all over her by the next day. Kicking him in the crotch had felt great, but being escorted out of the building hadn't.

His claims were nonsense. He had resources and family money…and a nasty reputation that people spoke about only in whispers and refused to confirm in public. She had documentation of the emails she'd sent after the incident and her complaint. No witnesses to what happened, unfortunately, but she guessed they'd be able to find a pattern of other women once they started digging.

Her lawyer was positive about her chances but cases cost money. She got that but employers weren't exactly lining up to hire a supposed human resources expert who had been fired for making a play for her boss. She could not let this go. Not when it was likely he would do this to someone else.

Thinking about Joe touched off that familiar spiraling sensation in her stomach. That mix of panic and worry. She liked to eat and have electricity. Which led her to the convoluted mess of an agreement on her lap.

Derrick's plan struck her as so odd. She had no idea if wealthy people usually did stuff like this, but she didn't.

She picked up her mug of now-cool tea and prepared to read through the agreement one more time. The doorbell stopped her in the middle of what looked like a never-ending sentence of legalese gobbledygook.

Grumbling, she put down the mug and stood. Slipping her feet into her fluffy pink slippers, she shuffled across the floor. That took about ten seconds since she lived in a studio.

When the doorbell rang again, she skipped her usual check in the mirror by the door. Anyone this impatient deserved to be greeted with the full hair-sliding-out-of-the-ponytail style she had going on.

She peeked through the peephole and froze. *Oh, no, no, no.*

He was here. Now. At her house.

"Open up, Ellie." Derrick's deep voice floated through the door.

She tried not to make a sound.

He sighed loud enough to shake the building. "I can see your shadow under the door."

"Fine." She performed the perfect eye roll as she undid the lock. "What?"

He started talking before she fully opened the door. "It's eleven."

"I own a clock." Though she guessed she looked as if she didn't own a brush. She could practically feel the tangles in her hair without touching it. Add in the shorts and oversize sweater that functioned as her pajamas and she was positive she made quite the picture.

"Are you sure?" His gaze wandered over her and stopped on her slippers. "Those are an unexpected choice."

"Imagine me kicking you with them." She stepped to the side and let him in. Why fight it? He was not exactly the type to scamper off.

He slipped past her, smelling all fresh and clean. Today's suit was navy blue and fit him, slid over every inch of him, perfectly.

He walked to the center of the room then turned around to face her. "You were supposed to be in my office at ten."

No doubt about it, he was much hotter when he didn't talk. "No, you commanded that I give you an answer to your absurd fake engagement suggestion by a stated time and I declined."

"Interesting."

Since that could refer to anything, she ignored it and focused on another annoying fact. "Hey, how did you know where I live?"

He shot her a look that suggested he found the question ridiculous. "Please."

That was not even a little reassuring. "Did Jackson follow me?"

"Jackson is in the car."

Okay... "Is that an answer?"

Derrick looked around the room, from the couch to the rows of bookcases lining the walls and holding her collection of romances and mysteries. He kept going, skipping over the kitchenette and falling on the unmade bed against the far wall.

He turned and stared at her again, his expression blank. "Yes or no, Ellie."

She didn't pretend to misunderstand. He was talking about the agreement. He needed a fake fiancée and, for whatever reason, thought she fit the description. "It's not that simple."

"It actually is."

Of course he would think so. The entire agreement benefitted him. "We don't know each other."

He frowned. "You said that already. So?"

Such a guy. "Really? That's your answer?"

"Again, for what feels like the tenth time, this is a business arrangement, not an actual romance."

She joined him by the couch. "Now you sound ticked off."

"I hate repetition."

Poor baby. "Do you want a fiancée or not? Because I would be doing this for you, not me."

"We both know that's not true. You benefit. Your brother benefits." Derrick shifted his weight and looked down. He stared at the magazines piled on her floor for a few seconds then pushed them to the side with his foot. "All you need to do is follow a few simple rules."

She didn't bother to debate his idea of a "few" because that could take them all day. From his scowl she guessed he wanted to add another provision to the agreement to forbid her slight tendency toward clutter.

"You say that but everyone I know needs to believe it's real." She scooped up the agreement and flipped through the pages then began pointing. "Here, look at this."

He didn't bother to glance down. "I'm familiar with the contract."

"Then you know we're supposed to live together." Which sounded as absurd this time as when she'd read it earlier.

"My house is big." His gaze wandered again. This time over to the boxes she'd gathered in case she needed to move in a hurry. "But I prefer you not live out of boxes. Haven't you been in this apartment for seven months, like right before Noah started working for me?"

She snapped her fingers. "Derrick."

"Don't do that. Ever." He put his hand over hers and lowered it. "What do you want to say?"

The touch, so simple and innocent, shot through her. She felt it vibrate through every cell.

She pulled her hand from his and forced her breathing to slow. "We've barely spent an hour together."

"We'll have separate bedrooms."

As if that were the only problem. "But you expect me to act like a fiancée."

"Whatever that means, yes."

"It's a direct quote from paragraph twenty of this thing." She shook the agreement at him.

"I've never been engaged, but I figure we can work out the details as we go. You know, like do the usual things engaged people do."

She suddenly couldn't breathe. A big lump clogged her throat and she had no idea why. "Usual?"

"Shows of...affection."

He may as well have said poison. "You should hear yourself."

He exhaled as he stepped back. His hand swept

through his hair and, for a brief moment, his thick wall of confidence slipped. He looked vulnerable and frustrated. She didn't think any of it was aimed at her. Not directly. This was more about the circumstances they'd gotten stuck in.

"We both need things, Ellie. You want to help your brother. You have some work issues that I can resolve for you."

"Are you going to give me a job?" She thought about her bills and her fears about losing her apartment. Growing up she never felt welcome or comfortable. Home hadn't been a sanctuary, but now it was. The idea she could lose that security left her shaken.

"Yes, as my fiancée."

With him that *did* sound like a full-time job. But pretending to have feelings might not be enough. They didn't run in the same circles. She didn't know anything about charity functions or season tickets to the Kennedy Center. "People aren't going to buy this."

He stepped closer again. This time his hands came up and his palms rubbed up and down her arms, gentle and warm. "We tell them we met while haggling about your brother. There was a spark and...boom."

"Did you just say *boom*?"

Instead of backing away, he leaned in. "The legal fees stop. Your brother gets some direction and guidance. Your bills get paid and my shareholders stop whining."

"You make it sound reasonable in a weird sort of way." She was practical and everything about this plan, including the very real problem of lying to her brother, was anything but.

"It is."

"My brother will go ballistic." And she feared that was an understatement.

"Trust me. We can sell this."

She didn't miss the fact his words sounded like a plea. She doubted he begged for anything. He probably didn't even ask others for help, but he was asking now.

The realization had her stomach tumbling. This close she could see the intensity in his gaze and feel the heat rolling off him.

"You can't fake a spark." Her voice sounded breathy even in her ears.

"Let's see if we need to."

He lowered his head as his hand slid into her hair. Fingers expertly massaged the back of her neck. His mouth lowered until it hovered over hers. For a second he hesitated, with his eyes searching her face, then his lips met hers. Mouth against mouth, he brushed over hers once. Twice. So enticing.

His scent wrapped around her and his fingers tightened on her. One second they stood a foot apart. The next he closed in. The caress turned to kissing, deep and alive with need. Energy arced between them. Every touch, every press of his lips, proved hot and inviting.

He pulled her tight against him and her common sense faltered. Heat burned through her as her arms slipped up to wrap around his neck. She'd just balanced against his body when he pulled back.

"Right." He cleared his throat as his chest rose and fell on harsh breaths. "There we go."

A haze covered her brain. *"There we go?"*

"Sure. That was fine." He set her away from him. Increased the distance between them to a few feet.

The man was an idiot.

"Fine?" She could barely feel her legs.

"Yes. I'm confident we can fake it." He started walking around the room, almost pacing. "We'll start with dates. In public. Let people see us together." He nodded as he continued the one-sided conversation. "I'd say in a week we move you into my place and announce the engagement."

"That's too fast." She was impressed her brain even spit that sentence out. Right now she couldn't think at all. The kiss had blown out every rational thought and had her wanting to slide that tie right off him.

"Well, it looks as if you're ready to pack."

"I need to sit." She plunked down hard on the armrest of the couch and struggled not to run her fingertips over her lips.

"We'll have a party—"

"No." Good grief, he was already planning. That was enough to snap her out of it.

"Not a big, flashy Christmas party. Just the normal engagement party."

It took a few seconds but her common sense came back. Doubt rushed in right behind it.

"First, it's March. Second, I'm Jewish." That seemed important to throw in there even in a fake engagement, so she did. "And third… I fear your idea of normal."

"We invite the people who need to see us."

People who would later wonder what happened and why it all ended, but he seemed to ignore that part. Fine. It was his problem and they were his friends, so he could figure it out. But she did have one issue she could not ignore. "And what do I tell my brother to keep him from killing you?"

"That we sparked. Tell him a one-night stand turned into something more."

Derrick. Sex. She blocked the thoughts that rolled through her head. The kiss had been enough to unravel her. Anything more would be a huge mistake. "You want me to lie to him?"

"That's the point. We lie to him and the public to diffuse Noah's claims."

She couldn't blame Derrick for that requirement. Noah hadn't exactly been subtle in his attack on Derrick to date. But something about his self-assurance about this agreement and all these details started an alarm bell ringing in her head. "You have this all figured out, don't you?"

"I thought so."

She swung her foot, letting the pink slipper flip through the air. "What does that mean?"

"You're not what I expected."

She stilled. "Right back at ya."

"Lucky for us, I can adapt."

Yeah, lucky her. "You don't exactly strike me as a guy who enjoys surprises."

Some of the tension drained from his face as he stared at her. That sexy little smile of his returned. "Maybe I can change."

She hadn't known that to work with any guy ever. "Oh, come on."

He walked up to her and picked the agreement off her lap. "Sign."

"You know you can't date anyone else while we're pretending to like each other, right?" For some reason it was suddenly very important to her that he know if she did this, they did it together. They'd both suffer.

He made a face. "Does it say that?"

"It will when we write in a bunch of notes in the margin and both initial them." She tapped the agreement. "Basically, every ridiculous provision that applies to me will now apply to you."

He didn't hesitate. "Fine."

That was almost too easy. "That means you're stuck with me for… Wait, there's no end time on this agreement."

His eyebrow lifted. "I'm aware."

For about the hundredth time since she'd met him yesterday she got the sense she was being outmaneuvered. She hated the sensation. "You get two months of fake fiancée time."

"That might not be enough. Say at least three."

She reached down and picked a pen up off her coffee table. She clicked the end and handed it to him. "I'm sure you can adapt to two."

"It seems you think I'll be adapting a lot over the next few weeks." He sounded stunned by the idea.

"I'm happy you realize that. It will make our time together, limited though it may be, more tolerable."

His smile widened. "We'll see."

Five

The DC Insider: *We are hearing that our Hottest Ticket in Town wants to get serious with his new lady but the lady's disgruntled baby brother is having none of it. He's making some big claims, all of which Derrick Jameson denies with a shrug. But can this budding romance bloom with all these distractions?*

Ellie was starting to think her headache would never go away. It thumped in her ears and over her eyes. Even the back of her neck ached.

She'd had two employment interviews today and nothing. Well, not nothing. In the second, the interviewer wanted to talk about Derrick. He didn't specifically ask about her dating life but he bounced around the topic, honing in on her "influence" over Derrick and his decisions and questioning if that would be a conflict. Since she was trying for a generalist HR position—one unrelated to Derrick or his habit of buying up most of the property in the city—she couldn't imagine what Derrick had to do with her possible paycheck.

Being a fake fiancée had sounded easy, two months of playtime while they went to dinner and she didn't panic about the water bill, but it was starting to take over her life. In addition to thinking about him and that voice…and that face…she had other issues. She'd splurged on a muffin at the coffee place around the corner that morning and two people took her photo.

And then there was the *Insider*. Her teeth ground together at the idea of being in the *Insider*'s daily round-up section for two more months. Derrick needed to knock that off. She knew she should have insisted on a "no talking to gossip sites" clause in that stupid agreement. But she hadn't, so now she nursed a glass of wine as she propped her feet on her coffee table and tried to pretend she was stuck in a bad dream.

She'd managed to kick her heels off and find her pink slippers. She had no idea where she'd thrown her suit jacket. Since she couldn't afford new clothes or a big dry-cleaning bill right now, not when she was saving every penny just in case, that could be a problem. She'd just leaned her head against the couch cushion when she heard the rattling. She stared at the ceiling for a second, trying to place the sound.

Jingling. Keys.

The mix of sounds had her jackknifing and jumping to her feet. The wine went *everywhere*. Down her shirt. On her couch. A line ran over her hand as more dripped onto the carpet, destroying any chance of getting that security deposit she so desperately needed back.

The door opened and she spun around, ready to throw the glass. She stopped just in time.

The wind rushed out of her. "Noah?"

Her brother stood there with a face flushed red with fury and his hands balled into fists at his sides. He looked ready to launch. She stepped back without thinking and rammed her calf into the edge of the coffee table.

"What are you thinking?" He hovered in the doorway, with the open hallway to her neighbors in the three-story, converted apartment building right there.

That tone, deep and shaking, brought back memories of the days before she'd found the right doctor for him. Once she'd understood that her parents had caused more trouble for him by not immediately seeking treatment and that the delay could lead to bigger issues later in life, she got Noah help.

But that didn't solve the problem completely. Even now, the more stressed, the more under fire he felt, the more skewed his boundaries became. The uncontrolled anger of the past when he would punch walls was gone, but the faint whisper of frustration remained.

Disregarding the way her shirt now stuck to her skin and the wet chilling her from the inside out, she inhaled and pitched her voice low. "Are you okay? It's not like you to barge in."

"I thought you might have someone in here and not let me open up," he said.

That struck her as the worst response ever. She set

her now-empty glass on a months-old magazine and stared him down. "And you thought that entitled you to use the emergency key?"

"Do you really care that I came in without knocking?"

That was a typical Noah response. He flipped things around to make her feel like the unreasonable one. "It's a matter of privacy."

"I want an explanation." He stepped into the apartment, leaving the door hanging open behind him.

"You mean Derrick." At the use of the name, she could see Noah's jaw clench. His features hardened.

With the straight brown hair and dark brown eyes, Noah looked like their father. While Dad's perpetual good looks and boyish charm had helped to launch him in hundreds of get-rich-schemes over the years, including the one her parents were flying to when they died, Noah tended to be aloof and always assessing.

He came around to the same side of the couch as her. "You're on a first-name basis with the guy who fired me and is trying to frame me?"

She wasn't sure how to broach this subject but she tried anyway… "Is it possible this thing between the two of you has gone off the tracks a bit?" When Noah's mouth dropped open, she hurried to finish the thought. "Maybe there was a miscommunication and then you—"

"He's brainwashed you." Noah sounded stunned at the idea.

She tried to ignore how insulting that was. Tried and couldn't. "What?"

"Is it the money?"

And he made it worse. "What are you talking about?"

"Look, I know you've had a tough time dating and stuff, but Derrick Jameson?" Noah asked. "People are asking me about you and Jameson in the comment sections of my videos. They're questioning *me* now."

So that was it. His precious videos. His crusade. Just once she wished someone would care about her. "That's what this is about? I'm messing up your revenge plans?"

"Having my sister sleep with my enemy is a problem, yes." Noah practically spat as he talked and stepped toward her.

Out of habit, she moved back. He wouldn't hurt her, but he sometimes still funneled his frustration into throwing things, and she did not want to be in the firing line. "You sound like you're twelve."

"He really does."

A now-familiar deep voice sounded from the doorway. Relief slammed into Ellie before she even looked over. It washed right through her, calming her down.

Derrick. He loomed there, wearing a dark suit and fierce frown. The glare did not waver away from Noah.

"You're here." Noah's shoulders fell as if a load of shock had replaced his anger. "In my sister's house."

"You always were very observant." Derrick stepped inside and closed the door behind him.

The soft thud snapped Ellie out of the haze enveloping her. That fast, she flipped from soothing mode to trying to wrestle control back. "Derrick, sarcasm is not helping here."

He looked at her then. His gaze traveled over her, hesitating on the stain plastering her silk blouse to her chest before bouncing up again. "Sorry."

The word sounded so sincere and heartfelt. As if he understood she was ten seconds away from shattering into a million pieces.

"You apologized to her?" Noah's full attention centered on Derrick. "What about me?"

"You stole from me and got caught." Derrick's voice stayed steady even as he shook his head. "If you needed money you could have asked for an advance on your salary." Derrick's eyes narrowed. "But I'm not sure any of this was about money."

Noah turned to face her again. "Do you hear him? His accusations?"

She did. Saw him, too. Watching Derrick was a revelation. If he carried around any guilt, he hid it well. If he had falsely blamed Noah...no, that didn't make sense. It had never made sense, but seeing Derrick now, in full de-escalation mode, made her brother's story even less believable.

She inhaled, trying to calm the last of her frayed nerves, and pointed toward the now wine-stained couch. "Maybe we could all sit down."

"Not with him." Noah pushed by Derrick. Shoved his shoulder into him and kept going. Didn't say anything until he reached the door. "Just wait until the next video."

As soon as Noah's hand hit the doorknob, Derrick spoke up. "Post whatever you want about me but keep your sister out of it."

Noah slowly turned around to face Derrick. "You think you get to order me around when I'm not working for you?"

"If you have a problem, you come for me." He pointed toward Ellie. "Not her. Not ever."

Noah's face went blank. "She's my sister."

"Then act like it."

Derrick forced himself not to follow Noah out the door. He wanted to have it out, make the kid understand he was playing in an adult world now.

Instead he stood there, staring at the door and trying to ease his temper. Something had happened before he'd walked down that hallway and heard the shouting. Ellie was drenched in wine. Hell, it beaded in her hair. But nothing, no furniture or glass, appeared to be broken.

She shook her head. "So much for thinking I was going to be able to enjoy two months of fake engagement bliss."

"Did I promise that?"

"Honestly, no. But I knew my brother would be a bigger problem than you thought." Ellie said the words on a heavy sigh.

Derrick looked at her again. "Your brother is—"

"Still my brother, so be careful with what words you use."

That seemed like the Ellie he'd experienced so far—tough and sure—but the tone sounded defeated. He hated that. "Right."

"He's upset." She lifted the wineglass from the coffee table and a magazine page stuck to it.

"Yeah, I picked up on that."

"He was diagnosed years ago with this disorder you've likely never heard of. Believe it or not, this is a thousand times better than he used to be." She held the glass in midair, peeling the paper off with a loud ripping sound. "His teen years were exhausting."

That was enough of that. Derrick stepped over to her and put his hand over hers. With one quick tug, he liberated the glass then carried it to her kitchen sink. "He's not a teen now, so don't make excuses for him."

"I'm explaining that this is not a matter of him being spoiled."

"Are you willing to concede that, maybe, you make it easy for him to not deal with his issues as an adult?" He stopped for a second with his hands wrapped around the edge of the counter.

Noah was nothing like Derrick's father, Eldrick, except that people rushed to forgive both of them. That innate ability to have people fall all over themselves trying to make things rights and ease any burden... Derrick didn't get it. No one had ever done that for him, which was probably a good thing.

"My point is that he doesn't always handle his anger and frustration the way others do."

Derrick turned around and watched her pick the soaked edge of her shirt up with two fingers and wave it around a little as if trying to dry it. Another button popped open under the strain of all that flapping. He couldn't imagine that move would dry her shirt, but it sure as hell was making him think about things other than this conversation.

From this angle he could see a sliver of skin and the outline of her bra, all lacy and, from the few peeks she'd given him, pink. This dating, no-touching, possible fake-engagement thing might be the death of him.

"Ellie, I have an office full of Noah types. I don't mind odd comments, social awkwardness or even controllable behavioral issues. But I do get pissed off when people steal from me."

She sat on the couch's armrest. "He insists you're lying."

"And I insist he is."

"So, we're at a stalemate."

"Are we?" He appreciated her loyalty to her brother, but she wore emotional blinders when it came to Noah.

He got it. He had brothers, too. Even though, thanks to their father, they didn't see each other much these days, he would do anything for them, including pushing them to take responsibility for their actions.

"If you had evidence…" With her head down, she picked at the couch's material.

"I'm not accustomed to having to prove myself. Most people take my word." Derrick heard his voice rising in volume and lowered it again. "It's one of those things I'm known for, which is why your brother's actions are doubly problematic."

"Any chance you could bend your rules and maybe…" She winced. "I don't know, review the evidence again? With me?"

It was a fair request but this sudden unexplained need to have her trust hit him. It wasn't rational. He hadn't earned it, but still. "We already have a deal, Ellie."

"I don't appreciate being made to choose."

She wasn't getting this. He pushed off from the counter and walked into the living room area. Stopped right in front of her so she had to look up to give him eye contact. "The point of the agreement is to defuse the issue with the public. Noah will either stop with the videos or he won't."

"And if he doesn't?"

The urge to reach out and brush his fingers over

her cheek almost overwhelmed him. He shoved his hand into his pants pocket to prevent any touching.

It was bad enough he was there. That he had this odd need to see her, to make sure she hadn't changed her mind. He had a phone. He knew how to text. Hell, when he'd first thought about a fake engagement and how it would work, he'd assumed his assistant would be the one in contact with Ellie. That his time with her would be for public view only and a complete farce. Yet, here he was. In her house. Talking family drama.

There was nothing disconnected about this arrangement that he could see.

"With us being together, Noah won't be able to hide from me. I'm confident I can get him to understand. I hired him, young and untested, because I saw something in him." He crossed his arms over his chest and scanned the room, not doing anything to hide his long look. "So...this."

"You're changing the topic." She stood as she talked.

The move put her so close. He could smell the shampoo clinging to her hair and the sharp scent of the wine.

"Obviously." His gaze drifted to her shirt. "Do you want to change?"

"I probably have to throw it away." She winced as she plucked at the material. "And I love this shirt."

He didn't become attached to clothes, so he had no idea how to respond to that. "Go ahead."

Without another word, she slipped into the bathroom, hesitating only long enough to grab a balled-up sweatshirt off the top of one of the boxes piled around the room.

He took the few minutes of alone time to study her apartment again. Tiny and cluttered but homey. There were things everywhere. Shoes piled under the window. A stack of magazines under the coffee table. A… was that a suit jacket on the floor? He scooped it up and draped it over the clean part of the couch. That took him to his next errand. Into the kitchen area to find something to clean up the wine on the cushion.

He was kneeling on the only clean and open part of the floor, doing a combination of dabbing and scrubbing on the stain. He was pretty sure it grew the more he worked on it.

Just as he decided it would be easier to buy her a new couch, she stepped into the room.

"Okay, I'm relatively dry…" Her laser gaze honed in on him right away. "You don't have to do that."

"I know."

"You probably have a team of humans who clean for you."

"Are we fighting again?" He hoped not because there was no way for him to win this battle. She clearly thought he was inept at anything but running a business, and since her brother was trying to ruin that, she might not even find him competent in that regard.

"No, but is there a reason you didn't tell me I had wine in my hair?"

This seemed like slightly safer ground. "I wasn't sure you cared."

She frowned at him. "You are an odd man."

That wasn't a topic he wanted to explore, so he stood with the wet rag still in his hand. "You have two choices."

"You're not planning on testing me on the agreement provisions, are you? I didn't memorize the thing."

Her mind really did bounce from topic to topic. Sometimes it took him a few minutes to catch up. He didn't want to admit that or how invigorating he found the entire verbal battle. "This evening we either can go to dinner or I can help you get packed."

"You make those sound like reasonable options."

She stood right in front of him now. Blame the pink slippers, but he towered over her. She wasn't petite or even short. She likely stood around five-seven. But compared to his six-one, he had the definite height advantage. "I can be reasonable."

"I haven't seen much evidence of that." Her voice took on a breathy quality.

He chalked it up to the room or dust or the boxes or something, because his breathing didn't sound right in his ears, either. "Well, I'm told the early days of fake dating can be rough. We'll both adjust."

"That almost sounded like a joke, but you're not wrong. There really should be a handbook."

"No kidding." He'd be studying that thing nonstop if it did exist.

"Dinner sounds fine, but I know there will be a reporter or photographer lurking somewhere, so what you're proposing is a setup with a side of food."

He sighed at her. "You're paranoid."

"Gee, I wonder why." She added an eye roll as if she didn't think he picked up on the sarcasm dripping from her voice. "And the packing thing…"

Any other time. Any other woman, he wouldn't ask. "Yes?"

The oversize gray college sweatshirt shouldn't even

earn a second of thought from him. But on her, with her sexy mouth and those invigorating comebacks and her refusal to take any crap from him, he got reeled in. She talked and he wanted to know more. He'd studied her background in preparation for making their agreement, but now he wanted to hear the details straight from her, in her time.

"That suggests I'm moving in with you now, and I'm not," she said.

About that…he'd rethought that portion of the agreement. He didn't have much time to meet his father's conditions. His father demanded Derrick get this public fight with Noah wrapped up or he'd lose his chance at owning the company. Never mind that he'd brought it back from the brink of bankruptcy or that the Jameson coffers were now full due to Derrick's efforts. His father insisted, once again, that Derrick prove himself.

There were other conditions about bringing his brothers home and repairing the damage dear old dad had done to his sons' relationships. Derrick liked that part. Running the family business with his brothers and without his father's interference had always been his dream.

But the one issue Derrick had to handle first, the one he'd signed an agreement to fix, related to Ellie. She was the only one he could think about at the moment. That and her mouth and those big eyes.

"We should discuss the timing of your move," he said.

She exhaled long and loud and added another eye roll at the end. "Here we go."

Derrick decided to ignore the dramatics and go

right to the heart of the issue. "You are out of work. Your brother clearly is not contained."

"You aren't exactly wooing me so far."

"I was *telling* you, not trying to convince you."

This time she made a clicking sound with her tongue. "Again with the blind obedience thing. So romantic."

He'd had girlfriends, dated other women, even managed to have sex now and then despite his over-whelming workload. None of that had prepared him for Ellie. He'd never met a woman less impressed with his wealth, position and power than her. It was endearing in some ways but it also messed with his usual way of winning an argument. "Should I call you lovely again?"

"Get to the point."

And now a third eye roll. Great.

He heard a noise and was pretty sure she was tapping her slipper against the floor. In his view, he was the one with the reason to want to move this along, but fine. "We should shift the engagement and—"

"Fake engagement."

"Those are words we only use with each other and when no one else is around."

Her eyes widened as she looked around the room. "Do you see someone else here?"

"I'm just saying." Her glare really could melt stone. He wasn't a fan, but he had to admit it was persua-sive. "Fine. Anyway, we should get you settled in."

When he finally got all the words out, she stood there. Silence screamed through the room. Even the foot tapping stopped.

Then... "Wow."

He gave up. "Now what did I say?"

"It's the way you say things. Like, everything is an order."

Damn right. He realized too late he should have made that much more clear in the agreement. "I'm the boss."

"I don't work for you."

"Technically, you do." But he decided not to talk about the fact he was paying for her time, or was about to. She didn't seem to be in the mood to discuss that topic.

"You would be wise not to put this fake engagement in those terms right now."

Yeah, he gave up. "So, dinner?"

She shook her head. "Tomorrow, or maybe the day after. I need a bit of time."

Another zig when he expected a zag. He never thought she'd say no. "Ellie, come on."

"It's not a test." She rested a hand on his chest. "I haven't showered. If people are going to be taking my photograph every two seconds, I should have the opportunity to brush my hair."

He looked down at her fingers and the nails polished a soft pink. Felt the weight of her palm over his heart. "Is this a woman thing?"

"I don't even know what that means."

"Are you still upset about your brother?"

She hesitated then nodded. "Almost always."

"Listen—" Derrick put his hand over hers "—I'll talk to him."

"He'll kill you." And for once she didn't sound excited by the idea.

Still, it wasn't as if he hadn't dealt with trouble before. Compared to the financial crew that wanted to dismantle the company when he became CEO over four years ago and all the fellow businessmen who mistook his youth for weakness, Noah was nothing more than a blip. A small nuisance. "Oh, please."

"I don't think any part of this charade will be as easy as you think it will."

He squeezed her hand. "Trust me."

Six

The DC Insider: *We are concerned, dear readers. It's been five days without a sighting of, or peep about, the most interesting romance in town. Did it already fizzle? There are some nasty whispers out there about the lady's last job. Goodness knows playboy Derrick Jameson has had some interesting things printed about him over the years but it's believed he's put those drinking and carousing days behind him. Maybe Ellie was too wild for her billionaire?*

Derrick sensed Jackson hovering by the door. He'd stepped inside the office but remained quiet. No surprise since Jackson had an uncanny ability to blend in. He overheard more than he should but wasn't the type to start rumors. His loyalty never wavered, which was only one reason Derrick considered Jackson his best friend.

After less than a minute of silence, Jackson cleared his throat. "Is everything okay?"

"With what?" Derrick didn't look up. It was the universal sign for "not now" but he knew Jackson would ignore it.

"Only you would answer that way." Jackson walked into the office. Sat in the chair across from Derrick without waiting for an invitation. "I meant with you... in general."

"I'm fine."

"Is that why you have a woman's shirt in a dry cleaning bag hanging on your office door?"

At the mention of the shirt, Derrick thought about the woman who owned it. Days had passed since they'd talked, and that was no accident. A bit of distance struck him as a smart move. Something about her had him spun around. He wanted her in his home. He'd visited her house for no obvious reason. He never did stuff like that.

"The shirt belongs to Ellie." Not that Derrick wanted to make a big deal about it.

"Yeah, I was hoping you didn't have a second fake fiancée wandering around here."

The comment got Derrick's attention. He settled in his chair as he looked at Jackson. "She had a fight with her brother and spilled wine."

Jackson's eyes narrowed. "Is she okay?"

"In what way?"

Jackson exhaled. "The human way, Derrick."

Derrick had no idea what that meant, but he did get Ellie. At least a little. She played the role of protector. She was the person who came in to clean up the mess, regardless if that meant she didn't have energy left to rescue herself.

"She's overly committed to babysitting her brother. She's been job hunting and I've gotten calls curious about the implications of our relationship. As if I'd get her hired to get the inside scoop on a company. And to top it all off, she's not that excited about moving in with me." The part about her brother should have been the most annoying part, but the last really ticked him off.

"I can't imagine why she doesn't have her bags packed. You're charming."

"It's a big house." Derrick wasn't sure why he needed to keep explaining that.

"Because that was my point." Jackson shook his head as he shifted in his chair. "Is that why you haven't been seeing her? Is she being punished for not jumping to obey your command?"

"What are you talking about?"

"It's as if you're hiding in your office to avoid her… and everything else."

"That's ridiculous." Derrick rubbed his thumb over the leather seam at the edge of the armrest. "I've been slammed with work and am still trying to unravel this Noah mess. It's almost as if he finished his work every day in about an hour and then spent the rest of the time working around our security and protocols and generally searching out every document and email ever sent around here."

"That's scary."

Derrick couldn't disagree with that assessment. "Understatement."

Boredom. That could be the explanation for why Noah had turned on him. Derrick originally assumed greed, but the more he learned about Ellie, inadvertently the more he learned about Noah. From what Derrick could tell, Ellie had eased Noah's way in the world. Maybe too much. It was all something a fake fiancé shouldn't worry about, yet he did. He told himself it was because Noah had stolen from him and he had to fix this, not because he cared.

"He's a genius, right?" Jackson asked.

Derrick was getting tired of hearing that excuse. He knew a lot of really bright people and none of them ever stole from him. "I guess you think that explains his behavior."

"Let's find a new topic. Have you seen the *Insider* today?" Jackson took his cell phone out of his jacket pocket and tapped the screen a few times.

"There shouldn't be anything worth reading about me since I didn't leak a story." Which made him realize he really had ignored Ellie and their arrangement. He should be two steps from putting a fake engagement announcement in the paper. Yet he couldn't pull that trigger, at least not until his brothers hit town and they were on their way.

The hesitancy wasn't based on fear. It was something else…a feeling he couldn't name. This flashing warning signal in his brain that told him to slow down and think things through.

He never expected to want her. This deal was supposed to exist on paper only. He should be able to leave her and not think about her. This whole thing where he wanted to drop by and see her, to call her and talk with her about nothing, made him desperate to create distance between them.

"That's the point. Someone did leak a story and it's not all that flattering to Ellie." Jackson turned his phone around and slid it across the desk toward Derrick.

"What?" Derrick glanced down, skimming the post. Then he read it again. One phrase stuck out: "nasty whispers out there about the lady's last job."

"Damn it."

"You're not the type to let details slip by you, so I'm guessing you knew about Ellie's job issue before you entered into your agreement?"

"Of course. It's all bullshit." He'd made it a point to investigate Ellie before offering her the agreement.

At first, he'd hoped to win her to his side with logic or even bribery, if needed. But the more he'd studied her photo and some bits and pieces of her history, the more the PR firm's offhanded comment about needing an old-fashioned, fake-relationship arrangement to make the Noah problem go away had sounded like the right answer.

And that's how he'd ended up in this mess, wanting her in his bed and at his breakfast table. Smelling her, touching her...tasting her.

"It still sucks for Ellie to have it out there, so public," Jackson said.

"I'll take care of Ellie."

"Did someone mention my name?" Ellie smiled at how the sound of her voice made two grown men freeze in their chairs. Just a handful of words and she had them spinning around and stopping. Now, that was power.

A few seconds later they both continued to stare at her. Jackson recovered first and returned the smile as he rose to his feet. Derrick's reaction was not as welcoming.

"How did you get in here?" Derrick practically barked the question.

Every single day she came up with more things she should have added to their ridiculous agreement. Today? A "no shouting" clause.

"I walked." And she did that again after closing the office door. In a few steps she joined the men by Derrick's desk.

"I'm serious. The protocol and security lapses are starting to annoy me."

Derrick's voice sounded low and growly. She refused to find that sexy. "So, I've been subjected to your nonannoyed personality to date?"

"Ellie." That's it. He said her name in a flat, monotone voice.

He truly was exhausting.

"A very nice woman showed me back. I told her my name and said we were dating—it's weird how much attention that attracted, by the way—and that I needed to talk to you about what was posted in the *Insider*." It had been the first time she talked to anyone about dating Derrick. The way the words had rolled out of her scared her. The lies should have caught in her throat, but no. "I think she took pity on me, probably because I said the part about us dating."

Derrick picked up his phone. "Who was it?"

"Why?"

"She should have called me first."

Truly exhausting. "Then I'm not telling you."

Derrick lowered the handset again. "The person works for me."

Every conversation with him turned into a debate. The few days apart hadn't done anything for his bossiness. She'd hoped he'd also magically turn less attractive. No luck there, either. "The person *helped* me. I'm not tattling on her."

"Tattling?"

She sighed, letting him know she was done with this topic, then glanced over at Jackson. "Did he really forget about dating me like the gossip post said?"

Jackson winced. "That's unclear at the moment."

"Trust me, ignoring you would be impossible," Derrick said.

"It's been days since we signed the agreement, then we had the canceled dinner plans because of your work emergency and then you went into hibernation mode. Even the *Insider* noticed, which is weird because I thought you were the one who fed them their intel."

She'd tried not to let the newest post bother her. Her ex-boss's accusations bordered on horrifying. They were the type to disqualify her for a human resources positions if they were true, which they were not. But no one would care about the veracity of his claims. It was his word versus hers, and now that her supposed relationship with Derrick fueled the town's gossip machine, those untrue accusations would grow even louder.

"Did you need something?" Derrick asked her.

She noticed he skipped right over her comment

about the gossip post. She turned to Jackson for assistance. "Do you think he hears his tone when he talks?"

"I can only hope not." Jackson shook his head. "You should hear him when he actually yells."

She snorted. "No, thanks."

"Ellie!"

This time Jackson laughed. "There, that was close."

Yeah, it looked as if they fully had Derrick's attention now. He held the edge of his desk in a death grip.

Ellie took pity on him. From the exhaustion tugging at the corner of his eyes to the rumpled shirt to the loosened tie, he seemed to be working nearly round the clock after all. "I'm going to ignore the near shouting because I was purposely trying to prick your temper."

"Good Lord. Why?"

She hated to admit it but part of her was testing him. After a few tough years with Noah, running through their parents' life insurance and holding on to the family home only with the help of an aging aunt who lived with them to satisfy a well-meaning social worker, she needed to see if Derrick could control his temper. Then there was the issue of being ignored. "I texted you yesterday and you didn't text back."

Jackson cleared his throat. "So that we're clear, I really want to stay and listen to the rest of this and see how it turns out, but I sense you two need to hash this out without me."

Something in his tone, a mix of amusement and general fondness for Derrick, broke through, making Ellie smile. "Does that mean you'll make him tell you later?"

Jackson nodded. "Definitely."

With a final wink at her and a small nod in Derrick's direction, Jackson took off. He slipped out, closing the door behind him.

"I like him." She did a second glance when something about the door caught her eye. The shirt. The dry cleaning bag.

"I was working."

Derrick's comment dragged her attention to the conversation. She slipped into the seat Jackson had vacated. "Oh, you're answering my previous question now? No texting because you're a busy, busy man?"

"Yes."

"Just so you know, being ignored is frustrating even in a fake dating situation."

For a few seconds Derrick didn't say anything. His gaze searched her face then he leaned into his chair. "I'll do better."

"I'm impressed that's your response." Stunned was more like it. But at his words, she relaxed into the chair, letting her hand fall over the edge of the armrest.

"You strike me as the type who could bolt at any time, so I'm being careful."

Which lead her to another one of the reasons for her visit. "You should know my brother keeps calling me to complain about you. Fair warning, I think another video is coming."

"I'll try to talk to him."

She wanted to believe Derrick could get through to Noah before his behavior spiraled much more. He was fixated on Derrick. Part of her wondered if it was the shock of being fired. But she loved that Derrick promised to try and was holding firm to that vow. Her father used to promise a lot and never follow through. She sensed Derrick was not that kind of man.

"It's not easy to win him over." She hesitated, not sure who much more she should share. "I've tried."

"I get that, but let someone else carry the load for a change."

That sounded so good, so promising, that a wave of relief rolled through her. "We lived together for so long. Right up until he got a job with you and moved into his own studio. Even in college I commuted and went home to him each night."

"You raised him by yourself after you lost your parents?" He sounded horrified at the thought.

"A great-aunt lived with us, which made the court happy. Little did the judge know she chain-smoked, spent her days watching baseball and swearing at the television and was really eighty, even though she looked at least a decade younger." Just thinking about Aunt Lizzy made Ellie smile. "She died my senior year of college. By then I was old enough that the social worker didn't make a fuss."

"You haven't had it easy."

She didn't know anyone who did.

"We have this other thing we need to deal with." She bit her bottom lip as she tried to come up with the right words to describe what really happened. "Joe Cantor. The *Insider* brought up my work history. That can only mean people are whispering about it and making up details... Joe was my boss... He's been saying... I mean, it's not as if it actually happened."

Derrick reached his arm across his expansive desk. "Ellie? Breathe."

She did. "I did not come on to him."

Saying the words brought the frustration crashing down on her again. She had enough to deal with without Joe and his lies. But what she really wanted was to reach out, to grab on to the lifeline Derrick offered. Fighting that urge, she stayed still in the chair.

"Of course not."

"Yeah, that's…" Her brain caught up with the conversation and the air whooshed right out of her body. "Wait, you believe me?"

Derrick's chair squeaked when he got up. Footsteps thudded against the floor as he came around the desk to sit on the edge right in front of her. "Your former boss is a raving jackass."

"I could insert a general snide comment here about businessmen in DC." One that fit a lot of the men she'd met and worked both with and for in the two jobs she'd had since college, the first at a department store then the last one with Joe. But it didn't fit Derrick.

He folded his arms in front of him. "Please refrain."

"I'm stunned you're taking my side. I thought you rich sit-behind-a-desk dudes stuck together."

"And I'm ignoring that description." He continued to watch her. "But the firing was not news to me."

She wrapped her fingers around the edges of the armrests. The wood dug into her palms but she held on. "Technically, I was laid off."

"*Actually*, you were marched out of the office building by security."

She felt something inside her deflate. "Gossip really does run wild in this town."

"There's also rumor you kicked Joe during this argument?" There was no judgment in Derrick's tone. If anything, he sounded amused by the thought.

"Right between the legs." She sighed. "Yeah, that happened."

"Well, there you go."

"Excuse me?"

"Joe is said to enjoy the chase but he clearly doesn't like a woman escalating it to the point of kicking his…"

She laughed. "You can say it."

He smiled at her. Big and beautiful and warm. "Balls."

The amusement died down, leaving behind one unanswered question. "You know about how Joe acts but…"

"What?"

"Are you friends?"

"Hell, no." Derrick made a face that suggested he was appalled at the idea. "And since I hired four women in management positions away from his office years ago, before you were there, he's not my biggest fan."

"You did? I might need their names for my employment attorney. And maybe your testimony."

He nodded. "No problem."

Score one more for Derrick Jameson. He wasn't anything like she expected…well, in some ways, yes. The bossy, intimidating, totally hot part—yes. The kind of sweet side that peeked through now and then? Nope. She had not been prepared for that at all.

"You almost sound likable." More than almost, but that was enough to admit for now.

"Don't start that rumor." He gave her a conspiratorial wink. "Really, though, I'm surprised you lasted with him for more than a day. I can't imagine you taking his nonsense for five seconds without lecturing him to death."

"See, I think there was a compliment in there somewhere, so I'll just say thank you."

"You're welcome." He dropped his arms and let his hands rest on his lap. "And I'm sorry I ignored your text."

"I believe you." But that left one big question. "So, who planted the gossip in the *Insider*? It sounds like someone wants to discredit me."

"I don't know but I'll find out."

An edge had moved into his tone. Usually that sort of thing touched off her guard and her defenses rose. But not this time. She knew the temper wasn't directed at her. "Now you sound angry. Why?"

"Why?"

He sure did enjoy raising his voice. "It's a simple question."

"I don't want anyone messing with you."

"But this is…us…it's fake." She sputtered through the explanation.

"That doesn't mean I want people to spread false rumors about you. How much of a jackass do you think I am?"

"That's kind of sweet."

He frowned at her. "What is?"

"The protective thing. Well, so long as you don't go nuclear about it." She felt obliged to add that caveat since he tended to do things in a *big* way. The last thing she needed was him following her around threatening people.

"Let's say I know what it's like to be on the wrong end of gossip."

Her shoulders fell as some of the comfort that had seeped into her bones seeped right out again. "You're talking about Noah."

"I wasn't." Derrick stood, looming over her. "I don't want to fight with you tonight, and talking about your brother is a guaranteed way to get you fired up."

"What do you want?"

He inhaled deep enough to move his chest up and down. "This."

Then he reached for her. Those strong hands wrapped around her arms and pulled her out of the chair. The move was smooth and gentle; she was on her feet before she even knew what was happening.

He stopped right before kissing her, so she took over. Slipped her arms around his neck and pulled him in closer. He clearly took that as a yes because he regained control from there.

His mouth slid over hers in an explosive kiss that had her pushing up on her tiptoes. Heat washed over her and her muscles went lax. The soft sounds of their kisses mixed with a low grumble at the back of his throat.

This wasn't a test. This kiss lingered and heated. It seared through her, burned a trail right through the heart of her. Stole her breath and left her dizzy and more than a little achy.

When they finally broke apart, her brain had scrambled as her insides turned mushy. Seconds later, she still clung to him, half hanging off him. Those dark eyes searched her face, focused on her mouth, until she could barely breathe.

"Was that to make the engagement seem more real?" The question came out as a whisper. She regretted it a second later, sure that he would use it as an excuse to switch to the cool, in-control Derrick she'd met that first night.

He smiled at her. "Do you think there are cameras in here?"

"I meant were you trying to get me accustomed to kissing you."

"I kissed you because I wanted to kiss you." He skimmed his thumb over her lower lip. "For the record, fake engagement or not, I don't want you to kiss me unless you want to."

"We seem to be stepping into dangerous territory."

"Agreed." He pressed one last quick kiss on her mouth then stepped back. "Dinner?"

The sudden space between them had her emotionally flailing. She tried to act detached. Unaffected. "Okay, is *that* for the fake engagement?"

"You're going to make my head explode."

"Very sexy."

He cupped her cheek and his fingers slipped into her hair. "Yes, you are."

The simple touch, so light, felt so good...and so scary.

This was fake. This was about saving Noah and restoring Derrick's reputation. But still. "Derrick."

"Just dinner. For anything else I'll need a clear green light." He dropped his hand again.

"Wait, do you—"

"Since talking tends to get us in trouble, let's eat." He slipped around to his side of his desk and opened the top drawer. Out came his wallet and keys.

"This feels unsettled." Probably because she wanted

to jump on top of him, wrap her legs around his waist and keep kissing him.

"That's my reaction every second since I met you." He headed toward the door, clearly expecting her to follow him.

She still was not a fan of the way he assumed she'd acquiesce like everyone else seemed to do for him. "Is that my shirt?"

"Well, it isn't mine." He took the hanger off the hook on the door and handed it to her. "Here you go."

She decided to ignore the sarcastic part of his response. "I've been looking for it."

"I had it cleaned."

The bag crinkled in her fingers. "For me?"

"I don't plan to wear it."

It sounded like they were back to the clipped sentences and defensive tone. She wondered if he was going to slip into that mode every time they kissed. "Are you being grumpy because I caught you doing a nice thing?"

"Don't get used to it."

She wasn't sure if he meant the grumpiness or the nice gesture. Right then, she didn't care.

Seven

The DC Insider: What happens when a nice dinner turns into a near fistfight? We're not sure, either, but we think we came close to witnessing such an event. Rumors have been swirling about Ellie Gold's last job and her unceremonious firing, but Derrick Jameson set us straight. She's the innocent party, he insists. We would have asked more questions but he was busy taking his lady home for the evening—his home.

Ellie Gold had him completely rattled. Just when Derrick thought he'd figured her out, she said something unexpected. He'd cleaned her shirt—a random, simple thing—and she'd cradled it in her hands as if it were an expensive diamond.

And that kiss.

Before that first one in her apartment about a week ago, he'd planned to keep things on a friendly, non-kissing level. But then his lips had met hers and his brain misfired. He hadn't been able to speak or to think. All he'd wanted to do was to hold on and keep going. He told himself it was because Noah had stolen from him and he had to fix this, not because he cared, but even he was having trouble buying that.

He didn't do overwhelmed. He didn't believe in rainbows or stars or whatever people claimed to see when they experienced a great kiss. He certainly didn't get all breathless and confused when a woman's lips touched his. Not usually, anyway. But with Ellie his body and brain went into free fall.

And it wasn't a onetime thing. The second kiss today nearly scrambled every bit of common sense he possessed. He had been two seconds away from pinning her to the wall and tunneling his hand up that slim skirt when he forced his body to pull back.

She messed him up. Took his balance and his control and ground them into nothing.

Now he watched her study the dinner menu. She even managed to make that look sexy. Her fingers slid along the edge. She lifted her chin as she scanned the page.

He was beginning to think he was losing it.

They sat at a small table near the window of a wildly popular French bistro near Logan Circle. It hadn't been hard to get a last-minute reservation because Derrick had a financial interest in the place. A chance he took on a chef he knew with some of the money he'd stockpiled over the years and it worked out. It also meant there was always room for him. He had to assume the position of the table, out in the open, was the overeager manager's way of capitalizing on his presence there tonight.

People noticed. Quite a few businessmen turned around when he entered the restaurant with Ellie on his arm. Some came over and said hello. One let his gaze linger a bit too long on Ellie's chest for Derrick's liking.

Bottom line—he didn't like being on display. "I feel exposed."

Ellie hummed as she continued to scan the food options. "You picked the game."

"What does that mean?"

"I'm assuming you chose this place, one of the hardest restaurants to get a reservation at right now, to be seen." She peeked at him over the top of the menu. "I'm not even going to ask how you got us in on such short notice. I'll assume this is a case of you being ready at all times for a photo op."

He reached over and lowered her menu so he could meet her eyes without anything getting in the way. "This is dinner, not a photo op."

"That's a first."

"And I'm part owner of this place. The behind-the-scenes money guy."

Her mouth opened a few times before she actually spat out any words. "Well, of course you are."

"Sarcasm?"

"More like *is there any part of this town you don't own* awe." She folded her menu and set it on the space in front of her. "You seem to have an interest in everything."

She was joking but he decided to give her a real

answer. "For the record, I am a minority owner in the family business. My father has the largest stake, and likes to hold that over me. I've tried to branch out with some other investments so I'm prepared."

She frowned. "For what?"

"His whims."

And that's exactly how Derrick saw it. His father played games. He liked to make his sons prove themselves over and over.

Derrick refused to be pushed aside or run off because he viewed the family business as his legacy. He'd worked there during college summers and all throughout business school. After that, he'd come on board full-time and worked his way up. Spent months in every department.

His father demanded perfection and when he didn't get it he'd resort to public humiliation. So, Derrick learned quickly not to make any mistakes. Four years ago his father offered more responsibility and Derrick grabbed at the chance. He'd expanded the family's commercial real estate and construction business and personal holdings.

Ellie watched him for a second then rested her hand on the table. "He's difficult."

"Understatement." Derrick noticed she didn't ask it as a question, so she must have heard at least some of the rumors about his notoriously demanding father. "He put me in charge of expansion, sure I'd fail. He questioned every decision, every strategy. Made it nearly impossible to move forward then yelled because we weren't moving forward."

He was going to say more but stopped. He never talked about family stuff with anyone except Jackson and his brothers. Battling for the business he dreamed of running since he was eighteen was a constant frustration for him. He thought he'd earned it, but no.

"But you eventually convinced him." She leaned in. "You're the big boss now. Right?"

"I'm in charge of the day-to-day operations, but there's no guarantee it's permanent. There are some… things I need to accomplish first." Derrick pivoted off that subject before he divulged something he didn't mean to divulge. "The only reason my father isn't here, picking every move apart, is because he's in love."

Derrick heard the snide edge to his voice but didn't bother trying to hide it. The idea of his father spending his days laughing and drinking after having spent so many years making his sons' lives a constant competition, pitting them against each other and punishing them for any perceived failure, rubbed Derrick raw.

Ellie blinked. "Excuse me?"

"Wife number four."

"Oh." Ellie's mouth dropped open. "Do we like her?"

"Thanks to Jackie, my father is testing out possible retirement far away on a beach in Tortola." He laughed. "So, yes."

"Your family is not dull."

No kidding. "And since you commented on my businesses, you should know I have no financial interest in the gas station across the street. I wish I did because I think my tank is almost empty."

"You'll probably buy that next week."

Since she sounded amused by his comments he played along, happy to move off a subject that kept him up at night worrying. Off the fear his father would show up and take it all away without warning. Derrick would survive, of course, but he wanted the family business and the family that went with it. "If I find some extra time at lunch to buy a multimillion-dollar venture, sure."

"Ellie."

Her smile disappeared as she looked up at their unwanted dinner guest. "Mr. Cantor."

Joe Cantor, Ellie's former boss, stood at the edge of the table. A guy known to have a wandering eye and a big mouth. He wasn't half the businessman he thought he was. The only thing that saved him was a mix of old family money and a forgiving wife. As far as Derrick was concerned, the wife could do a lot better than Joe—a man still trying to live off his former reputation as a big-man-on-campus almost two decades later.

Joe glanced at Derrick then focused on Ellie again. "I've been reading about the two of you."

Yeah, Derrick was done. "And I've been reading about you."

Joe's eyes narrowed. "What?"

"I thought you'd like to explain why Ellie was fired." Derrick didn't bother lowering his voice. He wanted people to know how little he thought about Joe's fake dismissal story. "Right here. To my face. In front of her. Let her finally tell her side."

Joe's smirk didn't waver. "Look, it's over. You two are together now."

"Clearly." Before tonight Derrick didn't think much of Joe. Now he thought even less. This intimidation tactic was a clear misstep. A smart guy wouldn't have tried it.

"Whatever happened between us—"

"Nothing." Ellie's eyebrow lifted as she stared Joe down. "Nothing happened between us. Ever."

Joe shook his head. "Ellie, it's okay. It's done."

"Not really." Derrick hated this guy now. "She's still waiting on your apology."

For the first time Joe's mouth fell into a flat line. "What?"

"I don't like when people make up stories about my woman."

Ellie made a humming noise. "*My woman*? Do we like that phrase?"

"Too much?" Derrick asked, seeing in Ellie's eyes that she was enjoying Joe's public takedown. Derrick looked at Joe again, who didn't appear as smug now. "Then ignore the word choice, but the result is the same. One more false word about her coming on to you—which we both know is complete bullshit—and you get to fight me."

Joe let out a pathetic strangled laugh and did a quick glance around. "Are you threatening me, Derrick?"

"I'm actually threatening your business. I thought that was obvious." He glanced at Ellie. "No?"

She put her hand over his. "I thought you were very clear."

"Thank you, dear." Derrick winked at Ellie then turned to Joe again. "Clean up the *misunderstanding* about her firing and then keep your mouth shut, and we're good. Maybe she'll even decide not to sue you."

She shrugged. "I can't promise that."

Joe glared at Derrick. "You can't be serious."

"We're done here." Derrick slid his hand out from under Ellie's and picked up his menu again. "You hungry? I am."

Joe closed in on Ellie. "Tell him the truth."

She didn't even flinch. "Your wife went out of town, you came on to me, I kicked you and then I got fired."

"That's not—"

"Illegal?" More than one table of restaurant patrons was watching now. The manager even made a move toward the table, but Derrick gave a small shake of his head to keep him back. He had this handled. "Yes, Joe. I think it is."

She shrugged. "My lawyer says it is."

Fury flashed in Joe's eyes. "You can't outlast me and you know it."

Ellie deserved better and this show. Even though they kept it respectable, Derrick knew the gossip would make the rounds. They'd proved their point. Now it was time for Joe to get the message and slink away. "For us, it's a date. For you? This is a chance to move without increasing your liability. I'd take it."

Joe gave them one last stare then turned and walked off. He was smart enough to not cause a bigger scene or to storm away. He slipped through the tables with a smile on his face as if they'd been having a nice dinner talk.

The second after he was gone the restaurant's noise level rose again. People seated nearby returned to eating and servers ran around getting food and drinks to the crowded tables.

When Derrick finally glanced across the table

again he saw Ellie staring at him. A smile played on her lips. A sexy smile that jolted through him.

"That was thoroughly satisfying," she said.

"Now that's the sort of thing I like to hear from a date."

The rest of the dinner consisted of talking and some verbal sparring, but the fun kind. Ellie finished her meal in a satisfied haze. She enjoyed letting her guard down and ignoring all the stress for an hour.

After her parents died she'd juggled college and Noah. She'd waded through their mess of an estate. All those failed ventures her father had started and driven into bankruptcy. All the debts that had to be paid and the questions people had looked to her to answer.

She'd handled all of it. Put her personal life on hold, limited dating to brief flings and friendships to a minimum. She'd worked hard, kept her head down and never expected anything from anyone. That's why her friendship with Vanessa meant so much.

Vanessa was the kind of best friend you could call in the middle of the night and she'd come running. She was smart and supportive. They could sit in silence for hours and watch movies. Gossip. Ellie was comfortable around Vanessa when Ellie wasn't all that comfortable with most people. Not on a deep level. Not enough to trust.

It's why Derrick's near automatic defense took Ellie by surprise. For the first time in ages, she had someone other than Vanessa looking out for *her*. Willing to stand up to someone else and protect her from the fallout. Willing to take care of her. It was a heady and humbling feeling.

That was the only explanation she had for why she stood in the middle of his kitchen at after nine that night instead of in her apartment. That and the fact she wanted to be there. Wanted to spend time with him. Wanted to know more about the man who fought so hard against his father.

She'd seen the stark ache in Derrick's eyes at dinner as he talked about the business. He tried to joke about finances, but she'd heard the roughness in his voice. She tried to imagine what it was like to be the oldest son of a man who enjoyed demeaning people, including his own children.

They'd walked in from the garage with the lights clicking on as they'd moved through the high-ceilinged, expertly-carved-moldings, man-this-is-expensive Georgetown house. Even in the dark she had seen rows of impeccably kept brick town houses as they'd driven through the tree-lined streets. The whole area dripped with wealth.

By the time they'd pulled off a narrow street and into Derrick's garage—a thing she didn't really think existed in this part of town outside of huge mansions—she'd confirmed she was way out of her league.

Now she looked around the pristine kitchen with the gray cabinets and swirling white-and-gray-marble countertops that looked like they should be on the cover of some fancy home magazine. Not a pot out of place. Not a glass in the sink.

For the fourth time since they'd left the restaurant, confusion crashed into her. She'd been riding this emotional roller coaster for most of her life but with

Derrick the ride turned wild. She flipped between interest and frustration. One minute she wanted to kiss him. The next, punch him.

They were supposed to be in a business arrangement and nothing more. But those kisses and the way he touched her, looked at her…how her heart thundered in her ears when he smiled. How she wanted to peel away the layers and peek beneath to see the real man.

Her attraction to him in more than an objective "oh, he's good-looking" way was unexpected and kind of unwanted. It clouded everything. They were from different worlds and using each other. But the glimpses she'd seen weren't of a thoughtless playboy who liked to throw money around. He was deeper than that. Far too likeable. Very tempting.

She sat on the stool at the massive kitchen island then stood again. "I feel like we're inviting trouble being here alone."

"You're going to be moving in here soon." Derrick took off his suit jacket and loosened his tie. Next he reached for one of the big double doors to the refrigerator and brought out two bottles of water. "You should get used to the place."

"Not that soon."

He set the bottles next to her on the countertop. "I'm thinking within days."

"I'm saying within weeks." She tried to mentally slam the brakes on all of this. The move, the engagement, the agreement. If the attraction she felt for him was real, should she really mix in the parts that weren't? She really didn't know anymore.

Life whizzed by her so quickly since she'd met him.

Her brain rushed to keep up, but when that failed, her emotions took over. Her wants and needs won out. She wanted him to touch her again. To give in and take something for herself for a change.

"You really do thrive on being difficult," he said.

She thought they were well matched on that score, but she didn't bother to argue since that would only prove his point. "Maybe, but I'm still grateful."

He put his hands on the counter on either side of her, trapping her there in a warm cocoon. "For what?"

Tension spun up inside her. She knew she could break out of his hold but the problem was she didn't want to. That's how little it took. He moved in, close enough for her to smell the soap on his skin, and her heartbeat took off in an all-out race. She wanted to run her fingers over the light stubble on his chin. Feel his mouth on hers.

She fought for breath as she pretended to stare at the white farmhouse sink behind him. "Look at this kitchen. My entire apartment would fit in here."

His gaze searched hers until she looked at him again. "For what, Ellie?"

"What you said to Joe. How you stuck up for me without making me prove my side of the story." She gave in to the need to touch him then. Let her fingers trail over his tie, follow it to the end and hang there. "For the nice dinner."

"I don't want your gratitude."

Her stomach took off on a frenzy of somersaults. "What do you want?"

"You."

The deep voice, having that laser-like focus trained on her, the combination pushed the fight out of her.

She'd been running and making excuses and coming up with arguments. But there, staring up at him, seeing the intensity in those eyes, she gave in.

She tugged on his tie and brought him in even closer. The air between them burned with a new energy. His mouth met hers and the rest of the world blinked out.

Heat roared through her as his lips crossed hers. Firm kisses. The sweep of his tongue over hers. One minute she stood there and the next he lifted her onto the counter. Her tight skirt bunched high on her thighs as he pushed them apart to stand between them.

His hands roamed over her back then to her neck. Fingers slid through her hair. His touch managed to be soothing and demanding at the same time. Heat radiated off him as she unknotted his tie. And when his mouth moved to her cheek then to her ear, a shiver stole her balance. She fell hard against him as his tongue traced a line down her neck.

They both made hungry, growling sounds and she ached for more. Her heels closed around his thighs, tightening his body against hers.

"Ellie?"

"Yes. Green light." She caught his mouth again. The kiss seared through her, destroying her worries.

His hands skimmed around her body, over her breasts. She almost sighed in relief when she felt his fingers on her shirt buttons. The voice inside her head screamed for him to hurry, but a part of her wanted to savor every minute. Every lingering touch.

"Oh, damn. Sorry!"

The deep male voice rang out in the kitchen. Ellie heard it but it took her another few seconds to realize what was happening.

Someone was there, in the house. As soon as that thought registered in her brain, she shoved against Derrick's chest. Their legs tangled together and his hand got caught in her shirt. When he stepped to the side, turned around and stood in front of her like a human shield, he almost ripped her silk blouse.

Derrick's shoulders went from stiff to relaxed as he looked at the intruder. "Spence?"

She didn't have the same reaction as she worked in double time to line up her shirt buttons and get them closed again.

The other man held up a hand but he didn't try to hide his smile. "I can leave."

"Of course not." Derrick glanced at her over his shoulder. His gaze bounced to her shirt and he nodded before stepping to the side and helping her from the counter. "Ellie Gold, this is one of my brothers, Spencer."

She grabbed for her skirt and tugged it down before she gave his brother an unexpected show. "Right."

Heat flamed in her cheeks. She could only imagine the force of her blush, but she pushed through and gave him eye contact. She should have done that first because she would have known the two men were related.

Spencer was a slightly stockier version of Derrick. They both towered over her and were blessed with that's-almost-unfair good looks. The Jameson family had a heck of an impressive gene pool. Their father might be a jerk but he churned out dark-haired hotties without trouble.

Spencer's smile reached his eyes, which made her think he did it more than his brother. That might also explain the lightness about him. Derrick walked around as if he carried the responsibility for the world on his shoulders. Spencer didn't give off that vibe.

"I'm Spence." He held out his hand. "The middle Jameson brother."

Derrick snorted as they shook hands. "The one with the shitty timing."

"I didn't know… See, Derrick never really brings… Okay then." Spence made a hissing sound. "I'll stand here and not talk."

His stumbling eased her discomfort at having been caught like a naughty teen on prom night. "What were you trying not to say?"

"He's pointing out that I'm not in the habit of bringing women to my house," Derrick said.

Spence nodded. "Yeah, that."

"Ellie is different." Derrick picked up one of the water bottles off the counter and offered it to her. "She's moving in."

Spence's eyes grew even wider. "Really?"

She waited for Derrick to explain about the agreement and Noah and all the trouble they were trying to fix. When Derrick didn't say anything, she glanced over at him. "And?"

He wrapped an arm around her shoulders. "We're still fighting over the date."

Her mind jumbled again. "Wait…"

"Ah, now I get it," Spence said.

That made one of them. She was still lost. "Want to explain it to me?"

Derrick moved then. He put down the water and reached for his suit jacket. His keys jangled in his hand a second later. "Let me run Ellie home then we'll catch up."

Spence frowned. "She's the one who should stay."

She wanted some air…and an explanation. "No, it's fine." She glanced at Derrick, sending him a we-need-to-talk glare. "You ready?"

If she knew her way around the house she would have taken off without him. Instead she followed him along a hallway and a set of stairs to the bottom level of the grand three-story home.

Her head was pounding too hard for her to concentrate but as soon as they were in the garage with the door shut behind them, she spun around to confront Derrick. "Your brother doesn't know."

He had the nerve to stare at his keys and not her. "About what?"

She put her hand over his. "That this is a fake arrangement, Derrick."

"It didn't feel fake a second ago." He hit her with intense eye contact. The kind that made her breath catch in her throat.

"I refuse to regret that."

"I hope not since I'm planning on finishing it very soon." He blew out a long breath. "Look, if you can't tell your brother, I can't tell mine. That seemed fair to me."

He said it as if the logic made perfect sense. She didn't buy it. Jackson knew. She had every intention of telling Vanessa when they met for lunch tomorrow as planned. She had no idea how she held it in this long, except that Vanessa had gone away on a work trip for four days.

No way did Derrick's brother need to be kept in the dark about something this big. He should know he wasn't really about to get a sister-in-law. "I hate when you sound reasonable because it convinces me you're hiding something."

"I think our agreement makes it clear we both are."

It was hard to argue with that. "Okay, but when it comes to this agreement and what we both get out of it, we'll be honest with each other, right? We need each other, and I'm not talking about the kissing."

"I'm happy to talk about the kissing."

Her stomach did a little tumble. "I'm not kidding, Derrick."

"Trust me."

He made it sound so easy, but he had no idea. Her father used to say that, too. *We'll be fine, Ellie. This time the plan will work. You won't have to switch schools.* Then he broke the promises almost as quickly as he made them.

"You've been in charge and getting your way for too long." She'd thought that from the first minute she'd met him and she still believed that was true.

"I have a feeling that's about to change."

Sounds as if he was finally getting it. "Count on it."

Eight

The DC Insider: *There is a lot happening in the Jameson household these days. Middle brother and perennial black sheep, Spencer, has returned to the nest. Does that mean baby brother Carter is on his way? Bigger question: if the family is coming into town, do Derrick and Ellie have big news to share?*

Derrick couldn't fight off the very strong feeling he'd screwed things up tonight. He didn't regret kissing Ellie, touching her. Hell, he'd been five seconds away from slipping her underwear off and carrying her upstairs when Spence showed up.

Them in bed. Sex. All that was going to happen. When he'd first met her, he'd thought he could keep the attraction separate, but since it sparked both ways, why fight it? They could enjoy each other, help each other with their family issues and have a good time. Win, win.

The only problem, as usual, came from his father. Those damn requirements of his. The ones that stood between Derrick and the business he'd always wanted.

In Derrick's head it made sense to hide from Ellie the fact that he could lose the business. Why give her that much power over him? It also made sense to hide the fake engagement part from Spence and Carter, because they would never agree with his decision to make that choice.

But all the half-truths, the partial information, meant lying to the people around him. He'd never out-and-out deceived his brothers before. Sure, when they were younger, he'd downplayed their father's crappy actions and how poorly he'd treated their mom before she died. What kind of man went to his wife's deathbed and asked for a divorce so he could marry his mistress sooner?

This was different. He wasn't protecting them as much as trying to handle everything his own way without interference. He worried that made him the asshole this time.

"So." Spence made the word last for three syllables. "I think you left something out of our weekly phone call. We talked about Dad's stupid business agreement, but I don't remember you mentioning Ellie."

That call was a tradition Derrick would not let die. Their father had tried to drive the brothers apart by making them compete over everything from sports to his affection. Derrick refused to let the bond break. He hadn't always been a great brother. At times he'd outright failed at keeping the family running, but Carter and Spence mattered to him and losing them was not an option. Ever.

They were both welcome in his house anytime. He'd bought a five bedroom so they'd have a place to stay when they were in town. Carter rarely came in from the West Coast. Not since the huge falling-out with their father over the running of the family estate in Virginia—the Jameson property no Jameson currently lived in.

Spence had been bouncing around from place to place, but stopped in for a few days now and then. His timing kind of sucked this time because Ellie was moving in and the fake engagement was moving forward. Having Spence there and not telling him the whole story would only make that all the more awkward.

"Ellie was a surprise." Derrick turned the words over in his head and decided that might be the most truthful statement he'd ever made.

"Women are like that."

Derrick leaned against the sink, facing Spence. "Not for me. Not usually."

"So, let me get this straight." Spence balanced his palms on the counter behind him. "Right now you're dealing with Dad and the business. He's insisting you bring Carter and me home or he'll sell it out from under you."

That was the biggest of the moving parts. "About that—"

"Wait, I'm not done." Spence paused, as if he needed more drama here. "Some kid has launched a campaign to paint you as a...what, bad boss? And on top of that and all the work you're putting in you found time to date. And not just date, to seriously date for the first time in…ever, right?"

That about summed it up. "Yes."

"Anything else I should know? Like maybe you invented something or cured cancer while I was gone."

"Ellie is his sister." That much Derrick could tell. Maybe Spence would have some ideas on how to shut down Noah without ticking off Ellie, because Derrick hadn't come up with one yet.

"Now you've lost me."

"The guy who worked for me, the one who stole, but insists I fired him out of spite and that I'm completely incompetent. His name is Noah and he's Ellie's little brother."

Spence whistled. "You do like to make your life as shitty as possible, don't you?"

"He's how I met Ellie."

"And now you're going to be living together."

"Yes." Unless she killed him first, which Derrick thought was a strong possibility.

"You, who has only ever introduced me to the women you dated after you stopped dating them and once they've moved into friend mode."

"I'm a complex guy."

Spence shook his head. "I'm not sure that's the word I'd use."

"Ellie is…" Man, Derrick didn't even know what to say next. Hot, special. Annoying yet energizing. He didn't get her at all or understand her hold on him. All he knew was that she'd flipped his life upside down and had him scrambling, and that a part of him enjoyed the chaos. "Different."

Derrick thought he found a nice, safe description until Spence frowned at him. And stared...then kept staring. "What?"

Spence made a groaning sound. "You should work on that."

"What?"

"How you describe Ellie and your feelings for her. An orange car is different. Your girlfriend should warrant a better word." Spence glanced at the very spot where Ellie had been on that counter. "If you plan to make out with her in the kitchen again, that is."

Oh, that was definitely happening. Derrick didn't even have to think about that. Forget hands-off and common sense. The next time he'd lock the door and strip her clothes off. "I was doing fine."

"I think I arrived just in time."

That's not how Derrick saw the situation at all. "Two hours from now would have been better."

Spence stepped away from the counter and headed for the living area off the kitchen. "Well, since neither of us is having sex tonight, you may as well fill me in."

"On what?"

"Ellie. I want details." Spence sank into one of the couches set up in front of the massive stone fireplace. "I can get them from you or I can ask her."

"Subtle."

"Start talking."

Breakfast with Vanessa went great, as usual, until Ellie mentioned Derrick and dating and the whole *big lie for good press* thing. Amazing how that brought all of the other conversations to a standstill. Even now, twenty minutes later as they walked to Ellie's apartment, Vanessa barely said anything.

Ellie was about to make a joke about how her timing of the news messed up any chance at getting more coffee when Vanessa finally piped up. "A fake engagement."

They turned the corner at the end of Ellie's block and headed toward her building. "I know it sounds ridiculous."

"You mean like we've stepped into some weird novel? Yeah."

"It's the best option for Noah."

Vanessa stopped stared at Ellie. The look on her face hinted at the confusion pinging around inside her.

"What about what's best for Ellie?" Vanessa asked.

That wasn't the reaction Ellie expected. Yelling, yes. Even a few well-placed "Are you out of your mind?" comments. But that? No. "What does that mean?"

"We need to talk about your propensity to look out for everyone but yourself." Vanessa sounded furious at the idea.

Cars whizzed by and Ellie could see the stoplight in the distance. She wanted to focus on all of that and drown out the voice inside her head that told her she was getting in deep with Derrick. That she would never be able to keep sex and her attraction separate from her growing feelings for him. That, most troubling of all, she was starting to like him and was desperate to spend time with him.

She focused on the practical instead. "I need a job, security and some relief from the ongoing Noah drama. Derrick provides that."

"At the risk of violating the Bechdel test and talking only about men, isn't Derrick the reason Noah is spinning right now?"

"I used to think so."

"And now?"

"As Derrick keeps reminding me, Noah is an adult. He's had therapy and needs to figure out how to control the frustration when it tries to overtake him. He won't be able to survive in the work world otherwise." Ellie hated to admit that.

After all these years of guiding him and handling the oppositional defiant disorder so that it didn't morph into something even more serious, she had to start to back away. Not completely. She'd always be there for him, but he needed to be in charge of his behavior and take responsibility for his actions. It was time to let him make mistakes like everyone else.

Even now he texted and called every day. He insisted he was about to break some new story about Derrick. Something awful that would make her see the man he really was. She begged him not to and so far he hadn't, but she sensed it was only a matter of time.

Vanessa exhaled and some of the concern seemed to leave her face. "Well, if Derrick convinced you to give Noah some space, then I might learn to like him, though I'm not promising."

Of course Vanessa liked the comment because she'd been suggesting the same thing for a while now.

"Derrick also went after Joe Cantor."

Vanessa smiled and started walking again. "I know. I read the *Insider*."

Ellie almost choked. "Good grief, why?"

"It's wildly entertaining. If I had known the business world was so full of gossip and sex, I might have traded in some of my art history classes for economics."

They dodged a group of men loading boxes into a truck and jogged up the steps to the front of her building. Kept going past the mailboxes and the elevator that seemed to be stuck with an open door and not moving.

"Derrick keeps planting stories. And now someone else is." She could barely handle Derrick's PR campaign, though she had to admit he had eased off a bit. Photographers weren't lurking around capturing pictures of them every second, as she once feared. But the *Insider* still churned out tidbits about their dinners and her movement every time she stepped outside.

"Who else?"

"Joe, more than likely." And that was the bigger concern. Someone wanted to discredit her. Derrick had vowed to stop it. But what happened to her once he was done with their fake arrangement? She still had to work. To eat. To find a real job.

Her stomach tumbled and a wave of nausea battered her. She wanted to think it related to the very real fear of not being able to support herself in the future, but she sensed it had something to do with the idea of waking up one day and not seeing Derrick again. Of losing the talking and arguing and zap of attraction that struck her whenever she saw him.

"The men in your life are exhausting," Vanessa said.

They turned the corner and moved into the hallway leading to her apartment door. Ellie reached for her keys and nearly dropped them. "Tell me about it."

Vanessa stopped in midstep. "What's going on?"

Ellie's head shot up. Her front door was open and two boxes were piled right outside in the hall. Panic surged through her as she ran to the doorway. "Hey!"

She didn't go in. There really was no reason to since the room, her studio, stood empty except for a few stray pieces of paper and what looked like a community of dust bunnies she'd missed living under her couch.

"Did you get evicted?" Vanessa asked, her gaze zooming from one end of the room to the other.

"No." At least she didn't think so.

Her mind flashed to the van outside. To the packed boxes. To the movers.

Derrick.

"Good afternoon." Jackson stepped out of her bathroom, carrying her robe.

Ellie wasn't sure what stunned her more, him being in her apartment or the sight of him holding a ball of pink fluff in his arms. "Jackson?"

"You know him?" Vanessa asked.

"He works for Derrick. They're friends…" Ellie didn't know how to describe their relationship. She knew Jackson was loyal to Derrick but there was a part of her that viewed him as an ally. Or she had until this. "It's complicated."

"Most things with Derrick are." Jackson put down the robe and shook Vanessa's hand.

Vanessa stared at their joined hands then at Jackson. Finally she shrugged. "What's happening?"

Jackson frowned. "Ellie is moving in to Derrick's place today."

He said the words slowly, as if he thought they were true at one time but now wasn't sure. Ellie blamed

Derrick. He had that effect on her, as well. "I didn't agree to do that now."

"He said…" Jackson's frown deepened. "Wait, you guys didn't agree today was the day? Then where did he get the key he gave me?"

"Good question." If Ellie had to guess she'd bet he somehow convinced her landlord to turn one over. Or he bought the building and now *was* her landlord.

"I figured you weren't here and weren't packed up because Derrick told you I'd handle it."

Yep, this was definitely Derrick's fault. He ordered and manipulated. Looked like Jackson got stuck in his trap this time, too.

"I'm going to kill him." Ellie had threatened it before but this time she just might do it.

Jackson swore under his breath. "I'll take that as a no. Derrick did this all on his own."

Ellie shouldered part of the blame. A very small part. She'd let Derrick lure her in. He did nice things for her. He kissed like he'd been born to do it. All that stopped now. She needed some control and she would wrestle him for it, if needed. "I'll handle this."

"Are you sure?" Jackson looked as skeptical about her statement as he sounded.

"Yeah, really?" Vanessa gestured toward Jackson. "Listen to him."

She got it. Vanessa was fighting a bout of friendly concern. Jackson likely thought this was one step too far, even for Derrick. They were both right and she appreciated it, but she and Derrick had an agreement. She also thought they had an understanding and possibly something bigger that might lead to getting naked.

"If Derrick wants a showdown, we'll have one."

This time Vanessa looked skeptical. Also a bit worried. "Is this a good idea? Derrick isn't exactly a lightweight. I'm guessing he barges in and gets his way a lot."

Ellie couldn't deny that, but he wouldn't hurt her. His yell didn't even scare her that much. No, this was about Derrick Jameson understanding how far he could push her. And he'd gone too far. "He needs to learn."

Jackson hadn't moved. It was as if he were rooted to that spot on her floor. "True, but…"

"I'm looking forward to meeting Derrick," Vanessa said. "Sounds like the guy needs a good kick."

Vanessa wasn't wrong on that, either. Ellie vowed to be the one who administered the blow.

"You will soon enough." Ellie looked at Jackson. "I need your help."

"I almost hate to ask what for." But he smiled.

"You'll see."

Nine

The DC Insider: *Living together? Why, Derrick Jameson. You are a fast worker. And, Ellie? You're our hero. Tame that rowdy billionaire.*

Jackson didn't sound an alarm unless something was really wrong. So, when he called from Derrick's house, insisting there was a problem, Derrick got his butt over there and fast.

Driving up outside, everything looked normal. The usual cars on the street. Nothing odd in his driveway. It wasn't until he got out of the garage and reached the bottom of the stairs to the main living area that he heard the deafening thumping. He didn't know how he'd missed it earlier.

Music. Blaring music.

After marching upstairs, he turned the corner and

stepped into the open kitchen and living room area...
and stopped. Both the television and stereo were on,
and at what sounded like full power. Magazines were
strewed all over his usually clutter-free space. There
were open boxes and balled-up piles of clothes. Books
everywhere. He couldn't see an inch of his hardwood
floor.

Ellie sat in the middle of it all, sprawled on his
couch with her feet propped up on the coffee table.
She wore a pink robe and matching slippers. Ate potato chips right out of the bag. Drank...was that red
wine? One wrong move and his light gray couch, the
one he'd owned for less than a year, wouldn't survive
the alcohol bath.

It took a few seconds for her to stop her off-key
singing and look up at him. "Hey, roomie."

So that's what this was. Payback. He had to give
her credit because little surprised him and this did.
He'd expected a series of nasty texts or an office visit.
Not this.

To avoid yelling over the song he didn't recognize,
he went to the stereo and turned it off. That left the
talk show, which raged in a circus of screaming. He
scanned the stacks of crap for his remote and didn't
see it. Realizing he had no idea how to turn the television off without it, he gave in. "Any chance you could
take care of that?"

She pretended not to hear. Put her hand behind her
ear, leaned in and everything. Apparently full drama
mode had been activated.

He tried again. "Turn. It. Off."

"Oh, sure." She reached under the chip bag and
produced the remote. The noise clicked off a second

later. "I'm recording this, anyway. Actually, I'm recording a lot of programs." She studied the remote and its buttons. "Did you know your DVR is empty? There's plenty of room for my stuff."

He inhaled, trying to hold on to the fleeting sense of control he'd had when he'd started the day. "I don't watch much TV."

"Then it's good I rented a whole bunch of movies. Your on-demand options are impressive."

He could hardly wait to see that bill. "Are you done?"

"Enjoying the house? Not even close." She continued to sit there with one leg crossed over the other, her pink slipper bouncing up and down.

The robe slipped, treating him to miles of toned thigh. When she didn't rush to close the material again, a new sensation hit him. She was making a point but she might also be making a play.

Now he needed to know what she had on under there and how long it would take him to peel it off her.

But he forced his mind to focus. He looked around again, wondering how long it had taken her to make this much mess and how many days it would take him to undo it. "I'm assuming this is your way of saying you don't appreciate the manner in which I moved you in here."

Even he had to admit he'd crossed a line, but he wasn't up for a debate about something he thought should be simple. Today, Spence had agreed to come into the office for a few hours, and Derrick knew Ellie had made plans to spend a few hours with Vanessa. It struck him as the perfect time to get the job done.

He'd taken care of it all, which meant delegating to

Jackson. The bigger benefit—he thought—was shutting down Ellie's attempts to stall by complaining about packing.

The plan may have worked if he hadn't gotten tied up in a meeting that ran long. He'd planned to meet up with Ellie *before* she'd headed to her apartment. To warn her. That had failed.

"Derrick, this is better than any hotel." She wore one of those sickeningly sweet smiles that silently telegraphed her desire to push someone in front of a speeding bus. "I plan to stay right here. And I mean *right here*. In this spot. With my boxes stacked all around me as I collect more and more stuff. Now that I know the official address for your house I can have even more boxes delivered."

"Okay, I get it."

Her head fell to the side as she stared up at him. "Do you?"

He should be furious or at least frustrated. He was turned on. Like, ten-seconds-from-stripping-that-robe-off-her turned on.

What he should do is explain the reason for his actions then get back to work. End any temptation and not go near her.

All good thoughts...smart. But he didn't intend to do any of it. No, they were going to be naked and soon. Her legs wrapped around him. Her mouth on his. The wall, the couch, the floor. He didn't care where so long as they got there soon.

He walked over to her. Maneuvered through the piles and kicked aside more than one stray shoe. No question her entire closet now rested on his floor.

She didn't bother to move the chips or the pillows

she had stacked on one side of her, so he picked the coffee table. Sliding some books aside, he sat across from her, right next to her legs.

Through it all, she watched him. Her expression bordered on a smile. A satisfied one. Clearly she enjoyed this moment and the statement she was making.

That seemed fair, because he was a reluctant fan, too. "I may have been a little heavy-handed in my approach to making your relocation happen."

She rolled her eyes. "Saying 'I'm sorry' would have been a shorter sentence."

He held in a smile. "True."

"Do you want to try it? I promise it won't hurt at all." Her voice dipped lower, grew sexier, as she finally put aside the chips and the magazine and folded her hands on her lap.

His mind went back to that robe. Her long, sexy legs were right next to him. He glanced over, taking in the bare skin and those muscles, all sleek and sexy. Suddenly he had only one question…

"What are you wearing under that?"

Amusement danced in her eyes as she reached for the belt and untied it. The slow reveal had his heart hammering in his chest. She must have sensed it because she took her time peeling the sides apart to reveal a pair of running shorts and a formfitting tank top. On her, the combination was just about the hottest thing ever.

His gaze traveled down her neck and over the slope of her shoulder. To her chest. Had she skipped the bra?

Damn…

She snapped her fingers. "That apology?"

Maybe it was the way she sat there, looking ready

to do battle, but his usual hate-to-lose-at-anything armor fell. "I should have talked to you first."

Silence thumped between them after he ended the sentence. For a few seconds they sat there.

"That's it?" she asked.

"Yes."

She sighed at him. "Try again."

Apparently his defenses hadn't fallen far enough for her liking. "I was attempting to honor our agreement."

"For the record, you're getting farther away from an actual apology, not closer." She glared at him.

He was surprised she didn't have a headache from doing that. "You said—"

"Nope."

On anyone else the refusal to back down would piss him off. He liked to be in control, to come out on top of any argument. But he loved that she pushed him. She didn't try to impress him. She didn't need to try because she did it naturally, just by sitting there.

He conceded this point to her, expecting it to cost him something. For it to grate against his nerves. "I apologize for unilaterally making the decision. I should have conferred with you."

Once it was out there, he waited for a kick of frustration to nail him. He should be running to work. He didn't spend afternoons hanging around at home. Hell, he spent most nights at his desk. Until he'd met her, that was the only answer. Push forward, drive in more business. But now, today, he was perfectly content to sit and look at her, to wait to see what she would say next.

Lately his frustration with his father's demands, the needs of the company, his brothers and his own instincts were pulling him in too many directions. Ellie cleared away all the noise and stress and let him relax. It had been a long time since he'd felt comfortable in his own skin—then again, it wasn't really comfort he was feeling.

But he was holding back details. They'd agreed to be honest with each other, but he hadn't told her all of it. She didn't know that him being successful in calming Noah down was part of a bigger plan to win the business. That, in reality, he needed her. He hated needing anything but this time he did.

"That sounded more like a presentation to your bankers than a real apology, but I'll take it."

He finally let out that laugh he'd been holding inside. Leave it to her to judge his apology and sincerity and find both lacking.

He glanced around. "So, how exactly did you make all this happen in such a short amount of time?"

"I told your movers to leave the boxes here then I dumped the contents all over your living room."

Joe Cantor was an idiot to fire her. If he'd harnessed her drive and talent, his business would be doing much better today. Derrick would bet the Jameson water properties on it. "By yourself?"

"It was my idea but I asked Jackson to help."

The idea of Jackson and Ellie teaming up against him hit Derrick like a shot to the chest. He would stand almost no chance against their joint forces. But he did like that they seemed friendly, that Jackson was protective of her.

Still, he was the boss and there should be limits, at least in theory. "He's fired."

"We both know that's not true."

He peeked at her legs again. Followed the long line to her knee then to the line where that soft skin disappeared under the shadow of the robe.

He dragged his gaze away. Moving forward meant letting her into his life in a real way. Not telling her everything risked her wrath.

He was torn and frustrated. He was also on fire for her.

Without thinking he reached over and slipped his hand under her ankles. Picked up her feet and put them on his lap, slippers and all. "You must be exhausted."

The move knocked her off-balance, but only for a second. Her hands went to the cushions on either side of her to steady herself. "I'm still on a bit of an adrenaline high."

That made two of them and Derrick didn't see the rush dying any time soon. "Interesting."

His palm skimmed up her leg from her ankle. He massaged first one calf then the other, with his thumb tracing gentle circles over her skin.

Her fingers flexed against the couch material. "Derrick Jameson, are you flirting with me?"

"I'm trying."

Heat flared in her eyes. "That's dangerous."

He'd skated way past that point. For him there was no longer an *if*. It was all about *when*. And if she showed any sign of agreeing, he'd have their clothes off in record time. "No, dangerous is what I *want* to do to you."

She didn't move. "Tell me."

He said goodbye to the idea of getting any work done today. "Any chance you'd let me show you?"

Her gaze went to the floor then to the boxes leaning against the end of the couch. "There's not much room in here."

"My bedroom is pretty spacious." Not his most subtle line, but it was out there now. "Unless you dumped boxes up there, as well."

"I was tempted, but now I'm happy I didn't."

His hand stilled on her calf. "Be sure, Ellie."

"The answer is yes, Derrick."

She didn't know how they made it upstairs without breaking something. The barriers she'd erected, the promises she'd made to herself about not getting involved and the need to ignore her attraction to him… it all floated away.

This was for her. For the first in a long time, she took something she needed and ignored all the sensible reasons to hold back. There, with him, she didn't want to be rational and careful. She wanted heat and passion. Touching and kissing.

She'd stripped his suit jacket off him before they'd gotten out of the living room. She'd had his tie unknotted and slipped off by the time they'd hit the bottom step of the staircase curving up to the second floor.

His footsteps thudded on the stairs as he walked backward, his hand curled around the banister.

He stopped when she dropped the robe. His chest rose and fell on heavy breaths as he stared at her. He didn't touch her, but his gaze traveled over her like a gentle caress.

Never breaking eye contact, he drew her closer, moving her to the step above him. Let his gaze dip to her stomach…to the tops of her legs. The anticipation burned through her. Labored breathing echoed in her ears, a mix of hers and his.

When he grabbed the back of her thighs and pulled her tight against him, her breath escaped her lungs with a hard punch. The next minute he lifted her off her feet. Without any thought from her brain, she wrapped her legs and arms around his firm body. Held him close.

Her fingers slipped into his hair. She loved the feel and smell of him. His strength. His determination.

She lowered her head and kissed him. Poured every ounce of need and want into it, and felt his arms tighten around her in response.

Boy, the man could kiss.

"Damn." He whispered the word when he finally lifted his head. Then he started moving.

There was something breathtakingly sexy about having Derrick carry her up the stairs. About the way his fingers clenched and unclenched against the bare skin on her thighs. He didn't break a sweat.

Their relationship had a ticking clock. For once, she didn't hear it thumping in her head, threatening to steal him out of her life.

The house whirled until everything blurred. At the top of the stairs they passed a doorway, then another. She saw a bed and, in another room, what looked like a desk and a wall of bookcases.

None of it stopped him. Derrick kept walking until they got to the shadowed room at the end of the hall. He hit the light switch with his elbow. A soft light bathed the room in white.

She could see the deep blue walls and closed curtains. So soothing. A huge bed sat smack in the middle

of the room with pillows stacked against the head-
board. It dominated the space.

The furniture was sleek. Clean lines that hinted at
a big price tag. Dark and mysterious…perfect for him.

"Are you sure?"

His question, asked in a deep, even voice, broke
through her gawking. She looked at him again. Saw
the warmth in his eyes, felt the need vibrating through
him. There was only one answer. "Yes."

His hold loosened and she slid down the front of
him, felt every inch of his excitement. As soon as her
feet hit the floor, her hands went to his chest and she
started unbuttoning his shirt. Once she got it open and
untucked, he captured her mouth in a kiss that made
her knees buckle.

He caught her around the waist and held her with
one hand while his other tunneled under her shirt.
Then both of his hands were on her, caressing her
breasts, learning her curves.

Tension ripped through her. The soft cotton of her
shirt suddenly scratched against her. She wanted it
up and off. As if she'd said the words out loud, he
peeled the shirt up, lifting it off her, leaving her exposed to his gaze.

His thumbs rubbed over her as he cupped her. That
intense gaze stayed locked on her breasts, on how they
fit his hands. "Ellie…"

He barely touched her and her skin caught on fire.
Every nerve ending snapped to life. Every instinct
told her to hold him again.

He sat on the edge of the bed and she wanted to slip
onto his lap, but he held her between his legs. Had her
stand there as he spread his hand over her stomach…

as he slid his fingertips under the band of shorts. With a tug, he had them skimming her body to the tops of her thighs. Wriggling her hips, she shimmied them the rest of the way off.

He stared at her white bikini bottoms. She knew they were see-through. She knew how much she wanted them off.

She climbed on him then. Straddled his lap and pressed her body against his. The way he inhaled, sharp almost as if on a gasp, empowered her. She loved the sound and his loss of control. When he fell onto the mattress, she went with him. They tumbled down and he shifted up on one elbow until he hovered over her.

He trailed his fingers over her stomach to the top of the bikini bottoms.

"You still have a lot of clothes on, big guy."

"I can be naked in two seconds." His palm flattened over the front of her underwear.

She could feel her body getting ready for him. Something inside her tightened and a tumbling started deep in her stomach. "Let's see."

For a second he didn't move. Then his eyebrow lifted. "Anything you want."

He sat up next to her and did a slow striptease, taking his time unbuttoning his dress shirt and sleeves before shucking it off. She couldn't really see anything but the firm muscles of his chest. She wanted to reach up and trail her fingers over that sexy dip between his collarbone and his shoulder. Over every pronounced angle.

"How does a man who spends all of his day at a desk look like you?"

"I don't spend *every* hour there." He winked at her then stood.

His hands went to his belt and that got her moving. She shifted to the side of the bed and dropped her legs over the side. Fit her hands over his and took over the task of undoing his belt. Slid the leather out of the loops and dropped it to the floor.

Next came the zipper. The ripping sound echoed through the room as she lowered it and pressed her palm against his bulge filling the space. Caressed him through his pants.

His fingers tightened against the side of her head. "Ellie, I'm not going to last very much longer."

"Good." She slid her legs beneath her and moved back. Lay against the mattress with her feet flat on the bed and her knees in the air.

He visibly swallowed. She watched him do it. Smiled when he nearly ripped his pants and boxer briefs getting them off. Then he was naked and so fit, so lean and sexy, as he crawled up the mattress to get to her.

That fast her heart flipped over. A revving sensation took off inside her. She slid her leg up the back of his, loving the burst of energy that flowed through her at the touch.

She wanted this. Him. That first time she'd seen him in person the air had left her lungs. Seeped out until she couldn't breathe. Every time since, her heartbeat did a little dance. His face, his body, even his grouchy personality combined in one intriguing package that she itched to open.

They had weeks left on the agreement and a need to make it look real. For whatever time they had left, she would. She'd put aside the worries and the ways it could go wrong and would dive in. And then she'd somehow walk away from him.

Right as he dipped his head to kiss her again he froze. "Damn."

She grabbed on to his upper arms. "What is it?"

The sound coming from him could only be described as a growl. "I bought condoms but I left them at work."

For some reason that made her laugh. "Did you think we were going to have sex on your desk?"

"It is a reoccurring fantasy of mine." He lifted up, just a fraction, and looked down her body. "But I can still touch you. Give you what you need."

Before she could say anything or even put a sentence together, his fingers slipped into her underwear. He skimmed his hand between her legs, over her. Gentle yet demanding. When one finger slid inside her, her breath caught in her throat.

His tongue swept over her nipple in a long lick that left her shaking. Sensations bombarded her from all directions. The mix of touching and tasting had her lower back lifting off the bed. When he did it again, all the air sucked out of her.

She felt light and dizzy and so ready for him. Her fingernails dug into his shoulders to hold him close. "Derrick, yes."

He pumped his finger inside her, bringing her body to snapping attention. Every intelligent thought left her head, leaving only one lingering fact. "I have an IUD."

His head shot up. "What?"

"Birth control."

His mouth dropped open before he said anything. "I got tested."

Now it was her turn to be confused. "I don't…"

"I have a report for you to see. You know, just in case. Not sure why I forgot the condoms."

His finger stayed inside her during the surreal and very not sexy conversation. But it was practical and smart…and it pushed out thoughts of risk and most of her common sense.

She slipped her hand down his body, between them, and circled his length. Her palm slid against him from base to tip.

"Ellie, please be sure." He shook his head. "We can wait if you—"

His words cut off when she wrapped her fingers around him and squeezed. "Now, Derrick."

Light flashed in his eyes as he nodded. Then he was on his knees between her legs. Her body hummed as he peeled her underwear off. Pushing her legs apart, he settled between them. His tongue replaced his fingers and excitement surged inside her.

Her heels dug into the mattress and she twisted the comforter in her balled hands as his mouth worked its magic. When he hit the right spot, her thighs pressed against his shoulders. A moan trapped in her throat begged to escape.

She shifted and twisted as the pleasure threatened to overtake her. Still, he didn't stop his sensual caress. That tongue. Those fingers. Every part of him, from the heat of his mouth to the expert use of his hands, had her straining to hold back as her body bucked.

Right as she hovered on the edge, he got to his knees. He was hard and ready and he didn't wait. She lost her breath as he pushed inside her, filling her. Her breath hiccupped as her inner muscles tightened around him. When he pulled out and pushed in again, she grabbed him and brought him closer.

He leaned over and his chest pressed against her. Heat pounded off his skin and a thin sheen of sweat appeared along his shoulders. She held on to him, traced a line of kisses up his throat.

Their bodies moved as he plunged in and out. The pressure built as she fought her release. She ached to make it last but Derrick's muscles began to shake. When he slipped his hand between their bodies and touched her again, her control broke.

The winding inside her shattered and her body let go. She rode out the pulses and pleasure, gasping as his head fell to her shoulder. She could hear the uptake in his breathing and feel the muscles across his back stiffen. She caressed and kissed him as he came. When his body finally stopped moving, he balanced against her. The weight made her feel warm and secure. Happy even.

After a few seconds he turned his head to the side and his breath blew across her neck. "That was pretty great."

Her fingers lingered in his damp hair. "It was the slippers. They're sexy."

She burst out laughing first, then he joined her. It took them almost a full minute to stop. But they didn't move for a lot longer. What scared her was she didn't want to. She was content to stay there forever.

Ten

Derrick knew he was in trouble the second he opened his office door. Both Spence and Jackson were in there. Spence looked at home in the big chair with his feet up on the desk. A bit too comfortable, but at least he was in the office, which was more than he'd been in months.

Spence made a show of looking at his watch. "You were gone for two hours."

Yeah, that was the last thing Derrick intended to talk about. "I had something I needed to do."

Truth was the sex had him reeling. He hadn't even used protection. That had never happened in his adult life. He'd never even been tempted to skip that step. With Ellie, he wanted it all. He ignored the risks.

The idea of a fake arrangement had backfired on him. He didn't want an on-paper-only relationship with Ellie. Then again, he didn't know *what* he wanted with her. Nothing made sense, including his choices, at the moment.

"How is Ellie adjusting to her new house?" Jackson asked.

Her house. Just the thought of that should have set off an explosion in Derrick's brain. He was not a guy to settle down. He rarely invited women to his house. That's what hotels were for.

He maintained a strict wall, keeping almost everyone but a select few out of his most personal space. But with Ellie the lines had blurred from the very start.

"She was less than impressed that I went ahead and scheduled the movers." Talk about an understatement.

"Women." Spence shook his head. "Man, you'd think they'd love having their stuff packed up without telling them first."

Derrick glared at Jackson. "You told him."

"It was too good not to share," Jackson said, not even bothering to deny it.

Spence leaned back with his arms folded behind his head. "Big brother, can I give you some advice?"

That wasn't what Derrick wanted right now. "Get up first."

Spence whistled. "You're grumpy for a guy who had sex. You did, right? I hate to think you look that disheveled just from talking."

"I was fine until I walked in here." That was pretty much all Derrick wanted to say on that topic, so he gestured for Spence to get up then took his seat.

"The advice?" Spence leaned on the edge of Derrick's desk.

"Right. From the guy who isn't dating anyone." Derrick held out a hand. "Please enlighten me."

"I talked with Ellie for fifteen minutes and I think you need to be careful."

That got Derrick's attention. "Of her?"

"Of losing her, dumb-ass. Don't mess this up."

Not bad brotherly advice. "I'm trying not to."

Spence shook his head. "Try harder."

The day had been this whirlwind of emotions. As soon as Derrick left the house to go back to work—because *of course he did*—panic set in. She worried about what would happen when he came home and what they'd say to each other tonight. The whole thing was now awkward and weird.

Planning the rest of the day after surprise sex was not easy. So, Ellie relied on the same thing she always did—Vanessa. She moved around Derrick's chef-caliber kitchen right now, cutting vegetables and making a salad.

Vanessa was there, just in case. Kind of like a shield against bumbling conversation. How Derrick would feel about guests in his house was a different question, one Ellie hadn't thought about until right now as she heard footsteps on the stairs. Well, if he didn't like it, that would teach him to move her in without talking to her first.

Ellie plastered on a smile as soon as she saw him. "You're home."

His gaze hesitated on her face before skipping to the counter and the stack of cutting boards and knives sitting there. "You're cooking?"

"Don't sound so surprised." Sure, it was fair, but still.

Vanessa popped her head around the corner. "Also, don't panic. I'm helping."

Derrick gave Vanessa a small wave as he stopped beside Ellie. "You can't cook?"

She snorted. "Can you?"

"I can grill. Men grill."

Vanessa winced. "Oh, boy."

"Typical," Ellie said at the same time. "Well, if you're done impressing us with your testosterone… Derrick, this is Vanessa, my best friend." She rushed to add one caveat. "The one person other than Jackson who knows this—us—isn't real."

His expression went blank. "It's not?"

"The contract thing." For some reason it hurt to say the words this time.

It's not as if they had some sort of miracle sex. It was great and her body still hummed, but she didn't think sex solved everything. Though she had to admit, something did change. Inside her, deep inside.

Together they were sexy and comfortable…they worked. The churning, that ramped-up feeling of being excited to see him and to hear his voice, didn't strike her as fake. She'd never experienced it before and it made her a little twitchy now because she hadn't had enough time to analyze it, but she knew it amounted to more than a practical agreement between friends.

She had such a short time to savor this feeling. She'd been the one who insisted on limiting the time of the agreement to two months. He had wanted more months and now she did, too.

Derrick still didn't show any reaction. His affect had gone flat and stayed there. "You told her."

She rewound the comment in her head, looking for any judgment, but didn't hear it. That didn't mean it wasn't there. "Is that a problem?"

For a second he just stood there, not talking. Then a lightness stole over him and he glanced at Vanessa. "You don't have a habit of gossiping or talking to the *Insider*, do you?"

The hint of amusement calmed Ellie. Her neck muscles unclenched as she relaxed again.

"Any secret Ellie tells me stays with me," Vanessa said.

"Happy to hear it." Derrick stopped in front of the lasagna pan and put his finger out as if he intended to poke it. "So, what's this—?"

"Stop." Ellie slapped his hand away. "You have to wait."

He smiled at her. "Should I order takeout to be safe?"

That look… His walls fell and he stopped being the commanding-man-in-charge-of-everything to be a man. This was at-home Derrick and she had no defense against this sexy side of him. This was the Derrick who had landed her in his bed—and would put her back there. This Derrick was dangerous.

But that didn't mean that she was ready to let him off the hook for his behavior earlier. Her arms still ached from the quick move she and Vanessa had made of most of her stuff to one of the extra bedrooms upstairs.

Oh, no. He'd be paying for that one for a while. "Tough talk from a guy who made a big mistake today."

Vanessa turned around, spoon in hand. "Yeah, you owe me for carrying all those books around."

"Technically, that's Ellie's fault since I hired movers. She sent them away," Derrick said.

Vanessa shook the long spoon at him. "I heard you were Mr. Bossy Pants."

Derrick groaned as he made his way around the counter and took a seat on one of the bar stools. "Oh, good. Now I get to fight two of you."

The byplay made Ellie smile. She hadn't been raised with banter in the kitchen. Her entire childhood had raged like a house on fire. There was always some new crisis and not enough money to handle it.

There were no settled moments of her parents joking with each other, or very few of them. Stealing a few now with Derrick had a warmth settling deep inside her. She'd always wanted this—a home and security. Someone who made her hot but also made her want to snuggle on the couch.

"Are we wrong?" she asked, wanting the moment to continue for just a bit longer.

"No." He rested his hands on the counter. "Today I was an overbearing jackass."

Ellie almost dropped the glass she'd picked up. "Whoa?"

Vanessa looked from Derrick to Ellie. "What?"

"What you heard was progress."

"I can learn." He shrugged as he stole a mushroom off the salad and popped it in his mouth.

Ellie wanted to believe that. She was desperate to believe that and she wasn't even sure why. "But can you set the table?"

He winked at her. "I'm on it."

She watched him meander around the kitchen. He rolled up his shirtsleeves and dug in. Grabbed the plates and silverware. Even hummed while he did it, which Ellie found oddly endearing.

And the man could move. Those long, determined strides. The long legs and that flat stomach. She'd seen him without his clothes and with them on, and she was a fan of both.

She glanced at the table. "Three? Isn't Spence coming home?"

"He's having dinner with Jackson. There was some thought tonight might be loud around here." Derrick shot her a sexy little smile. "From all the yelling, which Spence thinks I deserve."

"I like him."

"Yeah, I figured you would." Derrick finished with the table and walked back to the counter.

Ellie expected him to stand there or look at his watch, or even try to fit in a half hour of work before dinner. Instead he draped an arm loosely over her shoulder and brought her in close to his side.

Vanessa did a double take but didn't say anything.

"So, what else can I do?" he asked.

As far as Ellie was concerned, he was doing it.

* * *

Hours later dinner was over and the dishes were done and put away. Vanessa hung around, telling stories about the men they'd dated and some of their stranger travel adventures. To Derrick's credit, he listened and asked questions. He genuinely seemed to enjoy the night even though Ellie guessed he'd rather be tied to his desk working.

Now it was almost midnight. Vanessa had gone and Spence had come home. After a bit of small talk, he'd settled into the bedroom he always used when he was in town. Ellie started the night in Derrick's bedroom because it would have been weird for them to sleep separately if they were really dating.

Some of her clothes, the ones she and Vanessa managed to collect before dinner, hung in Derrick's oversize closet. The thing was as big as two rooms with shelves and racks and drawers and a chair.

A chair.

When the house went quiet, she'd snuck to the bedroom she intended to sleep in even though she wanted to stay with him, wanted to forget that Spence slept nearby and that stupid agreement. She craved his touch. Needed him to hold her, kiss her, roll around in that big bed with her.

She wasn't really the casual sex type. She needed a connection, a relationship. She didn't have a lot of experience but all of it included condoms.

So much had happened over the last few months. She couldn't even process it all. Her nerves were frazzled. A list of pros and cons kept cycling through her head.

With Derrick everything was different. More intense. Less clear. She'd bent her personal rules until they broke. Instead of feeling guilty or thinking she'd messed up, a wave of sadness hit her. A sense of loss at not being with him now. Of not being able to hold him, to touch him tonight, like she'd thought about all day.

She thought back to the first time he'd proposed this fake arrangement. The whole thing had confused and annoyed her, but something in his eyes and voice had compelled her. She'd agreed to an arrangement she'd never go for under any other circumstance.

Sure, there was the Noah piece. The part about her needing money and some bit of security. All that was real, but the truth was she'd signed that agreement because she'd *wanted* to. Because, for once, she took something she wanted—Derrick.

For the first time in her life she operated without a road map. She let emotion guide her. She saw the risks and accepted them, even knowing that the likelihood was this would end in pain and heartache. There really was no other way for a relationship built on fake facts to finish.

She was so lost in thought she almost missed the soft knock on the door. When it sounded the second time, she scooted out of bed, careful to make sure her shorts and T-shirt were in place when she opened the door in case the visitor was Spence.

Derrick stood there in what looked like lounge pants and a gray T-shirt that fit him like a second skin. That fast, her temperature spiked and her insides started to whirl.

She gripped the side of the door. "Are you okay?"

They'd worked out this plan about getting up early and keeping her bed made and door shut. Derrick had talked about using the excuse of her stacking her stuff in here until she could go through it all. She was accustomed to living with boxes, so having them around now didn't bother her.

"I wanted to check on you." Derrick shifted his weight from foot to foot.

The move struck her as uncharacteristic and a bit vulnerable. "I don't—"

"May I come in?"

Good grief, it was his house. She stepped back. "Of course."

He walked in and caught her up in his arms. His mouth covered hers in a kiss that had her forgetting about boxes and clothes and just about everything else. She grabbed his shoulders, dug in and held him close as pleasure pulsed through her. When he lifted his head a few seconds later, she felt breathless and weak. Her resolve had melted along with her resistance.

"I've wanted to do that since I got home from work," he said in a whisper against her lips.

Tonight had been incredibly special. She'd laughed until she couldn't breathe. She'd built memories. Discovered a warmth she'd never known growing up because everything had been so uncertain between her father's and Noah's moods.

She trusted and loved Vanessa. She was an integral part of Ellie's life. Derrick was supposed to be temporary, but her feelings for him, how she thought about him during the day, were anything but fake. They'd started this ruse by barely talking and now she texted him every day. Sometimes she made up silly things to ask, just to see his response. And he always responded.

"We are inviting trouble." She said it more to convince herself than him.

"I know." Derrick rested his forehead against hers. "I guess I can't convince you to join me in my bedroom?"

He could, so easily. That was the problem. "We should…"

"Right." He gave her arms a gentle squeeze then dropped his hands.

She felt the loss to her bones. It settled in and had her trembling. But she couldn't go overboard with her feelings. "Derrick."

"I'll let you get some sleep." He kissed her on the forehead, quick and simple.

Then he was gone and it was all she could do to keep from calling him back.

Eleven

The DC Insider: *We're hearing there are a few snags in the Derrick and Ellie forever plan. Her baby brother refuses to stay quiet. Her past continues to be a problem. And is our Hottest Ticket in Town having second thoughts about a serious relationship?*

Two days later Derrick sent Noah a message from Ellie's phone, asking him to meet her at her old apartment. This was the last day before she turned the keys over. Noah didn't know that, but Derrick did. He hoped that excused him sneaking her phone while she'd gone upstairs to shower this morning after their coffee together.

They'd done that for the past two days. No more sex, despite his attempts to make it happen. But she was holding back and having Spence hanging around turned out to be a bit of a mood killer. So did the calls from their father. All of a sudden he had work questions again, and that made Derrick nervous.

Through it all, she wandered around in her pajamas each morning. If that's how people acted when they lived together in a real relationship, Derrick kind of got it. There was something energizing about spending those fifteen minutes with her in the morning before he took off.

She didn't have to get up when he did or to fumble her way downstairs like she had this morning when she'd looked half-asleep and almost missed the bottom step. The coffee time didn't have to happen to prolong the ploy for Spence because he was still asleep at that time of the morning. That meant she did it for him, and that thrilled Derrick more than he wanted it to.

The door opened behind him and Noah stormed inside. He took a few steps then stopped. "Where is my sister?"

He sounded more concerned than angry, which may have saved him from the full-scale ass-kicking Derrick wanted to unleash. But they still had issues, and Derrick had promised Ellie he'd put those to bed, so he tried one more time. "We need to talk."

"Her stuff is gone from her apartment." Noah still frowned as he turned around in a circle in the middle of the room. "Her couch and her—"

"Noah, stop." He seemed locked in some sort of shock. "I called you here."

"But she's—"

"Living with me."

That got Noah's attention. He stopped moving and stared at Derrick. "You can't be serious."

"I am."

That familiar red flush of anger spread over Noah's face. "Nothing is off-limits with you."

The comment hit harder than Derrick expected. He felt the shot right to his gut. When it came to Ellie, he had crossed a bunch of lines, most Noah didn't even know about, but Derrick couldn't pretend he hadn't backed her into a corner and used her love for her brother against her.

He had to deal with that. Take it apart and assess it because now that he did, it seemed like an Eldrick Jameson move. Something his father would do to ensure he got his way. Derrick didn't like that comparison one bit.

"There aren't any cameras or videos in here. You don't need to pretend we had a confrontation at work. You can drop the bullshit." Derrick had to accept his part in a lot of sins where the Gold family was concerned, but not that one.

"I didn't steal anything."

"Noah, come on." Derrick didn't know how the guy could stand there and lie. How he could actually frown, curl his shoulders in and look like the injured party.

Derrick had taken a chance on him. They met when a friend from high school, now a college professor, called Derrick about a kid he found sneaking around the computer labs at George Washington University. The kid—Noah—had created a student ID and had been using university resources to play games and check out the internal supposedly confidential workings of the school.

Noah hadn't had the experience or the college requirements for the job he'd held at Derrick's company. But like the professor, Derrick had seen something in Noah. A need to prove himself. The brilliance waiting to be tapped. He'd given him a chance and brought him on. Thought of him as a mentee of sorts...then he'd stolen from the company and tried to turn Derrick's life upside down.

Noah shook his head. "You don't get it."

Something in his words and that tone got to Derrick. The sentence he was about to say died in his head. Now he wanted to know what was happening in Noah's head. "Explain it to me."

Noah went to the window and looked out. "I found out about you."

Other than the agreement with Ellie and his father's stipulations, Derrick didn't have much to hide. There were things he wished people didn't know, but he never had that luxury. "Noah, I hate to break this to you but my life is not exactly a big secret. I've had the press on me since I was in elementary school."

Thanks to his family, starting with his politician grandfather, the family got in the news and stayed there. Derrick started dating and the cameras were there to capture his young bachelor days. When they broke up, the girl's family sold a story about him to the tabloids.

The only time he ever got behind the wheel after drinking, the dumbest thing he'd ever done, the press had shown up then, too. He'd learned a harsh lesson that time, and many others.

His mistakes played out in public. His father excused them before the cameras and berated him behind the scenes. That's how it worked in the Jameson household.

"Did you cheat then, too?" Noah asked as he turned around to face Derrick.

Derrick's mind went blank. "What?"

"Abby."

There was an Abby who worked for him. She had a history with the Jameson men, but not him. He searched his mind for another woman with that name. Any woman named anything close. "Abby who?"

"My sister is going to find out who you really are." Noah nodded. All traces of uncertainty had disappeared. "She will. The people at the *Insider* will."

"Have you been talking with them, Noah?" If he'd planted that story about Ellie and her former job, his blood relationship to her would not save him. Derrick would move in and set him straight.

Noah shrugged. "What if I have?"

It took every ounce of willpower Derrick possessed to tamp down on his anger. "Do not ruin your sister's reputation."

"Me?"

Derrick tried reason one more time. "You stole from me and I caught you. You're trying to blow this up into something else and hurt Ellie, and I'm not sure why."

"Did you lead Abby on, too? Make her promises and then dump her?"

"What are you talking about?"

"I know what it's like to be one of your chosen few then get kicked aside." Noah was yelling now, but there was an underlying thread, an edge that suggested he'd been hurt.

The words crashed through Derrick. "Is that what this is really about? Because that did not happen."

"I'm leaving." Noah headed for the door.

Everything was so unsettled, maybe even worse than before they'd talked. Derrick wasn't sure what to say because nothing Noah mentioned made any sense to him. "You've got to stop, Noah. I don't want to hurt you and I certainly don't want Ellie hurt."

"This is your fault." Noah shook his head then slipped into the hallway, but not before taking one final shot. "You'll see."

It had been three days since they'd had sex. Every night they'd pretend to go into his bedroom together then she'd sneak out. Inevitably, about fifteen minutes later there would be a knock on the door. Derrick saying good-night. Derrick kissing her. Last night, Derrick tunneling his hands up her shirt and touching her, which she'd absolutely encouraged.

But when he showed an interest in more, she pulled back. She had to until she could get her thoughts in order. Being there, the domesticity, it all felt real. The first time together had been all consuming. She wanted to act like she could handle a no-strings fake relationship and walk away, but she wasn't sure.

She waited for those before-bed visits. Yearned for them with a fierceness that scared her. Last night she sat on her bed, staring at the doorknob, willing it to turn. It took him a full eighteen minutes to show up. She'd spent every one of those extra seconds counting down, trying to drown out the doubts welling inside her and making her jumpy.

That sort of unsettled sensation couldn't be normal. It had her reassessing, even as she knew she'd give in. Because she wanted to give in. She wanted more from him, for them…and that was the problem.

Now, they were out in public. All dressed up, with him in a tux that looked like he'd been born to wear. The black coat with his nearly black hair…she'd actually made a small *pfffing* sound when he'd come out of the bedroom. No one should look that good. Ever.

When Derrick mentioned a charity gala a few days ago, she'd told him she planned to be sick that day. Gala sounded like an opportunity for more cameras and she was about done with that part of their arrangement. He responded by threatening to drag her to it in her gym shorts, which left her no choice but to borrow a fancy dress from Vanessa. Thank goodness for those money-raising gallery events Vanessa hosted all the time.

The gown was beautiful in a princess sort of way. It had a fitted sleeveless top covered with beads and a long, flowing, light blue skirt in a fabric soft enough to beat out those expensive sheets Derrick had at the house. Vanessa was taller, so Ellie had on three-inch heels she was pretty sure would snap her ankle in two if she stepped the wrong way.

Vanessa also wore a smaller bra size, so the top of the dress, while stunning and sparkly, was also slowly strangling Ellie. She put her hand on her stomach and tried to figure out how to permanently suck it in. "I think I'm going to pop."

Derrick looked over at her. His gaze slipped to her

hand, which had moved to her chest. "I have no idea what to say to that."

"The bodice on this is a bit tight." It was choking her. But why be dramatic about it? "It has to be to hold everything in, but wow."

His gaze shifted to the tops of her breasts, which were spilling out more than they probably should be. "Well, we wouldn't want anything sliding out."

"It's Vanessa's fault. My boobs are bigger." She touched them as if she needed to emphasize the point.

"Okay, yeah. I'm purposely not going to talk about your best friend's body."

Ellie couldn't help but smile at that. He looked on the defensive and a little haunted by the idea. "Good call."

"I'm not a total dumb-ass." He took a sip of his champagne as he glanced at the dance floor.

A few couples moved around, looking stiff and out of place. Between this event and the one where she'd met Derrick, Ellie had come up with a theory. Many DC business people didn't exactly thrive in social situations.

Derrick looked perfectly suited to the room. Just as he looked great behind his desk and adorable in the morning in his lounge pants as he sipped his coffee in the kitchen. She'd never met anyone who "fit" into any situation like he did before.

"You are such a guy." The comment slipped out before she could think it through.

Derrick being Derrick, he did not let it slide by him. "I'm going to regret this but…what?"

"You look like *that*." She waved a hand over him, up and down as she took in every perfect inch. "You probably get up looking like that."

He followed her gaze. "I don't generally wear the tux to bed."

"Well, you should. You look ridiculously hot." When his eyebrow lifted and his attention switched from half scanning the room to full force on her, she snorted. "Oh, please. Don't look surprised. You own a mirror. I'm sure there will be a thousand photos of us all over the internet tomorrow and you can see for yourself."

She hoped her too-tight dress photographed okay. It would suck to stand next to him, looking all Hottest Ticket in Town, and her coming off as someone who snuck her way into the photo.

He put his mostly full glass on the tray held by a passing server. "If that's what it takes to get you in my bedroom, I will wear the tux all the time at home. Honestly, the going-to-bed-alone thing sucks."

She thought so, too. She also knew it was over. With him looking at her like that and her willpower gone, it was inevitable.

"Shh. There are ears everywhere." No one stared at them after his comment. Well, no one other than the ones already staring. Derrick did attract attention. "And cameras."

"Don't blame me this time. The charity hired them."

His hand brushed against her hers. She didn't realize what was happening until his warm fingers slid through hers. Hand holding. It was so innocent and sweet…she almost jumped him right there.

"What about the photographer who followed me home from the coffee place today?" The guy had stepped right in front of her. One second sooner and she would have thrown her coffee at him on instinct. "I had barely brushed my hair."

He lifted their joined hands and kissed the back of hers. "You look beautiful."

She was pretty sure she saw a camera bulb flash but she tried to ignore it. "I didn't then."

"I bet you did."

They stood in a room full of people and he made her feel like the only other person in the room. He had that gift. For a man who commanded his way through life, issuing orders, he didn't seem to get that just being there, looking like that, was enough to get people's attention.

A sudden case of nerves shot through her. She was out of her comfort zone and out with him, a man she'd started to dream about. People watched. Others whispered. Tomorrow every movement would be analyzed and dissected online.

It overwhelmed her, stole her breath. She rushed to find a non-Derrick thing to talk about. "My father would have loved this."

"He enjoyed parties?"

They still held hands and when she didn't answer right away, Derrick gave her fingers a gentle squeeze. That only confused her more. "Do you really not know?"

His smile lit up his face. "This cryptic thing you do is oddly endearing but it does confuse the hell out of me sometimes."

She refused to be sucked in by that sexy look. Talking about a harsh reality suddenly seemed easier than dealing with her growing and confusing feelings for Derrick. "My dad. He was *that* guy. The one who always had this big plan to make money. He met a man with a great idea here. He had a lead on something big there."

"Did anything ever pan out?" Derrick asked.

"No." She tried to remember a clear success and couldn't come up with one. "My entire childhood is filled with memories of him spending the last dollar on this dream or using the money for the electric bill to invest in some weird scheme."

She knew that sounded harsh. Maybe it was too much, but all she had was her perspective and the reality of moving around and never feeling secure.

"What about your mom?"

"She enabled it. I mean, she tried to talk to him. So much time was spent on dad's needs that I think maybe Noah's issues got overlooked." The pieces came together in her head. She'd tried for so long to keep it all separate but it did connect. Because of how her parents lived their lives, Ellie got stuck in a parental role that made her more sarcastic and less trusting. "I would hear her..."

Maybe that was enough of that. Ellie tried to concentrate on the music and the laughter floating through the room. To escape reality for a second.

"What?" he asked.

Derrick's gentle tone coaxed her on. "Crying."

"Ellie, I'm sorry." He slid his arm around her and pulled her closer.

"He always thought there was something better out there, you know. That if he could put the deals together the right way, he'd hit it big." No one could deliver the line like her dad. He had believed, or he'd sounded like he did. "He never understood that we didn't care about that. They died going to one last big event."

For a few seconds Derrick didn't say anything. He kept that reassuring hand on her lower back and they swayed to the music. People moved around them. A few stopped to say hello but didn't linger. They must have projected the couple-in-love vibe because most people just seemed to smile at them.

"It's possible he thought it was his job. You know, to make the family financially secure." Derrick made the comment without looking at her. He focused on a table of businessmen instead.

She saw Joe Cantor in the group. That explained Derrick's sudden interest. Since she didn't want another scene, she responded when she might otherwise have let it slip past her. "But he did the opposite."

Derrick glanced at her then. "That, I get."

"The rich boy understands being poor?" She tried to keep her voice light. Tried and failed. She regretted lashing out as soon as she did it. "Sorry. I didn't mean to take that shot."

"It's okay." He nodded toward the couples milling near them. "Dance?"

"Derrick." She reached for his hand and managed to snag it.

"We should dance, Ellie." With that, he pulled her into his arms and maneuvered them to the edge of the dance floor. After a few minutes the stiffness in his shoulders eased and the distance between them closed. Her body rested against his. The scent of his shampoo filled her senses.

She forgot about their conversation and the people watching them. The public ruse fell away until it was just the two of them—a man and a woman swaying on the dance floor. Holding each other, wrapped around each other.

She looked up and stared at his chin, those lips. "Derrick…"

"Keep that up and we're going to need to leave early." His voice sounded rough and lower than usual.

Feminine power surged through her. "Good."

The dance did it. He'd respected her boundaries and would keep doing so, but the dance brought her walls crashing down. He felt it as soon as it happened. Saw it in her eyes as she looked up at him.

He made a mental note to dance with her more often.

But that would come later. After all that touching he couldn't get them home fast enough. After the meal and the silent auction, both of which felt as if they lasted five lifetimes, he suggested they go. They'd said their goodbyes and scrambled for the door. He didn't think anyone noticed. The diced-up feeling came from inside him. He tried to hide it. They had that damn agreement to uphold, after all.

He stepped into the kitchen and dropped his tux jacket over the couch. His plan was to linger for a second, enough not to be rude, then head upstairs.

He got as far as the couch before Ellie started talking. "Have you forgiven me?"

He glanced over his shoulder, not really focusing on her during his quick look. Call it self-preservation. "What are you talking about?"

"I was a jerk tonight."

He hadn't expected that. Debating whether he should let it drop, he turned around to face her. "That's quite an admission."

"Derrick, I'm serious."

She stood there in a dress that showed off her curves and lit her face. It had taken all of his strength to resist her tonight. When she'd first come downstairs in that, he'd wanted to skip the public event that would help shore up their arrangement and drag her right up to bed. The temptation still punched at him.

He remembered her shot about being poor. She clearly thought that was the only problem that could happen to a family. "My family isn't a good subject for me."

He didn't know where that came from or why he said it. Well, he knew *why* but not *why now.*

"They're part of you. Your dad, your upbringing. It's all a piece of who you are."

She didn't know but that was the absolute worst thing she could have said. "I sure as hell hope not."

Her head shot back. "I don't get it."

How did he explain? Did he even want to? Every slight and every fault piled up over the years. He knew he had it easy compared to others. This wasn't a race but he hadn't exactly had a smooth time, either.

Some of that had changed with his father's new wife, Jackie. Or so people said. Derrick didn't spend much time with his father since he'd been the one to suggest his father think about retiring. He and Jackie had been living on an island, racing through money ever since.

"You guessed before that my dad was difficult. He's a… I can't even think of a nice way to put it. An ass?" His father wasn't a great man. He hurt women. A lot of women. He treated them like property. He'd ruined their mother's life. He acted as if his employees and friends were expendable. He saw his sons as disappointing playthings to bring out for photo ops but little else. "He ran through women, never quite finishing with one before moving on to the other. He sucked with money."

"Your family is...well, aren't you all millionaires, or billionaires or whatever comes after that?" Ellie took a quick look around the house as she spoke.

Derrick got it. He lived a certain way. Not over-the-top or even equal to a lot of other business people in town with his level of success, but he didn't suffer many hardships. But that was all thanks to his hard work, not his father's.

"Both of our fathers had issues with money."

Her eyes widened. "Really?"

"Mine spent money faster than he made it. He was always more impressed with the public version of the family and work than what was happening in private."

She took a few steps and ended up in front of him. "What does that mean?"

"He asked my mother for a divorce while she was dying in a hospital bed." Derrick didn't reach out for Ellie even though he wanted to. The idea of saying those words and touching anyone seemed wrong.

Her mouth twisted in a sour expression. "Who does that?"

"Exactly." She got it. She understood Dad wasn't just the handsome face that appeared in the news now and then. "He spent money and pretended he had an endless supply of it. Meanwhile, he failed to rein-vest in the company, retain good employees or expand when times changed."

She reached out first. Her palm flattened against his chest. "But you did. You rebuilt everything."

Derrick exhaled, liking the feel of her skin against his, even through his shirt. He folded his hand over hers. "Me and the people who work for me."

The start of a smile kicked up the corner of her mouth. "You're not going to take credit?"

Not out loud. Not ever. "I've spent my entire life trying not to be him, Ellie. I keep my head down and work. I don't get involved with people."

"Wait, that's not true." Her fingers curled into the material of his shirt as if she were willing him to listen to her. "You and Jackson are close. I sense you're close to your brothers."

"True."

Her second hand slipped to his waist to rest on the top edge of his pants. "You're a good man."

Derrick tried not to think about her fingers or how good they felt on him. "Am I? Your brother hates me and I forced you into a fake relationship."

She threw her hands out to the sides. "Do I look like I don't want to be here?"

The words slammed into him. He wanted her there. Agreement or no, he wanted her in his house, in his bed. In his life. To hell with the emotional consequences. "Then why are we sleeping in separate beds?"

Those hands slipped up his chest to his tie. It loosened a second later. "That's over."

Twelve

The DC Insider: *Dear readers...why are hot millionaire businessmen so hard to read?*

Derrick's hands shook as he lowered the zipper of her dress. Ellie couldn't think of a more satisfying reaction. Couldn't believe how right it felt to be in this bedroom with him. His bedroom.

His fingers brushed over her skin and his hot breath blew against her hair. She held on to the front of the gown, trying to catch it before the whole thing whooshed to the floor. If it were hers she wouldn't care, but it wasn't and that meant being extra careful.

"You're not wearing a bra." Derrick's voice carried a note of awe as he trailed his palm over her back.

Her breath caught and she fought to hold her voice steady. "The dress held everything in."

More like sucked it in and made her skin roll in places she preferred not to have rolls. None of that took away from the specialness of it all. She'd never dreamed about being a princess. She'd let her father do the unrealistic dreaming in the family.

Even with her practical streak, the memory of standing there on Derrick's arm, feeling his strong hand in hers as they'd danced under the lights with her dress swirling around her ran through her mind. She wanted to store away every moment and hold on to how freeing every moment had been.

"Any chance Vanessa has ten or fifteen more like this for you to borrow?" With the zipper the whole way down, Derrick's fingers lingered at the small dip of her lower back. He traced a pattern there.

Her entire body shivered in reaction. Every muscle shook as waves of pleasure ran through her.

She cleared her throat, trying to sound somewhat coherent. "Do we have more fancy events to attend?"

He kissed her bare shoulder. The move relaxed her, lured her in. Then he bit with only the barest of pressure, licked the wound and kissed the spot again. Her pulse took off on a wild race. She could feel it thump in her neck and under his mouth.

That mouth, so perfect, knew just where to nip and how to drive her wild.

He started to trail the kisses up the side of her neck. "I thought you could model them here, in private. With me as your only, but very eager, audience."

He was about to get *so* lucky.

"Aren't you naughty?" She asked the question as she turned in his arms. Seeing his face, running her finger over the stubble on his chin, set off a flurry of activity in her stomach.

On purpose, she let the top of the dress fall to her waist. Only the flare of her hips kept it up at all, and that balance was tenuous at best. She didn't cover herself. Didn't have to. He'd seen every inch of her. Toured his hands and mouth all over her. And when he saw her breasts now, all he could do was stare.

She couldn't imagine a better reaction. His pleasure became her pleasure.

Her feminine power exploded.

"I want to be a bad boy but I'm afraid of tearing the dress."

"Good call." She wiggled her hips and the material fell. She caught it before it hit the floor and handed it to him. "Here."

For a second he stood there with the dress draped over his arm. "Damn."

He wasn't looking at her face. No, his gaze traveled up and down her legs. To her thigh-high stockings with the lacy tops and the matching nude-colored underwear. She'd worn the combination for him.

"You like?" she asked, even though she knew from his expression he did.

"So that you're clear, I like you pretty much any way you'll let me have you." He used his finger to trace the lace pattern on the top of her thigh. "But damn."

Perfect reaction.

He'd stripped his tie off and shrugged out of his jacket. She went to work on his shirt. It took her about two seconds to get those small white buttons undone and to pull back the edges to reveal that firm, tanned chest. "Let's get this off you."

"I can do it." But he didn't make any move to help.

"I'll take care of you." She stripped the shirt off then sat on the edge of the bed.

She skipped the talking and asking and went right to the button at the top of his pants. His breathing kicked up as she lowered the zipper then pushed his dress pants to his knees. The boxer briefs went next.

When she took his length into her hand, his fingers slipped through her hair and held her close. The noise he made when she took him in her mouth, half moan, half yell for joy, sounded like music. It would stay in her head for a long time.

"Ellie." His voice dipped even lower than normal and held an extra-rough edge.

She licked her tongue over his tip then peeked up at him. "I didn't think you'd mind."

"I'm trying to figure out how I've stayed away from you for the past five nights."

"Sheer willpower on both our parts." Wasted time, as far as she was concerned. She wanted this. Wanted him. "To prove we could."

To continue the farce that this was fake and meant nothing…that was over. In reality, what they shared had started to mean everything.

She was falling for him. The words rolled through her head without a signal from her brain. They should have scared her and had her ducking for the toilet. She'd refrained from any real involvement up until now. Found excuses with other boyfriends to cut things off. With Derrick she wanted more, not less.

She understood him. They were good together. He made her rethink some of the views she held and things she took for granted. Made her assess Noah from a fresh perspective. And she smoothed out Derrick's rough parts. Had him thinking about something other than work every second of every day.

This—what they shared—may have started off as nothing, but it was something now. At least to her. The only fear, and it was a very real fear, was that this newfound reality only ran one way.

The room spun around her. He'd pulled her up and flopped onto the mattress, taking her with him. It was not the most dignified sprawl, but she landed on top of him—exactly where she wanted to be.

She scrambled to her knees and shimmied out of her underwear then took care of getting his pants and briefs the rest of the way off. He was left wearing socks and she had the thigh-highs on. That seemed like a pretty great combination to her.

She dipped her head to kiss him and he caught her face and held her steady. Cupped her cheeks in his palms and ran a thumb over her bottom lip. "I brought the condoms home."

The practical words shot through her. It took her a second to process what he was saying, but the choice was smart and made sense. They hadn't talked the "us" part of them through yet. That first time they'd had sex had been a risk. They could get it right now.

She looked around the bedroom. "Where?"

He pointed at the nightstand next to him. "Drawer."

That was the only word he could seem to get out, which only made him sexier. As she reached, he took advantage of her unguarded position and brought his mouth to her breast. Licked all around her nipple before sucking her.

She tried to slouch on the top of his thighs, but he

held her firm. His fingers traveled down her stomach and kept going lower. Between that hot mouth and those searching fingers, she lost all sense of time and what she wanted to do next. She got lost in a swirl of energy. It thrummed through her. The tension ratcheted up as her body got nearer to the edge.

"Ellie."

She looked at his determined expression and wet lips. "Yeah?"

"Ride me."

Yes. She thought it rather than said it. Without a word, she moved over his body. Straddled those impressive hips and pressed her hands to the rippled muscles of his stomach. "Have you been a good boy?"

"Very." His finger slipped inside her.

Her muscles strained as her head fell forward. Her hair slid off her shoulders and hung down. She could feel him curl a strand around his finger.

Heat radiated off their bodies. She tore open the packet and took out the condom. It should only have taken a second to roll it over his length, but she drew it out. Squeezed him as she covered him, inch by inch. By the time she was done, he squirmed on the bed. His fingers dug into her hips as he tried to draw her closer.

Then she lifted her body up and slid over him. Every cell screamed for her to finish it, but she didn't rush this part, either. She enveloped him. Measured each second before going lower. Waited until his back lifted off the bed and his eyes glazed with need.

She could feel him pulse inside her. After all those nights of limiting themselves, their bodies craved the completion now. She ached for it. When she lifted and returned to him again, her body started to shake. She was so close.

Tiny sounds escaped her throat. She hit a steady rhythm but she couldn't hold on. Her control shattered and the orgasm tore through her, surprising her with its intensity. She could hear Derrick saying her name and feel him lift his body to meet hers. Then she couldn't think about anything except how good he felt and how much she wanted this to last.

Derrick snuck down to the kitchen about a half hour later than usual the next morning. He wanted to get Ellie a cup of coffee and serve it to her in bed. The longer he could keep her there, the happier he would be.

He hit the bottom step and knew he'd miscalculated the time. Spence was already sitting at the bar, scrolling through his cell and drinking from a mug.

He didn't lift his head as he spoke. "You're tiptoeing around your own house. That's not sad or anything."

Derrick jerked at the unexpected sound but tried to hide it. Good thing he'd put pants on or Spence would have had quite the morning show. "You're up early."

"It's about time you two slept together." Spence just kept scrolling. "All that pretending was driving me nuts. I don't know how you stood it for all those nights."

Derrick froze. "Excuse me?"

"Oh, please." Spence put his cell to the side and smiled at his brother over the top of the mug. "My door is between your bedroom and the one she goes to…and you sneak off to each night."

So much for being stealthy. Derrick should have asked her to stay in his room and forget all the subterfuge. After last night, after the hangover from the personal information he'd shared with her, he was ticked off he hadn't ended the fake part of their relationship sooner.

Screw the agreement, he wanted to actually date her. He had no idea if she could make it work, but he really wanted to try.

But that didn't mean he wanted his brother knowing all about his sex life. "That's not—"

"I could never figure out why you didn't get right into bed with her." Spence shook his head as he made a tsking sound. "She's hot. You have to be smart enough to see that."

"Careful where you go with this." The brothers didn't touch each other's dates. Not ever. That was an unspoken rule. But the real problem for Derrick was that he wasn't in top form for sparring thanks to the lack of sleep, which he did not regret one bit.

"I have eyes. I hear the way you two talk to each other." Spence's smile was far too wide and snarky for this hour. "All tinged with unspent energy."

Tinged? Yeah, way too early. "You can stop talking now."

Spence had the nerve to shrug. "I'm reporting on what I've witnessed."

"You were spying on me?" For some reason that struck Derrick as ridiculous as he leaned against the sink.

Spence hadn't asked a lot of personal questions when he'd checked in by phone over the past few months. He wasn't the type to be up in someone else's business.

"I'm trying to figure out what's happening with you." Spence drained his mug. "I promised Carter I would find out and report back."

The alarm chimed and the front door downstairs opened and closed. Only a few people knew the code and had a key. Three of them were in the house right now and one was driving cross-country to get here for what appeared to be a brotherly interrogation. That left one other option.

Jackson stepped into the room. He carried a brown bag imprinted with the name of the nearby bagel chain.

This informal breakfast looked prearranged to Derrick. Jackson didn't just stop in with snacks. His smirk didn't make his surprise appearance any less annoying.

"What's going on?" Jackson asked the room in general as he unloaded the contents of the bag onto the counter.

"I'm digging into my brother's odd relationship to figure out why it's odd," Spence said.

Jackson hesitated for a second before reaching in and pulling out a tub of cream cheese. "Aren't we all?"

"He's got it bad for her."

Derrick put his mug down and took a step toward the staircase, making sure they didn't have nosy company hovering around upstairs. "Keep your voices low."

"Are you sure it's not that you're making this complicated?" Spence shook his head. "Because, I gotta tell you. From where I'm sitting, you seem to be messing this up."

Jackson opened two drawers before he found a knife for the cream cheese. Derrick was pretty sure it was a steak knife, but it worked.

"He's not wrong about the 'messing up' part," Jackson noted.

"You like her. A lot." Jackson pointed to the bagels and kept pointing until Spence picked up a specific one. "You're kind of stupid with how much you like her."

Jackson took care of slathering the spread on one side of the bagel then handed it to Spence before giving Derrick a quick glance. "Notice he's refraining from using the bigger L-word."

"I don't want to send him running." This time Spence focused on Derrick, too. "But, really, you've got it bad for her. You're living together. So what's the holdup? Why all the weirdness?"

Derrick didn't bother answering because they really weren't talking to him. This show was for the two of them and they really seemed to be enjoying it.

Jackson shrugged. "Don't look at me. I'm waiting for an answer, too."

"Well, you both think on it while I jump in the shower." Spence shoved a large piece of bagel into his mouth and took off for the stairs.

Derrick waited until the thumping on the steps faded and Spence disappeared upstairs before saying anything. "You didn't exactly help me there."

"You need to tell him the truth." Jackson dropped the uneaten half of the bagel on the counter. "Carter is on the way. You need to tell them both. They came back to town because you asked them to. They are trying to help you, even though neither wants back in the business as your dad is insisting."

Despite the annoying display of friends-gone-wild this morning, the advice was good. Derrick knew he had to come clean. He hated lying to his brothers, anyway. But he wasn't sure what to tell them now. The thing with Ellie had started off fake. Now it felt anything but. How the hell did he describe that state?

"I will. When they're together. There's no need to tell this tale more than once." And maybe he would know the right words to say when that day came.

"And Ellie? Are you going to tell her all of it?"

"One problem at a time." Derrick leaned over and picked up the uneaten bagel half. "Until I find the right opportunity, I'll continue to fumble my way through all of this."

"I told you this would be fun to watch."

Suddenly, Derrick wasn't that hungry. "Did you?"

"Maybe I just thought it."

"I could fire you."

Jackson laughed. "But you won't."

Thirteen

The DC Insider: *Word on the street is Ellie Gold is working miracles with Derrick Jameson. Is he getting soft? There are no signs of that in business, of course, but she has him jumping to her commands in private. So maybe those nasty rumors we're hearing aren't true?*

Two days later Ellie was still in a good mood. She even managed to ignore the guy taking her photo as she walked into the coffee shop a few blocks from Derrick's house.

They had hit a bit of a bump at the charity event but they'd ridden through it. She wanted that to mean something. They could talk about work and their arrangement and even their families. Right from the beginning they'd vowed not to lie to each other.

Despite all that, she couldn't think of a way to broach what, a few weeks ago when they'd first met, would have been unthinkable—talking about them. She knew it was easier to ignore the elephant standing in not only the room but also right on top of them than to deal with him. "Going along as is" meant dating and living together and getting to know each other.

For her, something deeper and meaningful had grown out of that. Derrick was so much harder to read.

And he wasn't the only one. She entered the coffee shop and slipped through the long line of people waiting to order. Noah sat at a table across the room, head down and not talking to or looking at anyone. He wore a baseball cap pulled low, like every other twenty-year-old in DC, and studied his phone.

Derrick told her he'd talked with Noah but hadn't been able to break through. Seeing her brother spin and knowing he would be in very big trouble without Derrick's interference was the kind of thing that kept her up at night.

She made it the whole way to the table without him looking up. Nothing new there. Eye contact was not one of his strengths.

She pulled out a chair and sat across from him. "Why did you want to meet here?"

She'd given him her new house address. The temporary one with Derrick. Suggested he come over and they talk in private. Noah had said no to all of it.

He kept tapping buttons on his phone, only sparing a glance or two in her direction. "To avoid Derrick."

"Are you afraid of him now?" When she didn't get an immediate answer, she put a hand over the screen and lowered the phone to the table. "Well?"

"Let's say I know he'll do almost anything to get his way."

"You might want to lay off the videos because you now talk in shortcuts. It's annoying."

"Then how about this." Noah leaned forward, his elbows on the table. "He's cheating on you."

The word bounced through her. A wave of nausea followed right behind it. "What?"

"There's a woman at work."

The accusation didn't make sense. "No way."

"I'm serious, Ellie."

If Derrick had a girlfriend, then why wasn't she visiting his house? Why wasn't he using this other woman as his fake girlfriend?

How could he sleep with her but be with someone else?

Ellie couldn't imagine any woman going along with that type of ruse and all the lies. Not if she cared about Derrick and vice versa. It was too dangerous and so disrespectful. Which brought her full circle. Derrick had a lot of flaws. She could spend an hour listing them, but being crappy to women wasn't one of them. Not that she'd seen.

Too many people would have to be quiet. She'd overheard the whispers at his office and none of them were about another woman. Someone at the *Insider* would know the truth and report it.

As soon as she reasoned it out, the choking sensation in her throat eased. So did the need to pound things.

She inhaled, trying to stay focused. If she let her mind wander, she'd be on the phone or in Derrick's office demanding an explanation and she didn't want to do that. He'd been accused of enough. "You're saying you know this because you worked there?"

"I never met her. This Abby. Apparently something happened with her months ago."

That barely sounded like a thing. A bit more of her anxiety disappeared. "Noah, you're talking about rumors and not facts."

Noah spun an empty coffee cup around between his palms. The edges clicked against the table. "I'm trying to make you see that he's not worth it."

"Why?"

He closed his fist over the cup with enough force to collapse the sides with a loud crunch. "What?"

"Why is it so important to you that I think that?" That part never made sense to her. It was one thing if he thought he was falsely accused and wanted revenge. But he seemed so determined for her to think *everything* about Derrick was awful. That he wasn't only a bad boss or a mean one, but a terrible cheating human being, as well.

The whole thing struck her as overkill. Like hurt feelings and crushed emotions.

"I know what it's like to be taken in by him." Noah continued to stare at his smashed cup.

"He hired you without any experience. Gave you a job and a place to go."

Noah's head shot up. "He abandoned me as soon as he needed a scapegoat."

The conversation pinged around. Noah seemed to move from one perceived Derrick sin to another. All of them seemed to come from the same place—somewhere personal. For the first time she realized this was about way more than work or a paycheck.

She slid her hand across the table, not quite touching Noah's. "Meet with him. I'll be there and we'll talk this out."

"We've talked. He tried to convince me I was wrong when the two of us met at your apartment."

"Try again."

"Can't you just believe me?" His voice grew louder until a few people sitting nearby glanced over at them.

She refused to be derailed. "I know you're angry with him."

"Forget it." He pulled the brim of his hat down even further and stood. The legs of the chair screeched against the hard floor.

"Noah."

He finally gave her full eye contact. "I never thought you'd pick some random guy over me."

Her heart hurt. "That's not what this is."

He shrugged. "Feels like it."

Then he walked away.

Ellie was waiting for him when he got home tonight. Not upstairs in the kitchen or sitting on the couch. Not even on her laptop searching for jobs. She was actually standing at the top of the steps.

He knew that was a really bad sign.

He barely reached the second floor when she launched into her question. "Who is Abby?"

She didn't move when he got to her. No, she stood there, arms crossed, wearing what looked like a day-long-practiced frown.

He should work from home while they were in this relationship. That would stop ambushes like this from happening. "You talked with your brother."

"I tried to get through to him again."

When she didn't move, he put a hand on her arm and gently guided her into the kitchen with him. "I thought we agreed I'd handle it."

They didn't even get to the counter before she turned and faced him again. Stopped them both in their tracks. "By putting our names in the paper all the time? That's defusing his impact, but it's not stopping him for good."

The *Insider* again. The gossip column proved useful. Everyone seemed more interested in his love life than in a dispute with a former employee. No one was taking Noah seriously and he was losing viewers, which meant losing some of his power.

Derrick didn't know how people could stand to sign on and hear Noah rave about one guy all the time. That thing had to get old. It certainly had for Derrick.

So did fighting with Ellie. Usually the verbal battles invigorated him. Not the ones about Noah. Talking about him seemed to suck the life out of both of them.

He set his briefcase on the counter and brushed his fingers through her soft hair. "Any chance you could trust me?"

"I do."

It sure as hell didn't feel like it. "You're asking about Abby. You're meeting with Noah without telling me."

"And you're sounding more like my boss than…"

"What?"

"The man I'm sleeping with."

Okay, he liked that answer and since he intended to keep doing just that, he loosened his rule on talking about this subject. The Abby issue went back to his father and their family dysfunction, but there was no way to explain that without blowing his relationship with Spence apart. "Abby has nothing to do with me."

Ellie frowned at him. "Derrick, that's not an answer."

He tried again. "She works for me."

"Okay." Ellie's eyebrow lifted as if she expected more.

But to him that's exactly what Abby was—a great employee he'd fought not to lose. "That's it."

Ellie stepped away from him. She walked around the counter to sit on one of the stools. "You are making this unnecessarily difficult."

"I'm answering you."

"Did you sleep with her?" Ellie ticked off the questions on her fingers. "Are the two of you having an affair?"

"When the hell would I have time for that? I'm here with you or at work with Jackson. That's it. That's all I do."

"That answer." She shook her head. "Good grief, Derrick."

He had no idea what she wanted from him. This part of a real relationship…he wasn't a fan. People trusted him. The idea that, after a brief meeting with her brother, she no longer did, made Derrick want to rip down the walls of his house with his bare hands.

"I haven't been with anyone since I met you. I haven't even thought of anyone else since I met you." The idea of touching another woman made everything inside him rebel. "You are it for me."

The words had slipped out. He didn't mean to say them, not like that. Certainly not out loud. He was talking about her being it *for now*…right?

There were many facts stacked against them. He hadn't told her everything. They had a mess with her brother. He needed to come clean with his brothers. Hell, he wasn't even sure she liked him all that much. He could ask, but he dreaded the answer.

She was supposed to be temporary. His focus had to stay on the business and meeting his father's requirements and getting the work part of his life settled. The company meant everything to him. He'd poured so much into it. He couldn't lose focus or his father would swoop in.

That reality of his whole life being up in the air scared the hell out of him. He tried to manage everything around him and suddenly his usual skills failed him. Admitting that he might be on a road that was off his plan made him want to head to work. Do something to burn off the odd sensation running through him. This unsettled feeling he was losing control of every single part of his life.

"Right now. I mean, I feel that way right now." He had no idea why he'd added that except that he'd been trying to convince himself it was true.

Her smile fell. "Interesting qualification."

"I'm not sure what you want me to do here. I feel like there isn't a right answer." If there was, he sure as hell couldn't find it.

She sighed at him in that way that told him he was missing the mark by a mile. "Who is Abby? A real answer this time."

"She and Spence had a thing. It's complicated, and messy, and my dad screwed it all up. Honestly, it's not my story to tell. I mean, I will if you want me to, but we have a bigger issue."

"Noah." She nodded. "He delivered some envelope to the *Insider* about you cheating on me, or is about to. I think this might be your new PR issue."

"No one is going to care that a single businessman is sleeping around."

She snorted. "How comforting."

He sensed trying to explain would only make it worse, so he skipped ahead. "My point is I can fix it."

"What?"

His heart thundered in his chest. It echoed in his ears. This wasn't supposed to mean anything. They had talked about it and she had known it was coming. But taking the step proved bigger than he thought.

He forced his fingers to work. Clicking the locks, he opened the briefcase and dug around until he found the small box. The one he'd had since the day after their first date.

"This is the way we start taking control." He took the blue box out and skidded it across the marble countertop in her general direction. "Here."

She stared at it but didn't pick it up. "What are you—?"

"An engagement ring."

When she looked up at him again... That was not happiness he saw. Her teeth clenched.

"Did you hand me a box with a fake diamond ring in it?"

What the hell? "It's not fake."

"You're offended by my comment about the cost?"

The conversation was spinning away from him. He could see it, feel it. Hear the thread of anger in her voice. He ignored every warning sign and dived in. "I picked the ring out for you."

"You did?" She didn't sound even a little impressed.

"Of course. It has to look real."

She glared at him then took a turn glaring at the box. "And now you've handed it to me."

"Okay, wait a second." He rested his palms against the counter. "I don't get this. Are you upset about it being real or do you need it to be fake? Fill me in here."

She looked ten seconds away from kicking him. Derrick appreciated that there was a heavy kitchen island between them right now.

"You shoved an unopened box at me and said 'here.'" Her eyebrow lifted in challenge. "Yes?"

Okay, that sounded bad. Even he could admit that. "Uh, yeah."

"Derrick, you have to know there's a better way to do this." She waved a hand in the air. "Forget that. You should see your face. You clearly don't get it."

"Do I look confused? Because that's kind of where I am."

"Fine. I'll take this." She grabbed the box and opened it.

She made a noise that sounded like a gasp. Hesitated before picking it up. But she did pick it up. Slid it on her finger as if it didn't matter to her at all.

Yeah, this was not going well. "Wait."

"I have the ring. Next provision of our agreement satisfied. Congratulations." She slid off the bar stool and headed toward the stairs.

He didn't even realize they were done talking. "You're upset?"

"Yes, genius. I am."

"But this is what we agreed to."

She shrugged. "Then I guess we're good."

She sounded far from good. And if the kicking in his gut was any indication, he wasn't doing so great, either. "I don't understand what's happening."

"Your fake fiancée is going outside."

It was nighttime and she had a rock on her finger and a heap of attitude. "Why?"

"Because you're not there."

Ellie managed to ignore him for the rest of the night and all of the next morning. Maybe it was immature but she needed a Derrick break. He hadn't even let her walk away from him in peace. He'd texted her the second she stepped outside and said he was worried about her safety. She stayed on the front steps until she cooled off enough to go inside and walk right by him.

For the first time since she'd moved in, she missed morning coffee with him. She decided to have it with Vanessa instead. They sat in the same coffee shop where she'd had it out with her brother.

Vanessa stirred her second sugar packet into her coffee. "So, let me get this straight. He gave you a ring for a fake engagement you agreed to and now you're ticked off at him for giving it to you."

Ellie had to admit her anger sounded ridiculous when her friend put it that way. "Please don't make me sound like the unreasonable party in this."

Vanessa held up a hand in mock surrender. "I'm on your side. Always."

Silence fell over the table as Ellie tried to find the right words. She was furious and hurt. This dragging sadness exhausted her.

She hated that battered-from-the-inside gnawing sensation that overtook her when she thought about the ring and Derrick. She was not the crying type, but right now she wished she was.

She didn't even know what to say to Derrick because he wasn't wrong. She had agreed to the fake arrangement. It had just taken him longer to launch into this part than she'd expected. She'd hoped that meant something.

"It was the way he did it." And that was true. Even a fake arrangement deserved some sense of importance. He'd handed her a ring without even bothering to open the box.

Thinking about it, reliving the moment in her head, had fury bubbling up inside her again. Really, the man was clueless.

"You're angry because he didn't get on one knee and ask you?"

Ellie didn't like that question, either. "Maybe I'm not telling this story right."

"Hey, listen to me." Vanessa reached her hand across the table. "There is an obvious problem here."

"Derrick."

"Him, too. But I think the real issue is you're in love with him." Vanessa winced as she said the words.

"This is about the way he—"

Vanessa fell back in her chair. "Oh, my God. You didn't deny it."

She couldn't because she was. Vanessa said the

words and they didn't sound wrong. The realization terrified Ellie. She'd tried to be smart and careful, but she'd fallen. It was stupid and dangerous and would likely break her heart, but it happened.

She thought the truth would hit with a jolt. Instead it settled in and snuggled around her. But she still wanted to throw up.

Rather than deal with any of that, she fell back on her anger. On Derrick's depressing choices. The least he could do was fall with her.

"You don't start a fake engagement by shoving a ring at someone." How could she not see that? Ellie thought for sure she would get an immediate agreement on that topic.

Vanessa nodded. "Okay."

"Stop smiling."

"I should because I'm worried about you." The amusement left her tone. "You changed the rules in this thing. You fell for him."

"I thought… I mean, we've slept together." When Ellie realized she'd yelled that bit of information, she immediately lowered her voice. "We've gone out on these dates. None of it feels fake."

"Maybe that's what the two of you need to talk—" Vanessa stopped herself midsentence then leaned in closer. "You're not confronting this because you're afraid the relationship didn't change for him."

Exactly. That was it. She should clear all this up. But what if the answer was something other than what she wanted it to be? "Maybe I should sell the ring and move to Alaska."

Vanessa's eyes bulged. "Wait, is that thing real?"

"He said it was." Ellie studied it for the fiftieth time. It was stunning. Big. But not too much. A solitaire surrounded by smaller diamonds, and a perfect fit. She didn't even want to know how he'd pulled that off.

"Damn. Go Derrick."

Anger or not, the ring made a statement. "Right?"

"I'm going to give you some advice."

Ellie didn't hide her groan. "About shoes? That's about all I can handle right now."

"You need to end this."

Her stomach went into free fall. "Did you miss the *in love with him* part?"

"That's my point. You guys need a do-over. Start fresh and honest."

"We've been honest with each other." With a few false starts, they had made a deal. They'd both known, going in, what this was and what it would mean: solving problems for both of them and little more.

Well, damn. Vanessa was right. She was the one who changed the deal.

"Since you're here and not with him, I think that's not true." Ellie started to talk and Vanessa talked over her. "You did storm out, right?"

"I do not storm."

She rolled her eyes. "I've seen you storm."

"He makes me want to throw things."

"Not the ring." Vanessa picked up Ellie's hand and gave the ring a closer inspection. "You're keeping that if the knucklehead doesn't get his act together. I mean, come on."

"The problem is I want to keep it all—his friends,

his house, his brother." The words ripped out of Ellie. It hurt to admit all of that.

"Oh, man. You have it bad."

Ellie was starting to realize that. "No kidding."

Fourteen

The DC Insider: They're engaged! You know who they are and what we're talking about. We're hoping for a September wedding. You?

"He didn't actually steal the money." Derrick said the comment more to himself than to any one person. He'd forgotten Jackson was sitting in the chair across from him, one leg crossed over the other, so he did have a captive audience.

He looked up. "Excuse me?"

Derrick wasn't sure how to explain how he'd come to that conclusion, but he tried, anyway. It was more of a feeling than any one specific grounded in fact. Still, he thought he'd stumbled over the right answer. "It was this thing Noah said. He talked about being my mentee."

From the beginning Derrick had assumed the situation with Noah was about money. That fact fit with what he knew about Ellie's precarious finances and now with what he knew about her unstable upbringing and the limited resources and attention given to Noah.

Noah hadn't been searching for easy money. He hadn't even tried to take the amount he'd managed to gather out of the account he'd created, which would have been easy. He'd moved the money the same way he'd moved around everything else in the company's system. Without one person noticing. And Derrick hired smart people. They knew what they were doing but their brains were no match for Noah's. He'd acted almost as if he were bored and looking for a better way to categorize things.

Derrick's tech people were still trying to figure out how the kid's mind worked so they could mimic it.

"You know you've been sitting for three hours without moving."

"So?"

"You worked late last night." Jackson nodded in the direction of Derrick's cell. "You haven't been texting with Ellie today like you usually do."

Derrick had no idea what that had to do with the information Jackson mentioned, except to question why he spent so much time tracking Derrick's movements. "I'm working."

"Are you sure you're not pouting?" Jackson dropped the file he was looking at on his lap. Closed the cover and focused on Derrick instead.

"Does that seem like something I'd do?"

Jackson snorted. "Not before Ellie."

Derrick didn't know how he felt about that answer,

either. He knew she'd turned his life upside down. He'd lost control of his office and his home but he'd hoped no one else had picked up on that.

While they were spinning around topics without finding answers, he figured he might as well add one more fact. "We're engaged, by the way."

Jackson's foot fell to the floor. "What?"

Derrick returned to looking at the printouts in front of him. "I need you to send out that press release and leak the info to the *Insider*."

That was the game, after all. A fake engagement to clean up his reputation and defuse Noah. The idea had once made sense but Derrick had grown to hate the words. Now he wanted a shot at making it real.

"Back up." Jackson knocked his fist against the desktop. "When did this big event happen?"

"Yesterday." A day that now ranked as one of the most confusing days of Derrick's life.

He'd thought he was doing the right thing when he'd taken out the box. Settling the unsettled between them. Giving Noah another reason to calm down. Feeding the PR machine. But he'd forgotten that Ellie didn't always do and say what he expected. She worked in this other world that he didn't get.

Bottom line, he'd hurt her and she didn't seem ready to let him fix the damage. That might have been good since he had no idea *how* to fix it.

"And we aren't celebrating the big event?" Jackson asked.

There would be a party. That was the point. A public coming-out of sorts. But he had one problem with arranging it right now... "She hasn't talked to me since."

Jackson laughed. "That sounds like a good start to a marriage."

"A fake marriage." For some reason everyone kept forgetting that part. Sure, the ring was real. It seemed like a dick move to get her a fake one of those. Besides, he liked the idea of her wearing his ring. Of seeing it on her finger.

He was totally losing it. He no longer knew exactly what he wanted. His emotions bounced back and forth along with his priorities.

Jackson exhaled long and loud. "We're back to that. The damn agreement you two signed."

"Did we ever leave it?"

Jackson tapped his pen against his folder. The clicking sound thumped through the room. "Derrick, what did you do?"

Derrick wanted to dig in to his work. Buying properties, selling properties, building properties. He could assess a piece of land and pinpoint its future value, see what it could be once he was done with it.

Figuring out Ellie? He needed a team of experts for that mission. Maybe Jackson could be on it. "What do you mean?"

Jackson exhaled a second time. "How did you ask her?"

"You're coming up with a lot of questions." For some reason that made Derrick nervous. Very little made him nervous.

"Maybe answer one."

"I gave her the ring." There. Simple.

Jackson's pen stopped midtap. "Gave?"

Since Ellie had treated him to a similar response, Derrick decided to stall. His delivery of the ring had been off. He got that now. Interesting how everyone seemed to know the fake engagement rules better than he did.

"Can you only talk in questions now?" he asked, ignoring the irony of that.

"What do you think?"

Some days it was hard to like Jackson. "Very funny."

"When you say 'gave,' you mean you asked her…" Jackson made a face. "Please mean that."

"No."

"Ah, I see." Jackson coughed, clearly trying to hide a smile. "How did that romantic gesture go over?"

"I slept alone last night, so not well." Derrick had walked to her door. Before they'd started sleeping together, every night he'd knock and go in. Once they were together and not fighting the sex, where she slept hadn't been a question…until yesterday.

"Do you really not see the problem or what your contribution to the mess you're in now actually was?" Jackson asked.

Of course he did. *Now*. "No."

"Damn it. I'm going to lose that bet."

That stopped Derrick. "What bet?"

"The one I made with Spence."

"Want to fill me in?"

"You'll figure it out." Jackson stood and took out his cell. "If you don't, I'm out two hundred dollars, so please figure it out fast."

"I'm here as ordered." Noah sat at Derrick's dining room table. "I'm not sure why we couldn't meet at the coffee place again."

"Because I can't go outside without having my picture taken." Ellie had about reached the end of her patience on that subject. She glanced to where Derrick sat at the head of the table. "We're going to talk about that, by the way."

His gaze went to her ring then bounced to her face. "What did you expect would happen?"

He had an uncanny knack for saying the wrong thing at the wrong time. The man built an impressive enterprise that churned out money, yet he failed on a simple people skills level some days. She might lecture him about that, too.

Noah frowned at both of them. "What's happening? Why am I here?"

"We're clearing the air."

Noah started to get up as soon as Derrick stopped speaking. "No, thanks."

"Sit." Derrick issued the order. "We're also engaged."

He really would be the death of her. Ignoring Noah's stunned expression, she glared at Derrick. "Really? That's how you drop that information?"

"If you have a script you want me to follow, please let me know."

He was in fine Derrick form today. He shot back the one-liners faster than she could come up with them on her end.

Noah sat hard in the chair again. The thud seemed to wake him out of his stupor. "What are you talking about? You can't marry him."

Through the haze of frustration winding around her, she could see him. She and Derrick might have an odd arrangement they worked out, but that didn't mean her brother was prepared for the roller coaster they'd all jumped on.

"Noah, let me explain." Though she had no idea what she could say.

"At least wait until you see this video." Noah slipped a thumb drive out of his jeans' pocket and dumped it on the table.

"What's on it?" Derrick asked.

Noah didn't even spare him a glance. "I bet you'd like to know."

"I can take it and watch it right now or you can save us some time and talk." Derrick snatched the drive and held it in the air.

"You and your father and a certain woman at work."

"This is old news." Derrick shook his head. "This is about Abby, right? I'm not sure where you're getting your information but Abby dated my brother. Not me."

Noah blinked a few times. "That's not what Joe—"

Ellie wasn't about to let Noah stop there. "Who?"

Noah shook his head. "Nothing."

"Joe Cantor? Is he the one who's been feeding you false intel, hoping you'd fall for it?" Derrick asked.

"Joe?" Ellie thought her head might explode.

The ramifications of what Noah admitted flowed through her brain. Joe had planted that story in the *Insider* about her work. He was trying to undermine Derrick and his relationship with Spence. And this poor Abby person was stuck in the middle. Sure, Derrick had made Joe look stupid, but the timing didn't seem right. And what kind of man would take that bait and go to all this trouble?

"You've been working with my former boss?" It sounded awful when she said it out loud. "The one who kicked me out of the office and sent me home without a paycheck?"

"It's not like that." Noah shook his head. "Only in the last few weeks when you guys started dating."

"Let's run through this." Derrick's firm voice broke through the room. "The *Insider* is not running anything about me cheating, because I'm not and they don't want to be sued."

"How did you—"

"And…" Derrick talked right over Noah's explanation or whatever else he was going to say. "If you put up that video, you'll hurt Abby. Not me. She deserves better than that. Honestly, she's been screwed over by my family enough without adding yours."

Noah shook his head. "Don't try—"

"Why did you move the money? Was Joe involved in that?"

Derrick's question came out of nowhere. Ellie had no idea what he was talking about.

But Noah didn't look even a little confused. "It's about time you figured it out, but Joe's not involved."

Ellie rushed to keep up. "What are you two talking about?"

"Noah moved money out of a bunch of work accounts and moved it into a fake client account he designed. Hid it all but didn't actually take it. I just figured that out." Derrick's gaze switched from her to Noah again. "So, did you run out of time to make a withdrawal?"

"I was never going to take it. I just wanted to prove I could do it."

It was such a Noah thing to say that Ellie's heart melted. He refused to see the results of his choices. He acted and let everyone else clean up his mess. Whatever his issues, he had to learn a new way. "Oh, Noah."

"You brought me on at the office then put me in that room." Noah ignored her and turned on Derrick. "I tried to talk with you about problems in your system, but you said I had to talk with my direct boss."

Derrick's eyes narrowed. "You were trying to get my attention."

"Don't flatter yourself." Noah returned to staring at the table.

That was it. Ellie knew Derrick was right. Something in Noah's reaction or Derrick's tone. In the middle of their fight and Noah's threats, Derrick had gotten to the bottom of the stealing question. He wasn't blaming. He was laying out facts. Because he was a good man. A man worth loving. The man she'd fallen for.

This time the realization didn't make her want to throw up. She wanted to tear up that ridiculous agreement so she'd never have to think about it again.

Derrick shifted in his chair, clearly trying to get Noah to look at him again. "I didn't mean to ignore you in the office."

Noah snorted. "Stop acting like I cared."

But he did. No matter what Noah was saying, he did. It all made sense now. So many people ignored Noah and passed him over. They didn't take the time to see what he could do. Derrick had taken an interest in him. Hired him without a load of experience or an advanced degree.

Derrick had taken a chance and Noah had taken that to mean something more than the usual employer/employee relationship. Derrick never could have seen this coming.

"I asked the prosecutor not to move ahead with the charges," Derrick said in a low voice.

The sound shot through her. The words...he'd kept his promise. Of course he did.

Derrick looked at her then. "For you and for him."

"You're not doing me any favors." But all of the anger had left Noah's voice. His outburst died as soon as the words were out. "Ellie, listen to me. You can't marry him."

"It's happening," Derrick said.

Noah stood. "I'll be back when he's not here."

That comment struck her as silly. "It's his house."

"Leave the video," Derrick said.

"Because you say so?"

Derrick shook his head. "Because I'm asking you not to release it."

"Fine." Noah slammed the drive onto the table and walked out.

Derrick watched Noah go. Apparently storming out in a huff was a Gold family tradition. Ellie did it better, but Noah was pretty good at it. Even slammed the front door.

Ellie stood. Derrick half expected her to go upstairs and not talk again this evening like a repeat of last night. He fought to find the right words to say but nothing came to him.

She stopped next to his chair. Her hand slipped into

his. When she gave his arm a gentle tug, he figured she wanted him to stand.

The change in her mood confused him. "Are you okay?"

Instead of answering him, she kissed him. Her arms slipped around his neck and she pulled his head to her. Then her mouth met his and speaking wasn't on his mind.

Her tongue licked out to caress his bottom lip. She had his brain misfiring and his pants growing tighter. It took all the strength he possessed to lift his head and stare at her, to drag his mouth away from hers. "You don't need to thank me this way."

He waited for her shoulders to stiffen, for her anger to rise.

She pressed a finger to his lips. Traced the outline before letting her finger trail down his throat to his chest. "You told me once that I should only kiss you if I wanted to kiss you."

The sound of her deep voice was enough to touch off something inside him. He got hard and his resistance to her, what little he still had, melted. "That's still the rule."

"I want to kiss you."

It took a second for her words to register in his brain. She wanted him. Through the missteps and the battles, after sleeping alone, she still wanted him.

Still, they'd been through some hard days. "Be sure."

She pressed her hand against his chest, backing him up until his butt hit the wall. "I am. I choose you, Derrick. Not because of an arrangement or money or my brother. I want you because of you."

That's all it took. The last of his defenses fell. Every argument for why he should hold back and not let this mean anything vanished.

His body vetoed his brain. They could talk later. They needed this now.

His mouth met hers in a kiss meant to possess. He wanted her to know this was real. There was nothing fake about how much he wanted to touch her, to be inside her. His hands traveled over her as she unbuttoned his shirt. She reached the bottom few and tugged. Buttons ripped off and pinged against the floor.

It was a wild frenzy to disrobe. He wanted her naked but settled for shoving her skirt up to her waist and tugging her bikini underwear down. Their legs tangled and he leaned against the wall for balance. When that didn't get him what he wanted, he spun them around.

With her spine pressed against the wall, he lifted her legs to his hips and settled his body between them. Her ankles balanced against his ass as he held her with one hand and rushed to unzip with the other.

Chaos filled his mind. A wild energy pounded through him. All he could think about was being inside her, of feeling her body wrap around his. At the last second, he slowed. His finger went to the very center of her. When he found her wet and ready, he slipped into fast forward again.

"I'm going to help your brother, Ellie," Derrick said between stinging kisses.

She put her palms against his cheeks and forced him to look at her. "Yes, but later."

"Much later."

Then he was inside her. He plunged in and stopped.

Ignored the sexy little growling sounds she made and just enjoyed the tight grip of her body around his.

She pinched his shoulder. "Derrick, move."

This one time he was happy to obey.

Fifteen

The DC Insider: *The party is on! We admit we were worried Derrick Jameson blew it, but friends and family are gathering. There's word of a sparkly dress and champagne being brought in by the truckload. Let the marriage plans begin.*

Two more weeks of tentative peace passed. Ellie returned to Derrick's bedroom. He hadn't proposed in a better way, but he did spend some time each night touching her ring. His finger smoothed over it with a near reverence. He'd spin it around on her finger as he watched in awe.

She still didn't understand him. His mood stayed relatively steady but he worked too much and continued to say the odd stray comment that made her wonder how often he dealt with actual human beings other than her.

A month had passed since they'd first slept together. After a detour to help a friend, Carter was on the way, which meant she would know both brothers soon. Even Derrick's father was flying in with his relatively new wife.

The idea of that made Ellie's stomach flip over. That was a lot of Jamesons in one house. She hoped they didn't kill each other. Even she thought about punching Derrick's father. The man had made a big mess of his family then snuck away to let Derrick clean it all up. What kind of man was that?

Friends and relatives officially would start pouring into town in two days. The party, the sheer scope of it, made no sense to Ellie. A hundred people. She didn't know five people she'd want in her house. This family had business associates and relatives everywhere.

This was the kind of shindig you threw when you really planned to walk down the aisle. Family met family. Friends traded stories. The happy couple showed off photos of their time together so far. None of that fit their situation, yet Derrick insisted.

He still hadn't filled Spence in about the truth of their relationship. Ellie hadn't because she no longer saw any part of what they shared as fake.

Jackson and Derrick had been trapped in the library all morning. There was talk of moving the party to the Jameson's Virginia property and holding it outside under the most expensive tent she had ever seen in her life. The thing had actual doors and windows.

She'd never seen the farm in person, but from the photos she thought it looked like a school. The idea that Derrick grew up there without his mom and with a distant father made her ache for him. The loneliness had to have been unbearable. Her parents had made a lot of mistakes, but they'd been around. Broke and confusing, but present.

She grabbed a mug of tea and headed for the library to see what ridiculous plans the men had dreamed up while she'd dressed this morning. She'd been dragging all week. She'd only ever needed about six hours of sleep each night. She'd swear she could use twice that much right now.

The stress was working on her. There was no other explanation. It also messed with her stomach. Coffee made it grumble these days.

If she were honest, she'd have to admit she didn't feel great. A terrible cold might be headed her way. When she'd mentioned that to Derrick last night he'd made her promise it would come after the party. As if she could control life like that.

She sipped on the herbal mixture of lemon and peppermint. The warm liquid poured through her on the chilly spring day. She'd thrown on one of Derrick's sweaters and it swamped her. She didn't care. The soft material made her think of a blanket.

The closer she got to the room, she expected the voices to grow louder. They didn't. The door was open an inch or two. She pushed it open a smidgen. Took the opportunity to watch them.

Even at home, Derrick stayed in command. He wore black pants and a simple white shirt. On him, the combination proved stunning. She was about to tell him that, maybe embarrass him a little in front of

Jackson, which was always fun, when she heard the ominous sentence.

You have to stop lying to Ellie.

She pushed the door open the whole way. Immediately she was greeted by the stares of the two men and Jackson's mouth dropped open. Derrick didn't show any reaction at all but his watchful eyes followed her.

"Lying about what?" That was the only question that ran through her head so she asked it.

Lies. The word stuck in her throat. She turned it over and tried to make it fit with everything she knew about Derrick and the upcoming party. Nothing matched the urgency she'd heard in Jackson's tone.

She couldn't ignore the comment. She'd grown up with lies. She'd lived with so many over the years and knew how they could burn away all the other good things in life. They stole security. She'd lost her job over one.

But Derrick had promised not to lie to her. He'd said it more than once. It was one of the underlying principles of their agreement.

Time ticked by and neither man answered her.

She stepped closer. For a second the room began to spin. The walls of books blurred and she would have stumbled but she fought for balance.

"Someone answer me," she said in a louder voice. She would yell if she had to.

Jackson looked at Derrick. "I should go."

"Don't move." She wasn't letting either of them off the hook because this was clearly big. "Someone start talking."

"There was another reason for our agreement."

Derrick's deep voice broke through the otherwise quiet room.

"The fake engagement." The words scraped against her throat.

"What started out as that, yes."

She ignored the comment. Pretended his words didn't echo what she'd wanted for the past few weeks—a real chance with him.

Her head started to pound. The drumming sensation started at the base of her neck. After a few more steps, it moved up to her nape. Her footsteps faltered. At first she thought her shoe had snagged the carpet, but no. Her balance was off. The room tilted on her.

"Explain." She somehow got the word out.

"My father said he would sell the business out from under me unless I met certain stipulations."

Eldrick Jameson. She should have known he was at the bottom of this. That bit of information fit everything Derrick had ever told her about his father. The man was pure trouble. He caused trouble, incited it.

But none of that explained Jackson's comment.

"What does that have to do with me?" She could no longer stand there. She set the mug down, ignoring her shaking hand.

"Are you okay?" Jackson asked, the concern obvious in his voice.

"Finish it, Derrick." Because she knew there was more. This all related to her. All that talk at the beginning of their relationship about how they were helping each other. Yes, she'd let herself get sucked in because he'd wanted to. But the reasoning rang hollow now.

"Each brother has an obligation they have to meet or we lose everything. My obligation was multipart.

I had to lure my brothers back to the business and I had to clean up my image."

That didn't sound so bad. It was close to what she knew with a few holes filled in. "Okay."

"I told you I needed your brother to stop. I didn't tell you my continued ownership of the business depended on it. Depended on you."

"The deal was pretty lopsided," Jackson said.

"I needed you more than you needed me. Without you, I lost everything." Derrick hesitated for a few seconds. "For me this wasn't about helping Noah. It was about keeping control of the business."

"That's pretty ruthless." The room started to blur along the edge. She looked at him through this strange haze.

She had no idea what was happening. It was as if her body was shutting down, abandoning her. But she refused to give in. She wanted all of this information out between them. No more secrets.

"I never pretended to be anything but ruthless," Derrick said.

That wasn't true. She'd thought so at first, but that was part of his perfectly crafted image. The real man was much more complex. Decent.

"Why not tell me the truth?" That part didn't make sense to her.

Derrick never left his place by the fireplace. He held on to the mantel as if it were the one thing holding him up. "I didn't know you and didn't want you to have the upper hand against me."

"Weeks ago. But now?" She shook her head and almost dropped to her knees.

Jackson got up from his chair and Derrick took

a step forward. She waved them both back. "Why, Derrick?"

"I didn't want what we had to stop."

The sex. He liked the sex and was willing to tell her half-truths and use her to keep getting it. "Maybe you are ruthless."

She saw Derrick rush forward and heard Jackson yell. Everything moved in slow motion as the air whooshed around her. Before she could call out, the pain closed over her and the room went dark.

Pregnant. Not just pregnant but a high-risk pregnancy.

Derrick sat beside Ellie's hospital bed and turned the doctor's words over in his head. He'd been pummeled with information since they'd arrived in the emergency room. Now she was settled in a private room and the facts still didn't make sense.

Spence and Jackson had stood next to him, taking it all in. Derrick had barely heard a thing. All he could think about was the ambulance ride. The first responders yelling, talking to the hospital. The noise as they'd driven at high speed. The beep of the machine next to him.

It had been a flurry of activity. Everyone rushed and ran. The stretcher. The blood from where her head had hit the floor before he could catch her. He'd thrown up twice while he'd waited for the doctor to come out and deliver some news.

And the news…pregnancy.

Now he had to tell her because this was not the ideal situation. Forget the state of their engagement. He would fix that as soon as she let him. He knew what he wanted now. Watching her fall, thinking he'd lost her, shifted his whole world into focus.

He'd told her he'd kept part of the truth about the agreement from her because he hadn't wanted their time together to end. What he hadn't said was that he loved her. He was couldn't-think-straight in love with her.

That losing her made him double over.

That he would forfeit the business if it meant she would stay with him.

His thumb slipped over the engagement ring on her finger and he thought back to the silly way he'd given it to her. So dismissive, ignoring her feelings. Jackson had unloaded, letting him know every way he'd messed up.

Derrick knew it was Jackson's way of handling his fear. Derrick's was to bury his brain in work and he couldn't do that now.

"Derrick?"

At the sound of her rough voice, he looked at her. Her eyes were open and filled with fear.

"Hey." He brushed her hair off her cheek. "You're okay."

"What happened?"

The worst. His nightmare. "You fainted."

But he'd thought it was something else. He'd never dreamed the answer would be pregnancy. He could handle that, or he would learn how to. But watching her drop…he never wanted to see that again.

"I did?" She tried to sit up.

He gently pushed her down. She'd be in the hospital for a few days. They had decisions to make. There were tests to run and precautions to take.

"My head is killing me." She lifted a hand and the tubes attached to her arm went with her.

"You're on an IV." He glanced at the bag hanging on the hook by his head. "You have some meds."

"What's wrong?"

He took a deep breath. "Well, here's some news. You can get pregnant with an IUD."

Her eyes widened. "What?"

"It's rare but it happens." He slipped his fingers through hers. "You're about five weeks along."

What little color was in her face drained away. Then her hand went to her stomach in a protective gesture that tugged at his heart.

"The first time we slept together," she said.

"Yeah." He didn't want her to be in danger but it was hard to want to call that night back. It had started them down this road.

She swallowed a few times before talking again. "Tell me all of it."

She deserved to know, so he didn't hide behind calls for her to wait or for rest.

"It means this is a risky pregnancy. Taking the IUD out now can be a problem. Leaving it in can, too." He swallowed before saying the part that made his voice break. "There's an increased chance of miscarrying and a lot of precautions we'll need to take if you decide you want to go through with the pregnancy."

Tears filled her eyes. "I understand."

So brave. No surprise there.

He leaned over and placed a sweet kiss on her forehead. "I will support whatever you want to do."

"You don't have to… I told you about the birth control, but…" This time the tears rolled down her cheeks.

"We created this baby together. Both of us."

She nodded but didn't say anything.

The quiet tears tore at him. "I will be with you no matter what."

She closed her eyes and nodded. The tears still fell harder. "I need to sleep."

"Okay." He had no idea if that was normal for her condition or if she was shutting off. He didn't want to ask. "I'll be right here."

"You do love her."

Derrick looked up an hour later to find Noah and Spence standing in the hospital room doorway.

"He wanted to see his sister," Spence said.

"Of course."

Derrick was more grateful for Jackson and Spence than ever. They stayed calm while he nearly lost it. He'd cradled Ellie, making sure she was breathing. They'd made the calls.

Noah came into the room then. He walked over to Ellie's bedside and stared at her. "She's really pregnant?"

Derrick couldn't believe it, either. "Yes, but it's risky."

Noah nodded without looking up. "Spence told me."

Spence. Interesting. Derrick hoped that meant they'd bonded. Noah needed guidance.

"Thanks."

The word came out soft. Derrick almost missed it.

"I'm not going to let anything happen to her, Noah." Derrick thought about what Noah had said about a mentee. "If you let me, I'll make it up to both of you."

"I shouldn't have moved the money."

"No."

"We can worry about that later," Spence said.

Noah nodded again as he stepped away from the bed. "I want to get her some flowers."

"I know the place for that." Spence gestured for Noah to follow then winked at Derrick.

He watched them go and thought about all that had happened. All the miscommunication and missed cues. He'd hidden behind his desk for so long, so focused on the business and not the people he cared about. But no more. He would do better. For her, he would try.

Sixteen

The DC Insider: *An ambulance. A family fight. These Jamesons know how to keep things interesting. But the fairy tale is back on! Congratulations to Derrick Jameson and Ellie Gold on their upcoming wedding...and the little surprise they've been keeping. We're hoping for a girl.*

Ellie was finally able to leave the hospital three days later. Not that anyone let her even take a step on her own. She'd tried to get off the couch for a drink of water this morning and men had come from every direction.

Derrick had turned away the engagement party guests. He'd explained that Ellie was sick. She didn't know much else because every time she opened her mouth Derrick tried to feed her or give her a pill.

The guy loved playing nurse. She let it happen because she worried about what would happen when he stopped. The game should be over. Everyone knew everything now. Noah had been by every day. He seemed connected to Spence's side and had made a tentative peace with Derrick.

She must have *really* been sick.

She heard male voices and Derrick's telling people to get out. His tone, frustrated and gruffer than usual, made her tense. She'd been waiting for bad news since she got home. Not that she needed to invite more.

Derrick hadn't been overstating what they faced with this pregnancy. It carried all sorts of risks. Not as bad as it could have been because she hadn't been that far along when they'd discovered it, but the risks were still pretty high. So she'd opted for keeping the IUD. Now she spent every day doubting the choice and worrying she'd lose the baby. Derrick's baby.

After everything that happened, she still wanted to build something with him. But could she trust him? He'd kept most of his promises to her, but he still lied. At the very least, he held information back because it benefitted him. She couldn't figure out a way to process that.

"Hey." That's all Derrick said as he walked into the room.

Just as he had since she'd come home, he seemed subdued and a bit on edge. Her insides churned and she half wondered if that rubbed off on him.

She tapped the couch cushion next to her. "Can you come sit with me for a second?"

He hesitated then nodded. "Everything okay?"

He'd asked her that so many times that she now dreaded the question. "Is it, Derrick?"

"What does that mean?"

The question had been right there, on her tongue. She'd bit it back for days. Didn't want to invite trouble. But she had to know. "Do you want me to leave?"

He made an odd face. "What?"

"This relationship was fake and now that—"

He swore under his breath. The sound of the harsh words made her jump. She wasn't afraid but he did let them fly. She started to get up, but he held her hands and pulled her closer to his side.

"Never."

The word didn't make any sense. "What?"

His chest visibly rose as he inhaled a deep breath. "Ellie, how can you not get this? I love you."

She didn't realize she was shaking her head until he touched her hair. "What?"

"I fell in love with you. Nothing about this or how I feel about you is fake."

Her mind refused to believe and that made his words that much sharper. "You don't mean that."

This was about guilt and the baby. He'd been moping around, not going to work. The pressure...she got it. It crushed her, too.

"We can figure something..." She didn't even know what to say. She'd practiced and now the words wouldn't come.

He slid off the couch and went to one knee. "Ellie Gold."

She froze. "What's happening?"

"Go ahead." Spence called out the encouragement from the top of the stairs. Jackson stood with him and Vanessa. Noah was there. And was Spence holding up a phone?

Jackson pointed at the cell's screen. "Carter didn't want to miss this. He's still ticked off that Derrick didn't tell the whole truth, either."

"You mention that now?" Derrick swore again. "You're all pains in the—"

"Keep going," Vanessa called out.

"Fine." But Derrick didn't sound fine. His voice was sharp and he was fidgeting. Something he rarely did. Then he looked at her and the scowl disappeared. A softness moved into his eyes. "Hi."

"Hi." She had no idea what else to say.

"I think I loved you from the first time I met you." He laughed then. "You were so unimpressed with me and who I was. So beautiful and not interested in anything I had to say. It was a potent combination."

The room started spinning again. This didn't have anything to do with her pregnancy or fainting. It was the punch of happiness—hope—that seared through her. It left her breathless.

"I should have told you everything from the start, but I didn't want you to find a new place to live." Derrick laughed as he bent to kiss her hand. "Hell, it took forever to get you to agree to share a bed with me."

He reached out a hand and fit it over her stomach. "Not that long, I guess."

"Derrick…" She didn't know what she wanted to say except his name.

"What I should have said when I gave you this ring." He held it up.

They'd taken it off her in the hospital and she hadn't dared ask for it. She felt naked and half-sick without it. Relief nearly swamped her at seeing it again.

He turned it over in his fingers. "I picked this because it reminded me of you. Bold, sparkly, beautiful. Different in every perfect way."

Her defenses, already shaky, collapsed. Seeing him kneeling there, usually so strong but now so vulnerable, won her over. He'd messed up but they could fix this. They could learn to communicate better, to share. Together, they'd unlearn some of the damaging interpersonal skills passed down from their parents. They would do better.

She reached out and cupped his cheek. "Yes."

He shook his head but this time he was smiling. "No, I'm asking this time."

She bit back a laugh because he seemed so determined.

"Ellie Gold, I love you more than anything. I loved you before I knew about the pregnancy and I'll love you forever, if you let me."

"Yes." The word rushed out of her. She was laughing and crying and nodding. One big weepy mess.

"Marry me."

This time she fell against his chest and felt his strong arms wrap around her. He whispered something into her hair. She could hear her name and the cheers from their family and friends who were sharing the moment. She loved all of it, all of them; mostly she loved Derrick.

She pulled back and stared up at him. Derrick, the strong and determined man who liked to boss her around and argue for no good reason. With him she felt the intoxicating mix of comfort and heat. She loved him and wanted him. She knew he would help protect their baby and they'd save each other if they lost it.

"I love you." Her voice was soft but mighty.

"About time you said that." He rested his forehead against hers. "I'm going to need to hear it a lot."

"You know, if this is a real engagement—"

"It is." He practically barked the response at her.

"You should know that I plan to be a bossy fiancée and an even bossier wife." And that was an understatement.

Once she checked with the doctor about what she could do and couldn't, she'd try to return to the work she loved. She'd also control his schedule a bit better than he did. No more all-nighters in the office or dinners at ten. She was going to get his life in line.

"Wait, what?" But he didn't sound even a little worried about the idea.

"We'll start with your work hours." She glanced over his head at Jackson. "They are decreasing."

He nodded. "Yes, ma'am."

Derrick cleared his throat. "We'll talk."

"I'll win." She looked around and realized she already had.

"I can hardly wait to negotiate our new agreement."

She heard groans that matched the one she was holding back. "You're not going to believe what provisions I add."

He kissed her then. Long and lingering. When he lifted his head, all the stress he'd carried on his face for the past few days was gone. "You can have everything you want."

Her heart swelled. "You're going to be a great husband."

Carter would arrive tomorrow, after what had turned out to be a ten-day trip across the country. Only his baby brother would draw out something like that.

"What are you laughing about?" Spence asked.

Derrick looked up to see Spence staring at him. He stood at the kitchen sink, nursing his morning coffee. Ellie wasn't up yet, which Derrick assumed would become a new thing now that she was pregnant.

They had a wedding and a baby ahead of them. His father was coming for the rescheduled engagement party in a few weeks. All of the things Derrick never thought he'd have, a family of his own and the stability of friends and family around him, were happening.

"Life is pretty good," he said in response to his brother's question.

"For you." Spence shook his head. "You've met Dad's conditions. Noah is quiet, your PR image is pristine, and Carter and I are both here, at least for the short-term. For as long as you need us, actually."

"Thanks."

"Yeah, well. Apparently, I'm up next. Dad has some stipulations Carter and I need before we can settle the business and get him out for good."

"You don't have to—"

Spence made a strange noise. "I do."

Derrick didn't want to subject his brothers to their father's stipulations, to have them run around trying to meet his conditions. He was willing to stop the nonsense. The business used to mean everything but his priorities had shifted. He knew he'd survive without the office now.

"This isn't up for debate, Derrick." Spence stared at him. "Got it? No more secrets or arguing."

That loyalty meant more to Derrick than he ever thought possible. "Yes."

"And the business is yours." Spence smiled over

his mug. "Just do a good job once Dad steps fully out so I can keep collecting the checks for my minority interest."

Derrick lifted his mug in a fake toast. "Happy to."

"And we'll be here for you and for Ellie." He made a groaning sound. "Even for Noah."

Noah was one more thing Derrick needed to deal with. But not today. For the next week, Ellie was his only priority. He was stepping aside and letting Jackson do what Jackson did best—run things.

He had a party to plan and a wedding to set. There were about a billion doctor's appointments they needed to go to. A bunch of specialists. He vowed that Ellie would not go through any of it alone.

"I appreciate that." Derrick let his mind wander to the one place he didn't want to go. "With this pregnancy—"

"She needs you. We'll take up the slack and do Dad's bidding."

Derrick had no idea how to thank Spence for that. He tried anyway. "I truly appreciate that."

Spence put down the mug and moved to the other side of the kitchen island, across from Derrick. "Stop doing that."

"What?"

"Being grateful." He snorted. "It's annoying."

"Only you would think so."

"We're going to get through this. She's going to be fine—so is the baby."

Derrick needed to hear the words. They might be empty, but he could tell Spence believed them. That was enough for now. "I believe I remember something about a bet?"

"Hell, no. You weren't in on it."

Derrick held out his hand. "Two hundred or I tell Ellie."

"Unbelievable." Spence slipped his wallet out of his pocket. "You only get this if I have a chance to win it back."

That sounded ominous but Derrick took the cash anyway. "How?"

"Give me the baby's due date so I have the inside scoop and can take a bunch of Carter's money."

"Sold." The sound of their laughter filled the kitchen.

For the first time ever, Derrick finally felt like he was home.

* * * * *

LET'S TALK

Romance

For exclusive extracts, competitions
and special offers, find us online:

MILLS & BOON

THE HEART OF ROMANCE

A ROMANCE FOR EVERY READER

MODERN

Prepare to be swept off your feet by sophisticated, sexy and seductive heroes, in some of the world's most glamourous and romantic locations, where power and passion collide.

HISTORICAL

Escape with historical heroes from time gone by. Whether your passion is for wicked Regency Rakes, muscled Vikings or rugged Highlanders, await the romance of the past.

MEDICAL

Set your pulse racing with dedicated, delectable doctors in the high-pressure world of medicine, where emotions run high and passion, comfort a love are the best medicine.

True Love

Celebrate true love with tender stories of heartfelt romance, from the rush of falling in love to the joy a new baby can bring, and a focus on the emotional heart of a relationship.

Desire

Indulge in secrets and scandal, intense drama and plenty of sizzling hot action with powerful and passionate heroes who have it all: wealth, status good looks…everything but the right woman.

HEROES

Experience all the excitement of a gripping thriller, with an intense romance at its heart. Resourceful, true-to-life women and strong, fearless m face danger and desire - a killer combination!

To see which titles are coming soon, please visit
millsandboon.co.uk/nextmonth

JOIN US ON SOCIAL MEDIA!

Stay up to date with our latest releases, author
news and gossip, special offers and discounts, and
all the behind-the-scenes action
from Mills & Boon...

 millsandboon

 millsandboonuk

 millsandboon

It might just be true love...

MILLS & BOON

MODERN

Power and Passion

Prepare to be swept off your feet by sophisticated, sexy and seductive heroes, in some of the world's most glamourous and romantic locations, where power and passion collide.

MILLS & BOON
True Love
Romance from the Heart

Celebrate true love with tender stories of heartfelt romance, from the rush of falling in love to the joy a new baby can bring, and a focus on the emotional heart of a relationship.

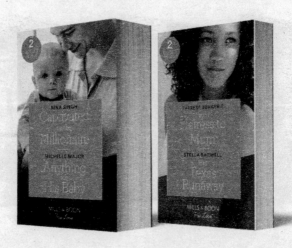

MILLS & BOON

HEROES

At Your Service

Experience all the excitement of a gripping thriller, with an intense romance at its heart. Resourceful, true-to-life women and strong, fearless men face danger and desire - a killer combination!